All
Is Vanity

ALSO BY
CHRISTINA SCHWARZ

Drowning Ruth

Doubleday Large Print Home Library Edition

D O U B L E D A Y

New York

London

Toronto

Sydney

Auckland

All Is Vanity

〜〜〜〜〜

A NOVEL

〜〜〜〜〜

CHRISTINA SCHWARZ

This Large Print Edition, prepared especially for Doubleday Large Print Home Library, contains the complete, unabridged text of the original Publisher's Edition.

PUBLISHED BY DOUBLEDAY
a division of Random House, Inc.
1540 Broadway, New York, New York 10036
DOUBDLEDAY and the portrayal of an anchor
with a dolphin are trademarks of Doubleday,
a division of Random House, Inc.

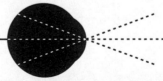

This Large Print Book carries the
Seal of Approval of N.A.V.H.

FOR BEN AND NICHOLAS

And in memory of Julia Sackin,
who taught me how to write a decent letter
when we were very young and whose
friendship I will always treasure

ACKNOWLEDGMENTS

I thank my editor, Deb Futter, for kindly but ruthlessly urging me to separate wheat from chaff, and my intrepid agent, Jennifer Rudolph Walsh. I also thank Anne Merrow for turning technological cartwheels so that I could make changes from a moving car. I'm grateful to the friends and relations, particularly Amy Halliday, David Kipen, Abby Pollitt, and Jennifer Stuart Wong, on whom I relied for crucial details about such things as treats for school parties, the L.A. transit system in the nineteen seventies, preferred plumbing materials, and the hot food currently sold in New York's all-night delis. Eliza Meyer Audley helped with the characters' wardrobes and the habits of young children; Robert Spoerl with real estate; Julian Fisher and Ginny and Steve Kaplan with the logistics of the plot; Elizabeth and Charlotte Krontiris with classical languages; Emily Parsons with internships; and the always amusing Jon Zobenica with obscure terms and rules of grammar. I thank Caitlin Flanagan for the humor and sympathy she applied to reading the manuscript, Mona Simpson for her decisive editorial advice, Jennifer Stuart Wong again for her fine-tooth combing, Carol and, especially, Barbara Faculjak for their generous and thoughtful responses, and Avril Cornel, whose good cheer is as unflagging as her printer. And once again I am indebted above all to Benjamin Schwarz, who helped me see what this novel should be about. His extraordinarily keen understanding of human behavior and maddening insistence on precise language informed every page of this book. He remains the best reader I know.

I made me great works; I builded me houses . . . And, behold, all was vanity and vexation of spirit, and there was no profit under the sun.

— ECCLESIASTES 2:4, 11

. . . people are greedy and foolish, and wish to have and to shine, because having and shining are held up to them by civilization as the chief good of life.

— WILLIAM DEAN HOWELLS,
A Hazard of New Fortunes

All
Is Vanity

CHAPTER 1

Margaret

I was a promising child. When I was seven, I spent an entire week hunkered down on the cranberry red carpeting in my father's study, building a scale model of the Temple of Athena at Paestum. I carved the columns out of Ivory soap with a paring knife and pushed red clay through my Play-Doh press to tile over the Styrofoam roof. I painted a frieze, which was cheating and ultimately unsatisfactory, since it was not authentically three-dimensional. My father wondered why not the Parthenon, but I wasn't interested in the obvious.

"Everyone knows the Parthenon, Dad," I said, in a superior tone, although, in fact, I knew no one other than he who was at all acquainted with the Greeks.

Three months after I'd finished my temple, my little brother, Warren, was parking his Hot Wheels in it.

When I was eight, I sewed two chamois I swiped from the garage into a little dress in the style of the Lakota Sioux. You'd think this would be less ambitious than the Temple of Athena, but the beadwork was extensive. Beads were very big then—my friends and I sat cross-legged on the driveway with little cups of color-coded plastic treasure near our knees and threaded them on elastic to give to one another as necklaces and bracelets. I had to cut apart five of the six chokers my very best friend, Letty, had given me to get enough beads just to finish the bodice of the dress.

My mother was less pleased with the Lakota costume than she'd been with the temple. Architecture, yes. Sewing, no. But at that point in my career, I didn't care what my mother or anyone else thought. I didn't care that the columns of my temple had bits of sticky string tied around them—to pump the gas, Warren explained—my pleasure was all in the making.

I could go on—I laid out the city of Ur in clay on the Ping-Pong table, rendered a map of Asia as experienced by Marco Polo, compiled a catalog of Scottish clans, and produced a page of medieval-looking illumination with hand-mixed inks—but I think my point is clear. I was precocious. I was enthusiastic, unswerving, creative. I had imagination. It took me only twenty years to realize that none of this mattered.

What you find out in your thirties is that clever children are a dime a dozen. It's what you do later that counts, and so far I had done nothing.

~~~~~~

But I was going to change that, starting right now, this morning, Saturday, June 15. I'd set the alarm for four forty-five and was at my desk by five. The sky over Lower Manhattan was the gray of used wash water. I would shower around nine, I decided, to refresh myself after logging a decent morning's work. I had easy to hand two new and newly sharpened pencils—the soft number ones I liked—and a legal pad for notes. The cursor pulsed eagerly on the blank screen before me. I drew my feet under me and sat on my heels. I leaned forward, ready, nearly holding my breath. It seemed as though, with just a nudge, my novel would spin from my pent-up imagination in skeins of gorgeous, moving words.

"Elaine pushed her fingers through her long, dark hair in the pearly dawn," I typed—it was the first sentence that came into my head—and then rested a moment, reaching to tease from my own hair a snarl the cat had painstakingly worked into it during the night. Why "Elaine"? Should my main character have the name that came first into my head? Shouldn't the name suit the character the way "Daisy" suited Daisy Buchanan? With one of my pencils, I printed neatly on the legal pad—"Buy baby-naming book."

"Margaret?" My husband's voice came from the bedroom, muffled by down comforter and sleep.

"Ted, I'm working," I said, a touch of righteous indignation in my tone.

"Come back to bed," he murmured dreamily.

Fourteen hours before, I'd been an English teacher at Gordonhurst Academy, a private school on the Upper East Side. The administration had put on a little party in the Marshall Room to send off all of us who weren't coming back in the fall with Chinese chicken salad, a favorite cafeteria offering, and grape juice made adult by the addition of cranberry and seltzer. One by one, we were called to stand before the portrait of Fitzhugh Marshall to collect a handshake and a gift—Suzy Cargill, an art teacher, who was having a baby and had decided to stay home for a year; Valerie Finkelstein, who was trading biology classes for med school; John Kingsley, who was moving to St. Louis to be with his girlfriend; and Penny Burich, who had won the outstanding teacher award the year before and was going to Columbia for a doctorate to become an even better teacher than she already was.

"One of our colleagues from the English department is leaving us to write the great American novel," the headmaster announced.

I blushed and began to push my chair back.

"And I'm just hoping for a run-of-the-mill novel," I think I said, as I shook his hand, although, oh, yes, in some shameful corner of my ego, never to be admitted in public and to be tasted only with the tiniest, most fleeting lick in private, was a hard little lozenge of belief that this grandiose idea was true. Why not? I was an American, wasn't I? That I had not submitted for publication a single line since *Cricket* magazine passed on "The Misplaced Mitten" when I was twelve only meant that I had reservoirs of untapped talent.

My gift was a pair of slim books—one titled *Character,* the other *Plot.* I was touched by this gesture of support, although I knew I would use them only for a laugh. I had paged through that kind of thing often in bookstores, mostly to reaffirm that I would be a writer different from their intended audience. I aspired to be an artist, to blaze a fresh trail in prose, not to write the kind of paint-by-numbers potboiler such manuals encouraged. "You know," Neil McCloskey, my department head, said to me, quietly, kindly, as I held the books up for

the teachers to admire, "you're always welcome back, if, you know, things don't work
out."

~~~~~

I complained about this to Letty on the
phone Saturday afternoon.

"But that's nice," she said. "He values
you."

"It isn't nice—he assumes I'll fail."

"That's not a reflection on you. Think of
all the great writers who couldn't get published. Think of Emily Dickinson."

"She was a genius, way ahead of her
time. I doubt I'll write something too good to
be published." There was, it seemed, some
limit to my arrogance.

"Well, anyway, I admire you. I'd never
have the guts."

"What you don't have is the time," I said,
and, as if on cue, a crash sounded somewhere in the background, followed by a
frantic wail.

"Gotta go," she said, and was gone.

~~~~~

Letty and I were so young when we met that neither of us can remember the occasion. Our mothers, so the story goes, deposited us in a playpen at Johnson campaign head- quarters in Pasadena and told us to amuse ourselves. Other than their sporadic loyalty to the Democratic Party, and the fact that both of them relish the entirely fictitious no- tion of themselves as young women so busy with the affairs of the world that they raised their daughters to be independent even as infants, my mother and Pam Larue have very little in common, and their friendship was long ago reduced to the exchange of nonre- ligious "holiday" cards. But Letty and I have ever since been as close as twins.

That's not to say we're alike. It's more that we're a sort of team, in the classic sense of hero and sidekick, and I don't think I'm being immodest, but only truthful, when I cast myself as the hero. Of course, she's much better than I am at many things, but her qualities—patience, for instance, and an easy laugh—are those that make for a good right-hand man. Even in our games, she was always Robin to my Batman, Watson to my Holmes, Boswell to my Johnson, and the times when she's been clearly the leader have been uncomfortable.

I remember distinctly an incident in first grade, when we were each assigned to render a tree in fall colors. It was work obviously well below my level of accomplishment—at home I'd recently completed a mosaic of painted macaroni that approximated one of the floors of Pompeii—but it was enjoyable to do something that didn't demand all of my resources, and I was quite pleased with the artful way I'd arranged and overlapped my swatches of construction paper.

Our teacher had been making the rounds of the room, peering over shoulders noncommittally, when suddenly she stopped.

"Look here!" she exclaimed, whisking Letty's paper off her desk and holding it up. Two or three construction paper "leaves" fluttered to the floor. "Now *this* is a tree!"

Letty's tree *was* good. She'd painstakingly shredded her paper into pieces so small and massed them with such intricate variation that the crown gave the effect of actual foliage. Her work was not only good, it was, I recognized with a pang, better than mine, which now looked clumsy and hap-

hazard—the efforts of a child—in comparison. Thankfully, I had the presence of mind
to beam at Letty, who kept her head bent,
shyly hiding a small, proud smile.
Nevertheless, I was not happy for her. I was
instead trying to console myself by noting
that she had had the advantage of the sort
of glue that dispensed only a small amount
when you pressed the rubber applicator
against the page, whereas I was forced to
use the much more difficult to manage
Elmer's. I even, for one brief second, dis-
paraged her in my mind for putting so much
energy into such a banal assignment.

Even as I experienced these feelings, I
was deeply ashamed of them, and that
shame is the only thing that now keeps me
from utterly despising my small self. But
while on the one hand I vowed never again
to begrudge Letty her success, on the
other, I promised myself that from that moment forward I would strain to the utmost,
no matter what the project, so as never to
be in a position to feel such chagrin again.
That was the lesson I learned from first
grade.

Letty was never so driven, which was at
least in part the fault of her family. I think her

parents must have had big plans for her when they named her Letitia, but there was never all that much get-up-and-go in the Larue household, and they let her name lapse into Letty almost immediately.

My mother was much more firm of purpose. "Please call her Margaret," she would say forbiddingly to everyone, even the well-intentioned mailman, who tried to shorten my name. My name, of course, presented a minefield of opportunities for corruptions—Meg, Peggy, Maggie, Margie, Maisie, Rita, Gretchen. She would accept none of them.

"Why?" I begged many times, especially during my *Little Women* period.

"Because your father and I named you Margaret," she said. "When you're older, you can let people call you whatever you decide, but I want to get a decent run out of the name we chose."

"Don't you like your name?" my father asked, puzzled and a little hurt.

I realize now that it wasn't the name I didn't like, but Margaret herself, whom I was beginning to find a little bossy. Margaret was admired, but Peggy, I believed, would be well liked. The way Letty was.

〜〜〜〜〜

When I'd told Ted over our very late breakfast that I planned to work that afternoon
and couldn't go with him on our regular
Saturday ramble through the city, he was
sweetly disappointed. "I thought you
worked this morning. You don't need to
write the whole thing the first week."

"I know, but I want to get a good bite out
of it. If I just get half a chapter done this
weekend, then I'll have a head start on
Monday, when I can really buckle down
while you're at work."

"You're right," he said. "If you think you'll
get something done, you should work.
Maybe we'll go to a movie tonight, then."

"Maybe," I said, "but I might be pretty far
into my story by then. I may not want another narrative intruding."

Our kiss at the door savored of our great
expectations for me.

I microwaved a cup of leftover coffee before I sat down at the table, turned on my
laptop, and retrieved the document I'd
named "Novel." Elaine with her ridiculous
hair leapt onto the screen. I read over the

single sentence I'd composed that morning. It seemed flat. It was going nowhere. "Pearly dawn" was pretentious. What had I been thinking, I wondered, pressing the delete key firmly? I couldn't write a novel just by stringing sentences together. I needed a plan, a sense of what I wanted to say. What did I want to say?

I pushed my laptop aside. I would take notes first, sketch out my ideas in old-fashioned ballpoint on solid paper. I noticed, as I bent to pick my pen off the floor where it had rolled, that the rug badly needed vacuuming. What with final exams and the deluge of grading, I hadn't cleaned the apartment in weeks. I tried to think of an important idea on which I could build a firm base for an important book, but the grit kept drawing my eyes to the floor. The windowsills, too, were fuzzy with dust, and the bottom of my coffee cup had collected some stickiness from the kitchen counter. I'd be able to think more clearly if my environment was less chaotic.

Around five-thirty, I sat down again at the computer. I'd cleaned all afternoon with satisfying concentration, interrupting my efforts between finishing the kitchen and starting the bathroom only for my call to Letty. I felt focused and relaxed, even a little weary. I was now ready to settle down for a few hours of mental exertion, so the sound of Ted's knock at the door was somewhat irritating.

"Why do you refuse to carry keys?"

In his hand was a small, plastic bag.

"What's that?"

"Just a little surprise."

I reached for the bag, but he held it back. "Later," he said. "It's not to be given without ceremony."

"So you had a good day of work?" he said, glancing into the closet with the window on an air shaft we both used as a study. But I'd been careful to turn off my laptop.

We ate that night at our favorite French bistro, a place that only took cash and where you had to bring your own wine. We knew if we eschewed a predinner salad and shared one dessert that we could leave there only twenty dollars poorer and infinitely richer in the feeling that we, too, were out and about in Manhattan, participating ever so modestly in the sybaritic pleasures of that hip metropolis, self-consciously being, in other words, real New Yorkers. When we'd pushed the cork back into the bottle to preserve the remainder of our five-dollar Argentinian red and were dueling over the single slice of chocolate hazelnut ganache, Ted laid a narrow cardboard box in front of me.

"Is this the ceremony?"

He nodded. "I know you use the computer, but I thought this would make you feel like a writer."

I lifted the lid. Inside was a Mont Blanc fountain pen, a rich, shiny black.

"The more expensive ones are prettier, but this one does have the gold nib," he said, reaching across the table to uncap it.

"No, no. This is perfect. The expensive one is too . . . nice," I said. "I'd never feel I could use it."

I pictured myself bent over a tiny café table, my intense concentration and the rain streaming romantically down the windows blocking out everything but the scene I was creating on the page. Except for the oversized cup at my elbow, I would be just like Hemingway.

"It does make me feel like a writer," I said, testing the weight between my fingers.

"There's ink, too. At home. I couldn't decide between blue and black, so I got blue-black."

"I know—black is too serious and blue isn't serious enough."

"Exactly."

We agreed about everything then.

When I'd told Ted a year ago on one of our marathon walks uptown to a free concert in Central Park that I wanted to quit my job to write a novel, he'd been more wary.

"A novel," he'd said, thoughtfully, and he grabbed my hand as we crossed Thirty-fourth Street to pull me out of the way of a cab that wasn't slowing definitely enough for his comfort. "Well, you are a very good writer."

"You think so?"

"Oh, no question. But a novel . . . don't most people publish some short stories first? I mean, build a reputation before they try a novel?"

"I don't know." I crossed my arms defensively. "I guess some do."

"Sally Sternforth published a piece in *The Atlantic* before she wrote her book. An editor from Basic Books called *her.*" Sally's husband was a program director, like Ted, at the Cabot Foundation. She'd been widely praised for her courage in writing a scathing account of her ancestors' role in driving Native Americans from their land, although to me her intrepidness was suspect. How harshly could she have been criticized for daring to expose the evils of Manifest Destiny, not to mention the embarrassment of family?

"Not that I don't understand your wanting to change careers. Teaching is noble, but not exactly ambitious. I can see why you might want a more prestigious job. But are you sure you specifically want to write? Or is it just that you want to do anything the world rewards more generously than teaching?"

Was I sure? No. I had to admit I liked the idea of being a lawyer, a district attorney, maybe. I was attracted to the notion of

being a doctor or a police detective or a reporter. As Ted had irritatingly ferreted out
over the course of the thirteen years he'd
known me, my problem, as far as careers
were concerned, was that I had remained a
perpetual ten-year-old: I had trouble imag-
ining jobs other than those depicted in television dramas, which severely narrowed the
field. Also, like a preteen, I half believed I
could do anything, as long as I set my mind
to it, but was never actually willing to set my
mind to anything that threatened to take up
a good portion of the rest of my life.

Those professions struck me as too difficult, requiring too much preparation and
commitment and grinding work, not to mention aptitudes I wasn't sure I possessed.
Writing a novel, on the other hand, seemed
almost a pleasure. Of course, I knew it
would take some application, but I imagined
it would be the sort of labor demanded by
the projects of my childhood, more entertainment than work. Writing a novel, I believed, would be a way to achieve glittering
success without the painful and humiliating
apprenticeship other well-regarded careers
required, and which I ought to have under-

gone in my twenties. Too late for that, I thought. I needed quick results.

I stalked on past the library, angry that Ted had not immediately applauded my courage at daring to attempt such a feat as becoming a writer. Wasn't he, as my husband, supposed to say "reach for your dream," "follow your bliss," "pursue your passion, no matter what it takes"? It was unhelpmatelike of him to poke at the vulnerable underbelly of my conviction. Hadn't I been preparing for this all my life, by reading, by teaching the fundamentals of composition, and mostly by simply living? He knew I was a decent prose stylist. What more did a writer need?

"The thing about writing," Ted said, "is that you've got to have a real gift for it. I mean it's like visual art or music or athletics. Lots of people can draw or play an instrument or a sport really well—just like you can write really well—but they don't try to make a living at it. And, you don't have to be an artist to do work that's creative and interesting. Look at Clinton—maybe he could have played professional saxophone, but he chose to fulfill his ambition in a different way, and he seems to have ended up with an interesting job, some might say even more interesting and fulfilling than being a jazz musician."

"So you're saying I'm more likely to become president than to write a novel?"

"I'm just saying that even if you don't have a gift, there are lots of things you can do that you might find more socially rewarding than teaching."

"So you're saying I don't have a gift?"

"I think," he said cautiously, "that maybe if you did, we might have noticed it by now. I mean, you haven't really written anything."

"I know I haven't written anything! I've been waiting for the right time. What could I possibly have written about before?"

Luckily, he didn't ask me what I planned to write about now, because I didn't have a clear answer.

"How long do you think a novel would take you?" he asked instead. Unfortunately, we were stopped at a light just then, so he was able to level the full power of his serious, I-don't-tolerate-sloppy-thinking gaze upon me.

"I'd say a year," I hazarded, indulging in my characteristic sloppy thinking. A year seemed to stretch so comfortably long.

People met, married, and divorced within a year; children were conceived and born within a year; the seasons exhausted an entire cycle. What couldn't be accomplished, given a whole year?

"Why not work on it in your spare time and take three or four years? Hedge your bet. Lots of famous writers had regular jobs, you know. Look at Wallace Stevens."

"He was a poet."

"So?"

"Well, I'd think you could write a good poem in a few days. Granted each word is precious, but let's say you give even a few hours' thought to every word, you don't need that many of them. I just don't think it takes the same kind of sustained concentration as a novel."

"Trollope then."

"Fine, if you want me to work in the post office, I'll work in the post office." We'd hit the fifties now and the crowds and scaffolding had thinned. I picked up the pace. "And he wasn't a wife. That takes time, you know, even though you don't see it. When you want to go to a movie, you want me to go with you. You want me to listen to you talk about your day. You want attention, which you should get, but that eats into my time. And that doesn't even count the dinner preparation and the cleanup, and all those other chores that take longer when you're doing them for two."

"I'd be happy to do more of the chores."

"I know you'd be happy to, but you won't do them. You don't even notice what needs doing."

At Fifty-ninth, we went east a block, as was our habit, so we could walk past the stores and restaurants on Madison Avenue. The park was pretty, but we'd come from northern Virginia; we craved urbanity, not greenery.

"You honestly believe you can write something good enough to be published? Not just want to, but can?"

"Yes," I said adamantly. Even in discussing the prospect of a novel, I could feel stirring within me the creative power that had carried me along effortlessly when I was a girl. I remembered those engrossing hours, when my hands confidently shaped whatever my brain envisioned, and one idea followed the last like rushing water. True, the results of my efforts were somewhat crude and clumsy—I had been just a child, after all. But now that I knew so much more, I had not a doubt that whatever emerged from my pen would be something spectacular.

"And I'm not suggesting I start right away," I assured Ted. "I'll teach this year and we'll save. We'll still have to cut back a little, I know that. But it's not like we're going to starve without my measly income. And I promise it'll only be a year. One year, and I'll have something salable."

He sighed. "OK, if you're that sure, I believe you. It would be great if it worked out. I wish, though, that you'd tried this experiment before we moved here, to the most expensive city in the country. We can't even afford our apartment."

"I wish that, too," I said fervently, but I was less concerned about our finances than how far behind I'd fallen. I'd been toying with this idea back in D.C. but had not felt such urgency until we moved to New York. Although at that point we'd been in this city only a month, I could sense already that here I, as an English teacher in her mid-thirties from bourgeois Glendale, California, by way of the suburbs of northern Virginia, was a half-witted, earnest, gray lump in a land of cynical, scintillating intellectuals. And that I could not stand.

Letty

Why did I listen to her? Everyone asks me this. My husband; my lawyer; my sister; my parents; Ramon, the gardener who came with our new house. Actually, "everyone" constitutes a small circle, thank God. The other mothers at my children's various schools only give me nervous half smiles as they climb into their SUVs. I'm not the woman they thought they knew. The neighbors, of course, sliding by in their sealed cars, say nothing. They're barely aware that I belong to this house, let alone of what I've done.

Why did I listen to her? I can only say in my defense that you have to know Margaret, maybe have to have known her for decades, like I have.

Margaret was always more sophisticated than I. The weekend my parents took my sister Charlotte and me dressed in our jammies to watch *The Wilderness Family* from the back of our LTD wagon, Margaret's father took her to *Dog Day Afternoon* at the Egyptian. Margaret talked about this movie as if I, too, might see it the following week. This was a kindness—she knew, as well as I, that it was the sort of film I'd never even catch a trailer of.

Margaret discussed movies in terms of actors and directors. She said Pacino had pathos. I nodded. "Absolutely," I said, although I'd thought that Pacino was some kind of Japanese pinball. When Lottie and I talked about movies, we described the action exhaustively, scene by scene. We said the bear was neat. We might even have said "neato."

Margaret wore her wavy hair in a ponytail secured with interlocking translucent plastic balls in colors like yellow, hot pink, and lime green. I begged my mother to buy me some like them, even though my hair was the thin kind that ridged along my scalp when it was pulled back. She came home with a strip of cardboard on which a pitiful example of what I'd requested was trapped under a plastic bubble. The balls were small, white, and opaque. "How can there be a wrong kind?" she asked. "These are tasteful."

Margaret let me borrow hers. I nearly cried when I lost an orange set in the grass. My mother was right; my hair really was too skimpy. "But you need that one," I sniffed. "It goes with your best shorts." Margaret shrugged. "You don't want to be too matchy-matchy," she said, and if I'd only admired her before, my gratitude made me love her then.

I saved my best beads—the turquoise blue and the iridescent crystals that looked like real diamonds—to string her a necklace. She wore it for two months, and then it was gone, replaced by a fine, pale line where it had sheltered her skin from the sun. I was afraid to ask what had happened to it. I didn't want to make her feel bad if she'd lost it. Those necklaces always broke eventually, Lottie assured me, especially if you wore them swimming. For a few days, I opened my eyes under the stinging water of the Glendale public pool, trying to spy a curl of blue-and-clear at the bottom. Even at the time, I recognized it was hopeless.

In sixth grade we were supposed to describe someone in the class so that the others could guess who it was. Her description wasn't like the other kids', who talked about obvious things, like hair color and height. "Good at basketball," Jimmy Murphy said, and everyone knew he was describing Howie Clay.

"The person I'm thinking of," she said, "is patient with animals and slow to anger. She has great integrity."

Nobody could guess.

"It's obvious." She crossed her arms and scowled at us.

"Can you tell us what integrity means, Margaret?" Miss Hartoonian said.

"Don't you know?"

Miss Hartoonian blushed. "I think it would be helpful to the class to hear it in your words."

"It means you do what you believe to be right."

"Then, I hope all of us in this class have integrity."

"Well, we don't. Letty does. It's Letty," she said, rolling her eyes and marching back to her desk.

"Class, what could Margaret have said to describe Letitia?"

"Short," Howie offered.

"Skinny," Mindy Birnbaum said.

"Average," someone else put in.

I preferred Margaret's description. It seems she was wrong, however.

When they ask why I listened to her, they don't want to know about Margaret. They want to know about me. They're right, of course. I can't blame Margaret entirely. Though she directed, I acted. The question is: who wrote the script? "It takes two to tango," as her father would say—he always played fast and loose with aphorisms.

Tango? Hardly. I feel too clumsy, oafish, and stupid ever to have been dancing.

I feel as I did the day Margaret made me climb over the fence that enclosed the tennis courts at East Mountain School. "Made me" is how I think of it, but in that case, too, there was no coercion.

It was the summer we were thirteen, on a Sunday morning, early.

"Those girls are never there early," she promised.

I was a good girl. I was the kind who said, "Please pick that up," in a haughty tone when my father dropped his gum wrapper on the sidewalk. The idea of sneaking someplace where we weren't allowed made my breathing shallow. Nevertheless, I was a little bit thrilled. I liked the idea of me, Letty Larue, sauntering onto the well-kept courts at the East Mountain School for Girls, casually swinging my Chris Evert racquet by its handle. I liked the idea that we'd be doing something daring. And I trusted world-wise Margaret to make it all right.

At six-thirty on Sunday morning, I zipped with difficulty the back of the tennis dress I'd bought with my birthday money the previous summer. I'd worn it to play tennis only once before, since it seemed pretentious on the scruffy public courts we normally used, but I often tried it on in the privacy of my room and admired its crisp, white fabric and its kicky little skirt appliquéd with strawberries. It was tight under the arms now and slightly shorter than it was meant to be, but it fit well enough to work as a disguise, to show I belonged. At seven, we met outside Margaret's house and rode our bikes to East Mountain.

Margaret and I lived in a nice neighborhood; but there was a distinct difference between our part of town and the area around East Mountain School. In Glendale, as in

Los Angeles at large, the greens of money and foliage run together. You know you're in the best sections when you can walk more than three contiguous steps in the dappled shade of overhanging branches. The shade at East Mountain was so dense that the grounds were practically dark and the air tingled with eucalyptus. The grass along the edge of the courts was thick and Margaret had to shove hard to jimmy our racquets underneath the fence. Then she tossed the balls over and scrambled up, over, and down the other side herself, her Jack Purcells needing only the lightest purchase on the chainlink to propel her forward, the bones jutting out from her wrists as she hooked her long fingers through the wire diamonds.

I couldn't move like that. Margaret always put my deliberateness in a good light; she would say I was careful and ladylike, but really I was scared, hesitant, and just plain slow when it came to using my body. I tried to jam the toes of my sneakers firmly into the links, though they would not fit; I glanced compulsively over my shoulder, scanning the smooth lawn for the principal (I hadn't heard of headmasters then) or the police. I had to drag myself up; the chain dug into the flesh of my fingers and my arms quivered with effort. At the top, I nearly lost my balance, as I inched first one leg, then the other, over the points of wire that threatened to grab the hem of my skirt. Then, even harder than going up, was the way down with the asphalt yards and yards below.

Margaret seemed to draw energy from our illicit play and whacked the ball like a demon, but I was nervous and couldn't concentrate. I tried to keep the ball from making noise when it bounced off my racquet, and I ran quietly on my toes, listening for the sirens and indignant shouts, knowing if anyone caught us there, we were trapped, literally caged, two obviously guilty specimens.

We were caught, actually, by a man with a girl about our age. An East Mountain girl. We stopped playing when we saw the orange BMW pull into the parking lot, but though Margaret might have made it, there was no time for me to work myself over the fence. We stood by the gate, waiting for our punishment, me with my head down, pushing at the strings of my racquet, Margaret nonchalantly bouncing and catching, bouncing and catching one of our balls. There was no question of our continuing to play, though there was plenty of court space.

It was the girl who mattered, the girl who made me wish I could slither right through the fence and hide in the bougainvillea. It was nothing she said, only the way she held herself, sure of her place. She was wearing boy's running shorts, loose and low on her hips, a T-shirt cropped with scissors, and scuffed leather tennis shoes. She paused before the gate, knowing we could not get out until she released us. She glanced at my dress, which was, I saw now, entirely wrong. She flipped her long, blond hair forward, and then tossed it back, gathering it with practiced fingers in a high, careless ponytail. The silver bangles on her wrist jangled elegantly as they fell down her arm.

Finally, cupping her hand behind the padlock, the girl lined up the numbers in the combination.

"Ready, Dad?" she said, looking away from us as she swung the gate open. She gave her head a little shake, so that her ponytail swished. We scurried out.

Now, remembering my humiliation as I

rooted among the fat blades of amaryllis leaves for a ball Margaret had earlier sent over the fence, while tugging down the hem of my too-short skirt, I suspect I may have been mistaken. The jangle of the girl's bracelets might not have been smug; her pause may have registered only confusion, as she wondered how the gate could be locked if we were inside; her glance at my dress might have been admiring. It's possible. Still, it was inevitable that I would see her the way I did, being as I was and as I would remain.

CHAPTER 2

Margaret

Everyone knows Sundays are ungraspable. I didn't really expect to accomplish anything. But Sunday night, I prepared to buck the unproductive trend the weekend had begun by placing the laptop open on the table, ready for the next morning. I filled my new Mont Blanc with ink and scratched out a schedule on the legal pad.

8:00–11:30 write
11:30–12:30 buy baby-naming book
12:30–3:30 write

3:30–4:30	run
4:30–5:30	grocery shop
5:30–7:00	write to middle of scene

My plans for that last hour and a half were inspired by Hemingway; I had read that he had always stopped when he knew what the next sentence would be so as to pick up the work easily the next day. It occurred to me that by this principle I should try to get a sentence or two down that night, but I liked the idea of starting fresh in the morning with a clean slate, so to speak. Clearly, Elaine and her hair had set me on the wrong path earlier and some unconsidered words now would surely do the same.

I starred the hour I planned to devote to exercise to remind myself not to forgo that physical refreshment—*mens sana in corpore sano,* as they say—no matter how involved I was in the writing. I made a mental note to start with a good breakfast, as well—maybe sardines and tomatoes on Swedish flatbread, a snack that looked bracing and wholesome in television commercials.

As it turned out, there were distractions at home Monday morning that I didn't antici-pate, used as I was to being out of the house by seven-fifteen. First, Ted dawdled over the paper, placed a few calls, and in myriad other ways made his presence un-conducive to my settling down to work. After he left, the cable company demanded access to the roof, and, because I seemed to be the only one home in the building, or at least the only one willing the answer the bell, I had to let men in jumpsuits in and out three times, which, since we don't even subscribe to cable, necessitated peevish calls to Benson Cable, to City Hall, to the landlady's answering machine, and to Ted to express my annoyance over having to fa-cilitate the money-making schemes of a giant corporation that was doing nothing for me.

It occurred to me when the stomping overhead was at its most distracting that this might not be the cable company at all, but some elaborately costumed and or-chestrated criminal gang, so I compared the number listed in the phone book with the one on the card the technician had given me, an operation that would have taken

very little time, if we did not live in an apartment so cramped that we had to store the
phone books behind the cookbooks behind
the large pots in the bottom cupboard.

Then, I had to eat something. We'd had
only toast for breakfast, there being, in fact,
no tomatoes, no flatbread, and no sardines.
We did have a tin of anchovies, but at
seven-thirty these had not seemed appetiz-
ing. At ten-thirty I made more toast and
spread peanut butter on it. I read the story
in that week's *New Yorker* as I ate: depressed man lives in crummy apartment;
pays much attention to grout between bathroom tiles; becomes more depressed.
Indignantly, I tore it out to send to Letty.

"I could have written this with one hand
tied behind my back!" I scrawled on a Post-
it with my Mont Blanc.

Right on schedule at eleven-thirty I was
standing in the childbirth aisle at the bookstore in Union Square, comparing *Multi-
cultural Baby Names for This Millennium
and the Next* with *Jack and Jill, Jeremy and
Jessica.*

"Ms. Snyder?"

At the end of the aisle, her boy-cut cor-
duroys slung low around her hips and flar-

ing out over her running shoes, was Chloe Brown, one of my tenth-graders. Former tenth-graders.

"Chloe. Hi. What are you up to?" It was always awkward to meet students outside of school, where I was not the teacher they knew. Presumably, they were not the students I knew either. I, at least, always felt as if I'd been caught doing something illicit.

"Mom is forcing me to read something," she said. As usual, the lift in her voice at the end turned her sentence into a question. "When we go to Nantucket." She reached to pull the elastic from her ponytail, smoothed her fine, light brown hair back from her face with both palms, and stretched the elastic around her hair again.

My WASP students had a habit of dropping the possessive pronoun when they referred to their parents, as if they were nurtured by some sort of universal progenitors. "Good idea," I said. This was, thank God, teacher territory.

I resisted the urge to suggest *Wuthering Heights* or *Sense and Sensibility.* She would not like them. "How about *The Shining*?"

She'd stepped closer to me and I could

smell stale smoke. Cigarettes were very in among upper-class New York children.

"I think you'd like it," I said. "Since you like scary stuff." This was a gross generalization drawn from the observation that the single piece of literature in which Chloe had shown any interest over the course of the previous year was *The Tell-Tale Heart.* Even William Carlos Williams, usually a great hit with tenth-grade girls, who, after reading him, earnestly believed they, too, could be poets, as long as they eschewed the rhyme they'd deemed essential when they were unsophisticated ninth-graders in favor of sensual imagery, had left her cold.

The Shining was, in fact, my standard recommendation for girls who wouldn't read; *The Firm* for boys. This annoyed parents who envisioned their offspring tearing through Henry James (although, they, themselves, had only the vaguest memories of a sinister governess—or was it a nanny?— from the high school class in which they'd been forced through *The Turn of the Screw* and found the classics too unnecessarily dense and old-fashioned for their own tastes). Of course, there were always a few students who did tear through James, or at least Edith Wharton, which made the inability of the rest to puzzle through even a paragraph of complex syntax and advanced vocabulary after ten years of the finest schooling money could buy (eleven or twelve, if you counted preschool) all the more exasperating.

"Ms. Snyder?"

"Yes?"

"No offense, but is that why you're not teaching next year?"

"Is what why?"

She lifted her eyes toward the bookshelves over our shoulders. "Are you having a baby?"

"Well, in a way," I laughed. "I'm writing a novel."

Her eyes actually got larger, something I had thought only happened in books. It was quite gratifying, and I had to remind myself that, contrary to popular opinion, it doesn't take much to impress a fifteen-year-old.

"That's really sick! What's it about?"

"Well, it's in the very early stages. I think I probably shouldn't try to describe it yet."

"Would I like it?"

"I hope so, Chloe." Actually, I sincerely hoped not. "Right now, I'm doing research, trying to find a meaningful name for a character. You know, the way Estella's name meant 'star,' and she was like a bright, cold star?" I said, shifting from insecure author to know-it-all didact, a guise in which I felt more comfortable.

"Cool. I'm probably going to be a writer, too. After I go to law school."

Her confidence would have been intensely irritating had it not been so ill-founded. At Chloe's age, I hadn't carried myself with anywhere near such assurance and would never have dared to ask a teacher whether she was pregnant or what the novel she was writing was about. Would never have dreamed, in fact, of uttering such a casual word as "cool" in conversation with her, and certainly would not have admitted to such a lofty goal as that of writer, or even law school. Did this reticence explain why I was so far behind now?

"Well, I'll look forward to your book, then," I said. "And your mother's right; if you want to be a writer, it would probably help to do some reading."

"Oh, I know," she said. "But I'm going to write about real life. I'll probably do a lot of traveling first."

"Well, that's good, too." I resisted my impulse to glance at the book I was holding as a hint that it was time she moved along. It would have been easy, but unkind, to take advantage of my superior status as an adult and a teacher in that way.

Chloe looked toward the escalator. "I should probably get my book."

As if I'd been keeping her! "Yes," I agreed. "Maybe we'll run into each other again this summer."

"I'll be in Nantucket. Until September." She pulled the elastic from her ponytail again.

"Right. Well, have a good summer, then."

But Chloe was already drifting away toward a table display. As I watched her flip through the pages of a book of sexually suggestive photographs and then study a collection of Calvin and Hobbes cartoons, I felt sorry that I was no longer a teacher. Observing the Chloes maneuver their way across the rickety bridge between childhood and adulthood had actually been one of the delights of my former profession. I felt fondness easily for those who looked up to me, who trusted me, who needed my help.

I reminded myself of how I'd chafed at

other aspects of private school teaching—
that sense of myself, for instance, as an
earnest, gray lump, unfit to interact as an
equal in the society for which my education
had prepared me, far below even all of
those "Moms." Sure, I'd read a lot of books
and could recognize a grammatical sentence, and these things were invaluable as
far as they could be applied to preparing
society's children for and getting them into
good colleges. This being an object second
only to keeping those children alive, I
ranked right up there with the pediatrician,
when my skills were wanted. But outside of
that narrow band of usefulness, respect for
my abilities waned along with people's interest in the "classics." My colleagues and I
were pitiable—we were intelligent people
who weren't bold enough to use our smarts
to earn real money. Had we been blue-
collar, we might have been romanticized as
creatures of another world. Instead, we
were condescended to as failures, glorified
servants to those who'd worked the world
better than we had, those who understood
that an annual rereading of *Leaves of Grass*
got you nowhere.

But that lump was not me at all, or at

least it hadn't been me. Back in D.C. in my twenties and even my very early thirties, I'd liked the idea, as well as the work, of teaching at a fancy, private school. In the spring of my senior year of college, when for the first time in my life I had to choose what to do next, I'd disdained the various corporations and consulting firms that had recruited at Penn, because I was too independent to indenture myself to the Man, not to mention too artistic to soil my hands with workaday business concerns. At the same time, I was too much the overachiever to fling myself into the currents of some exotic-sounding city and let them take me where they would. In the end, I'd applied for the teaching job because it was the only one I could think of that sounded challenging but did not involve the aforementioned tedious and humiliating apprenticeship—private schools did not even require an education degree— which I quite reasonably could not resign myself to until I'd decided on my true career.

And I enjoyed it. Since an inexperienced teacher does pretty much the same thing as an experienced one, albeit somewhat less smoothly, I had more authority than most of my contemporaries in other professions. I was immersed in the transcendent works of Western civilization, and what I said about them was pretty much the last word. The job connoted smarts without the stuffy specificity of the university professor, a dedication to the right values and an enviable rapport with the hip, younger generations.

But then, some time after I'd passed my thirtieth year, I began to see it differently. No longer was I dallying for a few years after college, passing on my freshly acquired knowledge and zest for learning, while I looked about me. I was a teacher. And what had been an absorbing game while I was only playing became a drab and repetitive chore. If it were only that I would spend every November with *The Scarlet Letter,* every February with *As I Lay Dying,* and every April with Huck, I might have been grateful at least to be in good company, but I feared the prospect of delineating the contrast between the wilderness and society and nodding sagely at the irony of going to hell for helping Jim year after year, as far as the eye could see. Worse, I would do this while my students, many of whom would never understand why Vardaman's mother is a fish, would nevertheless become doctors, lawyers, and Indian chiefs and pass me by.

On my way out of the store, I hurried past the new-fiction shelves. All those hopeful covers, putting a brave front on story after story about "the twisted, unbreakable bonds of love" and "the triumph of love over abuse in the South/in the Midwest/in Big Sky Country" and "man/woman/child coming to know himself/coming to love herself/coming of age" made me feel ill. This was only one season's crop. Authors were out there by the hundreds, ceaselessly writing, writing, writing. It seemed when I looked at those books, which would soon be replaced by more of their kind, that there could not be left for me a single plot unturned, a character undelved, or a situation unexamined. And these were only the lucky few that were published! How long would they last? A few months, most of them, with those that made the *New York Times* notable list hanging on a season longer. In short, there were too many books already. What made me think that it was worthwhile even to try to add to their number?

This, I told myself, scowling at a cyclist

who was riding on the sidewalk along University Avenue, was not the way to think. Marguerite Yourcenar and Barbara Pym would not have quailed at the sight of other people's books. A really good book, written with original style and a deep understanding of human nature, would find its way. That was the sort of book I had in mind.

A thick envelope from Letty awaited my return. The first page was written on the back of a school flyer announcing Dinosaur Day, February 27. I poured myself a glass of iced tea, rummaged unsuccessfully through the crisper for a lemon, and then settled on the couch. I anticipated a good read: Letty understood human nature.

Dear Margaret,
You'll notice that one corner is missing from this page. I think Noah ate it. Or possibly one of the cats. (I mean that one of the cats ate the corner, not that Noah ate the cat, of course!) I only left it alone for thirty seconds, but obviously I should have taken it into the bathroom with me. Anyway, I am now writ-

ing to you from the closet where I am hiding from 1. letter-consuming children and/or pets, 2. the room with the oven and refrigerator, which some maniac tried to use as a four-star pastry kitchen, 3. any activity that will highlight my glaring inadequacies in the eyes of other mothers.

The day after we'd last spoken, Marlo's school year had finally come to an end, and her class had scheduled a party for that final afternoon to which parents had been invited and for which Letty had cheerfully promised to produce "a treat to share." For both of her daughters, Letty's mother had always turned out perfectly serviceable devil's food cupcakes on similar occasions, and Letty assumed she'd make the same. "Although," she wrote, "I considered picking up a couple of bags of mini carrots, so as not to offend the health-conscious." But then Alex Prescott drove Marlo home from an afternoon of stages-of-metamorphosis poster construction with her daughter, Chelsea Prescott-Fang. Letty has felt a little defensive around Alex ever since "Take Your Daughter to Work Day." It was Chelsea's idea, not her mother's, that Marlo should accompany her to her mother's office, but Alex did give her permission.

"I felt so terrible," Letty'd said then, almost crying. "I mean, don't I work? I *feel* like I work! Why am I so tired if I'm not working!"

I assured her that certainly she worked, that I was sure Alex Prescott was only trying to secure entertainment for her daughter, who was probably dreading a boring day producing independent films with only her insensitive mother for company. I suggested Letty give permission for Chelsea to join Marlo on a day of work with her. Nevertheless, we both recognized that in this episode "Mothers Who Work Outside the Home" had scored.

The letter continued on a piece of paper that had obviously been torn from a Big Chief tablet.

So here she is now, leaning against the doorframe and crossing her arms over her perfectly cut raw silk jacket. The color of this jacket, by the way, is a violet next month's Vogue *will announce as the shade du jour, while I sport a rugby shirt in Lands' End–catalog grape circa 1986. "What're you bringing tomorrow?" she asks.*

She does not wait for my answer before producing hers. "I thought I'd make some tuiles," she says, and triumphantly dislodges the toy from a long-consumed Happy Meal from under our threshold with one pewter Ferragamo car moccasin.

I wouldn't have even known what a tuile was, except that Martha Stewart was rolling them about a month ago. From what I could see in the five minutes I watched while scrubbing out the dog dishes, it took about an hour to make four. Tuiles will prove that despite Alex's demanding profession she is not skimping on her child, and further that she's capable of pursuing domestic chores with the passion and perfectionism of the artist.

The "Mother Who Works Outside the Home" is going to shape cookies one by one by hand, whereas I, the "Stay At Home Mother," am planning to beat a box of cake mix and three eggs for four minutes with an electric mixer or swing by Ralphs for pre-washed, plastic-packaged produce. Don't I have anything more to show for all the time I've chosen to lavish on my child?

"Petit fours," I blurt out. "Petit fours with

candied sweet pea blossoms and angelica leaves." Where did that come from?

Alex lifts her wrist to check the time. The motion shows off her manicure, which is exquisite, the nails oval, pale pink. Her fingers, in fact, look like they could be on television. I think I'd like a manicure, Margaret. Is that a terrible thing to admit?

But here is the important part. Alex is wearing the very same watch I am. The one Hunter picked out for me, with the large red hearts on its face. The one that could be attractive only to a child under ten.

I hold my own wrist up. "Zeke?" I ask.

"Hunter?" she answers.

And in that moment, I wish I'd said mini carrots fast, fast, fast, before she'd announced the tuiles, so that she could have said "Chips Ahoy." Because now she must speed off in her vehicle capable of summiting Swiss Alps to spend all night creating her delicately flavored lesson in French culture, while I have exactly fifteen hours to produce twenty-seven too-pretty-to-eat teeny, tiny cakes.

After frantic consultation with Craig Claiborne and trusty, but often too heavy-handed with the sugar, Fanny Farmer, I find

that petit fours can be made relatively simply by baking a sheet cake and cutting it into
finger-sized portions. So simply, in fact, that
once I've fed the children their turkeyburg-
ers, played with Mr. Squeeky, Wally Whale,
and a slew of other bath toys, found The
World of Pooh, which had slipped behind
the couch, for Michael to read to Noah and
Hunter, and nursed Ivy while listening to
Marlo read chapter four of Caddie Wood-
lawn, I realize that all petit fours are not alike
and the product of my half measures won't
be impressively spectacular.

In retrospect, I cannot believe the folly of
this. We're talking about feeding a fourth-
grade class here! Nevertheless, I think of the
tuiles and decide to complicate my contribution by trisecting the cake with two layers
of jam and one of custard. But first, I must
purchase a jelly-roll pan and a fine-mesh
cake rack. And, as it turns out, my 24-hour
grocery doesn't stock a fine-mesh rack, but
ingenious chef that I am, I buy two regular-
meshes and stack them together crosswise.

As I scrape the bits of hardened pink
frosting from under the rack and put them
back in the pan to remelt, so I can give the
petit fours a third coat (this, by the way, is

only the first batch—I'm also doing a white and a yellow set), I'm actually pleased with my inspiration. Like the tuilles, these old-fashioned cakes project precisely the right image. They demonstrate that my children come first in that I'm devoting my time and creativity to delighting my daughter's class with ephemeral finger food, but at the same time they prove that I'm too sophisticated to be limited to a smiley-faced cupcake kiddie world. Not to mention that they all but scream "See the woman who can concoct with careless grace a sweet fit for presenta- tion at Le Cordon Bleu." Who would have thought a snack could say so much? And who will know the custard curdled twice and I had to drag Michael out of bed to go out for another dozen eggs? Who will know I was gathering rose petals with a flashlight at three-thirty a.m. (sweet peas, it seems, are poisonous) from the neighbor's yard and dipping them in sugar water at four?

At five, I gaze proudly at the cookie sheet checked pink, yellow, and white with the lit- tle square confections, each like a perfect ring box. Petit fours, I think, c'est moi!

If I'd not been so staggeringly tired today after lunch when I strapped Ivy and Noah into their car seats and adjusted the sun-screens so they wouldn't get too hot and inserted the tape of "Songs to Grow On" into the cassette player so we could all sing along, I might not have forgotten that I'd set the cookie sheet on the roof of the Tercel. It clanked onto the concrete just before I reached the corner.

I didn't even have time to go to the market for carrots and had to settle for Hostess Gems from the 7-Eleven. That the kids clearly preferred the mini doughnuts to the tuilles was no comfort. No comfort at all.

The letter covered other issues. Michael had purchased a computer "for the kids" and had already wasted two weekends that could otherwise have been spent on beach trips and backyard ball games unsuccessfully attempting to set up Internet access. Hunter had gone to a birthday party at which the favors—not the gifts!—the favors, which every child got, were CD Walkmans. Hunter, Letty explained, did not even own a CD, which seemed reasonable to me, since Ted and I have only about seven compact disks ourselves because we're unable to justify the extra expense when records have perfectly good sound quality. Of course, this means we can't buy any albums produced after 1981.

Ivy was teething. Marlo was angling for figure skating lessons. Letty enclosed a little drawing Noah had done that may have been one of the cats, or possibly some owl-like bird.

For both of us, I thought, magneting the cat-bird onto the refrigerator, it was good that the school year was over. Now that it was summer, Letty and I would be able to shake off the world beyond ourselves choc-a-block with continually assessing observers. Without Alex Prescott looming in the doorway, Letty would be free to mother along in her naturally excellent way, unconcerned about how that would appear to others. For my part, I would retreat into the universe of my novel. I would think nothing of what others thought of me, and in that way emerge with something that would stun them all.

CHAPTER 3

Margaret

I needed a compelling plot, a connected thread of events that could draw me, like Theseus, through the labyrinth. Back in my study, I pushed the laptop aside. Time to get to work. I uncapped my pen. "Her mind furiously churning, she uncapped her new Mont Blanc," I thought. "The nib hung quivering over the porous, yellow page, which waited, patient and still, laying itself open for her words."

Plot, I told myself sternly. I tried to think. "Theodore wants desperately to get through med school. (med school = Minotaur)," I wrote. "He comes from a long line of doctors. His father is demanding, controlling, sort of a Joe Kennedy with his eye on Mass General as his empire." I broke off here. Best if I used another color to represent motivating background material.

It took about half an hour to locate my colored pencils in a tin marked "Art Supplies" under my shoe boxes, but time devoted to organization is never wasted. At the top of the page I constructed a key. I would continue the plot in blue-black fountain pen; fill in character traits, tragic flaws, outside influences, etc., in red; insert secondary plots in green; note any quirky supporting details, symbols, particularly apt metaphors and allusions in pink.

"On his own, he's doomed to fail," I wrote in red. I could figure out why later.

"His wife, Anna, is brilliant. She helps him cheat on his exams so he passes."

"Problem." Problems would be blue. Why doesn't Anna just become a doctor herself, if she's so smart? I was stumped for a minute, and then I had a sensation surprisingly similar to the one cartoonists depict with a lightbulb. "Anna is doctor," I scribbled, in my excitement making a mess of my color scheme by continuing with the blue pen. Anna's being a doctor would make cheating easier and also cause conflict for her—she's not only loosing an incompetent doctor on an unsuspecting population of sick and injured, but also endangering her own career. Maybe the book should be from Anna's point of view.

Theseus left Ariadne. "Once Theodore has used Anna, he leaves her while she's sleeping, preferably on an island. Maybe Barbados?" Ted and I could take a research trip. "He can't stand to live with her knowing what she's done, even though she did it to help him."

It was a great plot. I could tell by the way the snags unraveled after only a moment's thought. I waltzed with the legal pad around the room. I passed my hand over the page of scribbled, colored lines in awe. Even by itself, it was a work of art I would be proud to have displayed someday among my collected letters and drafts.

Faulkner printed the plot of *As I Lay Dying* around the walls of his study in Oxford. I was reluctant to write directly on the walls myself—after all, we were renting—but I did have several large sheets of white paper left over from the "Literary Map of the United States" I'd done for my eleventh-grade class. If I transferred my diagram to those, using one sheet per pivotal event, I could tape them up along the hallway, around the bedroom, and in the space that remained between the bookcases and the windows in the living room. I would leave room to add the chapters in between once I'd decided what would happen in them.

Ted had a dinner meeting, so I worked without interruption. It was five-thirty on the West Coast by the time I taped the final sheet onto the closet/study door and called Letty.

"I've got the plot!"

"You're kidding. That's great! Not until you're done with your homework." The last was not to me, of course.

"Marlo?" Marlo was her eldest, my god-daughter.

She sighed. "Yes. She wants to go roller blading with Patrick and Conor." Neighbor kids. "But I told her—"

Marlo warbled in a high, faraway voice, "Help me, Auntie Margaret! I'm being held prisoner by an evil queen!" She stomped off in what I assumed was the direction of the tiny bedroom she shared with her infant sister, Ivy.

"No skates in the house! So," Letty said, "the book's going well?"

"No, better than that. I have the entire plot worked out, actually taped all over the apartment, like wallpaper."

"You should have written it right on the walls, like Faulkner." This was one of the many things I loved about Letty—she remembered everything I told her. "So? Tell me. What's going to happen?"

I told her, keeping the story as fluid as I could while still injecting the crucial background information. I walked around the apartment as I talked, moving from one segment to the next, just as I anticipated I would when I began to write. I'd easily be finished with this thing in six months. Or, I could work ten hours a day and polish it off in four or five. I wondered if the sculpture of the recumbent Ariadne could be photographed for the cover. Would that cost a publishing house more than a cover designed by their own art department?

"That's great, Margaret."

I ignored the fact that this was a response one would give to a recitation by a six-year-old. Letty hadn't much practice critiquing literary works. "I think it's a book I'd like to read," I said. "Don't you?"

"Definitely. I can't wait to read it. And when it comes out, I'll casually pick a copy off the shelf and say, 'Have you seen this book? My friend wrote it.' I can't wait to do that. I'll just spend the whole day in the bookstore."

I laughed. "Feel free to break for meals."

"Can I ask you about one tiny thing? It's no big deal, but I was just thinking—" She broke off. I could hear water filling the dishpan and small voices making the noise of gunning engines in the background.

"What's that?" I was open to suggestions. I'd come up with the idea in a single afternoon; there were bound to be some pesky details to tweak.

"Well, I just know, you know, from Lottie"—Letty's older sister was a hematologist—"that they're extremely careful with the boards. I mean, a lot of it's oral. I'm sure you've figured this out, but I can't really see how a person could cheat."

"What if Anna was one of his examiners?"

"That's a really good idea, but I'm not

sure it would be allowed. I mean, probably definitely not if anyone knew about their connection."

"Could she change the score later?"

"Maybe. I'm not sure. I mean, security is pretty tight. I guess it might be possible."

Maybe Letty just didn't want to believe there was any way to cheat on the test that her sister had passed. "What if she wasn't his wife, but secretly his girlfriend? Then could she be one of his examiners?"

"Well, that could happen, sure. But I'm just wondering, if he's not giving the right answers, how's she going to convince the rest of the panel to pass him?"

"Maybe she could kill them." She laughed at this and I joined her, but the walls of our apartment no longer looked like a masterpiece.

"Margaret, I really don't want to be a naysayer. I'm sure there's some way to make this work. Because it's such a great story, especially with the myth and all. And I really love the characters."

"No, no. I want you to be honest. What if I'd spent two months writing and then ran into this problem? You're saving me."

I yanked at the first of my drawings. The

tape peeled away from the wall, carrying with it a large swath of paint.

"Margaret, I've got to pick Hunter up from his play date. Let's talk in a couple of days. I'll call you."

"No, let me call you." What with the four children and Letty not earning an income, the MacMillans' finances were tighter than ours. It didn't seem right for her to have to spend money to be my cheerleader. Or wet blanket.

We hung up. I retraced my earlier, hopeful steps, pulling down my faulty framework. Every strip of tape left a ragged track, a dotted line leading only in a cramped circle around the apartment. My novel was still stuck at the beginning—Margaret = Minotaur?—and I was going to have to repaint the walls.

"It'll help me write," I told Ted. Three tenants ago the landlady had attempted an antique effect by painting the apartment a color akin to yellowing linen. As a writer, I was hyperattuned to my environment, and such surroundings were a drag on my wits.

Also, to be honest, I was desperate to destroy the evidence of my mistake. I'd noticed very early in my life that I couldn't tolerate being wrong. I was understanding when others erred, but, unfortunately, this was only in part from kindness. The rest of my forgiving instinct derived from the conviction that others couldn't live up to the towering expectations I set for myself. Everyone made mistakes, but I was not everyone.

When, in second grade, I relied on my own experiences with vegetables and recklessly colored the stem on a mimeographed picture of a pumpkin brown, rather than the requisite green, as the directions had clearly instructed, I begged Mrs. Reynolds for a chance to do it over. "No," she said, "one pumpkin to a customer."

During recess, she taped the pumpkins colored side out to the windows, blocking the afternoon sun so that the classroom took on the gloomy cast of the earth under an eclipse. Obviously, the whole pumpkin-coloring endeavor had been merely an attempt to provide seasonal, albeit prosaic, decoration. Still, she'd given my picture a C, which would now be prominently displayed in all its oversized scarlet shame—until the pumpkins were replaced by the inevitable trace-around-the-hand turkeys—to anyone waiting to board a schoolbus, in fact, to anyone casually strolling by the school, possibly even to those driving past, given the leisurely school-zone speed. Even Dougie Resnicki, who was still using fat crayons, had been granted a B.

Nevertheless, I would like the record to show that I did not wheedle to be taken to the supermarket that evening on a search for evidence to prove the accuracy of the brown stem position. My mother, however, discovered that we were out of spaghetti just as the Bolognese sauce had simmered to the proper consistency. My father was already jingling the car keys, this being a nearly nightly ritual that varied only in the identity of the missing essential ingredient, and since he seemed to enjoy my company, I abandoned the map of the autumnal night sky I was plotting on sixteenth-inch graph paper and went along. The Halloween pumpkins were piled unceremoniously in and around refrigerator-sized cardboard boxes in the Ralphs parking lot. I could not help but observe their stems. Their brown stems.

I felt at once vindicated and outraged. I had correctly rendered the pumpkin in living color and had been rewarded with ignominy.

I found my father already in the checkout line with the spaghetti and a shaker can of Parmesan cheese he'd thought to pick up just in case. "What color is this?" I held up the pumpkin I'd heaved inside and pointed at the stem.

He frowned, suspecting a trick. "Orange?"

"No, not the pumpkin, the stem."

"Who cares about the stem?"

I sighed. "Just what color is it? Brown or green?"

"I'd call it beige."

Beige, sand, dun—those were fine distinctions I, as a normal second-grader, was unwilling to make.

"So brown?"

"Brownish," my father conceded.

As we drove home, I complained at length about Mrs. Reynolds, as well as the creators of the pumpkin outline and its nonsensical instructions, accompanying my diatribe with much angry snapping open and shut of the ashtray on the armrest.

"That's exactly the way the world is, I'm sorry to say." My father's eyes flicked up to check the rearview mirror.

"How?"

"Objective reality counts less than what people say. How do we know what green and brown are anyway? They're just those colors because we, as a society, say so. Your class, as a society, agrees that stems on pumpkins colored by children should be green."

"I don't."

"Well, that's a common problem. Especially if the society is led by a cliché-dependent despot."

"Does that mean if Mrs. Reynolds says it, it's right?"

"Pretty much."

I hadn't needed his thirty-five years of life experience to understand that.

"Still," he said, turning into our driveway, "we can take comfort in the fact that we know better. We can gleefully sneer at those misguided fools." He looked at me as he turned off the engine. "That's what I recommend. A hearty dose of gleeful sneering. You may begin now."

At dinner, my mother explained the concept of poetic license. She also suggested irritatingly that the stem of a pumpkin while it's still in a pumpkin field might very well be green. I assured her that the picture was most definitely of a pumpkin long removed from a field and that Mrs. Reynolds was in no way a poet. Warren demanded to know what a poet was, which spelled the end of the pumpkin discussion. Not that anyone wanted more.

I was wrong in the case of my plot, of course, wrong because I'd been so inaccurate as to be unbelievable, affording me neither poetic license nor license to sneer. Clearly, I needed to do much better.

Ted did not agree that painting the apartment was the best use of my time. "I think you should get the book done first. Then, while you're waiting to hear from agents, you paint the apartment to keep your mind off the future."

"But what about this mess?"

"Sally Sternforth says a writer's surroundings don't matter, because a writer draws her material from within," he said.

"Remember that Annie Dillard essay where she draws a picture of the view from her window and tapes it over the glass, so she won't be distracted by what's going on outside?"

So I wasn't Annie Dillard, I thought the next day, as I draped the couch with an old sheet after Ted left. I worked energetically throughout the morning, pausing only for a restorative square of crumb cake, while I paged through *Samuel Johnson: Selected Poetry and Prose* for instructive essays on composition. By noon, I'd stacked all our books along the hallway and in orderly piles in the bedroom. There was, literally, no room to stand in the bedroom, except on the bed itself, from which our cat, Pickles, watched me somewhat critically. When the bookcases were bare, they, too, begged to be repainted, especially the one cobbled together from raw wood that we'd found discarded in SoHo.

Manhattan was the most affordable city we'd ever inhabited, in terms of acquiring furnishings. We'd been amazed and delighted in our first months to discover not only nearly uncreased magazines piled on the sidewalks, but also perfectly good, or only slightly damaged, furniture—the kind of items that in suburbia would have been shifted from the house to the garage or attic, until a large-enough collection was amassed to justify a yard sale. In Manhattan, we sensed that even had there been enough storage and a proper venue for rummage sales, people had too much money to bother. Why spend a weekend marking prices with a roll of masking tape and dickering with confused elderly women, when you could be brunching at your country house?

So far, Ted and I had dragged home, besides the bookshelf, a child-sized, six-drawer dresser containing three dozen rolls of Ace bandages and about two hundred packets of antibacterial cream; a sort of cupboard on wheels with an enamel top, produced, according to its metal label, in Nappanee, Indiana; and a reasonably clean rattan hamper. Our sidewalk shopping was governed by only one rule: nothing upholstered.

<hr>

"You're not painting the apartment, are you?" Ted asked at seven-twenty, after he'd

stood for an entire minute in silence just inside the door.

I was sanding bookshelves, a task that
would make anyone irritable.

"Not right at the moment. No."

"I thought I told you this was a bad idea."

I blew the dust that had accumulated
along the surface I'd been rasping into the
air. "And your opinion matters more than
mine because . . . ?"

He didn't answer. And then, in one nau-
seating instant, I realized something that
made me feel as if I were strapped in "The
Zipper"—an amusement park ride of my
youth—and had been abruptly turned up-
side down. Ted's opinion did matter more,
because he was paying for my book. He
was, in a sense, my patron. Although, theoretically, my income from the school would
continue throughout the summer, I'd taken
the remaining months of pay in one lump
check, which had already been deposited.
Financially, Ted and I had not been equal
partners for years, but, nevertheless, I'd always brought home a salary that could support me. I had, in other words, pulled my
weight. But now it was as if he were at the
top of a cliff with a rope around his waist

from which I dangled. If he said, "Reach for the rock on the right," did I owe it to him to obey? If I thought the left was better, should he trust me? What sort of a team were we exactly?

"Look, Margaret." Ted set his briefcase down, boosted himself onto the counter, and swung his legs out of the living room and into the kitchen. I seemed to have blocked the traditional passage between the two rooms with the couch. "I know you're having a little trouble getting started."

Luckily, he held up his hand as I opened my mouth to protest, since I had no idea how I intended to defend myself. "But you have to give yourself a chance." He took the Campari out of the refrigerator and held it up. "You want some?"

"Thanks," I said. "What do you mean, give myself a chance?"

"I mean you need to face the fact that you're probably going to have to just sit and think, which you can't stand to do." He twisted a plastic ice cube tray until the cubes surrendered with a crack. "These people, for instance," he said, tapping his briefcase to indicate those who'd submitted grant proposals to the Cabot Foundation, "they spent a lot of time observing and mulling over ideas. They didn't rush around like chickens with their heads cut off, distracting themselves with trivial make-work, hoping that a finished copy would eventually spring full-blown from their heads."

"I observe," I protested. "I mull." His comparing my novel to the proposals he evaluated made me uncomfortable on two fronts. First, concerned as they were with issues like the plight of the poor, these proposals were a continual reminder that others were directing their efforts and talents toward truly worthy causes. Much as I liked the idea of acting noble, such a sentiment could not be applied to anything I'd ever done, including my intermittent volunteer work, which would better be described as vaguely helpful. I didn't like to admit this, but, in all honesty, I undertook such work more so that I could see myself as a caring person and so assuage my guilt over being born among the privileged, than out of a burning sense of compassion or outrage over others' distress. And second—and here my discomfort collided with resentment—how many hours had Ted and I spent groaning over those pages almost universally filled with pompous and tortured jargon? And these were to be my models? "Literature," I said, "is different from your work."

He handed my drink over the counter. "I know it's hard," he said. Was the patron being patronizing already? "You need to give yourself some time, that's all. Don't panic. Don't distract yourself. If I were you, I'd lie on the bed all day. Or go sit by the river. Sally Sternforth wouldn't even do the dishes when she was working on her book. She didn't want any task other than writing to satisfy her drive to be productive."

I laughed, my hands in the air in a gesture of surrender. "All right. You can do the dishes. But, Ted, honestly, I think better when I'm busy. While I'm painting, I'll generate some good ideas. And in a week, I'll be done and we'll both be happier and more productive in bright rooms. Really, I know what I'm doing."

That night, I read Joan Didion's "Some Dreamers of the Golden Dream." I underscored passages lightly in pencil, keeping my lines straight and neat with an index card. "Buy index cards," I wrote on my legal pad, under the exhortation to "Buy baby-naming book," which was marked with a satisfying tick to indicate its completion.

Didion created an ominous mood and suggested an impending threat of suicide, divorce, and murder with her description of the Santa Ana winds, but when I thought about that weather the words that came to mind were "dry hair" and "allergic reactions." As in the case of the pumpkin stem, my own observations did not seem very reliable, if my goal was to produce A work.

"There's no drama in my life," I complained to Letty the following day.

"There's drama here," she sighed. "There's blood and tears, and sweat, too. Mostly mine," she added.

"What happened?" This would be another of the mini-misfortunes from which Letty was constantly bouncing cheerfully back. I sympathized, but sometimes the bid for attention that these scenes seemed to represent annoyed me. Particularly when I wanted to talk about myself.

"Noah pinched his finger in a door this morning."

"My God, Letty, is he all right?" I remembered when this had happened to me in nursery school, my tender, unsuspecting fingers clutching the doorframe during an overly wild game of hide-and-seek, and Jimmy Kaufman slamming the door shut as he ran by. The thought of it still made me gasp and pull my fingers into a tight, protected fist.

"*He* seems fine. He and Hunter are in the bathroom with the light off right now, trying to see if the bandage glows in the dark. I'm still a little tender though. Also, Zippy peed on the car seat on the way to the vet."

Zippy was the guinea pig that lived in Hunter's classroom. Letty had agreed to keep him for the summer, along with her two dogs, three cats, and tank of tropical fish.

"Shouldn't he have been in a carrier or a cage or something?"

"Apparently so. It's a zoo, here, Margaret. I love having all the kids home, but there's just so much . . . I don't know . . . activity."

"What's going on with the bigger-house plan?" We'd concocted the "bigger-house plan," which was actually not so much a plan as a wish, when Letty was last pregnant and realized that if she had another boy, her sons would eventually have to

sleep in some sort of triple bunk arrange-
ment suitable only for merchant marines or
Tokyo businessmen. Luckily, the baby
turned out to be Ivy.

"Well, I don't know if I should say anything yet, but there actually might be a
bigger-house plan this year."

"What? What are you talking about? Why
didn't you tell me?" I was a little ashamed
that in our last few calls I'd not thought to
ask about Letty's life, since I expected it
simply to jounce along in its established
way.

"Well, I was about to, actually. I mean this
all just happened yesterday. Michael got a
call from the director of the Otis Museum."

"The Otis! Would he be interested in
something like that?" The Otis was known
for its flamboyance. It had a gorgeous site,
magnificent buildings, a colossal endowment, and a relentlessly second-rate collection. Letty's husband, Michael, was a
tweedy art historian with a specialty in
nineteenth-century Lithuanian printmaking
who had just been tenured at Ramona
University. They hardly seemed a match,
and I had to admit that, though I'd phrased

my question sincerely, I also wondered if the Otis could really be interested in Michael.

"I don't know. I mean, we don't even know what the job is yet, exactly. It's really all just talk at this point."

"It would mean a lot more money, wouldn't it?"

"Oh, you know," she said dismissively, "we don't really care about money that much."

"Money's not such a bad thing." In fact, like Letty and many others in my comfortable class, I did think that work should be directed toward some more lofty goal than income. Ample money should be the happy, preferably unexpected, by-product of the passionate pursuit of a meaningful interest. However, if the big bucks were not forthcoming despite passion and obvious talent, what then?

"I'm sorry, Margaret, but I've . . ."

"I know. You've got to go."

"But we didn't talk about your book! Do you have a new idea?"

"Next time," I said.

I did not have a new idea. I'd been sanding all day with the notebook open beside me ready to catch any drop of inspiration, but so far the pages had collected nothing but dust. It turned out that, despite my claim to Ted, I didn't think better when I was busy. I did feel industrious, though, almost virtuous, sanding, listening to *Jude the Obscure* on audiotape turned up to maximum volume so I could hear it over the scrape of the paper against the wood.

Applying the primer, while the reader rumbled on about how Jude's misfortunes and ill-chosen associations drag him deeper and deeper into destitution, heartened me, though. The clean, white paint running like a milky river behind my brush renewed my confidence in my plan. Just as I was preparing the wood so that Codman Claret would cling to every grain, so I was preparing my mind for the right idea. But Ted was right, too, in a way. I'd been trying to force inspiration, grabbing like a drowning person at every twig. I would relax. I would float. I would let the ideas come to me.

Letty would approve of this. She'd always insisted that "wait and see" was not just a hopeful way of saying "lazy." If I hadn't filled out her college applications for her, she'd have missed all the deadlines. Of course, she wrote the essay herself, started and finished it in one short afternoon, something about how the values she'd learned as a Brownie had guided her behavior ever since. It had turned out quite well—clever, pithy, light—much better than the labored piece on California's hypocritical attitude toward illegal immigrants modeled on *A Modest Proposal* that I produced after three weeks of erasing and rewriting in my locked room.

Back in elementary school, when I told my mother that Mrs. Larue had signed Letty up for Brownies, she'd scoffed. She'd said she'd wasted enough hours for the both of us striving for inconsequential badges. She'd said the Girl Scouts was an organization designed to keep girls in their place. She'd also declared her unwillingness to iron the uniform. I yearned a little for that ugly chocolate-milk-colored dress and felt beanie on Tuesdays, when the Brownies met after school, but I had to side with my mother after I saw the "telescope" Letty made with her troop out of a paper towel tube. There were no mirrors, no lenses; they just decorated the cardboard with sequins and glitter. What good was that? And it was obvious from

Letty's creation that no one had taught them to apply glue with a toothpick.

Since the table was hemmed in by the shelves, which needed to stay away from the walls, and the kitchen counter was cluttered, Ted and I ate sitting on the bed, balancing a bottle of wine and our glasses within easy reach on pedestals of books. I may have enjoyed this picnic atmosphere and the sensation of inhabiting a work in progress more than he did.

"How much longer, do you think?" he said on the seventh night, picking a curl of sesame noodle off the pillow.

"Really just another day. I wanted to be sure the walls were dry before I put the masking tape around the windowsills."

"You're doing the windowsills, too?"

"They would look shabby, Ted, now that the walls are so nice. Believe me, you wouldn't like it. And then a week for the hall and the bedroom, and then I'm done."

"A week!"

"Well, I was thinking of doing something a little more interesting in here. Maybe a celadon with a light, springy green trim. And then the pale yellow base in the hallway, but with a subtle stencil about three inches above the molding, incorporating the green and the red of the bookshelves to draw the rooms together."

"Are you insane?"

"What? It won't be a Christmasy red and green."

He let his face fall forward into his hands and then tipped his head back again, raking his fingers through his hair. Ted tended toward the histrionic. He thrust his arm toward me, index finger aloft. "Margaret, you have one year. One year to write a novel, not to paint the apartment, not to read about writing, not to talk on the phone to Letty." We'd received a phone bill that afternoon listing a number of calls of surprising length to California during peak hours. "Do you think I would've said, 'Sure, go ahead, take the time,' if I'd thought you were going to spend it tarting up a rented apartment?"

"Tarting up?"

He shook his head. "No, I didn't mean that. It looks nice. But it's completely un-necessary, and it's taking you away from your work."

"All right," I said, my voice tightening as I got up from the bed in a self-righteous huff. My foot tumbled a stack of books, instigating a domino-like cascade of several more stacks. "I'll get back to work, right away, sir." I grabbed my notebook and flounced down the narrow path between the books that lined the hall. I tried to make enough noise with my bare heels to communicate my displeasure, but not so much that it would wake our downstairs neighbors.

Ted followed, a takeout box in each hand. He liked his environment to be orderly, even in the midst of internal turmoil. "Margaret, you're deliberately misunderstanding me."

I'd thrown myself into the corner of the skewed and sheet-covered couch and opened my notebook on my drawn-up knees. This was the closest I could get to demonstrating work, since I'd neglected to pick up any sort of writing implement. " 'Go ahead, take the time,' you said. As if I were your employee!"

"Listen, it was your plan. I liked the plan. I agreed to the plan. Now you have to do the plan! Not whatever you want."

"I'm not—"

"No! Let me finish. It's as if we agreed I could use my time, which is basically the same as our money—not your money, not my money, our money—so that I could build a boat, and instead I used it to reorganize my books. When the time was gone and there was no boat, you would feel cheated."

"If it were important to you to reorganize your books, I would want you to do that."

"No, you wouldn't! Not if you knew I really wanted to build a boat!"

"But Ted, it's not like type, type, type, type, done! You make it sound like if only I applied myself I'd be sliding into the denouement around now."

"*You* made it sound like you only needed to apply yourself."

"Well, I am applying myself. It's hard, that's all. It's art, not boatbuilding. I'm figuring it out as I go along."

"Margaret, I know it's hard. I couldn't do it." He sat down on the couch next to me. I pulled my nearly empty notebook against my chest. "But I believe you can, and I just don't want you to look back and see this as an opportunity wasted. I want you to give it your best shot."

How could I argue with that? Ted was right. The only reason I'd not made more progress was that I hadn't been giving it my best effort. I needed to buckle down. "You know what?" I said. "I think I'll just do a quick base coat to cover up the mess and be done with it. Save the celadon for when we buy a place."

"After you sell your book."

I got off to an excellent start the next day. Like Sally Sternforth, I ignored the growing ruin of dishes and I turned off the *Today* show before it was over. The shelves were dry, so I shimmied them back into position and reshelved the books. To discipline inspiration, I forced myself to write one thing in my notebook after every tenth trip to the bedroom to collect books. It didn't matter what I was writing, I told myself. As long as I got material down, I'd have something to work with later. Then I painted the windowsills.

Really, I got an enormous amount of both writing and apartment work done, so it was unfortunate that when Ted came in the door unexpectedly at three-fifteen, I was sprawled on the couch laughing at something Letty was saying. Our door was weighted so that it swung shut automatically, which it did with a wallop, as Ted stomped back down the stairs.

"This isn't good," I said into the phone.

"What? Did you paint the windows shut? I did that once."

"No, no, it's Ted." I explained the wrath of Ted, perhaps putting a bit more stress than was strictly accurate on his patronizing tone and unreasonable expectations and neglecting to mention the elaborate stencil work I'd proposed.

Letty was gratifyingly outraged. "It's not like you're making widgets! I mean, sometimes you'll produce pages, sometimes you won't. Just because there's no evidence doesn't mean you're not working. It's a process. Look at me; I must pick up twelve times a day, and the house is still a mess."

Though I appreciated Letty's attempt to empathize, I did not, I admit, relish her equating her work with mine.

"I think Ted has a point," I said. "Maybe I'm not doing as much as I could be. I'm working, but maybe I'm not working in the right way."

"What is the right way?"

"Well, for one thing, I should do more writing, generally. What about, instead of calling each other, we send e-mail. Writing might become a real habit for me then."

"And when Ted hears you pounding away at a letter to me, he'll think you're working."

"Letty, I'm not suggesting this to avoid work—it's to make myself work more!"

"I know."

"Well, I think it would be an excellent exercise for me. I could even imagine that in the course of writing to you about an idea, I might really develop it. I might end up writing my novel to you."

"Ooh, that would be neat," she said. "It would be like reading Dickens in the original serial form."

∿∿∿∿∿

That was my first mistake. If only we'd stuck with the phone and kept Letty's words off the page, I don't believe I would have done what I did.

Letty

Margaret always had to be different. Some people, my mother, for instance, thought she was showing off. "Why can't she just do like the rest of you girls?" she said the year we were nine and Margaret refused to remove the Socialist Workers Party button from her collar, even for the Christmas concert, and then again the next year when Margaret insisted on trying out for the football team. She wasn't showing off, though, when she did those things. She was just being Margaret.

The story is that Margaret and I met before we could understand what it meant to know someone else, and I suppose this is true. I can't remember the single occasion when I first became aware of her, because she was always there, like my own hand. She was more vivid, though, than other children, at least to me. My memories of nursery school are a jumble of unconnected details—penny loafers with a confusing dime in the penny slot, a dress in a Mondrian pattern of red, white, and blue rectangles, swinging around white tights, a boy's bristly brush cut, and the teacher with a bindi—although then I thought of it as a dot—guiding my fingers to form a papier-mâché bracelet for Mother's Day. I remember Margaret clearly, though. That morning Margaret made her mother something she said was the bust of Nefertiti, which made some boy, Buddy something, giggle. It looked like a ball with a blue cylinder on top. Miss Betty, the teacher's aide, frowned. "Wouldn't your mother like a nice bracelet," she asked, "like everyone else is making?" But Margaret shook her head, her gaze intent upon her sculpture.

I was never like that. If they said, "Make a bracelet," I made a bracelet. I was so pliable, so eager to please. It would never have occurred to me to do anything else.

Margaret told me my bracelet was the best. I didn't say anything about Nefertiti. I didn't know what a Nefertiti was. Maybe she'd made a good one.

Our high school offered Spanish and French, but Margaret petitioned the language department for permission to take Latin at Occidental College in Eagle Rock.

"It's the root of all Romance languages," she said, trying to convince me to go with her. "Once you know Latin, you'll pick up Spanish like that." She snapped her fingers. "Not to mention French and Italian."

I understood. It would be dull and sometimes even a little frightening to take the RTD to Occidental all by herself three days a week. But I wanted to learn Spanish. It was the language not of clean and cozy Glendale, but of the real city, Los Angeles. I may have had vague notions of social work. Mostly, though, I was attracted to Spanish because its speakers seemed to occupy a mysterious and, therefore, romantic world behind an invisible but nevertheless impenetrable curtain. When Lottie and I went downtown with my father, who wore a white shirt and a charcoal gray suit and did something incomprehensible behind a desk in a high-rise under buzzing fluorescent lights, we would loiter in the Central Market with five dollars in a little leather box that folded into a flat square. Instead of my prosaic existence, I wanted the life of the girl with the black hair who swayed to the music of the bright horns as she filled paper cups with horchata at her father's stand. She slipped before the curtain as easily as she made change and then ducked behind it again, turning to the woman I assumed was her mother with a laughing comment in her rapid, rolling tongue. Unlike Margaret, I had no interest in the words of the past. I wanted the words of the future. Also, Spanish was supposed to be easy.

"If you learn Latin with me," Margaret said, "we'll be able to have conversations no one else will understand."

That was how she talked me into it.

Such conversations were more difficult than we had imagined, given Latin's vocabulary of poetry and conquest. "Oh, the times; oh, the customs" was a handy phrase when we wanted to roll our eyes at our classmates' proclivities or our parents' demands, and occasionally we found opportunity to say, "I sing of arms and a man," but most of what we learned ran uselessly along the lines of "Gaul is divided into three parts."

However, as it turned out, I had a talent for Latin. Margaret dropped out after a year and a half, but I went on and on, throughout high school, riding the bus on my own, careful to keep my head far from the windows greasy with hair tonics. At first it was the neatness of translation that attracted me, the puzzle of the line that meant nothing until you broke it apart and applied the rules, moving each word into place. But later, it was the style that drew me on, the elegance of Tacitus, the slyness of Catullus. I felt I knew these writers, as personalities, as people, through their words.

Michael and I met in a class on St. Augustine, an advanced Latin course we were both taking our freshman year of college. At our wedding, Michael thanked Margaret.

CHAPTER 4

Margaret

I spent the next hour cleaning my brush and then dismantling the structure of dirty dishes we'd erected along the counter over the last two days. I eschewed the dishwasher so as to feed my self-righteous dudgeon, while I waited for Ted to return from his snit. It was helpful that many of the dishes with the most stubborn encrustations were Ted's. He had a habit of eating at the center of the plate, which somehow forced bits of food to the edges, as if they'd scrambled to the rim for safety. I'd always found this a charming idiosyncrasy. Now, it struck me as disgusting. My earlier admission to Letty that Ted's view might be valid didn't mitigate my sense of outrage.

Inside my head, my voice, ringing in round, powerful tones, delivered arguments worthy of Demosthenes as I scrubbed grains of petrified rice from the plates and quite effectively drowned out the notion that had the book, in fact, been going well, I'd not be taking such umbrage. I'd written three pages that day! (Granted, all in the form of incoherent notes, but still words! Filling pages! Three of them!) Letty was helping me! (Or, she would have been, had I had some material to discuss!) How dare he tell me that I shouldn't talk to my friend? Did I barge into his office to check his progress? This was *my* book! I would do it *my* way!

Inconveniently, I'd just finished washing the last fork when I heard his key in the lock. I plunged the utensil back into the dishwater and pretended to be dislodging material from between the tines as I gauged his intentions so as to marshal the most effective defense. He came up behind me and I tensed, if further tautness was possible, ready to let fly.

"You know what?" he said, putting his

arms around me. "I've been wrong about this. You should do it your way. What do I know about writing a novel?"

The rampart I'd constructed collapsed under his touch. "No," I protested, "I've just been thinking the opposite." I turned to face him. "From now on, I'm going to approach this in a businesslike fashion. No more phone calls. No more waiting for the muse. I'm going to leave the apartment with you in the morning, as if I had a real job. I'm going to produce 'deliverables.' Five pages per day."

I knew Ted would appreciate this plan. He was practical, a characteristic I admired in him, although I didn't covet it for myself.

Ted and I had met in our sophomore year at Penn at an October charity smorgasbord, during which students were supposed to explore avenues for "giving back" to the community to which we so comfortably did not belong. Ted was manning the Philadelphia Reads! booth, an organization he'd founded himself the year before, after he'd discovered that one of the cafeteria workers couldn't decipher the menu.

Technically, this was where we met. But I knew who he was. I'd noticed him in Poetry from Spenser to Yeats, even before the professor had pointed out, to our great embarrassment, that we'd been the only two to receive A's on the *Paradise Lost* paper.

Ted was a big believer in first things first. While I whirled from Life Drawing to Astrophysics 101 to Studies in the New Testament, lighting on whatever seemed interesting as I paged through the catalog, he slogged dutifully through courses like Marx and Engels, Victorian England, and The Novel from Eliot to Hardy, as if he were laying down bathroom tiles. I admit I'd disdained this approach. I liked to tell myself that I was a Renaissance woman, but this was not entirely accurate, since, as I've mentioned, I'd yet to do one thing well, let alone a varied handful.

By doing first things first, Ted had moved on to seconds and thirds. His success thrilled me. I was proud of his steady rise from research assistant, to researcher, to program officer, to program director, and the trail of exhaustively researched, gracefully written reports that followed him. Still, it was galling to think of how we'd started out just the same, each with a superior interpretation of Satan's fall, when I saw how he'd lapped me, lapped me again and again, while I reeled among the starting blocks, not sure even which lane I'd been assigned.

But no more. I would take a page from Ted's book. I would advance in a methodical fashion. The primary goal was neither to prepare to write, nor to think about writing, nor to talk about writing; it was to get words on the page. Therefore, that was where I would begin. As soon as I found a place to work.

On Monday evening, I'd promised myself I'd produce five pages a day. By Friday at three, after a weeklong search for rent-free "office" space, including trial runs in several cafés in which a nagging awareness that I appeared either pretentious or pathetic and probably both tended to subvert my concentration, I figured I was running a fifteen- to seventeen-page deficit, depending on how many of those daily five pages I could reasonably expect to complete in the last few hours of the afternoon. The summer heat had been radiating off the sidewalks and buildings all day and my bare shoulders were sizzling in the sun. As I waited to cross Eighth Street, smothered by a sidewalk vendor's incense, I felt like a roasting fowl, flavored with vanilla and basting in my own sweat.

My last hope for an office was the Jefferson Market branch of the New York Public Library. From the outside, it had romantic charm, with its turret and its reputation for having housed women prisoners in the nineteenth century (although that may have been a building behind it—the facts were difficult to pin down). Inside, beyond the nifty circular staircase and stained glass windows, it was really two linoleum-floored rooms with an unimpressive assortment of books, their covers grayed and softened by hundreds of hands, collapsing sideways on their shelves.

It was cool and fairly quiet. One of its beigy-yellowy tables was completely unoccupied. It seemed unlikely that any of the people poking at the computers or standing dazed in front of bookshelves, absently

rocking strollers, would think me pretentious and/or pathetic if I sat down and uncapped my Mont Blanc. Which I did.

It was three-twenty. Two pages, I decided, would be a decent beginning. I would
not leave my seat until I'd written two
pages. Unless I had to go to the bathroom.
Or get a drink. No, I would be fine without a
drink. Two pages, bathroom breaks only.
Double spaced.

I opened my notebook. Two pages, I saw
with relief, would be nothing, given the material I'd jotted down on my last day of
painting.

"Robert Martin ate a breakfast of grape
fruit, egg, bacon, and English muffin. He
needed to be prepared for what lay ahead."

I was drawn to this scene. The bright
kitchen, the deliberate chewing as Robert
Martin, brown hair neatly parted and
combed, moved from item to item, getting it
all in, under his belt, loading himself as if he
were a weapon. For what? What lay ahead?

I felt hungry myself. Should I run over to
Gray's Papaya for a hot dog?

At the next table, a man in a shrunken
white T-shirt—an undershirt, really—was
pushing a ballpoint steadily across a note-

book page. He was bent so low that his cheek was nearly pressed against the paper. Suddenly, he sat up, turned the page with an ostentatious rustle—obviously meant to show that *he* was getting some writing done—and then bent again to his work. He was the type who might very well be repeating, "All work and no play makes Jack a dull boy."

His industry irritated me. "Shh," I said. I frowned in his direction. He glanced up for the briefest of moments and shot a puzzled look around the room. When his gaze lighted on me, he smiled very slightly, very quickly, and then bent to the page again, his pen racing as if alive and highly caffeinated.

I bent to my own page, lowering my own cheek somewhat. I would pursue Robert Martin. I would generate two pages of close observation in poetic prose, revealing through a detailed study of his every mundane motion the character of this man. Then I would have him. And once I had him, I would know what to do with him.

"Robert Martin"—I would check the significance of this name later in my baby name book, but I would not pause now— "selected the last egg"—I crossed that out—"the last extralarge grade A egg from its cardboard nest and positioned it carefully four inches above the edge of the prewarmed skillet." This showed he was a deliberate man, not spontaneous. "He paused for an instant, and then, sure and quick as lightning, snapped the egg down upon the iron. A perfect crack." I crossed that last sentence out. I could do more with it. "He could achieve a perfect crack almost every time now, but it had taken some practice. The proper height at which to begin the stroke and the degree of force had been easy enough, but it had taken him quite a while to realize that to be exactly centered, the crack must actually fall"—would a crack "fall"?—"slightly closer to the fat, rounded end of the egg; there had to be extra length on the pointed end to make up for its narrowness. Once he had discovered this crucial element of position, Robert had rarely been dissatisfied with his fried egg." Robert's logic confused me here—how could the way an eggshell was cracked affect the fried egg itself?—but I pressed on. "While the egg was frying, he nestled the empty carton"—I liked that, "nestling" the cardboard nest. Or was it overdone?—

"onto a stack of others under the sink. Every few months he delivered these to his mother in Filmore, who fashioned them into tiny hats and Christmas trees and sold them at craft fairs." And was, I hoped to God, a more interesting character than her son.

With generous margins, this lucubration on a man self-conscious to what seemed likely to be the point of insanity filled a little over half a page. It was something, at least. I could go on to describe the kitchen—the precisely folded hand towel with its border of pineapples, the hiss and spit of the percolator, the sectioning of the grapefruit with a Swiss Army knife he'd carried over in 'Nam. I set my pen down. I needed a bathroom break.

There is such a thing as effortless concentration, when one is thinking so deeply and so fast that shouts of "fire" would only further color the dream. In that state, the ideas run from the brain more quickly than the hands can catch them and make them concrete. I'd experienced this often enough before to know that the condition in which I'd written about Robert Martin was nothing like it. This was a forced concentration, a grit-your-teeth-and-press-your-fist-to-your-

forehead-in-imitation-of-The-Thinker concentration, a concentration in which one
quarter of the brain dragged the rest
screeching with the hand brake pulled up
hard. It resulted in halting words, painfully
squeezed forth one by one, as in the prover-
bial blood from a turnip. It also caused a
tense, headachy trance, which made me
move stiffly and sluggishly toward the
ladies' room and then take my time in that
sanctuary. I washed my hands twice, once
on the way in because I didn't really have to
go and couldn't think what else to do, and
then again on the way out, after I'd determined that I might as well see if I didn't
really have to go. As I wiped up the water I'd
dripped on the counter to sanitize it for the
next person, I made a mental note to have
Robert Martin mop up the sink in a public
restroom.

I wound another brown paper towel out
of the dispenser to get a clear sense of the
texture. Was "brown" really the best way to
describe the color? I could more easily picture Robert in a service station washroom
on the way to Filmore, trying to dry his
hands on the semi-clean edge of an over-
used roller towel. It would make him feel

used and dirty. No! It would symbolize the impossibility of keeping one's hands clean in this world—thus providing a neat segue into a flashback to Vietnam.

I hurried back to my table, pregnant with this idea. Vietnam was admittedly a bit beyond my experience, but I could reread Tim O'Brien's books and take notes for atmosphere. Maybe Ted and I would rent *The Deer Hunter* tonight. Few women had written fiction about the Vietnam War—I would get points for my daring originality. I could already hear the choppers chopping—no, slicing—no, whipping up the humidity. "He remembered it as if he were still slogging through the water-heavy air," I wrote. Or I would have written had my pen been on the table where I'd left it.

I looked under my notebook, then picked it up by the wire binding and shook it. Nothing fell out. My breathing quickened. My armpits prickled. Ted's pen. The pen Ted gave me. The pen that made me a writer. I pushed my chair back and crawled under the table, scanning the floor in all directions. How could I have left it? This was New York, for God's sake! True, it was the cleaner, safer New York, as compared with the last few decades, but this applied only if you were a person, better yet a man, on certain subway routes and downtown streets, not if you were a gold-nibbed Mont Blanc on a public library table.

"Looking for this?"

The ostentatious scribbler was bending over so that his balding head was even with his knees. He waggled the pen in one ink-smudged hand. I grabbed it and shot out from under the table, nicking my head on the edge on my way up.

"Careful there."

"You took my pen!" As the words left my mouth, I realized I should have been more circumspect. I'd broken the first rule of the woman on the street, or, as it were, in the library: never engage. Although, had I not noticed his furious writing earlier, I'd have been less suspicious. He was scrawny and his skin and clothes had a somewhat grayish, unwashed cast, but they didn't appear to be literally lived in, nor did he seem schizophrenic or drunk. His eyes were clear, his face was unweathered, his beard was only a day or two old, and he was properly zipped. Still, he was likely to demand a reward or insist on talking to me in a vaguely threatening or bothersome manner. He might even follow me home. After all, he'd been scribbling with an unnatural intensity, he'd taken my pen, and he was a strange man. These things could not add up to anything pleasant.

"I was afraid someone might steal it," he said. His volume was not appropriate for a library.

I looked around, worried other patrons would be offended by his implication, but the only other person in the room now was slumped over a table, drooling on his arm.

"I meant to catch you right as you came in, so you wouldn't worry," the scribbler was saying, "but I got sort of engrossed."

He motioned toward his table. His own pen—blue with white lettering along the side, obviously purloined from some business—lay unattended on a page three-quarters full of densely packed writing. "I've gotta use this place as an office," he added. "My partner is writing an opera in our apartment." He put his hands over his ears and made a face. "So," he said, shrugging and giving the semi-smile he'd used when I shushed him, "back to work."

"Thanks," I said belatedly, when I was sure he wouldn't swerve back in my direction. I used a voiced pitched correctly for the library.

He waved his right hand, wafting my gratitude away, while his left picked up the pen and raced across the page at a speed incompatible with serious thought.

I tried to continue my novel, but the choppers were overwhelmed by the crack of the librarian's gum and the tender green rice paddies paled in the fluorescent light. I attempted a scene in which Mrs. Martin transformed a single egg carton cup into a whimsical fedora, but she, being quite obese, moved even more slowly than her son. I forced Robert to continue his drive to Filmore and sat him in his mother's kitchen in a vinyl-and-chrome chair from which the stuffing tufted out along one seam, but the two of them had nothing to say to one another.

"Care for some breakfast?" the mother finally brought out.

But, of course, Robert had already eaten.

I knew I could not drag the Martins across one more line that day. Altogether, I'd written three-quarters of a page, with plenty of space between the words to insert corrections. Maybe beginning my book with the minute details of morning routine was the trouble, I thought, winding my way down the circular staircase. It left the whole rest of the day yawning. On Monday I would thrust Robert directly into midafternoon.

CHAPTER 5

Margaret

My hopes for the summer were largely fulfilled, thanks to the strict regime I imposed on myself with a digital sports watch. I'd learned from a PBS documentary that James Thurber's wife had insisted he set an alarm clock at intervals to prod himself to work quickly. My fourth-grade teacher had employed a similar method.

Mrs. Larson's classroom was part of a new addition to the school, the linoleum hard and slick, the edges of the desks as yet unsoftened by the cuts of rulers and compass points, the seats made of some modern composite that would never wear away in comforting grooves. The days in that room passed in a series of terrifying quizzes, each beginning with an ominous clicking as Mrs. Larson set a kitchen timer and ending with a ringing that seized our hearts and stopped our pencils. With the smart movements of soldiers on maneuvers, we would pass our papers to the front, where she would collect and then impale them on her spindle. There were multiplication tests—increasingly difficult as we galloped from the twos times tables to the twelves; there were spelling quizzes, history quizzes, and geography quizzes, during which, each in turn, we ran to the front of the classroom, index finger outstretched, to identify on a huge, pull-down map of California the county Mrs. Larson had shouted out. No time to prepare, no time to think. "You know it or you don't," she barked. Some hours must have been devoted to learning the material on which we were quizzed, but the only other activities I remember from that class were singing "Yes, I Have No Bananas" and playing a plastic recorder.

Realizing that up until now I'd spent too

much time thinking at the expense of writing, I adapted Mrs. Larson's (and Mrs. Thurber's) technique to my book. Now that I'd created a couple of characters—Robert Martin and his mother—and a general sense of their situation, I wrote whatever came into my head about them in forty-five-minute intervals, punctuated by the bright beeping of my watch alarm. With a continual sense of the imminent "time's up," I tore forward without looking back. At the end of the summer, I would type this mass of pages into the computer and discover a richness and complexity I could never have consciously achieved.

The alarm bothered Simon at first. Simon was the ostentatious scribbler, although after my first week at the library, I didn't think of him that way anymore. He was, in fact, the writer of an actual novel published by a house with a predilection for first novelists with exquisite prose. Through interlibrary loan, I borrowed his book from the Bronx branch and read it carefully, searching for direction.

"The human relationships," I said, one day in August, as we walked down Charles Street eating slices, "they seem so real.

How did you come up with those characters?"

"Hmm," he answered, chewing, willing to
think this through. He was generous with his
writerly insights. "I don't know. It's not like
they emerged full-blown. But, you know,
after a while they start to come to life and
then it's easier to figure out how they'd be.
Are you going to eat your crust?"

The writing books also made it sound as
if a good writer need only take dictation
from bossy characters. Left to their own devices, however, Robert and his mother
would do nothing but eat.

Across the street, a man with matted hair,
wearing, despite the heat, a flannel shirt,
leaned over the trunk of a car. In his right
hand, he clutched what seemed to be a fat
marker or a wedge of chalk with which he
wrote in long, passionate, swooping flour-
ishes on a large sheet of paper. With his left
hand, he smoothed the paper over and
over, keeping it flat across the trunk.
Abruptly then, he stopped and straightened. The chalk dematerialized. There was,
in fact, no paper. The man walked away,
conversing with himself.

My alarm went off as we were about to cross Hudson.

"Just to the river," Simon begged. "Please, it's so hot. I need to see water."

"You go ahead," I said. "I must obey the watch." But he turned up the block toward Perry Street and trudged dutifully back with me.

In the evening, the oppressive heat of the day became the balminess that gives summer its good name. Ted and I strolled languorously east on Tenth Street in the dusk. In front of the 2nd Avenue Deli, we passed tourists folding a map and felt smug. The city was ours now that those who really owned it had gone to their country houses. And we were pleased with our possession, especially amid the quaint, exotic spectacle of an East Village August gloaming. A lumpy Ukrainian matron in a sprigged housedress stood sourly in her doorway, her arms crossed over her chest. A cat on a leash slunk along the wrought iron fence that bordered an outdoor café. Indian restaurateurs beckoned us into their Christmas-lit establishments. Ted studied the shelves in a used bookstore, while I perched on a vinyl chair with a split seat under a ceiling fan and read scattered pages of *Goodbye, Columbus.*

On such an evening, the sense that I was a writer—and even that I was the kind of writer who might be considered an artist—was palpable. I had the giddy feeling that this city was both my home—which meant I could claim its attendant rich human drama as my own—and a piece of theater I could view at a remove, a spectacle from which I could borrow shades and tones and a succession of characters who would, if I listened closely enough, whisper to me their amusing or poignant narratives. It seemed on such evenings that capturing life on paper would be almost as easy as observing it.

My novel bubbled from me as we luxuriated in all New York had to offer. I would outline for Ted the various maneuvers I'd put Robert through each day, while we dodged Rollerbladers along the riverside promenade to Battery Park or walked block after block uptown. I proposed options for the next day's charge as we combed the bricks near the Metropolitan Museum for metal admission buttons casually discarded on the way out by those who'd paid the suggested amount. Ted, who in high school had gone through a period of intense interest in the Vietnam War, gave me details about what battles Robert could have been in and what military rank he could have achieved while we held hands perched on the balustrade under the trees in Bryant Park, waiting for the free movie to begin, or two-stepped under the stars at Lincoln Plaza to the open-air bands. On the Staten Island Ferry with our faces turned to the breeze, and strolling late at night past Korean groceries overflowing with plums and green onions and black-eyed Susans, we debated whether Mrs. Martin would have called her son "Bob" or "Rob" and bandied army nicknames about.

I believe I would have been content never to finish, never to publish, only to work, if the limbo that was August had lasted forever. In August, when all of those people who, by their very existence, made me feel like a dull penny under their shoes were in places like Martha's Vineyard, I was happy—in the deep way engrossing work makes one happy—simply to be dreaming scenes for Robert to play. I was satisfied when I caught hold of one of his moods and coaxed it to stick to the page in a way that seemed sure to call forth that very sensation in a reader's mind. I was ecstatic when occasionally such moments seemed to dance across the paper in particularly graceful or vivid phrases. At times I forgot to reset my alarm and still I kept on, searching for words, crossing them out, straining my brain to conjure Robert Martin from scant impression and overtaxed imagination, trying to draw his very fibers through my fingers delicately, so as not to scare him off.

Looking back now, I suspect that in that brief, sweltering period, I was, in fact, a writer. But cooler weather was inevitable. And with it returned the real Manhattanites, the sort of people who called a messenger to deliver a package to the building across the street, and I was merely a hanger-on again, cringing and grinning and well aware that if I had not been attached to Ted, I would never have been asked out.

We were invited to dinner in September, the first occasion at which I had ample opportunity to appreciate the words of Harold Nicolson, whose slim book of essays I'd read back in July, when it was already far too late for me to heed this advice: "Unless . . . you possess a strong will and a large private income I should not recommend you to announce your first book before you have written at least a third of it."

Opening rounds went well. We were able to admire our hosts' apartment without excessive chagrin, since it was only one room larger and a few hundred dollars less expensive than ours. (Being far better connected than we, they'd been able to take advantage of the city's generous rent control policy, and so could afford to put a good deal of their money into their country house.) Then, while wine was poured, I leaned against the bright orange counter (cheap, 1970s renovations were the scourge of even the best apartments) and listened while other guests compared the fingerlings available at the farmers' markets in Rhinebeck with those on sale at Union Square. People were either weary of summer and relieved to be back in the city or were already exhausted by the city and longed to be back in the country. That Ted and I had stayed in town was exclaimed over as an eccentric novelty, although several people agreed that the summer months they'd spent in town were among the best they'd experienced. Of course, they'd been students at the time.

When Ted and our host began to discuss the merits and liabilities of mutual acquaintances, I bravely struck off on my own and wandered into the living room where two women seated in easy chairs were engrossing one another.

Changing rooms at parties is risky. You have done something purposeful and so are forced to look as though you indeed have a purpose. If you're lucky, a kind stranger will welcome you into her conversation. If you're extremely lucky, an acquaintance will hail you from across the room. Most often, you must resort to feigning an overwhelming interest in the knickknacks or pressing your nose against a dark window so as to be able to see beyond your own abject face. For me, the tide of the party was about to turn.

I suspected that the women in the chairs registered my presence with triumph, pleased that they were involved in an animated conversation and not, like me, standing awkwardly too far into the room to retreat, but neither of them faltered in the pretense that I did not exist. Luckily, a plate of baguette rounds spread with marinated goat cheese was lying hospitably on the coffee table, so rather than scanning the bookshelves or acting as if I'd forgotten something essential in the kitchen, I availed myself of this prop to jimmy myself into their tête-à-tête.

"Have you tried these?" I said, committing myself to the couch and raising a baguette to my mouth.

"No," said the woman nearest me. She pushed the plate slightly in my direction and turned back to her conversation. I considered chugging the contents of my wine glass.

"I hear you're writing a novel," said a bright voice behind me.

"Yes," I said, turning with relief. Sally Sternforth crooked her knees and perched beside me on the couch. "Who's your publisher?"

"For a first novel," I explained, sliding into the space between the couch and the coffee table to retrieve the hors d'oeuvre I'd dropped on the rug, "you don't usually have a publisher until the whole thing is done."

I tried to deliver this as if it were insider's

knowledge to which I was privy, but it came out as an apologetic squeak.

"Really? Well, you know, with nonfiction . . ."

I interrupted her as I regained my position on the couch. "Yes, the proposal, the contract, the advance, all before the book is written. Have you tried the goat cheese? It's delicious." Secretly, I thought goat cheese had run its course. When we gave a party, I intended to reintroduce sharp cheddar, perhaps the sort with wine stirred in.

Sally forged on. She would not be waylaid. "Well, I admire you," she said. She did not admire me. If she was kind, she pitied me, and if, instead, she was like most people, she felt superior. "It was such a relief when I'd been writing for months without validation to know that at least my book was sold." A profile of Sally, replete with photos in various stylish outfits, had appeared in the *New York Times Magazine* two weeks before.

"Yes," I said, "that would be nice." I tore at my baguette round with my teeth.

There are those, and I like to count myself among them, who will graciously change the subject when they sense a particular line of conversation may cause embarrassment for another. Others, however, close in, licking their lips, like hyenas who sniff the blood of a wounded gazelle. "But you've published short stories?" Sally suggested, delicately retrieving a crumb of cheese from the corner of her mouth with her tongue.

I was tempted to lie. I might say, "Certainly, a few pieces. In small periodicals mostly. You know, the *Hoe and Spindle, Blue Dragon Review,* that kind of thing." I could even mention a big quarterly or two— *Prairie Schooner, Grand Street*—as long as I avoided the national magazines. It was a pretty safe bet that Sally Sternforth didn't have back issues of the *Sewanee Review* piled by her bed. But I'm excruciatingly honest. It's a fault really. "No," I admitted. "I really just started this."

"But Ted says you quit your job. Someone must have told you that you have potential." She nodded encouragingly. I thought of my ninth-grade teacher, who'd written "Very good! You'll be an author someday!" at the bottom of my five-paragraph sketch about a frog vacationing in Baja. I was sure that Mrs. Hammerstein was not who Sally had in mind. Did she really picture Paul Auster plucking one of my paltry, albeit well-written, student evaluations off the kitchen counter in a friend's house and calling to beg me to share my talent with the world?

"According to John Gardner," I said, "I'm a novelist."

"Oh, you studied with John Gardner?" She said it matter-of-factly, but I could tell by the way she leaned toward me and smoothed the cocktail napkin lovingly over her knee that she was impressed. Even one of the women in the chairs glanced my way.

But what good was impressing people with lies?

"I mean his description of a novelist—in *On Becoming a Novelist*—it fits me."

"Oh." She put the napkin on the table. "We should mingle," she said brightly.

Parties had long been a problem for me. People had an annoying habit of asking what I "did"—a question I had been brought up to think rude. My old answer, that I taught high school English, elicited a predictable response. First, as my companion realized that he or she was stuck talking to someone who exercised power only over sixteen-year-olds, there would be a subtle shift in stance, coupled with a fleeting scan of the other guests, in preparation for a smooth getaway. This was generally followed by the well-intentioned rally, the patronizing forward tilt of the head. "I really admire that kind of dedication," he or she would say, "the way schools are now." And then I would be forced to explain with excruciating honesty that, no, I was not selflessly redirecting the lives of disadvantaged students from the ghetto by introducing them to the eternal wisdom of Shakespeare, rather I was further advantaging those who were already so well clamped upon the track that led to success that they could hardly derail themselves if they tried.

In a different crowd, the comment on the current state of public education might be replaced by a hearty "I better watch my grammar!" by which the speaker meant that he, unlike me, had more important things to do than pay attention to usage. But, in either case, the mention of my former profession had never incited lively interest and spirited conversation, except to the extent to which I could reveal tidbits about the failings of children with socially prominent parents, which hardly seemed fair or dignified.

In short, I was used to others' sudden need to mingle.

My new answer, on the other hand, provoked much interest, but of a kind that made me squirm.

"So what do you do?" the fortyish woman seated beside me at the dinner table asked. Her midriff, slightly plump, showed between her tube top and her spandex, hip-hugging skirt, and her black hair had a chic, slept-in look. I briefly regretted using a brush before leaving home.

"I'm, um, working on a novel." I was surprised at how difficult it was to choke these words out. In private, I was proud of my efforts.

She threw her head back and rolled her eyes. "Oh, God, who isn't?" she said bitterly and reached in front of me for the wine.

"Who's your agent?" Zachary Roth asked. Zachary wrote a column about Washington gossip for a weekly political magazine. I could feel the winds of the savanna; the hyena's hot breath at my heels.

"She doesn't have an agent yet, of course," Ted said, rescuing me and even managing with his tone to suggest the question was ridiculous. "Fiction doesn't work that way. You have to write the book first."

"So what's it about?" one of the easy chair women asked. She leaned across Zachary, who was seated to my left, finally interested enough to look at me.

These questions! I wanted to throw my hands up to block them. Of course, this last was perfectly reasonable. I would ask it, if someone told me she was writing a novel.

For a second or two I made divots in my shrimp risotto, as I summoned my descriptive and analytical skills. "Well, there's a guy, a man," I began, "who was in Vietnam. And he's home now. In southern California."

"Margaret's from L.A.," Ted put in.

"Well, Glendale, really," I said, relieved to be on firmer ground. "More Middle America on the West Coast."

"So what happens?" slept-in-hair woman asked.

"Well, he comes home," I continued. "Actually, he is home, already. When the novel starts. In southern California."

"There are flashbacks to the war," Ted tried again, helpfully.

"But what happens?" slept-in-hair asked

again, forking a generous helping of rice and shrimp into her mouth.

"Well, he seems to be doing a lot of cooking," I said. "Maybe he should try making risotto." I laughed to show this was a joke. No one joined in, not even Ted. I couldn't blame them. I wasn't even sure how it was funny myself. "And he shops for groceries. To support the cooking." I was losing them. The host was refilling wine glasses. The hostess was heading for the kitchen. "I guess it's really about aimlessness in post-Vietnam America," I ventured in desperation.

"Oh, that's interesting," Zachary said. "Would you say that the seventies were aimless? I'd say they were full of purpose."

"Misguided purpose," someone said. There was general laughter and for a few blessed moments discussion detoured into the reintroduction of the crocheted vest, but they were not through with me yet.

"Where have your stories been published?" asked the other easy chair woman, who was, I suddenly remembered with acute embarrassment, an editor at the *Paris Review.*

"I've never," I said, glancing apologetically at Ted, "been published."

"Oh, well," Sally said cheerfully, "you know Emily Dickinson never got published!" She took a swig of her wine, as if toasting the prospect of a similar fate for me.

If at times during my previous career I'd felt I'd been living some of the more pitiful moments of *Good-bye, Mr. Chips,* this clearly was *Lord of the Flies,* and I was Piggy.

Over dessert, someone complimented Sally on her *New York Times* profile, and she launched into a story about the photographer's obsession with finding backgrounds that would provide strong contrast to her clothes. She revealed that one photo had, in fact, been taken in the bathroom. I could not fault Sally Sternforth. She had not, after all, written a multiple-prize-winning book simply to spite me. Yet, she had sized me up and satisfied herself that I was nowhere near her stature, and for that I gave myself permission to wish that the tarte Tatin would give her heartburn.

"I just never imagined," Sally concluded, beaming, "that anything like this would happen before I was forty."

As we walked home along those same East Village blocks that had made me feel like a true writer only a week before, the first fall breeze rose off the East River and swept the stray food wrappers and pages of *The Village Voice* toward the gutters. I shivered.

"What kind of writer would want that kind of attention?" Ted asked loyally, putting his arm around me. A man was peeing in the middle of St. Mark's Place. I thought longingly of Washington, D.C., a place where people's pictures were taken in their bathrooms only when they were caught in the midst of criminal or compromising activity.

On Ninth Street, Ted paused to riffle through a stack of magazines waiting on the curb for the next morning's recycling pickup, and I sounded my depths. Was Sally's my idea of success? Was I as arrogant as she, believing it was only a matter of time and a judiciously placed call from my publicist before the world fell at my feet? Such a person deserved to be struck down and that Sally had been rewarded was simply a prime example of the way society actually worked, not a lesson to guide the course of my own life.

A professional magazine scavenger had swooped up on his bike and was trying to trade last month's *Architectural Digest* for the current *Vogue* Ted had just picked up. I shook my head. *Architectural Digest*s were thick on the ground; we'd already read it.

At home, I flipped my laptop open, slipped off my shoes, and drew my feet under me in my traditional writing position.

"You're not going to work now, are you?" Ted protested.

"I just had an idea," I said, "on the way home."

I did not have an idea. I wanted to rail to Letty about my disgrace. When I accessed my e-mail, however, I saw that she had beaten me to the punch.

Margaret—
Well, now I hate our house. Four hours ago it was fine, maybe a little cramped, certainly not architecturally distinctive, but fine. Now it shames me, every bit of it.

"But what about those curtains?" you'll protest, because you are my friend. Those curtains you made for the living room with the aqua-and-yellow vintage material from Fabric and Foam? "Shabby," I will say to

you. "And two of them are crooked." "What about the mint green Formica kitchen counters with the silver stars and moons and asteroids? You chose this house above all the other nondescript boxes in Beverlywood because of that Formica," you will say to me. And I will say to you—"Tacky."

Face it, Margaret, 23 Hummingbird Lane is a starter house, and anyone living in a starter house this far into the race is a loser.

We went to a party tonight as part of the vetting process for this job Michael may or may not want. (He's decided, at least, to be vetted.) The hosts were some people in Sherman Oaks—she does museum development; he's in the industry—some kind of studio executive—anyway, something I have no concrete concept of.

It's not that I've never been in a nice house before. We grew up in nice houses, didn't we? Not as nice as this house in Sherman Oaks, but still, decent-sized with a good scale to the rooms and some attention to detail. That my parents' house is nicer than mine never bothered me, though. That's a different generation. Everyone knows housing is more expensive now. Even that people only ten or even five years older

than we are have nicer houses never bothered me. We would catch up, I thought,
when Michael got tenure.

These people—Zoe and Brad—they're
younger, Margaret. They're younger and
they have a better house. Not just better. It's
so vastly superior that the two structures
should not even be classified as the same
species.

Their house, for instance, is built into the
canyon and has a redwood deck from which
you overlook the Valley—an ocean of lights
like iridescent plankton. Our house has a
cement slab with a clear view of 24
Hummingbird Lane, a beige ranch with a
dominant garage door. Their house has an
entry area, a formal dining room, a family
room, a Sub-Zero refrigerator, and a blue
enamel Viking oven. We have Sears appliances, a dining el, and no version at all of
the rest of that stuff.

"Stuff!" you say disdainfully. "Why should
you care about stuff?" And you're right. It's
not the stuff so much as the graciousness
that seems to go with it, the careless way
Zoe stuck the knife in the marinated goat
cheese, the unstudied fan of green cocktail
napkins on the oak buffet, Brad's generous

hand with the single malt, the cleanliness of their infant, Hannah, in her pale pink Baby Guess sleeper.

If I were the kind of person that lived in that house, I wouldn't have painted my toenails in the car on the way to the party; I would not have told my babysitter to microwave frozen enchiladas for my children's dinner; I would not have hemmed my trousers with Scotch tape. I would be serene; I would be respectable; I would be a better Letty.

You scoff. Yes, I can hear you scoffing away. But you have to agree that surroundings are important. If you feel sunnier in a bright room than in a murky one, wouldn't it follow that in a spacious, well-organized house, you'd feel generous and in control?

It's not just that, though. I admit that the reason I most hate my house now is that if Michael takes this job, we'll have to invite Zoe and Brad into it. And then they will see that we are not as good as they are. "That's not true," you say. I know. I know. But they'll think it anyway; you know they will. There will be a supercilious smile behind their eyes as they admire the "creative" way I've converted footlockers into end tables and the "artsy" look of our fabric-draped couch and the fact that I've produced sushi and grapefruit Campari granité in a kitchen without counter space. As they drive up Beverly Glen, they will talk about how warm Michael is and how kind I am, and then they will say, "Yes, it's too bad." She will incline her head lovingly toward him and he will give the varnished wooden stick shift of his luxury coupe a fond caress, and they both will feel relieved that they each chose to marry someone perhaps a little less warm and a little less kind, but infinitely more at home with high-end appliances.

Your green friend,
L

I shared with Letty the benefits of my own insights that evening, my fingers sprightly on the keyboard.

Letty—
Do not doubt yourself! Brad and Zoe will doubtless be fighting for custody of Baby Guessed Hannah when he discovers she can't do a thing with a footlocker and she realizes he loves his car more than his wife. I do agree, however, that surroundings are

important, and I'm sure you would feel bet-
ter in a better house—although you would
not be better, since you already are the best
Letty there is. Just wondering—if Michael
takes the job, wouldn't you be able to move
into a house that more closely reflects the
true Letty?

I continued with a two-page account of my
own humiliation and determination to seek
revenge, until Ted begged me to come to
bed.

"It's going well, huh?" he asked, holding
the blanket open for me. For the first time in
a month, the night was quiet, free of the air
conditioner's roar, and we needed more
than a sheet.

"I hope so," I said. Tomorrow, I'd decided, I would read all that I had written that
summer. I would bravely lay out my pages
and pull my story from them. After all, I'd
filled two legal pads in the library, not to
mention the twenty or so pages I'd generated during odd hours at home. Somewhere
among all those words, the core of a really
fine novel lurked, a piece of writing better,
more daring, more moving, more socially
relevant, than anything someone as insensi-

tive and attention-hungry as Sally Sternforth could possibly have written.

"I bet you never expected anything like this would happen to you before you were forty," Ted whispered, pulling me toward him.

CHAPTER 6

Margaret

A ten o'clock the following Monday I placed before me on the false wood grain of the library table everything I'd written all through July and August. Having matured over the summer, and thus no longer believing that any sentence I constructed was necessarily publishable, I had purchased a set of multi-hued highlighters to mark the "good" (orange), the "passable" (blue), and the "needs work!" (green).

I expected, in fact, that entire paragraphs might be unsalvageable and so deserve no highlighting at all. I warned myself not to let this upset me. I did not, after all, aspire to be one of those writers who get by on brilliant prose style alone. I was attempting to capture the essence of a man who'd been through America's most reviled war, a man who'd suffered cruel self-revelations when called upon to give his all, a man who'd returned to an unwelcoming country, but was getting on with his life all the same. This, I reminded myself, would certainly take several drafts.

"Getting On," I scribbled in the top margin of the first page. It might be a good title, suggesting as it did the sort of colorless plodding I had come to see as Robert's chief characteristic.

Simon smiled at me encouragingly before bending his head to his page. This would be one of our last days together and we planned to have a real lunch to lament his going and to celebrate the reason for it. He'd been offered a job as editor in chief of a new magazine called *In Your Dreams,* dedicated to publishing the rambling stories, interesting only to those who personally dreamed them, with which people bored their analysts.

I uncapped my highlighters.

At eleven-thirty I recapped my high-lighters. I had used the orange "good" marker four times. Once to highlight a piece of punctuation. In two months I had written altogether four pages and six lines of usable material. Unable to face my "work" another instant, I retreated to the circular staircase and slumped on the steps until some child insisted on using the handrail to which my nearly supine body was blocking access.

"This is the end," I said wanly at lunch. Simon and I were seated in the back room of the sort of place beloved for its rough "authenticity" and its cheeseburgers. The air stank of authentic smoke. I might have let my head sink onto the well-inscribed table had several of the initials not been filled with ketchup.

"We can still have lunch," Simon said, and I realized that he assumed I was mourn-ing his leaving.

And I *was* mourning his leaving. That, too.

"Your office is on the Upper East Side," I said. But, after all, what would stop me from taking an entire afternoon to subway up, eat a leisurely lunch, test perfumes at Bloomingdale's, and walk back fifty blocks?

It wasn't like I was doing anything productive.

"You're leaving me and my book isn't going well," I confessed. I kept my eyes down, watching my finger push grains of salt along the dark varnished table.

"Maybe you should take a class," Simon suggested.

"A class? What class?"

"There's a good one at the New School Extension this coming semester. With Peter Berginsky. He's written at least fifteen novels and he normally teaches in the master of fine arts program at Columbia." Simon tapped the air with a french fry, as if instructing me with a pointer. "Some people go to Columbia just to get into his class."

"So why is he teaching a continuing education course?"

"For the money, I assume." He touched the remainder of my cheeseburger with the tip of another fry. "Are you going to finish that?"

This was discouraging. I knew better than to think that novel writing could be a money-making scheme, so earning was hardly my primary purpose, but I did hope that after fifteen books an author wouldn't have to scramble for extra cash.

The reasonable, competent half of my psyche agreed with Simon that a course would be good for me. Surely, the strict environment of a classroom and the pressing deadlines, not to mention the threat of public humiliation if I did not produce, would push me to come up with a sheaf of coherent pages to snap into my three-ring binder, and thus would give me the running start I apparently needed to get this project solidly under way. My other half, however, was divided. On the one hand, I feared that my classmates would guffaw as they paged through my offerings in the elevator and later pass each other knowing looks over my head. On the other, I was pretty sure I would be Mr. Berginsky's star pupil. I imagined him (as well as I could without having seen the man) giving me a special glance when we read my chapters, as if to say, "I would praise this as it deserves, but you know we must be fair to the others." I decided to apply.

The pumpkin incident aside, I had done reasonably well in grade school, although on occasion my natural abilities had been hampered by my lack of interest in the make-work my teachers had arbitrarily deemed necessary. That same fourth-grade year-of-the-timer, for instance, I chose one evening not to waste an hour memorizing the nines times tables. I was, at that point, engrossed in compiling an exhaustive catalog, complete with full-color sketches, of the flora and fauna of Glendale and believed that I could not afford to lose a minute, if I hoped to complete it by Christmas, when I planned to present it to my father as my gift. I knew the eights, I reasoned; when it came time for the test, I would just do those and add one.

"Why should we have to become human adding machines?" I said to Letty on the phone, when she tried to quiz me. This was before every student owned a calculator, in the days when, despite the steady encroachment of the sets and subsets of new math, most teachers and parents still did, in fact, think the safest course was for students to become human adding machines.

"Look," she said, "we've learned every number up to nine, so most of them should be easy. I mean, if you know seven times nine, then you know nine times seven, right?"

"Right!" I agreed, although I, in fact, had already forgotten seven times nine. I sketched a royal palm on the scrap paper near the phone. I had not yet decided whether to use examples of all local plants and animals or only indigenous species, and was leaning toward inclusiveness because I was good at drawing our dog, Scout.

"So just remember nine times nine is eighty-one and nine times twelve is one hundred and eight and you'll do fine. Ten and eleven are easy."

"OK," I said. "Eighty-one, a hundred and eight." But even as I spoke I was forgetting, since I was now focused on the brown rats that were rumored to nest in the trees on our street.

The next day, in a panic induced by the very act of sitting at my hard desk, pencil poised above my rectangle of pulp-flecked paper, the reverse side of which had already been used for a spelling test—Mrs. Larson abhorred waste—waiting for the timer to ratchet into position, I recognized with a wave of horror the flaw in my plan. Eight times two and nine times two weren't separated by one, but by two, and eight times three and nine times three were separated by three. I could not remember nine times four. Was it thirty-five, or was that seven times six? Or, no, it was only the fives that ended in five, so maybe thirty-five was nine times five.

Mrs. Larson sandwiched the timer between her large-knuckled hands. "Ready, class?"

No, I wanted to shout. I could feel my body lifting slightly from my chair, my pencil raised in protest. No! But that, I knew, was not an appropriate response.

Click, click, click went the timer, marking off sixty seconds, sixty fleeting seconds in which the well-rehearsed answers were supposed to hurl themselves eagerly from our minds onto the page.

For a few blessed moments, my pencil moved down the paper just like everyone else's while I wrote out the equations, leaving a blank where the answer should go. I filled in the first three and then decided to trust the pattern and add four to eight times four. Thirty-six, forty-five, it was working, I thought; I prayed. But six and forty-eight were hard to add and I couldn't remember eight times seven. I knew eight times eight was sixty-four, so maybe I could subtract from that. But subtract what?

For the first and last time in my entire academic career, I failed to keep my eyes on my own paper. I glanced generally around the room, my eyes darting from the shelf of songbooks to the *World Book* encyclopedias to the rolled-up maps. Except for the clock, the beige walls were bare. Either Mrs. Larson didn't believe in the educational efficacy of colorful posters or she couldn't get anything to stick to the chilly cinderblocks. Furtively, I looked left. Melanie Parker had one hand cupped protectively over her answers. I looked right. Letty was just finishing. She erased one answer, wrote another number in its place, and neatly brushed the eraser bits from her paper. I could see her answers perfectly.

Immediately, I was overcome by a moral outrage that made me blush. I looked away and fixed my eyes on the blank spaces on my own page. Cheating is worse than failing, I told myself. And copying from your best friend is worse than cheating.

Failing, however, was quite bad. I thought of the way Mrs. Larson made us stand up so she could record our grades. "How many had none wrong?" she'd say. I'd be the last, the very last, to stand.

Unfortunately, I've always had an excellent visual memory. Staring at my paper, I could not help but see Letty's answers there, hovering, at the ends of my equations. It was almost as if I knew those answers myself. I had just needed a little boost, a reminder. Now I could even hear Letty's voice from the night before saying, "Nine times nine is eighty-three and nine times twelve is one hundred and eight."

Lightly, at first, I sketched the numbers I'd seen on her paper onto my page. Lightly, at first, but then, once they were there in my own handwriting, I shaded them in darker. I had finished by the time the buzzer went off.

"Pencils down!" Mrs. Larson said sternly.

Letty, I saw, had been about to erase the answer she'd already fixed. Biting her lip, she replaced her pencil neatly in the indentation at the top of her desk made for such a purpose. My pencil, less well stored, rolled onto the floor.

We exchanged papers with our neighbor, and Mrs. Larson briskly recited the answers. Letty, who was grading my work, gave me a puzzled frown before marking my paper with a neat red check, when it turned out that nine times nine was eighty-one. We both had only that one wrong, and as only Chuckie Toll and Patty Pennerson had gotten them all right, we had performed decently. Letty, I thought, must have told me the incorrect answer on the phone the night before. I gave her a forgiving little shrug, but knew that I would, in future, check her information for myself.

"Pass your papers to the front," Mrs. Larson said.

The rest of the morning was filled with a review of the tens (easy, as Letty had promised) to be tested the next day, a presentation of the basic food groups and a spirited discussion of where Space Sticks fit into them, Donna Kim's oral book report on a biography of Julia Ward Howe, the copying down of homonymic spelling words, and a smattering of recorder practice. When the bell rang for recess, Mrs. Larson called

Letty and me to her desk. A sound wafted through the room, half taunt and half sigh, but she squelched it with a look and the rest of our classmates scattered.

"You girls both did pretty well on the multiplication quiz this morning," she said, when we were standing as close to her desk as we dared, which was a few steps away. Mrs. Larson was efficient. She had recorded grades during the book report. She sat with her hands clasped together, resting on her spotless green blotter, as if in prayer. "Pretty well," we knew, was the best we could hope for if we failed to earn less than one hundred percent. "What interests me, however," she went on, glancing down at our papers through her bifocals, "is that you both got the same answer wrong. Nine times nine!" she barked, suddenly, raising her eyes to us.

"Eighty-one," Letty shot back.

I said nothing. It seemed wrong, somehow, to respond, even though I knew the answer now.

"But you both wrote eighty-three. What are the chances of that?"

It seemed an unfair question, seeing as how we'd not yet studied statistics.

"What might have happened," Letty said, "is that last night I called Margaret. I told her to remember nine times nine and nine times twelve. I told her all the rest should be easy, because, you know, we'd done the eights. I must have told her nine times nine wrong then."

"Well, I think Margaret should be responsible for her own work, Letty," Mrs. Larson said.

"No," I said. I pushed the toe of my sneaker into the unyielding linoleum.

"No, you should not be responsible for your own work?"

"No, that isn't what happened," I said. "Letty told me eighty-one last night. She got it wrong today and I copied her. I also copied many of her correct answers. From nine times six on."

"Is this true, Letitia?"

Letty shook her head, terrified. "I don't know," she said.

"Mrs. Larson," I said. "May I approach?" Without waiting for her answer, I stepped forward and put my hands on the edge of her desk. I leaned toward her for emphasis, my chest inches from the spindle. "Letty had nothing to do with this, Mrs. Larson.

She had no idea I was copying from her. She keeps her eyes on her work."

Mrs. Larson sighed. "Well, then it hardly seems fair to punish Letty."

"That's what I believe," I said, nodding vigorously.

"But you girls will have to be separated. Margaret, you will trade seats with Donna. And you will receive an F on this quiz, as well as on the tens and elevens. Which, by the way, are easy. Also, tomorrow I would like a two-page explanation of why you will never cheat again. Using complete sentences."

∽∽∽∽∽

This incident, when I'd padded it with some fictional material about Mrs. Larson and a few of the other more colorful members of our class and typed it out double spaced with wide margins, came to eight pages and two lines, which I figured was close enough to the ten pages the New School catalog indicated were required to be considered for the class. Besides, having been a teacher, I knew that Mr. Berginsky might appreciate brevity.

Now I needed only to convince Ted that a class was worth the price of admission. Obviously, we were not poor—we had enough money to live in Manhattan—but Ted had a horror of profligacy and was convinced that the seemly way to live was never to spend more than was absolutely necessary. To this end, he'd kept track of his expenses ever since I'd known him, when they'd run heavily to books and cheese steaks. Since we'd married, one of my Christmas presents was invariably a ten-by-fourteen-inch, forest green, vinyl-bound ledger in which we both were to record every purchase, including items like shoelaces and Tic Tacs. I balked in the first few months of married life, and then often simply forgot, but when I neglected to make entries he spent hours searching for receipts, making estimates, and quizzing me four days after a meal about whether I'd had the chef or the garden salad, so disturbed was he by the notion of not knowing where our money had gone. Out of compassion for us both, I became more vigilant.

"What do you think of writing courses?" I asked casually, forcing a stack of newspapers into a brown paper bag at midnight on

Sunday. We were tackling the IQ test that was New York garbage disposal. "Only cans in the blue bag, Ted!"

"Where does this go?" he held up the wastebasket from the bedroom.

I sighed impatiently. "Paper in clear, Q-Tips in black."

"What about gum wrappers?"

"Foil or paper?" I was in charge of reading the bimonthly modifications and exhortations from the sanitation department. "And is that plastic from hot and sour soup? Because Chinese food plastic is apparently not the same as other plastic."

"What writing course?" Ted started down the stairs with a black plastic bag in one hand and a blue one in the other.

"Just, in general, I mean," I said, leaning over the railing. "Do you think they're a good idea?" I wasn't sure he'd heard me. It was late, and I spoke quietly so as not to disturb the other tenants.

At the bottom of the stairs the door clicked shut, swung open again, and then feet tramped back up.

"Do I think someone can teach you how to write?" he whispered from the landing.

Ted had an annoying habit of cutting to the heart of a discussion.

"No," I said, sidling past him at our apartment door with a load of newspapers, "but don't you think that having an audience, deadlines, comments from someone who teaches in the Columbia MFA program, could be helpful?"

"It could be." Ted followed me down with a clear bag bulging with yellow pages covered in my handwriting. "You're throwing all this out?"

"It's just early drafts."

"Wow!" He looked pleased and held the door open for me with his foot. "Then you must be pretty far along."

"Pretty far," I said. "Not done yet, though."

"I've heard Anita Brookner writes a novel every summer," he said. "But I'd think your first one would probably take a little longer."

"Ted." I looked at him seriously. "It's going to take quite a while longer, you know."

"Oh, I know. I know." He was holding the recycling bag at eye level, trying to read from the crumpled pages. Firmly, I wrenched the sack from his grip and set it on the sidewalk.

"Simon thinks I should take this class at the New School. Just to give me some feedback."

"Feedback?" Ted and I agreed that jargon was one of the banes of the modern world.

"You know what I mean." We were wandering down the street now, as was our custom.

"But won't you have to read other people's work, then?"

"Of course. That would be fun."

"Well, sure it would be fun, but that's time you could be spending on your own writing." We'd turned into the Korean grocer's, and he picked up a package of sesame candies. "Do I like these?"

"You like the ones from the place on Fifth Avenue better."

He put them back, and we inspected the mélange of specialties from many lands available at the hot food buffet, including but certainly not limited to baked ziti, Swedish meatballs, corned beef and cabbage, turkey with gravy, and teriyaki chicken, and then circled the compact but impressively varied produce display. I was delighted to discover that I could buy shallots at three in the morning.

"I think I'll get the sesame candies," Ted said finally.

"I'd have to submit something to see if I could get in," I began, when we were out on the street again.

"I'm sure you could get in!" Ted exclaimed. Ted also had an endearing way of letting me know he was on my side.

"I'd like to do it," I said. "I think it would help to have other people read my work."

"But, Margaret, how can they help you? These people will be lawyers and accountants; they won't be writers. They'll be . . ." He hesitated.

"Just like me? Except currently embarked on successful alternate careers? Is that what you were going to say?"

"Why can't you just ask Simon to read your work without taking the class?"

"Ted! I can't do that! He's a published writer. We're not equals." I stopped. "Why do I have to fight you every step of the way with this? I'm trying to do something extremely difficult, probably the most difficult thing I've ever done, and all you do is hamper, hamper, hamper. We're not talking about a lifetime commitment here. This is one night a week."

"All right, all right," Ted said, "you asked what I thought. How much does it cost?"

When I told him, he held up his package of sesame candies ruefully. "Shouldn't have bought these," he said.

That evening, when I logged on to explain to Letty that the external discipline and structure of a class were the key to whipping my novel together, I collected a letter from her.

M—

Should one accept a job because one has fallen in love with a blond office?

"The finish on the paneling is . . . how can I describe it? . . ." (remember this is Michael, a man who has no trouble assigning a name to Titian's favorite blue) ". . . sort of a clover honey. No, more of a maple sugar with bronze undertones." This is what he said when he got home from another "get-acquainted" meeting tonight.

It's wood, Margaret. It is not edible. But there is a private chef for the staff, who serves, as far as I can tell from the menu Michael described, a sort of Asian/French/Italian/Southwestern mélange. Fusion with a twist—or a tornado.

"I can bring a guest," he said.

The ultimate selling point is Paul, who would be Michael's assistant and is engaged to the Xerox man. I sincerely believe that Michael would do anything to escape the daily strain of his relationship with the departmental secretary at Ramona. She has this habit of sighing heavily—it's really, at least according to Michael's imitation, almost a groan, as if someone were pushing a letter opener into her abdomen—whenever anyone other than the chair gives her work, and Michael's afraid to ask her to do anything for him. In fact, I once caught him addressing envelopes for her. He always makes his own copies and the machine inevitably breaks down and then he has to sneak away and spend the rest of the afternoon peeking out of his office at half-hour intervals to see if someone's come along who knows how to fix the thing.

And, honestly, I can't blame him for being dazzled by a fancy office, given the grimy, dank slot he's working in now.

"It doesn't matter where I work," I remember him saying his first week there—I'd come in to help him arrange the furniture, and I think may actually have burst into tears when I realized that I was looking not at some sort of oddly speckled gray wall, but at the sole window (university policy dictates window washing only once every three years). It was only because they wanted him so badly that he got any window at all. As far as arranging the furniture, by the way, we'd had no options; everything had to be pressed in a line against the cinderblock. That afternoon, he'd tapped his head and told me not to worry. "It's what goes on in here that counts," he'd said.

This, of course, is exactly what I worry about in the case of this new wood-paneled, cuisines-of-the-world, helpful-and-well-connected-secretary job. The point of this position, as far as I can make out—which, I admit, is not extremely far, given that the only details I've been given are the perks— seems to be making art more accessible to the public, when what Michael's always been happiest doing is his theoretical work, which, quite frankly, makes art less accessible. As an academician, Michael has always been of the opinion that art exists for its own sake—whether people see it is irrelevant. (Feel free to be aghast at this—everyone else is.) But now he's going to have to believe, or at least pretend to believe, just the opposite.

"You're sure there'll be enough for you up here?" I asked, tapping my own head. Sadly, he seemed unable to recall the gesture.

"Sure," he said, "I'll be helping people experience art."

"Pod person!" I shrieked, pointing an accusatory finger. "What have you done with my husband?"

"What do you mean?" he asked. All innocent. They're clever, those pod people.

"Michael," I reminded him, "you don't care about people."

"I care about some people," he said, wrapping his arms around me. "I care about my wife and my children and I'd like them to have a decent life for a change."

You see what I mean about their cleverness?

But here's the thing, Margaret. Already I was hoping he would persuade me that it was right, that it would be good for art, for humanity, for us. I wanted him to take that job. I wanted to be a pod, too. Not for the sake of the office, of course; I would not have the office, or even very much of the food, despite the guest privileges and what I anticipate to be a liberal use of doggie bags, but because I could already sense the relief it would bring. I've felt for years—how can I describe this?—like I've been trying to stretch the double-bed-sized sheet of our resources over the king-sized mattress of our needs. It's exhausting. Not only that, it's impossible. And now it seems that Michael will be bringing home several large shopping bags from Bed Bath & Beyond. Also, I can imagine that it might be quite delightful when conversing with, say, Alex Prescott, to know she knows my husband has a job with a touch of glamour and puissance.

"Wait!" you say. "Michael will be working for a museum," you say. "He will not be the CEO of a major corporation." And I say to you: "this is the Otis. You know the Otis. No one has a bigger endowment than the Otis. Plus, Michael will be up there, the number four, or at the very least, the number five guy." He explained it to me like this: the people on the next rung down have espresso makers in their offices. Michael's espresso *maker is in his assistant's office, and Michael will not have to learn to operate it to enjoy a teeny cup of superstrong coffee with a twist of lemon peel whenever he desires. (During regular business hours, of course. Michael would never ask an assistant to stay late just to make coffee.)*

"Well," I said (this is to Michael, not to you), "it would be a change. Maybe we can put in a dishwasher."

This is the way it is, Margaret, after four children. My first thoughts are for appliances.

Yours, with dreams of high thread counts and low-energy drying cycles,

L

My admission letter arrived one week later. I was ecstatic at the confirmation of my skill as a writer I believed it implied and had even decided that it meant I could easily get into Columbia's MFA program if I so chose, when the credit card receipt also slid from the envelope and I remembered that this class was a moneymaker for the New School and for Professor Berginsky, so they were unlikely to turn many prospective students away. Nevertheless, I was in and was eager to see how quickly my novel would shoot forward, now that I would have guidance, supervision, and like-minded companionship.

"First," Peter Berginsky said, "I'd like to go around the room and have each of you tell the rest of us your name and say something about why you chose to take this class."

Four tables were pushed together in the seminar room, forming one giant rectangle. We had arranged ourselves around three sides, leaving the head for the professor. We looked dismayingly eager, more like earnest students than jaded writers. Every one of us sat with a pen hovering over blank paper, ready to inscribe the wise words of our teacher, and so emerge from this hour with a two-dimensional talisman that would somehow coax our latent talents into the light. I was glad that I'd at least pulled my hair back severely into an Emily Dickinson–ish bun.

"My name is Bathsheba," the large woman next to me was saying, "but most people call me Bathy. I'm a lawyer. I mean, that's how I make my money, but spiritually, I'm a writer. I'm working on a novel right now that's sort of loosely based on a period of my life that was very difficult for me. You could say that I'm trying to work through some issues by writing it. Really, I don't care if it ever gets published. I just want it to be the best I can make it." She beamed at the rest of us.

Obviously, she said this only to protect her feelings in the face of possible future rejection. A novel had to be published; otherwise it was pointless. Her prevarication made me suspicious, and I reacted in my usual extreme manner. "My name is Margaret, and I'm working full-time on my first novel," I announced defiantly when my turn came, daring the rest of the class to snicker. All of the others had fully formed, respectable identities and, with the exception of a retiree, were managing to squeeze this project around serious careers. Most of them, in fact, were lawyers, a job I had always believed to be quite time-consuming. One ran a company that matched freelance professionals with businesses. Businesses too cheap to pay benefits, I thought. He handed each of us a card, even Peter Berginsky, who put it into his wallet.

Inexplicably, and so, I assured myself, randomly, it seemed that Mr. Berginsky had asked a management consultant, thin and supple, with luminous toffee-colored skin and Botticelli hair to come prepared with pages for all of us to read over the following week. She exemplified the triumphant mix of races that, according to the Gap and Coke and other such arbiters of popular culture, symbolized her generation, which, irritatingly, was the one that followed mine. However, she was so charming as she modestly slid a paper-clipped sheaf of fresh, white papers before each of us, and begged us to be gentle, that I resolved to treat her work with the indulgence I'd give my students'.

I volunteered to submit my work at the next class meeting.

"Thank you . . ." He consulted the legal pad on the table in front of him, "Marge. We'll look forward to your twenty pages."

If I reserved a day for revision, that left five days to write. Four pages a day, that didn't sound so bad.

"Oh, and please put it in my box the day

before class," he added, "so I can get it copied."

Five pages a day then. Pressure was what I needed, I told myself, jabbing a slipping hairpin back into my scalp. Fear of leaving Professor Berginsky in the lurch, not to mention shaming myself in front of the rest of the class, would spur me on. "I'll do that," I promised.

M—
We just found out that Michael will not have exactly the job the museum has dangled before him but only a facsimile thereof, in that he will do all the work but not begin to collect the whole of the pay "for approximately nine months." Something to do with budget approval and taxes and several obscure, at least to me, legal issues. "It's because it's a new position," Michael says. "They're creating it just for me, so they didn't figure it in." It's not clear to me whether we understand what it is they didn't figure it into, but Michael insists there's nothing to worry about. "It's not like this is some fly-by-night company," he says. "This is the Otis." He's also very taken with the director, who took him out for a drink the other night and

ended up talking to him for five hours. It seems the fellow's read all of Michael's books, or at least looked at enough of them to be able to fake it convincingly. Michael appreciates that. "Duncan Bishop wouldn't make a promise he couldn't keep," he says. "He's that kind of guy." Michael's faith is touching, but the word "approximately" bothers me. Apparently, however, this is standard. "That's just so we can't sue them," Michael says, which is exactly why I worry. But the bottom line is that the minute he starts work at the Otis, he'll be making much more than he's making now, so I feel kind of ashamed obsessing over whether he'll eventually be getting the whole amount. It's not like we need it.

Love, L

P.S. Michael can't take donors to lunch in a 1980 Honda CVC, so we're test driving a Saab convertible, his "dream car," tonight. It's not nearly as expensive as it seems, since I'm pretty sure we can write it off.

CHAPTER 7

Margaret

Of course I could not do it. Three days later, I had written two paragraphs.

Late on the fourth night, I escaped the apartment and in desperation wandered the aisles of the A&P.

"We need capers," I'd told Ted.

"OK," he'd answered distractedly from the bedroom where his fingers had been pounding the keyboard with infuriating speed all night.

In college, I'd done this sort of thing often, prowled Wawa's, the twenty-four-hour convenience store, in my sweat pants, searching for inexpensive snacks and praying that an idea for the paper that had stalled between paragraphs five and six would come to me if I looked the other way. Generally, I was, in fact, inspired, somewhere between the purchase of a nickel chocolate Ice Cube and my return to my dorm, doubtless thanks to the trickle of adrenaline that began the moment I started down the dark sidewalk. But New York in the nineties was, alas, much less scary than Philadelphia in the eighties.

I had chosen the University of Pennsylvania because in tenth grade I'd decided that I wanted to become an archaeologist, and according to the literature, Penn's program was probably the best in the country. I planned during the course of my career to explain the extinction of the Neanderthals, as well as trace the influence of the ancient Assyrians on the Archaic Greeks. I don't blame myself for having grandiose ideas. I know from teaching that many students have them and are able to sustain them for years until, like me, they run smack against a course like statistics.

I say that only for effect. My disintegration, in fact, was under way long before that particular course entirely dissolved the

Margaret I'd known for so many years. My decline is not an interesting story (or perhaps I would have tried to get it down on paper and passed it off as my "novel in progress"). It began when my roommate, Annabel Huggins, let slip as she snapped her violin into its case, that she'd written a symphony. I was pretty sure that I'd never even heard a symphony in its entirety. I'd brought my saxophone intending to join the jazz band, but after I'd heard Annabel play, I stuffed the instrument in the back of my closet and piled my shoes on top of it for the rest of the semester. At Christmas, I took it home and left it there.

Discovering that I would never be a musician only scratched my facade. I'd never really believed that I had a great talent for the horn. Even back in Glendale, there were kids who were better than I on all sorts of instruments. But not so much better that my notes didn't even sound like music in comparison, the way it was with Annabel.

It turned out that I knew nothing about movies, although that had been an area I'd been surer of. I was an expert on silent films, thanks to the theater on Fairfax, but no one cared about those, and when it came to talkies, it seemed I'd only seen the standards. In the dining hall, when opinions about obscure prints and foreign releases were bandied about, I had nothing to say.

English, a discipline in which I'd always excelled, baffled me, although it became my major, since I believed I understood the texts, at least before entering the class-room. In seminar, we often spent a full hour and a half discussing the word order in a single phrase, seemingly chosen at random by the professor, who would in the final min-utes of class gleefully and inconclusively draw our attention to a pun at some entirely different point in the text. Along with the others, I pretended to laugh when it came time for the pun, but I worried about the exam.

Swiftly and incessantly, college life chipped away at my sense of myself as a high achiever. Until those years, I admit, I had, as quietly and modestly as possible, considered myself to be exceptional. Even brilliant. I now realized that I, like a million other people, was merely smart.

As I said, I'd chosen Penn strictly for its reputation in archaeology. With overween-ing confidence in my own abilities, I'd not

cared a whit about the school's membership in the Ivy League and the fact that its
name attached to mine would, in future, ensure a specific status. Had I given this issue
a moment's thought, it was only to assert
that I would never need such false distinctions.

Most of my classmates clearly thought
otherwise. Brooke Wickerson, my neighbor
across the hall freshman year, for instance,
had never made a move without calculating
its effect on her résumé. Back when she
was twelve, she explained, she'd dropped
tennis in favor of fencing. "More unusual,"
she said, "especially for a girl." She told me
that Penn was more prestigious than
Cornell but not as good as Columbia, where
she'd really wanted to go. When she found
out I'd been admitted to Stanford, to which
I'd applied simply to placate my father, who
hated the idea of my living in downtown
Philadelphia, she actually looked ill.

"But Stanford doesn't offer advanced
classes in Near Eastern archaeology," I
protested.

"Well," she answered, pouring boiling
water from her hotpot into two crimson
mugs stamped "Veritas" with tea bag

strings dangling from their lips and handing one to me with a look of pity, "I guess we just have different ideas about the purpose of college."

I was rather dense in the ways of the world then, and despite Brooke's example, it took me more than a year to realize that for most people, college was an opportunity not to learn but to position oneself. In retrospect, given what little I retained about the rise of the city-state and elementary Akkadian, I suspect that those who were not like me had the more reasonable attitude, and I'm ashamed of the contempt I felt for them our senior year, as I watched them dash from recruitment meeting to recruitment meeting, collecting folders full of indecipherable corporate propaganda.

"I got an offer from J. P. Morgan," Brooke confided, lighting a cigarette, while we sat on the library steps in the lingering spring evening.

"Congratulations," I said, "what will you do there?"

She shrugged her pretty shoulders beneath her cotton sweater and picked a fleck of tobacco off the tip of her pink tongue.

"Something with money, I guess," she said. "It should help me get into Tuck."

"I didn't know you wanted to go to business school."

"You have to have an MBA if you want to be an international investment banker."

"Which has something to do with money and travel?"

She laughed, tipping her head back so that her hair brushed the pebbly concrete step behind her. "Oh, Margaret, you'll never change, will you? It's, you know, deciding how to invest money internationally. It's really the best field to go into right now."

I saw what she meant now or, since I couldn't literally see what she meant, having no access to that world, I could at least imagine it.

But that sort of high-powered glamour wasn't what I wanted, I reminded myself as I reached for a jar of nonpareil capers and checked the price. I could see the numbers taking shape in the ledger. "For this little jar?" Ted would say.

What did I want exactly? I replaced the capers and strolled the narrow aisles past olive oils and dry cereals and mint-flavored cocoa mix, the soles of my shoes sticking disconcertingly to the linoleum in front of the pickle display. I didn't want fortune. As I've said, we weren't poor—we had plenty of money for our needs. I could even have splurged on the capers, if I chose. And not fame either, although I could see how others, also wanting what I wanted, would believe it was fame they craved. But I, and I would bet most of them, didn't really care to gain the attention of strangers. What I desired was far more fundamental and far less grand. I wanted people to meet me and think, "Ah, someone worth my notice." I wanted them when speaking to me to stop gazing absently over my shoulder, hoping someone more interesting would arrive. Simply, I wanted them to recognize me for the person I believed I truly was. I can't imagine that this is a particularly unusual wish. Emily Dickinson may have disdained an admiring bog, but she did hope that Thomas Wentworth Higginson would take her seriously.

"Why do you care what others think?" This is what my mother would say. But I did care. I suppose because I, unlike my mother, would never be quite sure that I was

someone to be reckoned with until someone else told me so.

Margaret—
We have braved Circuit City on a Saturday
and survived—nay, triumphed—for we
parked in the nether reaches of the lot, in
fact, in the far corner of the TJ Maxx lot, two
grotesquely oversized stores away, our pale
yellow Tercel bravely tiring the asphalt be-
tween a navy Navigator and a bronze
Suburban; we slipped past those in ties who
would entice us with DVD and large screen
TV, stopped our ears against the siren song
of Surround Sound and steered hard past
Circe's aisle from which PlayStations beck-
oned. For forty-five minutes, we languished
among the dishwashers, searching and
waiting, crying out for a knowledgeable
sales associate. But, at last, guided by clues
gleaned from plastic-coated cards affixed
with impossible-to-remove sticky stuff to
the door of each machine, we made our se-
lection: the Maytag Superwasher, Model
#1247, with pot-scrubbing, glass-shining,
and copper-polishing capabilities. Obsidian,
stainless steel, or faux cherry finish? Well
might you ask. The choice was agonizing,

rusty as our taste has become after years of avocado, harvest gold, and almond. But at last, I saw myself in the shiny one—it was I and I it; I glisten, therefore I am—and we joined the snaking line of pilgrims at the register, our yellow copy of the order slip trembling in our hands.

Have never before made major purchase without consulting the Pennysaver.

Delivery in three days.

Letty

P.S. Also, am beginning to research private schools for Marlo. This will basically mean blowing the college fund on middle school, but she started to teach herself Latin this summer out of my old Wheelock, so it seems that now that we can afford to give her a really rigorous education, we probably should.

CHAPTER 8

Margaret

I'd had to focus so single-mindedly on my own submission that I didn't lift the cover page of "The Leaf Blowers: A Novel" by Zelda Jackson until late the night before class. Within two pages, I wished with a desperation so intense that it brought tears to my eyes that I could snatch my offering back from Kinko's. Zelda's prose read like a published book, every phrase exquisite, measured, angled together to form a gem-like whole. The story moved forward, not with the inexorable, crude pull of a thriller, but with a steady accretion of carefully observed moments. It rendered gorgeous the gritty, secret lives of Mexican gardeners in Rancho Santa Fe, who conversed in perfectly captured accents between the roars of their signature tool—the leaf blower. I wanted to hate it, but it drew me on, through descriptions of dirt that glinted like mica under broken fingernails and pickup trucks rumbling like heartbeats through gated communities at dawn.

On page seven, I spotted a comma splice and circled it with relief. On page ten, I wrote in the margin, "Would Pablo be eating grapes in December, given the fruit's expense, not to mention the solidarity he would feel with his countrymen laboring in northern California? Perhaps a rice and bean dish would be more authentic." And then I crossed it out. It was obvious that Zelda knew about these people. If she said they ate grapes in the off-season, that is what they did.

In the end, I could in all honesty only gush, which I did, three single-spaced pages' worth. The next evening, the rest of the class, including Peter Berginsky, universally agreed with my assessment. We all urged her to finish quickly, to secure an agent, to collect her Pulitzer. Some of us— Peter Berginsky, I've no doubt, and perhaps the retiree—probably did so without jealous claws tearing at their guts. Maybe others, too. Maybe I, in fact, was the only one who felt diminished and defeated by her talent, who in some dark, locked cupboard of my soul wished her ill.

"Where did you get all this stuff?" Bathsheba dared to ask.

I winced, waiting for some haughty reply declaring her intimacy with oppressed peoples everywhere.

"I don't know," Zelda answered, shrugging her slender shoulders winningly. "We had a gardener, but he was Japanese, and I never really talked to him. I guess I just made it up."

I reprimanded myself sternly for my selfishness on the way home. Wouldn't someone who truly loved writing feel only delight in the presence of such obvious natural skill? Apparently not. Apparently she would find room in her heart only for bitter reflection on the unfairness of a world that bestowed every advantage on one random and undeserving creature. No, I thought, catching a glimpse of myself among the scraps of cardboard and mismatched shoes that formed a display in the window of the Parsons School of Design, that was not strictly true. Part of me could not help but admire Zelda. And, I reminded myself, as a trench-coated man jostled me off the curb in his eagerness to hurl himself into the crosswalk and elicit furious honking, that Zelda had been born with a genius for arranging words on the page did not mean that I could not also produce a perfectly readable novel.

It occurred to me that meeting Zelda might make taking this class worthwhile, even beyond the tutelage of Peter Berginsky. Anne Lamott often mentioned the value of the writing group as a source of artistic and emotional sustenance. Perhaps Zelda, after she read my chapter, would be interested in forming such a group with me. We could meet in the lobby of the Algonquin Hotel on Thursday evenings and critique each other's work.

Letty's e-mail that evening was a refreshing distraction.

M,

Blue or yellow? What do you like for a kitchen? I'm also thinking about tangerine. Or we could go all sophisticated yet warm with granite and cherry, in which case I probably should have chosen the cherry-paneled dishwasher.

Can you please get out here and help me choose a floor?

Have I told you that Michael took the job? We agreed that he's published so much that he could always go back to the groves—or brambles—of academe, so why not take a chance, try something new?

So we got the dishwasher to celebrate, except it turns out that a dishwasher is impossible given this awkward kitchen design. There's no room for a dishwasher, unless we install a hanging rack for the pots, which would either obscure the view of the driveway out the kitchen window or collect grease over the stove. And now it seems there's some trouble with the pipes that we never had occasion to discern before. Apparently, the previous owner routed them in an idiosyncratic way, so as to install the hot tub that was in the backyard when we moved in.

"Michael is going to help me re-envision the museum's role. We're going to make it a significant national presence," Duncan Bishop told me yesterday.

I was in Michael's office to help him decide where to hang his "office art": Marlo's charcoal "Wild Horse," Hunter's tempera "Daddy in a Yellow Jacket," and Noah's fingerpainted "Sunset on the Pacific" or "Egg on the Carpet," depending on your mood.

Duncan Bishop had to stoop to shake my hand. He is tall enough to make you want to estimate—6´2´´?, 6´3´´?—and his fingers are so long my hand seemed not to fit properly in his. "We're extremely lucky to get your husband over here," he said. He was looking not at me, as he spoke, but at some spot to my right. Possibly Ivy, who was kicking at the desk from underneath, was distracting him.

"Well, I know he's happy to be here," I said. Or some such thing.

"You should take Letitia to lunch," he said to Michael. "Copper River salmon today."

So last night, when Michael got home, he

said, "Let's redo the kitchen!" in the happy-go-lucky way he's had since he started working at a place that serves Copper River salmon in the cafeteria. And I said, "Whee!," which, as you know, is not like me, or hasn't been like me for several years now.

Not that I haven't been happy. You know I've been happy. I've just not been . . . giddy, I guess is how I feel just now, a bit as if the rug's been pulled out from under my feet, which you'd think would be uncomfortable, but it turns out that the rug was some sort of brown shag crusted with Cream of Wheat and underneath was this golden-stained, highly polished oak. (That's one of the floors we're considering for the remodeled kitchen. What do you think?)

I didn't want to complain, Margaret, that we were not where we should have been in life (although, in fact, I know I did complain, it was only to you, which doesn't count, does it?). I mean we'd made choices: academe over business for Michael, children over a career for me, and that entailed certain sacrifices. That's the way life is. There are compromises. There are trade-offs. And yet . . . and yet . . . what had I done to be cursed with an apartment-sized electric *oven? In L.A.! Almost no one has electric in L.A.!*

We're running a gas line to the kitchen, and I'm going to Koreatown to find one of those big old O'Keefe & Merritts. With two ovens and a griddle. And maybe a working clock, although those are expensive. This Thanksgiving, I'll be able to roast a twenty-pound turkey without cutting it in half first.

Seriously, Margaret, I need your help with this. I'm sending you some blueprints and paint chips, and a couple of pages from the Williams-Sonoma catalog (now that we have more cupboards, I might buy a croque-monsieur maker and an asparagus pot—you know, the sort of gadget that performs a single function perfectly twice a year and takes up an inordinate amount of space the rest of the time). Perhaps the children's art will look nice in the new kitchen. It didn't work, in the end, in the new office.

L

Silently, I thanked Letty for allowing me to feel again like the generous, warmhearted person I hoped I was. In my imagination, I bestowed upon her the finest kitchen ever conceived. Nothing could be better for Letty than a new kitchen, a kitchen that would not do its best to thwart her every omelette. In high school, Letty had taken home ec, defying her mother, who, like mine, believed that a woman with domestic skills would end up chained to her house. (That neither of them was particularly good at keeping a house, and nevertheless both were, aside from an odd job here and there, primarily homemakers, didn't shake their conviction.) Even in that bland environment with its exact measurements and its oversimplified substitutions Letty had shown signs of becoming a gourmet chef. While her classmates were learning to keep skin from forming on the surface of pudding, she was making pots de crème. While they mastered the twist of the wrist essential for releasing dough from a cardboard tube, she was practicing puff pastry.

In general, Letty had developed into the sort of person who appreciated fine touches. If you put a carton of cream on her table, she'd surreptitiously whisk it away and pour the cream into a squat pitcher. She knew how to garnish plates with lemon wedges and sprigs of fresh herbs from the herb garden she'd cultivated in the grassless ring that remained after they'd had the hot tub removed. On her dining room table, she kept a big bowl of oranges for juicing, their luxurious color and abundance belying their provenance: a shopping cart parked in the median at the intersection of Venice and Robertson and manned by a rotating team of Guatemalans, who pushed a bag of fruit through her open car window in exchange for two dollars while the light was red.

A gift from Letty was always small and inexpensive, but exquisite: a set of four antique linen cocktail napkins; a stainless steel moderne key chain; art deco book plates. This sensibility had not been learned from her family. I remember hanging over the front seat of our car on the way home from a sleepover and asking my parents why the Larues had a giant teak fork and spoon hanging on their gold-flocked kitchen wall. I had recently been reading about the inclusion of useful items for the afterlife in Egyptian tombs and thought the monster utensils might have some similar significance.

"Some people just don't have an eye for decor," my mother said cheerfully. "Take the Chinese."

"Don't teach the children to stereotype, Alice," my father said.

"I'm not saying the Chinese don't have many fine qualities, but taste is just not one of them. For heaven's sake, Albert, look at their restaurants."

Although I understood from this that my mother didn't admire the Larues' sense of style, for some years I had a confused sense that Letty's grandparents had been colonials in Shanghai and had come to America to escape the Boxer Rebellion, carrying with them the fork and spoon with which they'd established their identity as suave Westerners in a land of chopstick-wielding, gauche Easterners.

I had one foot on the bottommost stair in the New School building, when I saw Zelda step into the elevator. "Going up?" I called, and she held the door.

"Hi," I chirped, as I slipped inside.

She nodded and the doors shut, encapsulating us.

"Your chapters the other week were so

great," I said, my diction disturbingly reminiscent of that of my former students.

"Thanks," she said.

I pressed on with another insightful observation. "I think class is going really well so far, don't you?"

"I suppose," she said, glancing above the door, where, if the elevator had been in a fancier building, the number of the floors we passed would have lighted up. "I'm really just taking it because of Peter."

I frowned, not recognizing by first name alone the man I thought of in no terms other than the complete "Peter Berginsky." Zelda, it seemed, knew him by more than reputation, or at least she hoped to give this impression.

The elevator doors opened. "I was wondering," I said boldly, stepping aside to allow her to exit first, "if you had any interest in forming a writing group. You know," I went on, when she did not immediately respond, "outside of class."

"A writing group?" We were entering the classroom now. About three-quarters of the class were already sitting around the table. "Who would be in it?"

"Well, me," I said, "and, I don't know, maybe there's someone you'd like to ask."

She slid my pages from a manila folder and placed them on the table in front of her. "I prefer to work by myself," she said.

∽∽∽∽∽

The class was not optimistic about *my* chances for a Pulitzer.

I managed at the end of the two hours to scrape into a spiky pile the pages and pages of critical notes printed in perky fonts that my classmates shoved toward me across the table. "Good work!" Bathy had printed in red at the bottom of her list of objections.

Reeling down lower Fifth Avenue after class, I had difficulty gaining a purchase on my emotions, overwhelmed as I was by shame and despair and the desire to wander with eyes closed into onrushing traffic. What besides my own hubris had made me think that I could concoct from the scanty resources of my imagination and the even scantier store of my experience an actual novel? Bitterly, I now recalled the cautions Ted had raised a year ago, as I'd stalked, full of confidence and outrage at his doubts, up Madison Avenue. There were steps you were expected to take to prove yourself before attempting a book. Others wrote short stories, building credibility page by page for years before they burst forth with full-fledged novels. They'd collected prizes: Buntings and Whitings and Aga Khans. They'd sweated for MFAs, garnering the favor of their esteemed and well-connected professors. They'd secured places in artists' colonies and dined on watercress sandwiches left on the doorsteps of their isolated cabins, because their efforts had been deemed worthy of nourishment. They did not enroll in extension courses with a bunch of other unpublished professionals and hope that these people would help to make them writers.

But like a sandbag flung before a flood, this last thought gave me hope once again. What, after all, did those who had criticized me so fiercely know about writing? If my classmates understood the rudiments of good composition, would they not be spending their Thursday evenings polishing the most recent in a series of well-acclaimed novels, instead of carping in a windowless seminar room, borrowed from undergraduates?

This idea buoyed me up the six flights to our apartment. What do they know? What do they know? I chanted on every step until I pushed the key into our door, at which point I remembered that I, too, was an unpublished professional attending an adult education class. What did I know?

I was, therefore, collapsed facedown on the couch twenty minutes later when Ted came in with Imperial Szechuan.

"I take it your classmates are blind fools when it comes to recognizing talent," he said, sinking onto the couch himself and pulling my feet onto his lap.

"No," I groaned. "They're right." I sat up and looked at him. "What made me think I could write a novel?"

"What makes you think you can't?" he answered.

At least I'd not been mistaken in my choice of husbands.

I ran through my classmates' objections: the confusing structure, the boring opening, the suspect bamboo basket, the impracticality of journaling in blood, and the myriad other faults that rendered my efforts a colossal waste of time. "They don't even like my character's name!" I wailed.

"Those sound like details to me," Ted said. "You shouldn't be concerned with details yet."

Perhaps he was right. Perhaps I shouldn't be distracted by petty issues like nomenclature and authentic weaving materials. All that could easily be changed or added later. "What about the lack of focus?" I sniffed. But now I was fishing for reassurance, rather than presenting a true concern. Had Ted thought this a problem, he would have said so immediately.

"That's not a detail, but the book isn't finished yet. Is it?" He said this last somewhat wistfully.

"No, of course it isn't finished." I didn't add that despite a full summer's work, it was barely begun.

"So, it seems to me that any novel that's not formulaic—"

"Not formulaic—yes!" I interrupted, sitting up straighter against the sofa arm.

"Well, it's bound to lack focus for a while. I mean you're exploring your characters, trying to discover their full natures. You shouldn't know exactly how they'll behave and where their story will go yet."

Of course, Ted was right. I'd ambitiously chosen a character whose experience, gender, and social milieu were completely foreign to me. In fact, the only common ground between Robert and me was grocery shopping, which was perhaps why he so often found himself at the supermarket.

"What did Berginsky think?"

I glanced at Ted, fearful. I pulled my feet off his lap and put them firmly on the floor. Both of us cared what Peter Berginsky thought. He was, after all, a real writer. Swamped as I was by doubt and misery, I had not, however, read the page of comments he'd given me. From the prickly mass in my purse, I drew a sheet of onionskin. It seemed that Peter Berginsky still used a typewriter, one that needed cleaning. The *a*'s and *o*'s were filled, as if the sort of fourth-grade girl who dotted her *i*'s with hearts had decorated the page.

"You seem," his comments began, "to be working within the framework of the word and its antithesis: the deed for which there are no words, the unspeakable, so to speak. The protagonist cannot even name himself, much as in Lear we see Edgar (the holy counterpart of evil Edmund) babble as a lunatic, not to mention Lear himself, who is rendered incoherent when the natural order becomes disorderly. (But what, after all, is natural, when it is Edmund, who is the child of 'nature'?)"

"Well, what does he say?" Ted was craning his neck around the page.

"I'm not sure. Either he thinks I'm insane or he's comparing me to Shakespeare."

"You juxtapose two worlds," the note went on, "the despoiled paradise and the paradise utterly lost, the oriental and the occidental. Some reference might perhaps be made to the Native American experience, as compared, for instance, with the Khmer Rouge—the Red Man and the Reds, as it were."

Was he saying I should set the novel in Cambodia?

"My advice to you"—I snapped the page as I read these direct words to bring it into sharper focus—"is to juggle the odd sizes. Swim with the chickens. Turn the details inside out until they smoke, threatening combustion. Also, don't use so many adverbs. PB."

And then there was a postscript: "How do the cheating little girls fit in?"

"I'm sorry, Ted," I said, "but I really don't feel like dinner tonight. I'm just going to lie down for a while."

Drained, I shuffled dramatically to the bedroom, dragging my purse full of cavils and worse behind me by the shoulder strap. I pulled back the tablecloth that served as a curtain and lay listlessly on the bed watching the people in the building behind ours enjoying lives Ted and I suspected had been scripted by a screenwriter who was smitten with lush interiors. These people occupied not an apartment, but an entire house on the next block. The man we thought of as the father was lighting votives on a table spread for guests on the flagstone-covered patio. The woman we'd decided was the mother moved back and forth between their wood-paneled refrigerator and their restaurant-sized stove. Between the picture window and a floor-to-ceiling painting on the third floor, in a room that, as far as we could tell, was completely devoted to exercise, the daughter pushed and pulled at some large piece of equipment, while a trainer stood beside her, spotting her now and then with a judiciously placed hand. I was sure that such people had never tried to write a novel and they, with their imminently arriving friends and their painstakingly prepared or at least carefully chosen meals and their well-toned bodies, were clearly the better for it.

Letty was also having educational difficulties.

Margaret—
Just got a call from the principal's office at Hunter's school. I have to come in at three o'clock to discuss "a matter of grave concern." I'm afraid I shrieked into the phone when I heard this. I suppose I feared some child had carried a gun into the second grade, or perhaps attempted to distribute Tylenol. "We'd prefer to discuss this with a parent in person," the secretary said. Michael assures me that if Hunter had been kidnapped or molested, they wouldn't wait for a three o'clock appointment to tell me. I guess that makes sense.

L

M—

Me, again. It's two-fifteen. Over the course of the last two hours I've had to breathe into a paper bag several times. Could the "matter of grave concern" be a horrible brain disease detected by a specially designed spelling quiz? A fall from the jungle gym? A fight in which precious tiny teeth have been lost? "Letty," Michael said, the third time I called him out of a meeting, "calm down. I'm sure he's all right. He probably walked into the girls' bathroom by mistake." When I worried that this might be considered sexual harassment, Michael was impatient. He was never impatient when I called him out of meetings at Ramona. In fact, back then he was pleased. He would stretch the conversation, ask what we'd had for lunch and whether I'd remembered to give the dogs their flea medication. He would inquire about the progress of potty training. Now it seems a museum meeting is more important than his child's health and incipient criminality.

L

M—

Hi. Me, yet again. I got to the school office at 2:45 and tried to be chummy with the *secretary. "Hi," I said, as casually as I could. "I'm Letty MacMillan. Some problem in class today?"*

She refused to be chummed. "Mrs. Henderson will discuss that with you," she said. She looked at the clock disapprovingly. "At three."

So I had to wait, shrinking into a fragile second-grader myself as I sat in that office, waiting to be summoned.

Mrs. Henderson has wispy, home-permed hair and a wide waist. She wears flowered dresses and inexpensive navy or beige pumps. In other words, she is a reas-suring figure and I'd never had cause to fear her before. Today, however, she didn't smile when she opened her door to me. "Mrs. MacMillan," she said. "Thank you for com-ing in."

"Of course," I said. "What happened? Is Hunter all right?"

"Physically, yes," Mrs. Henderson assured me, "but we've had a worrisome episode in the classroom today." She indicated that I should take the chair in front of her desk and sat down behind the desk herself. The vinyl padded seat sighed beneath her, as if weary of troublesome children and their anxious,

obviously ineffective, mothers. Lying precisely across the center of the desktop was a purple pen. Positioning an index finger at tip and base (presumably to avoid leaving fingerprints), she lifted the pen and held it toward me. "Have you ever seen this before?"

I shook my head. Was it a knife, cleverly disguised? Was it a bomb?

"You see, we do not allow these sorts of pens in school," she said, replacing the implement at the center of her desk.

I nodded, though I didn't understand the point of this nor its application to Hunter. How could pens not be allowed in school?

"The ink," she said, "is erasable." She smiled, then, as if she pitied me, and sat back in her chair. "You see, we like to allow the children to correct their own exercises out of a master book. We believe that encouraging the student to seek his or her own correct answers fosters a sense of independence and intellectual initiative, and allows the student to view the educator as a facilitator in the search for knowledge rather than as a dictator of right and wrong. It also," she added, "saves the teacher a great deal of time."

I continued to nod. Again, I wasn't sure exactly what she meant, but it sounded friendly.

"The children are supposed to mark incorrect answers with a check. Hunter," she leaned toward me here, "your son," she added, as if I might try to disclaim our connection, "has been using this pen to erase his incorrect answers and replace them with the correct ones."

"He's cheating?"

"Well," she leaned back again and waved one hand dismissively, "there seems to be some possibility that he misunderstood the purpose of checking his answers, but we believe it's best to nip this sort of thing in the bud. You can see why we'd rather he not use this pen in the classroom." She picked it up again, this time with one hand in a normal fashion, and handed it to me.

"Of course," I said, quickly dropping the pen in my purse. "How about pencil?"

"Pencil is fine. Young children, we find, are not very adept at cheating with pencil," she said. "They press too hard."

Hunter and I had a little talk on the way home from school. It turned out that I didn't even have to broach the subject.

"Mom," he said, "did you know that you're not supposed to change your answers if they're wrong in the book?"

"I found that out today," I said.

"Me, too."

He'd traded his mechanical pencil with Bailey for the pen. Michael was more upset about the choice of color than the possible cheating. "I can't believe a child of mine would want to write in purple," he said. "It's undignified."

While I'm on the school subject, did you know there were tests for private ones? I mean, just to get in? (Obviously, there are tests once you get there. It wouldn't be school without tests.) Marlo has to take a three-hour exam on English and math. "It's really designed for seventh-graders," one of the admissions directors told me, "but we like to see them give it a try in fifth. Of course, we don't expect our fifth-graders to ace it." Then she pulled open a drawer of her Mission-style oak file cabinet. "I don't give this to everyone," she said, "but your daughter seems like such a nice girl." She leaned a little to her left to look out the door—I suppose to make sure no one was spying on us from the hall—then slipped me *a vocabulary list. "Study this," she said. I'm not sure if she meant Marlo or me. What does "termagant" mean? How about "perspicacious"? "Otios"? Also, we both have to write essays.*

I hate private school already, but Marlo is so excited. At night, under the covers with her Hello Kitty flashlight, she's paging through glossy brochures. I can't blame her. All the children look so happy and attentive in those pictures. I don't remember smiling in middle school. Do you?

Love, Letty

P.S. I'm looking for a good nursery school for Noah for next year. There's a kindergarten I'd like him to go to and he might not get in if he does preschool in a church basement like Marlo and Hunter did.

CHAPTER 9

Margaret

M—
Our kitchen is a disaster. Or rather our kitchen is a superb example of Italian design, French sensibilities, American cherry and granite, and German knives, cunningly arranged in a 9 x 4 foot space that now makes the rest of the house the equivalent of the cheap cardboard and plastic photo album that I purchased at a yard sale in 1987—I remember because I was so pregnant with Marlo at the time I could not bend properly to pick it up—and used to hold recipe cards. We resold said album to a

Honduran family at our own yard sale last weekend.

The historical refrigerator was reclaimed by the people we bought it from—remember that day? We've replaced it with a supersized model of the brand everyone agrees is best. Never previously owned! Any dried egg, mustard, or inexplicable pinkish stains original to us! It's pristine and spacious and full of clever compartments that I suspect are for items like pâté. Also, it's energy efficient and installed flush with the cabinetry. It seems to take offense when you refer to it as the "fridge."

Remember the cupboards that were covered in fake wood grain Con-Tact paper when we bought this house? We've replaced them with deep, ceiling-high, glass-fronted "cabinets." Change begets change, however—now we must go to the Rose Bowl flea market on Sunday to replace plastic Tom-and-Jerry-ware, as mouse and cat do not look elegant behind glass.

I would take photos—have, in fact, taken photos—before and after, so what I mean is I would send photos, if you were not planning to be here at Christmas. Right? You are

*planning to be here at Christmas? I want
very much to see you. Stunning as this
kitchen is—and conducive to cooking,
which is, after all, the point of a kitchen—it's
making me at the moment a little sad, since
it's so far removed from our former life.*

*Your friend, the proud operator of a
garbage disposal,*

L

It made me sad, too, to think of what was
gone. Ted and I had shopped the second-
hand (fifthhand would be more accurate)
appliance stores—free pickup and delivery—on Western with Letty and Michael for
that refrigerator. We'd rejected several
round-shouldered ones with the kind of
handle that snaps satisfyingly open and
shut as niftily vintage but impractical. We'd
finally selected a largish, somewhat more
up-to-date model in hideous harvest gold at
a price Ted approved. A cockroach scurried
to hide from the light when I slid open the
crisper, but I kept that observation to myself
and used the bleach liberally when the appliance was safely in Letty and Michael's
kitchen. The four of us made up a history for
that refrigerator, the family of six for whom it

sturdily held gallon jugs of whole milk; the single mother who juggled baby, toddler, and string cheese while pushing the door shut with one flip-flopped foot; the fraternity, who'd let it grow a lining of mold in their basement, while they forced it to open wide for case after case of Heineken.

Letty and I had peeled the Con-Tact paper from those cupboards and then chipped away with our putty knives at the layers of paint—yellow and cream and pink and beige, down to the original green—just to see—and then smoothed our own green, Letty's custom color, over it all. Where was the silver-star-spangled mint linoleum now?

I looked forward to Christmas not only because we would see Letty and my parents and possibly even Warren, if we could lure him away from his phone, but also because a government-sanctioned holiday would provide a legitimate break from the drudgery of my solitary work, or rather the drudgery of my solitary not-work.

I'd taped PB's notes to the table beside me. Ted had several times set his coffee mug on the page, but I could read around the rings. After my early debacle, the specter of the class's response dogged me as I wrote, but I kept my apprehensions at bay by reminding myself that I'd have plenty of time for meticulous editing, since I wouldn't have to distribute pages again until early December. Unfortunately, the balm of "plenty of time" also soothed the itch to rush forward. Freed from the pressure to produce quickly, I spent many hours composing insightful and witty notes to my classmates about their work.

M—

I just spent an enormous sum on a dress. Just the dress. Not the shoes necessitated by the dress nor the bag necessitated by the shoes. Not the shawl the saleswoman said I might like to throw over my shoulders, because for a price I once spent on a car I don't even get sleeves. Granted the car had been worn. It was also a Chevette. The dress is much nicer—it's black, ankle-length. It has hematite beading on the bodice. But it is, as my mother would say, just a dress.

Michael made me buy it. I balked at the door—actually, I balked at that block on Wilshire where the little brown sign says "Beverly Hills," but I was in the passenger seat. My feet jammed against the floor did nothing to slow our progress. "You need it," Michael said. "For the Christmas party." He did not need to remind me that at the last Otis event we attended—a cocktail party to celebrate the acquisition of the new curator for painting restoration—the caterer's assistant, a gawky nineteen-year-old, was wearing a black velvet skirt identical to mine, right down to the unstylish length and the slightly off-seam zipper.

We went into the kind of store in which a jacket on sale costs $850. And, no, that does not include the pants. I hovered near the escalator, so as to make a quick getaway when we were found out, while Michael methodically worked his way through the display racks, holding each dress out at arm's length and studying it—eyes slightly squinted, mouth a little ajar—with the same degree of concentration he devotes to a work of art. Outfitting me is his new hobby, Margaret. He's already made several trips to the mall that's on his way home from work and purchased clothes for me—khakis and a pair of black capris, a jersey skirt and a bright white poplin blouse that reminds me of a pajama top—casual things that cost

*what I would normally have spent on some-
thing special for my sister's wedding.
"They're just basics," he says. "Trust me,
you need nice basics." And it's true that I am
better-looking in an azure cashmere turtleneck than in a faded cotton T-shirt, spotted
with bleach from an errant spray of toilet
cleaner. But now what do I wear to clean the
toilet?*

Love, L

On November 1, a letter arrived from
Brooke, my college friend now in London,
who had already excelled, although she had
not, in fact, become an international investment banker as she'd planned. She'd discovered during her second year at Tuck that
she'd been "born to be a management consultant," a career that, as far as I could
make out, demanded she convince execu-
tives nearly twice her age to restructure corporations in industries and services in which
they'd spent their entire working lives and in
which she'd invested a few months.

Her envelope—not airmail tissue, but the
regular, thick sort—sliced my finger as I
opened it. Clutching a damp paper towel to
the wound, I read that she would be in New

York in two weeks and hoped I could join her on Tuesday for breakfast.

Prime work time, I thought resentfully. Between the meal itself and the hair drying, outfit choosing, and discreet makeup application I'd need to make myself presentable for breakfast wherever she'd propose, probably her hotel (where I'd have to limit myself to coffee and an English muffin and still end up spending fifteen dollars, actually more like thirty, since I'd feel obliged to treat her, which would mean closer to fifty dollars, since she'd certainly order juice and an egg-white omelette), the entire morning would be used up by the time I subwayed home, and I would be too drained and depressed to be productive in the afternoon. I decided to start immediately making up for the anticipated lost time.

I turned off the computer that evening after four hours of steady application, perhaps the most focused period I'd spent working on the novel since I'd had to deliver the twenty pages for class, and stood up from a table spotted with blood, coffee, and crumbs. The thought of seeing Brooke had spurred me on. If only the book could be comfortably published before our breakfast!

I wished this again two weeks later as, in a subway-induced stupor, I clung with an upraised hand to a metal triangle in the aisle of the number 4 express train that hurled me uptown. Brooke I imagined in the sitting room of her suite, paging through *The Wall Street Journal* or perhaps that pink financial paper, her stylishly hosed legs crossed, her Manolo Blahniks (did people wear such shoes to breakfast?), one tipped coquettishly on its side, waiting beside her. I was wearing clogs, purchased in 1985.

I reminded myself that I, deep underground, pressed and jostled by elbows and shoulders padded in damp wool and leather and some stifling-looking blend of nylon and rayon, bombarded with smells of mustard and wet newsprint and patchouli and aging perspiration, was a part of the city's lifeblood. A Coach briefcase banged against the back of my knees, a plastic bag containing a pointy-edged object poked me in the ribs, a sharp-heeled woman danced on my toes whenever the train changed speed, and the man beside me rested his paperback on the top of my head. I would have to remember to wash my hands before eating.

I was sorry to be dreading this reunion. After all, despite our antithetical outlooks, Brooke and I had become fond of one another in college and, simply by virtue of the fact that we had maintained contact, our bond had strengthened now that the circle of acquaintances who shared our four-year history had naturally thinned over the years. I admired her directness and her abhorrence of the sentimental, and while I wasn't sure what she liked about me, I appreciated her feeling all the same. I should, I knew, have felt merely warm anticipation at the chance to see her for the first time in at least eight years. I should have been looking forward to cheering her on, hearing about her life in England, her current beau, and her impressive career. Instead, I prayed the car would squeal to a stop, and I and all these people, exuding our smells and stamping our heavily shod feet, would be stuck here in the dark for three hours, a fate preferable to sipping coffee across the table from obvious success.

At Fifty-ninth Street I wormed my way out of the train and onto the grease-and-gum-dotted concrete platform, shoved through the turnstile, and escalated toward the gray

November light. I would not, I decided, even mention my novel, only say that Ted and I were doing well, that we liked New York, that we hoped to visit Brooke in London someday, when we were not so busy. I would talk about the Hopper exhibit at the Whitney. I would ask questions; I would express delight; I would sigh when the plates were cleared and wish we had more time.

I'd been meanly pleased when Brooke mentioned a hotel I'd never heard of. How highly could her company value her if it wasn't putting her up at the Plaza? The doorman at the Daniel, a male model in a loose-fitting, black crepe Calvin Klein suit, who nodded condescendingly as I shouldered my way in, made me realize my mistake. This was a place too hip to be staffed by friendly graying fellows from Queens in broken shoes and stiff maroon crested jackets. It was, I realized with chagrin, a place too "in" for me to have heard of.

I phoned Brooke from the black glass lobby as we'd planned.

"You're here!" she squealed, so sincerely happy to hear my voice that I was at once ashamed of my cynical roilings.

She emerged from the elevator as polished as I'd imagined, although her shoes were flats. Her hair somehow managed to be both stylish and careless; her clothes were so current and so London, as to look almost wrong in New York. When she hugged me, though, she was the person I'd known in school, back when we were girls pretending to be women and then actually becoming such. I was glad I'd come.

"So how's London?" I asked, when we'd been seated in the suede-walled dining room.

"It's completely spoiled every other city for me. It's so . . ." she faltered, searching for the right adjective.

"English?" I offered.

"No, not at all. That's what makes it so great."

We traded information about various mutual acquaintances at Penn—who'd had children, who owned his own software company, who'd already been divorced three times, who'd been arrested for drug dealing—which sustained us until the food arrived.

"So, what do you do here?" she asked, slicing with the side of her fork through the glistening mass of egg on her plate.

"Well, Thursday nights—" I began, ready to explain that admission to the Whitney Museum was free on that particular evening and then to launch into my detailed critique of the current show.

"Are you going to that opening at the Gardner Gallery on Thursday? I said I couldn't make it, but if you're going, I'll call and say I've changed my mind."

The Gardner, I guessed, was a private gallery, probably in Chelsea. One would not have to pay for a ticket to attend, but one would need to be invited.

"I think we might have other plans," I answered vaguely. Surreptitiously, I began to push the tiny pots of jam and honey that had come with my English muffin close to the edge of the table, so as to more easily whisk them into my bag if the opportunity arose. Around us, the murmur of the other diners swelled. All of them, I realized, had invitations to openings and premieres. They didn't poke about in the ashtrays outside the Metropolitan Museum, hoping to turn up a discarded admission button. They didn't go early to Bryant Park to stake out a free mosquito-infested seat for a movie like *Casablanca* that everyone on earth had al-

ready seen a dozen times. They danced in
the meatpacking district, behind unmarked
doors, not in the plaza at Lincoln Center,
open to anyone who wandered down
Columbus Avenue. They wore clothes like
the doorman's suit to galas and benefits
and birthday parties and screenings. They
bought makeup brushes in SoHo at stores
that looked like art galleries. I was not even
sure what galas were. I wouldn't know what
to do with a makeup brush if I owned one.

These people, parrying their heavy utensils in the chic, pinkish light of the dining
room, were the lifeblood of the city; these
people, who thought nothing of ordering
nineteen-dollar bowls of granola, not we
who spirited jam pots into our purses, not
the worker bees who grabbed cellophane-
wrapped bagels from the deli counters to
chew in the airless tunnels, as they waited
on the pleasure of the trains that would
hurry them with numbing daily regularity
into the maws of their spirit-sucking jobs,
but these. A woman at a table to my right
dropped a spoon that hit the carpet with a
gentle thud. She raised one discreet finger
toward the waiter and with the other hand

adjusted her so-chic-as-to-be-ugly eye-
glasses.

"I'm working on a novel," I announced, in
a desperate attempt to wrench myself free
from those with whom I'd spewed onto
Lexington Avenue an hour before. (Of
course, half of them were probably working
on novels of their own.)

"Really?" Brooke sighed and discreetly
raised her own finger for the waiter.
"Sometimes," she said, "I feel like I put in all
this time and effort and what do I have to
show for it? Nothing you can put your
hands around. Nothing that's really me."

I nodded, gazing affectionately at my
friend. Her regrets made me feel closer to
her.

"You know," she went on, "I've got an
idea for a novel or two in mind. Someday,
I'm just going to have to take a summer off
and write one up."

I waved indiscreetly at the waiter, knocking a jar of black currant jam off the table
with my elbow. How many people believe
they have a novel fully formed in the backs
of their brains, I thought, ducking below the
table for the jar, and are convinced that if
only they could manage to tear themselves

away from much more important work, they would just "write it up"? I would say one in two. That's fifty percent of the population who believe that they could easily do what I was discovering every other day to be impossible and who, because they would never actually try it, would remain infuriatingly oblivious to this truth. I dropped the jam jar into my purse on my way back to the surface of the table. Brooke was already handing her American Express card to the waiter.

"I wanted to treat you," I protested.

Brooke held up one hand dismissively. "Don't be silly. Jones and Cartwright will get it."

I could have ordered the eggs Benedict or even the Japanese breakfast box.

"Speaking of money," she said, "you should look into this stock I just bought—Genslen—my financial adviser is very high on it and I don't think he's been excited about a stock since Xerox."

"What do they do?" I asked. Although I did not have investments and so didn't understand exactly what people looked for in a stock, my conversations with Warren had led me to believe this was a reasonable question. It was not, apparently.

"Oh, you know," Brooke said, and paused to calculate the tip, "it's a drug stock. Something with genetic engineering, I guess."

She kissed me goodbye in the French way, swearing she would call if a moment opened in her schedule. I, we both understood, would always be free.

It was beginning to rain when I reached the sidewalk, and the concrete exuded a sharp smell, as if it objected to the wetting. Twice on the way to the subway, I was offered five-dollar umbrellas, but I knew a vendor downtown who sold them for three, so I marched on, my hair first covered in a veil of fine mist and then dripping down my forehead. What did it matter if I was unpresentable, I sulked, plunging at last down the subway's urine-scented stairs? I had nowhere to present myself. Ted and I, it turned out, were not imbibing New York, experiencing the delights of the most powerful, arguably the most culturally exciting metropolis in the world. We were not, in other words, at the center of the universe. We were instead clinging to the city's edges by our fingernails like poor tourists. We may as well have been buying shot glasses with a picture of the Empire State Building stamped on them or climbing the Statue of Liberty. Perhaps in some past decade, we might have been bohemians, but it was difficult now that the sort of restaurants in which Dawn Powell's characters treated each other to bottles of wine charged twelve dollars for a plate of pommes frites. Had we been twenty-three, it would have been fitting, exciting even, that a night out in Gotham meant cutlets and plantains at the Puerto Rican lunch counter on Eighth Avenue or chicken vindaloo on Sixth Street, but how could we consider ourselves New Yorkers—how could we say we were any sort of real people at all—when we were skulking in the fringes at this time in our lives?

At home, I stood over my notes in my closet/office, eating leftover lo mein from the box and willing my novel, the vehicle that would transform me into a real person, to coalesce. If Brooke called, I told myself, I would be busy. I would be writing.

I spent the remainder of the week weeding through my school files, admiring the discussion topics I'd teased from *The House of Mirth* and chuckling at the clever sentences I'd composed for spelling quizzes. Brooke did not call.

M—
Do you and Ted ever take people out to dinner? This is what we do with the people Michael has been meeting recently. We don't always, or even usually, mean to take them out, but they call and say, "Let's get together." And then we're all supposed to think about what we should do. Sometimes people suggest a new play in one of the little theaters on Santa Monica Boulevard. "But then we won't be able to talk!" someone always says, "and we want to get to know you," which is so flattering, so we decide to go to a restaurant they've been dying to try or absolutely love or just read a review of. I've yet to get anyone to agree to the chicken and waffle place Michael and I have always been partial to.

We get Delaney to babysit and we take the Saab, because the Saab is fun, but also because of the Tercel's embarrassment factor. Once, when the Saab was in the shop, we almost canceled. We valet park, because when the other husband hands the valet their ticket, it's also too embarrassing to trek off into the night as if we hitchhiked there. (Although the night we had to take the Tercel, we pretended we hadn't managed to get our workouts in that day and so had deliberately parked twelve blocks away to force ourselves to exercise—people understand an obsessive need to exercise far more easily than they understand owning a ten-year-old Tercel or refusing to valet park.)

Once safely inside the restaurant, we order a bottle of mineral water for the table, and start with things like frisée with Asiago and balsamic vinegar, and crab cakes with corn salsa and cilantro, and tuna tartare dressed in hazelnut oil, and then move on to the kumquat-crusted roast duck breast and the sea bass, lightly seared, and throw in some pancetta and some onion confit, and maybe a risotto with broccoli rabe. We get a Willamette Valley Syrah, two bottles—even though we never even half finish the second, and two desserts, perhaps a coconut crème brûlée and a flourless chocolate cake, accompanied by a small pile of forks and spoons, so everyone can taste, and espresso all round. And all the while we've been talking about Los Angeles real estate and private schools and museum gossip and traffic patterns. And then Michael always makes that little motion to the waiter or waitress, which means "bring the check here," and the other husband halfheartedly opens his wallet and gives the top edge of his credit card a peek at the outside world. Occasionally, we'll split a bill, but Michael usually insists on treating. He's scared of being seen as poor and/or chintzy. "Our treat next time," the other couple will say. "Yes, next time," we say. We all nod, we smile, and Michael's pen makes a great many figures on the credit card slip.

The next morning the wife calls and says what a lovely evening they had and how much they hope we can get together again soon, and I say the same, even though, four out of five times, we both know we're lying, and that all we've done is spent an evening enriching a chef or a restaurateur, who still will probably not make enough money to keep the establishment going for more than another eighteen months. And even if we do go out again, it will be so many weeks from now that they will have forgotten that they intended to pay "next time." Having money, *it turns out, is very expensive. Luckily, the funding to increase Michael's salary should be coming in soon—so we'll be able to treat even more people to dinner, like you and Ted, I hope. Duncan says he wants Michael to help define the overarching vision of the museum, which obviously needs definition, since I, for one, have no idea what this means.*

Also, the consensus among our dinner companions seems to be that soccer camp is a must for Marlo and Hunter. Must look into that.

Love, Letty

CHAPTER 10

Margaret

We'd agreed to make our Christmas trip to Los Angeles between December 12 and 17, to avoid the airline's holiday price gouging. Also, this meant that Ted could arrange to spend a couple days talking to people at a Santa Monica think tank, so that we could write the whole trip off our taxes. The several hundred dollars we were thereby saving made Ted's sighs as he studied the ledger in bed particularly irksome. I pulled my knees up firmly and lifted my own book, *The Best and the Brightest*, closer to my face.

Ted sighed again. "What's this?" he

asked, tilting the ledger toward me, so I could see the list of figures. The difference in our entries was striking; Ted always wrote in the ledger with the same black Razor Point, whereas I used whatever implement came most quickly to hand. During the month of November that had often been a green wax marking pencil, left over from a creative spurt in October, during which I'd spent a week and a half chutneying cranberries. Being rather thick, the wax numbers were not exceptionally clear.

"What's what?" I asked.

"This number." He pointed to a scribble of wax labeled "linoleum tiles." Letty's kitchen remodeling had inspired me to buy the cheapest, thinnest, most-prone-to-scratching, "appropriate for a rental" variety of black-and-white sticky-back squares to paste over the worn, dark, and dated faux brick that until then had covered our own kitchen floor. While Ted had admired the effect, and even spent an hour discussing the pros and cons of a diagonal versus a straight pattern, he hadn't entirely approved, maintaining that since the mottled brick appeared dirty even when clean, it demanded less upkeep than a floor that would show every grain of sugar and every turn of a black rubber heel. Also, the landlady would not pay for the new floor, the kitchen having been renovated as recently as 1975. "How much did I pay for those tiles?" Ted asked.

I felt a flash of angry heat, as if the vulnerable underside of my arm had pressed for a sizzling moment against the oven rack. "How much did *who* pay for those tiles?"

"That isn't the issue," he said. "The issue is whether those cheap tiles—which we now do not even own, I might add, unless you intend to pry them off the floor with a butter knife when we move out—cost a hundred and fifty dollars!"

I leaned over the ledger and with a fingernail flicked the hundred off the page. "Piece of spinach," I said. "Try fifty."

Mollified, he leaned back against the pillows. "Fifty is better."

I tried to return to Johnson and his cronies but read the first half of a single page several times, without grasping its meaning. Mightn't it be Ted's fault, what with his continual anxiety about how the work was progressing, that the novel was

not in better shape at this point? It was certainly his fault that I was now stewing over
his attitude toward our finances—specifically, his apparent conviction that he was
magnanimously keeping me in overdeco-
rated splendor—rather than attending to my
research on Vietnam.

I snapped my book shut. "So it's beginning, is it?"

"What's beginning?"

"The inevitable resentment, the veiled demands, the erection of attention-wasting
roadblocks."

"What are you talking about?"

"Do you want me to quit, Ted? Because if
that's what you want, you should have the
courage and the courtesy to say so."

"What do you mean? Quit?"

"Give up on this novel. Get a job. A paying job, I mean. One that would allow me to
spend fifty dollars to 'remodel' our kitchen
without guilt." A sliver of me, paper thin,
wished he would say yes. I could imagine
myself, years hence, sighing pensively and
talking about the book that might have
been, that was really quite well along, but in
the end could not be finished "because we
simply didn't have the money." I could be

the artist stymied by the exigencies of the modern economy. I could be a woman who understood and forgave her selfish husband.

"I said fifty was OK."

"What gives you the right to 'say' anything? You may at this particular moment be filling the purse, but that doesn't mean it belongs to you. What if I were taking care of our children, instead of earning a wage— would you still think you could 'say' how I could spend money?" This argument was safe. I knew we both abhorred the idea of a patriarchal marriage. "What if I were going to school?" I said. But the fact remained that I was doing neither of these things. I hadn't stopped earning money to nurture our family or to increase my ability to make a better living later. I wasn't even attending art or music appreciation classes and enriching myself. I might as well have quit my job to play the slots.

"I just thought a hundred and fifty dollars was excessive for eighteen square feet of instantly scratchable plastic. I thought maybe we should complain to the manufacturer or the Better Business Bureau. That's all. I wasn't blaming you."

"Oh," I said. I opened my book. Luckily, I'd kept a finger in the page I'd been reading.

Ted returned to sighing over the ledger. "A baby would be cheaper than these birth control pills, unless it had to go to college," he muttered, toting up a line of figures he'd inked neatly onto one of the sheets of scrap paper he filched in bulk whenever he visited the NYU library. "Aha, now here's something! What would you say to doing without Parmesan? Isn't it really just superfluous topping? And shampoo! Look here, if we replaced shampoo with plain bar soap and cut out the conditioner altogether—*I* don't use conditioner as it is—" He glanced meaningfully at me, "look how much that would save in a year." He circled the figure he'd written on the scrap paper and pushed it toward me. "Also, you know, don't you, that it's ultimately more expensive to turn your computer on and off all day than just to leave it running, right? We've discussed that."

"Yes, we've discussed it." I did, in fact, turn my computer off frequently. It was vexing to see those fish swimming serenely across the screen, reminding me that I'd not touched the keyboard in at least four minutes.

Our early departure demanded early holiday preparation, but, as I told my laptop and notebook when they reproached me with their stiff, closed covers, when everyone else was still Christmasing it up on December 25, I'd be virtuously back at work, refreshed by a period of celebration that had not been unnecessarily and enervatingly dragged across an entire month. And so, with a clear conscience, I paddled along in the exhilarating current of pre-Christmas New York, breathing in the Midtown air, permeated by what I imagined to be a Victorian charcoaly smell of chestnuts roasting and pretzels toasting on pushcarts, striding purposefully along with the rest of the crowds, and nearly weeping at the sight of the giant Rockefeller Center tree, that had, precisely because it had struggled upward so long and so well in some small, upstate backyard, been sacrificed merely to please shoppers. I was not a shopper. Months ago, I'd justified my chutney experiment by telling Ted the jars would make good—and inexpensive—gifts. My results were somewhat thin; some ingredient, as Ted said, had not "chutted properly." But we agreed this was no matter, since no one actually consumed such gifts. Even Ted thought, however, that the jars alone looked too stark for presentation, despite the holly leaves I'd sketched on the label with my green wax pen.

I was not a shopper but I was a scavenger, and a few afternoons spent perusing the Hanukkah refuse bundled in recycling bags along the sidewalks produced paper of various colors and textures and five yards of ribbon, string, and twine. In Washington Square I collected a boxful of twigs. Then I spent two pleasant days listening to carols on the radio, tearing the wrapping paper into strips, sewing the strips around the jars with large, loose artistic stitches, and attaching a crown of twigs to the rims with Scotch tape. I hid the tape under a bow and hung cranberries strung on thread in the "branches."

"Like a little tree," I said proudly, presenting one to Simon the night before we were to leave.

"Looks hard to pack," Ted said, and the three of us spent the rest of the evening unhooking the cranberry ornaments and un-

taping the twigs, which we placed in a separate box ready for reassembly in Los
Angeles.

"Wow, Margaret! This is great," Letty said,
shifting Ivy on her hip to reach for my "tree."
Some of the twigs had broken in transit and
their edges looked raw in the hard, clear Los
Angeles light. "What is it?" This was our traditional remark upon receiving gifts from
one another, ever since I'd given her a poem
composed in runes for her ninth birthday. "I
don't have anything for you yet, though."

"The only thing I need," I said, holding up
both hands as if to prevent her from bom-
barding me with presents, "is a few chapters of this stupid novel."

"It's not going well?"

Ivy was pulling at one of the cranberry ornaments. "Here, sweetie," I said, prying her
little hooked fingers away, "let me take
that." Letty expertly replaced the prohibited
cranberries with a plastic crescent that
began to heave forth "Twinkle, Twinkle,
Little Star" at a dragging pace. Ivy was not
fooled. She dropped the moon and leaned

away from her mother, reaching with both hands for the better toy, the object she observed Letty and I wanted for ourselves, a jar wrapped in refuse with dirty sticks taped to its lid.

"Trade you the chutney for the child," I said, and, setting the jar on the seat of Letty's Tercel, I reached for Ivy, who came to me willingly and was instantly distracted by something around the area of my mouth, possibly my teeth.

We were waiting for a real estate agent outside of a Cape in Brentwood. Letty'd explained that Brentwood was closer to Michael's office, but we both understood that no one moved to Brentwood for the sake of proximity. Although Beverlywood had a prettier name, Brentwood was brighter. The lawns had that brilliant, jeweled, somewhat stiff lushness characteristic of well-tended Los Angeles landscapes, where each vibrantly colored plant reserves a distinct spot all to itself, often with a ring of brown earth around it, unlike in the East, where various shades of green leaves, runners, mosses, and blades tend to rat together. It smelled clean, too, with eucalyptus leaves tanging the blue air. A newlywed could announce with pride that she'd just bought a house in Beverlywood, but later she would have to spin a list of extenuating circumstances—her children's close friends, a $200,000 addition, nearby aged parents—to justify staying there. Personally, I would feel vaguely ashamed to admit I lived in Brentwood, but then, thanks to Ted, I have socialist tendencies. Most people declare that address with a silver note of triumph in their voices.

"Now remember," Letty said, half to me and half to herself, when a white Grand Cherokee zipped into the driveway, "this is way overpriced. We're not planning to buy. We're just taking a look at what's out there."

The door swung open and a tiny woman slid carefully off her perch to the ground.

"Letitia!" she exclaimed, hurrying toward us in a pair of suede shoes of the type that make valuing comfort over attractiveness fashionable. "So glad you decided to keep going with this project. Peri Scott," she said, turning to me. She grinned for a moment at all three of us to solidify the atmosphere of good cheer and then drew from her purse a pink, reptile-skinned pouch, from which she drew one of her cards and handed it to me. "Peri" was short for "Periwinkle." "Now don't," she cautioned, raising one finger, "hesitate to tell me if this is not at all the kind of thing you're looking for. At this point, I'm just trying to learn what you're all about."

"Good," Letty said.

"Yes," I said. "We want to see what we're all about, too."

Letty gave me a tiny frown, but Peri said, "Exactly!" She brought her hands together and then opened them out, like a blossoming flower, as she spoke. "I like to think of home buying as a process of self-discovery. What could be more personal than your home, the place where you'll raise your family?" She shook Ivy's hand playfully, and then reached into her bag for a tissue to wipe her fingertips. She could not be blamed for this. I, too, had noticed that Ivy was going through a stage in which her hands were continually sticky though she'd had no access to sugary substances. "Shall we go inside?"

"A foyer," Letty breathed into my ear, as we stepped into the coolness. The house had been shut against the sun, and Peri flitted around, roughly tugging open the Roman shades.

Tiny gray veins and sketchy corners had been painted on the rose-tinted entryway walls to suggest marble blocks. To the left was the living room, really too small and with a ceiling too low to do justice to the two squat columns that had been erected with artistic randomness in the space.

I kissed Ivy's soft head to keep from smiling, but kept my eyes on Letty, waiting for a private moment, when we could exchange sardonic glances. Who could possibly want this house? But Letty was trying to fold back a corner of white carpeting with the toe of her sneaker. "Do you know what kind of flooring is under here?" she asked.

Peri frowned and flipped the pages of her specification sheets. "I'll ask," she said. Skillfully, she drew our attention to the French doors that opened onto a tiny side patio, draped in pink bougainvillea and furnished with an iron bistro table and two chairs. "Isn't this precious? I would have my coffee out here every day. You know, after the kids have left for school, when the house is quiet?"

Letty had been encouraging the

bougainvillea in her yard for years, but the dogs kept digging it up.

We passed back through the living room into an awkward, poky room on the other side of the entry. "Formal dining room," Peri said, "and then here," she announced, with a grand, Carol Merrill sweep of the arm, "is the kitchen. Completely renovated."

The kitchen, with its shiny black counters and shiny black floor, resembled the lobby of the Daniel Hotel. Letty opened an oven door. "Double ovens," Peri said. "And, of course, the Sub-Zero and the Miele are included."

Ivy pressed a sticky palm against the refrigerator door. Her fingers made a squeaky sound as I pulled her hand away.

"What's a mee-lee?" I whispered in her ear and she laughed at the feel of my breath.

"This kitchen can almost cook for you," Peri said. "And look, around here is a breakfast nook."

I scrubbed at Ivy's prints with my shirtsleeve, but they only smeared.

Letty tapped an experimental finger on the door between the kitchen and the laundry room. Finally, she looked at me. "Hollow," she mouthed.

I felt more relaxed then as we went upstairs and tried not to look too closely at the wedding photos of the strangers who, presumably, had only hours before dragged themselves out from under the chocolate brown duvet in the dark master suite. Letty exclaimed over the double sink and the Jacuzzi tub and the slate-walled shower, but I knew she was only being polite.

"You have to see the grounds," Peri said, herding us down the stairs. She ushered us along a back hall and out the door into what was, as I'd suspected, only a yard. "Great possibilities, don't you think? I'd put a terracotta patio here," she said, pacing the area directly behind the house. "And then . . . well, I don't know how you feel about pools." She looked expectantly at Letty.

"A pool would be nice," Letty admitted.

"I have to warn you, it can be a detriment when it comes to resale. But I say, why live in southern California if you don't have a pool? I had one put in and use it every day. Sometimes twice. I figure it's already paid for itself, since I don't have to keep up a gym membership anymore. Of course, we still belong to the club, but that's more for social reasons and the tennis. Plus, we'd already paid the initiation fee, which is really the killer, isn't it?" She looked at us as if we understood.

"That's how they get you," I ventured, which turned out to be an appropriate response, because she lifted her eyebrows and nodded.

Even I could imagine the "grounds" as Peri saw them: the four children, plus a friend or two, frolicking wholesomely in the water, the littlest ones encircled in life rings or water wings, or whatever floating aid children used now; multiethnic adults, freshly showered, stylishly attired, the women pedicured, the men in sandals, all spread on lounge chairs beside the gas barbecue and sipping from sweating highball glasses in fun, garish colors. If one had a pool, one would have the kind of friends who knew how to choose wines and grill swordfish.

My father understood neither. "Who invented fire?" he grumbled from the concrete strip that stretched between the back door and the garage, while he pumped a miniature set of bellows ineffectually over the coals. "It was a bad idea."

Inside the house, my father was content to sit before the ubiquitous southern California gas-fed fire that spurted festively around a ceramic log at varying heights in response to the turn of a dimmer switch, but when cooking outside, he believed it was important to use "real coals." "Otherwise, what's the point?" he would say. Of course, in his quest for authenticity and mesquite flavor, he often failed to make food edible, which some might argue was the larger point.

I was chopping garlic, waiting for the first possible moment when Ted and I could leave for Burbank to pick Warren up at the airport.

"Honey, are you sure you want to waste time with that chopping? I've got the powdered stuff somewhere in here." My mother, who was enamored of time-saving substitutions, began rummaging through the junk drawer that also served as her spice cabinet.

In the far corner of the kitchen, Ted was scuffling with the blender. My parents, apparently needing to define Ted for themselves in reassuring ways, had years ago arbitrarily decided that he knew how to mix drinks. He may once have offered to open a bottle of wine.

"What are you making?" I asked.

"Something your mother found in a magazine." He slid a soggy *McCall's* toward me along the counter with one elbow. Ted was always embarrassed to call my mother's discoveries, which usually included ingredients like grenadine and coconut cream, by their names. "When did you say Warren was coming?"

When Warren arrived, we would outnumber them.

"We're off to get Warren," I said, holding the screen door open for Ted with my back. My parents had dragged the plastic patio chairs over to the grill and were both just sitting, staring at the flames, as if the driveway were a ski lodge.

"Mmmm, thank you." My mother reached for the pink-filled glass Ted held out to her. "Isn't it early yet? Why don't you two have one of these?"

"You try them," I said. "If you're still alive when we get back, we'll have another with you." I set the guacamole I'd made on the arm of my mother's chair and a basket of tortilla chips on the arm of my father's. "Isn't there something about a watched grill?"

"That's only pots," my father answered, taking a tentative sip from his glass.

"We thought we'd take a little drive first," Ted said. "Take a look at downtown Glendale and Burbank. See if there's anything new."

My parents nodded and smiled. They'd also decided that Ted adored driving. "Take the Skylark," my father said, shifting in his chair to dig the keys from his pocket. "It's zippy."

We drove aimlessly for a while, picking out houses we'd like for ourselves. I told Ted about the places Letty and I had once constructed out of cardboard boxes and filled with cardboard furniture.

"We made half-inch boxes of Kleenex," I said, "with little Kleenexes inside. And tiny rolls of toilet paper. When Letty's parents were building a guest room over their garage, we also tried to make miniature furniture out of scraps of wood. I probably spent three weeks filing away at one chair leg, trying to make it perfect."

"How did the chair turn out?"

"All right," I said. "A little wobbly. It was a

Louis XIV. I upholstered it with blue poly-
ester from the hem of my mother's
bathrobe." I looked out the window at the
ficus trees with their huge, sidewalk-
buckling roots. I'd never lied to Ted like that
before. Yes, I'd told him I was making
progress on days when I'd not even opened
the computer, but that wasn't lying so much
as reassuring. On other days, the book was
truly moving forward, and my subconscious, I reasoned, was constantly refining
it. Those were vague, indeterminate lies.
What did "going all right" mean, after all?
Maybe it *was* "going all right"; maybe this
halting slog was the way all novels got written. But I'd never finished that chair.

Neither of us had. We'd sat on Letty's
back stoop day after day, filing and sanding,
sometimes making tiny nicks with a saw,
each working away at a single, two-inch leg.
We talked the whole time, of course, about
other things, about kids in our class and
episodes of *The Partridge Family*. We had
fun. But we couldn't make those chairs.
Somehow, that summer, we'd become too
old for the suggestion of reality that would
have satisfied us before. We were using real
materials, after all, real wood and real tools,

not cardboard and tape. It had to be right. It had to look real, and try as we would, we were not skilled enough for that.

What scared me now was remembering how well I'd envisioned that chair when I'd held the stump of wood in my hands. I'd imagined, in fact, whole roomfuls of furniture fashioned from those plywood bits. Nevertheless, I hadn't been able to make them appear. Thinking of that chair, I realized I'd believed that I could fashion a novel, too, simply because I could envision its existence. But like my chair, though I whittled and sanded and scraped, the novel refused to chut. Scenes that were fluid and vibrant in my head clunked stolidly on the page. And just as Letty and I would have had no idea how to attach the legs to a base and the base to a back, had we ever constructed such essential chair elements, I now had no notion of how to attach bits of story together, even were I able to write them in any way close to the way I experienced them in my mind.

I doubt Ted would have drawn such a connection. But I felt a new reluctance to admit even to trivial failure, even with him. Serious failure seemed all too close at hand.

"Let's go to the airport," I said. "We might as well meet Warren at the gate." And so we drove on with a purpose, which in itself made me feel somewhat more optimistic. Perhaps I was too close to the novel. When we returned to New York, after I had stood back from it and gained some perspective, it would go better.

It was easy enough to push the novel from my own mind, but harder to steer my family from it.

Warren always sat in the back because traffic made him nervous. "So how's the book coming?" he asked, leaning into the space created by the elbow rest between the two front seats. We weren't even out of the parking lot yet. "Are you about halfway done now?"

"In a sense," I said.

"Because you said you'd be done in a year," he pressed on. "So I figure you should be about halfway done now, give or take a few chapters."

"Give or take a few chapters." This may have been true, if you counted notes and vague plans and general intentions. It was certainly not true, if you counted pages. "Why didn't Missy come down?" I countered, turning on my brother in a manner more reminiscent of a cornered rat than a wounded gazelle.

Missy had been Warren's girlfriend for nine years. It was unclear which of them was in charge of permanently postponing marriage, but their relationship was one of the few areas in Warren's life akin to an unfinished novel. Otherwise, he had exhibited extraordinary life-planning skills, the various aspects of which my parents rolled in like dogs in manure. But who could blame them for being proud? I, too, was proud of my brother's galling success. If we'd ever had any extra money, I would without hesitation have given it to my little brother to invest.

Warren, unlike Brooke, had become an investment banker, not only that, but he did so purely because the market fascinated him. He might have become an economics professor, but he modestly claimed he was not smart enough, so he was instead well on his way toward becoming inconceivably rich as a portfolio manager in a small San Francisco firm.

"Nice work with those midcap funds," my father said, pouring wine—opened by Ted—into Warren's glass. He often spoke as if his close connection with Warren made him an expert on the market, as well, even though before my brother had this job, my parents both used the word "portfolio" only to refer to two-pocket folders made of stiff, colored paper.

"Mmm, yeah, I think we might sell," Warren said, mounding his mashed potatoes along the rim of his plate away from the fish. Warren didn't like his foods to touch one another. He looked worriedly at the rivulets of chutney, which refused to be contained.

"Really?" my father said.

"Al, if he wants to sell, let him sell. Warren knows what he's doing," my mother said.

"I know he knows what he's doing. Hasn't he quadrupled our portfolio in five years? And that Genslen you had us buy. Whoo-ee!"

"What is that?" I asked. "My friend Brooke was talking about it, too."

"Oh, it's a biotech stock," Warren said. "The product's done really well in clinical trials so far and it's got potential, if they can get it on the market."

"It's a fat pill!" my father announced gleefully. "It's going to sell like hotcakes!"

"The thing is they're not targeting it just toward the morbidly obese. Doctors could prescribe this to almost anyone who wants to drop a few pounds, so the market should be sizable," Warren said. He looked up from his plate to see if any of us had registered his joke.

"That's a good one, Warren," Ted said. I married an extremely kind man.

"So how's Jim Barnes doing? How's the leg?" While my father enjoyed "talking stocks," my mother preferred probing for personal details about the head of the firm, with whom she'd shaken hands twice during tours of Warren's office. "Skiing accident," she added knowingly for Ted's and my benefit. "In Vail."

"He's having some kind of special therapy," Warren said, spearing a broccoli floweret. Since he was about twelve, he'd always eaten in a specific order: first green vegetables, then vegetables of other colors, then starches, and finally meat. It occurred to me that it might be useful to give Robert this habit as a manifestation of his efforts to keep his drifting life under control. I wondered, for the first time, if this was what my brother's habit manifested. "This woman comes into the office every day with a cartful of stuff," he was saying, "like medicine balls and giant rubber bands and industrial-sized cans of pineapple juice."

"Could that be Pie-lates?" my mother asked, doubtfully.

"I don't think so, Mom," I said, suddenly feeling a sisterly instinct to rescue Warren.

"Now, Margaret," my father said, "how's the Great American Novel coming along?" Of course, by that he meant to make my ambition appear foolish. Unless he meant to be supportive. In the time it took me to sip the mediocre and probably overpriced Chilean wine, I swung wildly to both contradictory conclusions.

"It's all right," I said.

"Margaret's halfway done," Warren said.

"Really? Already?" my mother said. "Maybe you're going a little too fast, honey. You want to write something lasting, you know."

"Oh, it's very good," Ted said.

"You've been reading it?" My mother sounded slightly hurt.

"Just a few bits here and there. Mostly, Margaret's told me about it." Ted smiled at me. "Actually, I didn't realize it was so far along." Was he trying to tell me he was onto my game, or did he really think I was halfway through? Who could possibly finish half a novel in five months?

"What's it about?" Warren asked.

"Well, the main character is a Vietnam vet," I began. "He lives in Pomona. Or, no, I guess it's Ventura now," I stumbled. "I wanted to use the ocean. For metaphorical reasons." I could not now remember what those reasons were. Looking at my parents nodding and smiling, I suddenly saw how ridiculous, how juvenile, this whole project sounded. I was going to write a novel, I'd announced, just as in sixth grade I'd sworn I would be a professional jazz saxophonist; just as in ninth grade, I'd been sure I'd be the next Pauline Kael; just as in my junior year of high school I'd declared my firm intention to become a Near Eastern archaeologist; just as at twenty-two I'd said I'd be joining the Peace Corps. These people knew way too much about me. And what did I know about Vietnam? My parents were well aware that I'd been eleven when the U.S. pulled out of Indochina. How could I have anything to say about the repercussions of modern American warfare? I was only their daughter, after all.

"The important thing," my mother said, "is that you're writing it. Remember Emily Dickinson couldn't get published."

"And you can always go back to teaching," my father said, refilling my glass.

"You know what I heard?" Warren said. He had started in on his fish now. "At the end of the day, Ernest Hemingway always stopped in the middle of a sentence, so he'd have something to get him going the next morning. Maybe you should try that."

I wanted to tell about the newsmagazine show I'd seen in which a chimp, pointing to various companies on the New York Stock Exchange, made more money than twenty-five top financial advisers, but I pushed a dry corner of swordfish into my mouth instead.

"Maybe we should live in Paris like Hemingway, too," Ted said. This was the sort of remark that made my parents anxious and spawned their compulsion to fashion Ted into a more predictable joy-riding drinks mixer.

"Heh, heh," my father said experimentally.

I laughed to give the others their cue.

"There are lots of writers in New York, aren't there?" Warren asked.

"Plenty," I said. "Too many."

"Well, I know I couldn't do it," my mother said.

I looked at her gratefully, but then I wondered if what she really meant was that she was pretty sure I couldn't do it either. This is the way you get when you feel yourself sliding quietly but inexorably downhill. Every comment is fraught with significance. Everyone, even people who aren't sure whether "fatuous" has something to do with humor or gas, is secretly laughing at you.

"How many pages do you write a day?" my father asked. "I remember when I wrote papers in college, I did a page an hour. Of course, that was in the days of the manual typewriter; I suppose you can go faster now with a computer."

"Did you make an outline, Margaret?" my mother asked. "I think it always helps to have an outline."

I seemed to be pushing mashed potatoes into my mouth without pausing to swallow. The problem with writing was that pretty much everyone had done it in one form or another. It wasn't like what Warren did, drawing conclusions from factors beyond the realm of normal human understanding.

"You know what author I like?" Warren said. "Charles Dickens. You should write a book like *David Copperfield,* Margaret. Then I would read it."

"Warren! You're going to read your sister's book!" my father said.

"I meant, I'd read it even if she wasn't my sister."

"Oh, Margaret, I forgot to tell you!" My mother set her flatware firmly on her plate for emphasis, the tines of the fork crossed correctly over the blade of the knife. "Guess who's writing screenplays now? Allison Pumphrey! Don't you remember her? She was in your modern dance class. Remember? Her mother has the big teeth? And that eye problem, you know, like Marty Feldman. Anyway, she went to USC film school and now she's writing screenplays. Her mother says some people are very excited about one of them, at Disney, maybe, or

DreamWorks, one of the 'D' studios. If your book becomes a movie, maybe she could write the screenplay."

That night I slipped out of bed in the room that had been mine before it had become an impersonal guest room. I made my way into the hall, where I stood on a chair to reach the knotted cord that dangled from the ceiling. Quietly, I yanked open the trap door, unfolded the ladder, and climbed to the attic. At the top, I swung my arm in a wide arc in front of my face, waiting for the brush of string against my skin. I knew it was there; it had always been there, but I felt nothing. My fingers grasped only warm, dry air, until I went back down the ladder, turned on the hall light, and climbed back up again. The grimy string with its metal pull dangled just where I'd been reaching. I tugged, two, three times. The bulb had burned out. While I rifled the contents of several kitchen drawers and searched the back of the liquor cabinet and the shelves of the hall closet, wondering if my parents even had any extra bulbs—unlike Letty's family, who always kept a supply of toothbrushes under the bathroom sink and a larder of canned goods in the garage, mine was not the kind that stocked up—I tried to convince myself to go back to bed.

Pressed into the back of the closet was the navy nylon Pan Am flight bag, in which more than twenty years before I'd packed supplies in case of an earthquake. Inside, between the rancid peanut butter and the duct tape (for use in constructing a tent out of thirty-gallon garbage bags), I found a flashlight, full of long-expired batteries. But I'd seen batteries among my parents' scant supply of cloth napkins, while looking for a lightbulb. Finally, back up the ladder I went and, crouching under the beams, shone my light along the tumbled stacks of boxes. I was searching for my promise.

The box I remembered was closed only by the trick of fitting flap corners under and over one another to allow for easy access. There had been a time when first my mother and then I had added lovingly to its contents, preserving the one-dimensional evidence of my artistry and imagination and intelligence, if not under glass, at least under cardboard, keeping hold, the way a mother saves a tooth or a lock from her baby's first haircut, of the little sproutings and shavings of me, as I grew steadily beyond them.

I pulled open the flaps, soft and pliable as cloth from all the times they'd been pried apart and fitted back together again, and lifted the top item, a stack of typed pages, so thick as to require a binder clip to hold it together, entitled "Bewildered: The Juxtaposition of Wilderness and Civilization in American Literature from Hawthorne to Wharton." This had been my senior project. Next to the red "B-" under the title the professor who'd read it had written in tiny script: "Although your writing is assured and your insights surprisingly original, this is far too broad a topic for a senior essay. You ought to have been advised to tackle something more manageable, say, Whitman's use of bird imagery in the first six stanzas of 'Out of the Cradle Endlessly Rocking.' "

I had been so advised. Professor Lindsay, my adviser, had pleaded with me every time we met to focus and trim. "At least concentrate on a single author!" she'd begged, but I pressed stubbornly on, wanting to say something consequential, even perhaps to make a real, nonstudentlike contribution to the study of American literature. Proud of my work at the time, I hadn't minded the grade. What important point could I possibly have made had I limited myself to six stanzas of a single poem? Now, having long since forgotten whatever points I had made about nineteenth- and early-twentieth-century American literature as a whole, I was most impressed by the paper's physical heft—how had I managed to string so many sentences together?

Hoping to catch hold of that old, jaunty, productive Margaret, I picked a few more relics from the box: a charcoal self-portrait from Art 101, drawn while staring into the back of a spoon; the labeled sketch of an imaginary downtown plaza, in slightly skewed perspective, from a course on urban planning; a biographical poem about Leonardo da Vinci in rhyming couplets, composed in seventh grade; a construction paper Valentine I'd made for my father. Madeleine-like, they evoked for me the hours of their creation. I remembered my mother and me in a thick pond of yellow light, the dark windows showing only our reflections, as if nothing existed beyond our kitchen. She tore apart a head of iceberg lettuce with her long, sure fingers, the bangles clinking on her thin wrists, a sound that I would always equate with femininity, while I cut construction paper, making a noise not quite as rich as that which Captain Kangaroo's scissors made on TV, but still satisfying. It was hard to get the hearts right, though I knew to fold the paper in half to make both sides even. They often came out too thin or too fat, and they were always marred by that fold down the center.

I remembered the scorn I'd felt for "Roses Are Red," especially since, as I'd pointed out to my mother, roses were only sometimes red and violets were obviously violet, not blue, although they could also be white or even yellow. Being a California girl, I'd not, at that stage of my life, actually observed a violet firsthand, but I had looked them up in a guide to eastern flowers, after I'd noticed the rose inaccuracy. Missing entirely the point of the standard verse, in which the loved one is at least described in complimentary terms, I had proudly printed my version of the non sequitur: "Birds-of-paradise are orange and also purple at the spine. I hope you will be my Valentine."

When I wrote the da Vinci biography, Letty was working on Benjamin Franklin. She sat at the foot of my bed, I at the head. We tossed our rhymes back and forth, screaming and breathless with laughter, collapsing sideways on the mattress, digging our heels into the bedspread against the pain of our hilarity. I still had a tiny gray-blue spot imbedded in the skin of my knee from accidentally stabbing myself with my pencil as, in response to one particularly amusing couplet—whether hers or mine, I don't remember now—I slipped completely off the bed onto the carpet.

These grease-spotted and dog-eared papers were not what I'd remembered them to be. I'd gone to them to be reminded of my earlier, better self. I'd hoped, I suppose, to duct tape them together into a sort of paper reservoir of reassurance and inspiration from which I could draw when faced again with the tedium of the sluggish keyboard and the despair brought on by the nearly blank screen. I'd assumed that among them I'd find evidence of incipient genius. What instead leapt from these pages to grab me by the throat was at best precocity and at worst self-conscious straining. Had I been, after all, only an overachiever type, who, in fact, had not managed even to over-achieve?

One more try, I thought, digging gamely into the dark box. My hand emerged clutch-ing a handful of envelopes, thick as two bricks, bound in a disintegrating rubber band, my name and address on each in Letty's round script. The camp years.

My impatience with most organized ac-tivities precluded any serious interest in camp, but Letty, who liked team sports and even marching band practice and who had a predilection for crafts, was different. She began going to overnight camp the summer we finished third grade and went year after year for longer and longer, even into high school, when she became a counselor, while I doused cornbread-coated wieners in boiling oil at Hot Dog on a Stick. For me, these months were, if not exactly miserable, marred, and she missed me, as well. Whatever talent I may possess as a writer, however, I owe in large part to our separa-tion.

Letty was born knowing how to write let-ters. She never said, "How are you? I am fine." She never delivered a long dull list of the day's activities or described a setting in brochure terms. Instead, she jumped into the good stuff—"Rachel and I had another fight today"—or, if nothing was happening, she made just sitting around counting mosquito bites sound interesting. The secret, I realized, was in the detail. She did not just paint her toenails, she painted them "Very Cherry," which did not, as it turned out, go with her new pink sandals. I am not ashamed to say that I modeled my own missives after hers, stuffing them with colors and textures and crumbs of conversation I'd never otherwise have noted even to myself. Thanks to her lead, when I was writing to Letty, my own everyday world became surprisingly full and amusing, nearly as fascinating as those of past civilizations. Sometimes, before I sealed the envelope, I marveled at all that had happened to me.

I piled my own papers back into the box and wove the corners closed. Letty's stack of envelopes, however, I took with me downstairs and tucked into the underwear pouch of my suitcase. I had no illusions that a twelve-year-old could teach me anything about writing now. I just thought it might be comforting to have her old voice near me.

Letty's adult voice betrayed an edge of desperation, as she opened the front door. "Will
Christmas never end?" she said. "I know we
were going to have lunch, but you have to
help me with the gifts." A thin but rising wail,
akin to her own but somewhat louder, is-
sued from down the hall, and she hurried
after it, handing me half a sandwich as she
went. I bit tentatively into the soft white
bread. American cheese and mayo.

"Don't eat that!" Letty was back with
Noah on her hip. She looked into his face to
check that the crying had stopped and
brushed some strands of hair back from his
warm forehead with two motherly fingers. "I
mean, you can if you want, but you don't
want to, do you? I mean, it's kind of gross.
Not that it isn't absolutely delicious," she
added for Noah's benefit, taking the sandwich from me and putting it into his outstretched hand.

"Sorry, Noah," I said. "I didn't mean to be
eating your food."

"Have you ever made jam?"

"Well, that chutney . . ." I began.

"That's right, it's your fault. If you hadn't given me that chutney, I'd have just bought some gourmet baskets at Gelsons and been done with it. You have to help me." She started for the kitchen.

"What are we doing?"

"We're jamming."

Letty's new granite kitchen counters, which I'd not yet had time to admire, were covered with unaffordable fruits. Teeny wild blueberries, raspberries, currants, gooseberries, and champagne grapes were heaped in pint-sized plastic baskets next to cardboard trays of apricots, each globe nested safely in its own molded depression. A green glass bowl I recognized from the Williams-Sonoma catalog was mounded with ripe persimmons. Blood oranges were packed in excelsior in two small wooden crates. Letty rolled her eyes. "I thought I'd save money if I did it myself," she said.

"What's this?" I asked, my hand on a greenish, lumpy, elliptical object.

"Papaya."

"No, I mean, what's all this? What are you doing?"

"You mean what are *we* doing."

I nodded.

"We are daringly combining exotic fruits to fill cunning antique ceramic pots with homemade jam and marmalade, matching as closely as possible the flavor to the personality of the recipient. We will then nestle said cunning pots among various packaged delights from foreign lands with bright amusing labels in baskets made to resemble wattle and tied with French ribbon available exclusively at a store in Malibu that's open only on Tuesday and Thursday afternoons. Can you come over tomorrow, too?"

"Where are the ceramic pots?"

"I don't know, Margaret." Letty's voice was again overcome with despair. She let Noah slither to the floor and he scampered off, no doubt to play again at whatever had caused his earlier tears. "I've been to five different stores and called seven others, but they seem to exist only in my mind."

"Who are you giving these things to?" I asked. "Not the kids, obviously. And not us, I hope."

She laughed. "No! Would you want such a thing? I'll probably give you and Ted a loaf of Wonder Bread and a package of sliced cheese, if I get around to it. There's no time to find gifts for people I like. This," she said, waving dismissively at the spread on the counters, "is for people Michael has met through work. People we've eaten with at La Limonade. People who have given us this." She reached into the cupboard over the refrigerator and pulled out a bottle of champagne so expensive I'd only read about the brand in novels. Ivy, who'd been throwing Cheerios one by one onto the kitchen floor from her high chair, ran out of cereal and began to scream.

"Does anything need to be washed?" I said, moving toward the new, deep "farm kitchen" sink.

"All of it."

M,

You despise me now, don't you? Admit it! How can you not when the actual words "at least glass will allow the jewel tones of the cooked fruit to show through" came from my actual mouth. Was I drunk? What did I offer you to drink anyway? I seem to remember apple juice in a sippy cup.

They're there, those jars of jam, massing on the dining el table, squat, perky, gorgeous little monsters. I woke from a sound sleep with the idea that they must each be swaddled in thick, Victorian reproduction gift wrap sold exclusively in the Otis's gift shop, before they can leave the house.

What's happened to me? Last Christmas I made fudge and wrapped it in red and green Saran. But the thought of giving Jeanette Peabody a square of plastic-wrapped fudge makes me choke.

I told you, didn't I, that I'm not giving these jars over which we sweated all day, jars that made my children cry for attention and forced my husband to dine on boxed macaroni and cheese, jars that cost—oh, God, I can't even tell you how much that fruit was—and the blueberries that Hunter put down the garbage disposal were the most expensive of all (I keep telling myself that if I hadn't redone the kitchen, I wouldn't have had a disposal to grind them up! But then, if we'd had a disposal all along, it wouldn't be so fascinating to Hunter now)— where was I? oh, yes . . . I'm not giving these to dear friends, who'll remember me with every sweet spoonful. No, I will present them to people who think my name might be "Leslie" or possibly "Lexie." And I will give the finest one—the guava/damson/sat-

suma—to Jeanette Peabody. That'll show her.

I'm not sure you ever met Jeanette. We were both production assistants at KSMC right after college. We did things like help set up the mikes in bowling alleys and in front of the Federal Building to record background sound effects. This is what one does after college with degrees in music theory and sociology. And then we got that apartment together in Palms, the one Michael and I lived in after we were married.

Someone's crying—hang on.

Noah fell out of bed—he was just startled, but then he had to tell me his dream, which was long and complex, and I suspect he was just making it up as he went along. This is why you can do nothing other than pay attention to your children when you're a mother, because if you're dying to get back to something else—your own endless story, for instance—you just feel impatient, whereas otherwise you would be utterly charmed by this little creature who really hasn't been talking for all that long wanting to tell you and tell you and tell you things he's made up out of his clever little brain. You wouldn't then feel the urge to say, "Yes, sweetheart, that's very interesting, but maybe we should save a little of it for tomorrow," which is what I did and now feel guilty about. "How to Squelch Creativity in the Early Years" by Letty MacMillan.

So, anyway, I had the bedroom, because I had a steady boyfriend, even though Michael didn't technically live with us because he had his graduate housing, and we partitioned off a piece of the living room for Jeanette with the Indian-print bedspread— Yes! Yes! the one covering the hideous brown, inherited-from-Aunt-Louise couch! My life! My life!—and she and I spent a lot of time sitting in beanbag chairs after work with bottles of beer between our bare feet analyzing her dates and the possibility of these encounters developing into relationships and decrying the general poor state of available men—the usual thing. Except then I felt just a teeny bit smug. Because I had Michael, you see, and we already knew we were getting married, and it seemed my life was going along pretty well, that I was maybe even a little ahead, what with my desirable, artsy, public-radio, vaguely "save the world" type of low-paying job and my *right to talk about china patterns and color schemes for bridesmaids' dresses.*

So I can't say it isn't a contest now, can I? It wouldn't be fair to say it was when I was winning and now say, no, of course it isn't, when I'm so far behind Jeanette that it's like we inhabit two different worlds. I can hear you saying, "Different, yes, but equal." But that is where you're wrong. Hers is much, much better.

Our worlds converged last month. It turns out she's an events consultant—do you have any idea what that is? It seems to be a professional party thrower. She's eventing the Norton Simon in February, and she recognized Michael at some interart-museum meeting. I can't believe he's now going to meetings about parties! He hates parties! So she and I arranged to have lunch, and it was one of those awkward things where she suggested a place with a chef who makes appearances on Charlie Rose and then I just couldn't bring myself to say, "How about the Cuban place on Venice where the roasted garlic chicken is $5.95," so I ended up saying, "Why don't you come over here?" Which, of course, turned out to be worse than spending sixty dollars on lunch be-

cause not only did I feel compelled to spend over three hours in the car driving to the Santa Monica farmers' market for teeny-tiny purple potatoes and then to this new gourmet place on Third Street for tarragon mustard and then back to Santa Monica for a quarter pound of the best niçoise olives, I also had then to create something with these ingredients that appeared to be casually yet elegantly tossed off between committee meetings—no, I am not on any committees! It's just that I had to seem busy with the right things, not, in fact, busy, as I actually am, with mopping up vomit, reinstalling a mini-blind, and trying to convince Noah that he'll like a red Popsicle as much as a purple one.

Altogether it took three days to prepare this special lunch—if you include the trip to Pier 1 to buy fish-shaped plates, one chartreuse and one turquoise, and coordinating placemats and napkins, and the evening of homemade crouton preparation—and then I got a call at eleven-thirty this morning. Jeanette had an "event planning emergency." Something about candles or canned dal.

I'd like to say that it didn't turn out so bad,

that Marlo and I put on dresses and ate the salad, like ladies-who-lunch, and the boys were delighted with fish sticks on the fish plates, and I fashioned the napkins into a charming poncho for Ivy, but no. Marlo tasted the salad niçoise and declared her preference for "plain tuna"; Hunter and Noah fought over who would use the blue plate, which then, perhaps predictably, fell off the counter and shattered on the new slate floor—which is murder on the calves, by the way, when you stand on it for any length of time; Ivy threw up on a coordinating place mat. Lunch is overrated, anyway.

I take comfort in the fact that Jeanette can't be doing a good job with her children. She cannot possibly be touching them as much as she should be—her linen shirts would be spoiled. (I can tell by the way her voice sounds on the phone that she wears linen shirts—or possibly those stretchy sort of shrunken-down blouses which appear not to allow you to move your arms. And her hair is straightened or crimped or layered or razored, or however hair is supposed to be right now.) And while I'm sure she's got a hand in all the big decisions, like what schools her children will attend and whether they'll join the soccer league (her son, it turns out, will be on Hunter's team this year), those, at least in my opinion, are not the moments of true mothering. No, it's the little things that crop up hourly, the six hundred daily trips to the potty, the singing in the car on the way to the grocery store, the debate over the amount of jelly that should rightfully go on a peanut butter sandwich, the kissing of the stubbed toe, that's when you do the real work of helping your child grow into a thoughtful and sensitive adult. At least this is why I've chosen the path I've taken, isn't it?

Please let her children be brats.

Love, Letty

CHAPTER 11

Margaret

Ted waited until we were on the plane to ask. "So," he said, shaking the last of his Bloody Mary mix from the can into his plastic cup, "are you really halfway through?"

I was engrossed in *Alias Grace,* but I did hear the question.

Ted tilted his head forward to look into my face. "It's all right, you know, if you aren't. A third of the way would really be just fine at this point."

When I didn't answer, I could tell he was worried that he might once again have said something I would think he had no right to say. Which, in fact, he had. "I mean, I would think the later stuff would come more quickly, once you've got your characters established," he went on, trying to gain a purchase. And then he gave up altogether. "Are you going to eat your peanuts?"

"Yes," I said. I bit down on the crinkled edge of the stubborn little bag the flight attendant had dropped on the napkin beside my club soda.

" 'Yes' you're halfway through or 'yes' you're going to eat your nuts?" Evidently, he had not given up altogether.

And, I, evidently, was no longer a scrupulously honest person. "Yes to both," I said. This book had made a liar of me. Which could be good, I thought, staring down at the Great Basin. Maybe my habit of truthfulness had been standing in the way of my being able to fabricate a story.

"Well, that's great, Margaret. Really great." Ted sat back for a moment and then turned to me again. "Can I read it?"

The man in the seat ahead of me tilted his chair back so that his head hung just over my tray table, squeezing my space down to the compact L my body made pressed against the upholstery. "I think," I said slowly, as if I were actually considering Ted's question, "that I'd rather if you waited until I had a whole draft done. That's when your response would really be constructive." As opposed to now, when your response would be moaning and shouting, I thought.

"Sure," he said. "That makes sense. It would just be fun to read." He closed his hand over mine on the armrest. "It sounds so good."

I wished it were possible to open the scratched rectangle of Plexiglas at my shoulder and allow myself to be sucked into the blue oxygenless air. I felt, for the first time in my married life, utterly alone, as if I were not sitting pinched in a plane with my husband on one side holding my hand and some stranger in front of me with his head in my lap but was instead dragging my way across the hard sands of the endless, empty beige desert below. Deliberately, one by one, I ate all of my peanuts. At least I would make good on that.

Getting back to work in our unfestive apartment was more difficult than I'd imagined. A

week after our return I was poring over the
Federal Truth in Lending Disclosure Upon
Renewal of Annual Fee statement, written in
fine print on the back of our credit card bill,
instead of extracting Robert from a warren
of North Vietnamese tunnels, when Ted interrupted me.

"Come here, Margaret. There's something
I want to show you."

Warily, I advanced as far as the doorway.
"Shouldn't you be going to your office?"

"Not yet. Just come over here." He spoke
calmly, but there was obviously nothing
pleasant over on his side of the room.

"What?" I said again, as casually as possible. I stood beside him at the table now.

"I just want you to see this," he said.
"Just so we're on the same page."

"Literally," I said, as he opened the
ledger.

He smiled weakly and patted the seat of
the chair beside him. I sat in it.

"See here?" he said. He actually wanted
me to look at the back of an envelope. The
ledger was only to support his case. On the
envelope, he'd printed with his Razor Point
the months from January through July. "I'm
going to make two columns."

"Would you like to use my markers?" I suggested, jumping up. "Sometimes things look more organized when you use color."

"Black will be fine."

So I had to sit down again.

"We'll call one column," he said as he wrote, "monthly credits and the other monthly debits."

"Ted." I was getting annoyed now. "I have to get back to work. What's the bottom line?"

He raised his finger. He had an infuriating way of raising his finger. "You see," he said, "I don't know yet. I want us to do this together. I don't want it to be me telling you. You're perfectly free to check the ledger, you know. Any time you want to take some responsibility."

I closed my eyes so as to keep from closing my teeth around that finger.

"All right," I said. "Let's see."

"OK, here's my monthly salary, minus FICA and taxes and so forth." The figure he wrote beside each of the months included pennies.

"You know the cents?"

"Of course." He looked at me as if I were the crazy one. "Then there's a little interest on our savings." He knew this figure by heart, as well. He wrote it next to January.

"What about the other months?"

"We'll have to see. If our savings drop, the interest will be less."

"What do you mean, 'If our savings drop'? We're saving to buy a place. We don't want to spend that."

"No," he agreed, "we don't want to, but . . ." He made a little box in the lower left-hand corner and labeled it "Savings as of January 1." The envelope was getting crowded and it really would have looked much better in colors. "What's our savings at right now?"

I shrugged.

He shook his head. "You see, Margaret! This is exactly what I mean!"

"I know what it is approximately," I said defensively.

"Approximately is no good here! We need exact figures! Are you going to say to the scary guy at the A&P, 'I'll pay you approximately what I owe'? I don't think so!"

The analogy was not at all clear to me, but I forbore pointing that out.

"All right. This is what we have in savings right now. And this is what we have in the checking account. Of course, there's no interest on that." He wrote both these figures in the corner box. "We can draw on the money in the savings account. If we have to." He looked at me. "Now, let's see if we have to." He opened the ledger. "We can estimate our expenses for January will be very similar to December's," he began, but I interrupted.

"But we were away for a week in December."

"Good thinking. So, in fact, we'll have to add more for the paper we stopped and for the electricity we didn't use." He scribbled some figures on the envelope.

"But we can't count the plane tickets!" I said, "We won't be buying plane tickets in January!" I was feeling a little frantic. When it suited his purposes, Ted seemed to think approximation was perfectly acceptable.

"Actually, we bought those in November."

"All right," I agreed, sullenly. "January will be a little more than December. Approximately," I couldn't resist adding.

He wrote that figure in the monthly debits column. "Which will mean . . ." he said, looking at me significantly.

Ted was right. Black was fine. It looked

like red anyway when the debit number was larger than the credit number. Which it would be, according to Ted's projections, beginning in July.

"We'll have to borrow from our savings," I admitted.

"And you see how the interest will then dwindle," he added, officiously.

It was always difficult for me to believe that there weren't plenty of ways for us to spend less. We bought things we didn't desperately need—candles, for instance, and health insurance. We ate better than we had to, and we contributed regularly to retirement funds. We were middle class, for God's sake. If we were willing to eke by for a while, how could we not have enough money? "Fine!" I said. "You've convinced me! I'll give up shampoo!"

"Margaret, I'm not trying to convince you of anything. I wanted to work on this together, remember? But you can see, can't you, that dirty hair isn't going to make all that much of a difference?"

"What about," I whispered, my eyes fixed on a clump of cat fur under the table, "credit cards?"

"Margaret, you don't mean that." Ted

equated credit card borrowing with selling a firstborn child. "Anyway," he said, resting his hand on my shoulder, "we'll be fine as long as you're finished by June, which it sounds like you will be. And if you need another month or two, I could probably sell an article."

I squeezed my head between my palms to create a counterpressure. I could imagine the conversation we'd have in June when there was no book and no money.

"You know," I said, as Ted neatly inserted the envelope of figures between two pages of the ledger for safekeeping, "maybe I should look for a part-time job. Trollope, you know, worked in the post office, and look how much he produced."

"I don't know if that's such a great idea. You don't want to slow the work down. Sally Sternforth turned down an assignment to do a piece on Cuba once she got into her book. She didn't want other projects distracting her."

"But just because I'm into it," I argued, following him to the door, "I could probably afford the distraction. I think it's only a matter of organizing my time efficiently."

"Let's think about it," he said and kissed

me goodbye. At the landing, he turned back. I was closing the door, but I heard his words distinctly. "Work hard," he said.

Work hard! I would have been happy to work hard. It wasn't that I was lazy. It was just that I didn't know what, exactly, to do. Telling a person to work hard on a novel is like telling a person to think. You can't just do it on command. I slumped in the chair and laid my head for a moment on the table, my face in the figures Ted had written. Why not get a job, I thought, something part-time? If I were making money, finishing the novel by June—which was obviously not going to happen—would be less crucial. Also, it might in fact be true, as I'd argued to Ted, that curtailing my hours could actually help me to focus and get more done in the remaining time. I clearly didn't need to keep the entire day free so that I could peruse the back of the credit card bill.

I remembered the card the freelance guy had given me. Having been a student and a teacher, wasn't I qualified to do all manner of research, writing, and editing, or even perhaps seminar or conference running, what with my experience in front of a class? I could freelance as a communications specialist. I was not sure what "communications" meant in the business world, having previously thought of the term only as a long way to say "talk," but I could learn.

Dear M—
The children and I were invited to swim today. At Jeanette's. When she gave me directions and it was clear we'd be crossing Sunset, I suspected her house would be nice, maybe even nicer than Zoe and Brad's, so I thought I was prepared, but, in fact, a person like me cannot be prepared for such a place. I may have left some drool on her windows.

The house was hidden from the road, of course. And the driveway was blocked with the usual mechanical gate, the security device of choice among those living north of Sunset and aesthetically preferable to the bars people south of Pico install over their windows. I spoke into the intercom, as if ordering hamburgers, and then the gate swung slowly open, its little motor humming.

"Hurry, Mom," Hunter said. He was worried that the gate would close on us before we were through (in disgust, I suppose,

when it realized it was admitting a car equipped with crank windows). The drive-way slipped gracefully through a small grove of eucalyptus to a parking area where we left the Tercel next to a silver Lexus SUV and a bronze BMW coupe. (Jeanette's husband must drive the gold car.) Along the walls of the house huge terra-cotta pots held flowering trees. Do you have any idea how expensive a pot large enough to hold a tree is? Not to mention the trees themselves. I counted ten of them.

Jeanette came out to meet us in a chic little sunsuit, wincing as her bare, pedicured feet touched the hot brick of the back patio. Jake and India, her children, gamboled beside her in all-cotton bathing suits available in Neiman Marcus and certain Malibu boutiques. Needless to say, I was shuffling along in gym shorts and rubber flip-flops from the drugstore, as were my children.

How can I describe the tastefulness of her house? The gracious width of the hallways between unscuffed, custard-colored walls. The brown-sugar-stained floorboards. The whimsically hung paintings by California artists. The buttery leather couch cushions. The grand piano with its slightly yellow keys.

Jeanette had assured me that her house, like mine, was full of junk. There is, however, absolutely no similarity between the Peabodys' furnishings and ours. Her children's desks are made of "reclaimed" pine, their well-grained surfaces gently "distressed." They evoke history: the farmwife scrubbing, one hand spreading the scouring sand, scooped from the creek bed at dawn, the other wielding the rough, homespun cloth, dipped in clear water, also scooped from the creek at dawn. Or the young scholar, sleeve secured in an elastic band, polishing the wood with his elbow, as he declines his Greek nouns with a quill dipped in ink. Indeed, a discreet and lovely blotch of black ink near one corner endowed Jake's desk with character. Marlo (thus far, the only child of ours with her own desk) works on plastic laminated "wood," produced when sawdust left over after boards have been cut is pressed into an incredibly heavy slab that bears no resemblance to the tree from which it came. Her brothers' trucks and her mother's X-acto knife have painfully scored its hard, impersonal finish, and markers, overreaching the page they were coloring, have fringed the surface here and there with their unnatural hues.

The field of chocolate leather on Jeanette's horsehair fainting couch is artfully broken by a paisley cashmere throw in subtle golds and muted reds that the Peabodys picked up in London. The grape juice stains on our foam-core loveseat, on the other hand, are hidden by an afghan crocheted in hot pink and lime green acrylic by my grandmother. Most impressive is the huge Oriental carpet that covers their living room floor. Even I, who know almost nothing about carpets except to avoid those of the zebra patterns and acrylic sheens that hang for sale over the chain-link fence on La Cienega and Olympic, can tell that this is the real thing. The colors are faded—obviously nothing but vegetable dye touched these yarns—and the pattern is intensely intricate, more detailed the closer you look. (I know this because I knelt to examine the fibers while the others were in the kitchen. They smelled vaguely of camel.) A really good carpet makes all the difference, Margaret.

"Where are the dolls with the matted hair?" I wanted to ask. "Where are the ac-

tion figures and the dinosaurs? Where is the plastic truck with the missing wheel?" In the bathroom, wild grasses were suspended in the soap, and the bar was clear all the way through, not white and gummy underneath. The house overlooks the ninth hole of a golf course so exquisitely landscaped that the green appears to be a fairy glen nestled among tree-covered hills.

"This looks familiar," I said as we approached the pool, where a twelve-foot sculpture of a woman lounged on her side, her head propped in one hand. "Is it a copy of the Dumeule that was at the Armand Hammer?"

Jeanette playfully covered her face with her hands and shook her head, "Oh, I was so annoyed when they got one. Theirs is the fifth cast. Ours is the second."

Jeanette and I lay on teak pool chairs, sipping ginger iced tea. I actually lay on my chair only intermittently and for scant seconds at a time, since Ivy, who was supposed to be entertaining herself with an assortment of hand-carved wooden farm animals, kept toddling off in the direction of the water.

"So what have you been doing since

KSMC?" Jeanette asked. "Tell me everything."

With four children, two dogs, and three
cats, I have mostly been picking up poop.
"Oh, this sort of thing," I said, jumping up to
herd Ivy back to the farm.

Marlo was practicing her dives and India
and Noah were splashing contentedly on
the steps at the shallow end, but Jake
seemed to be dunking Hunter relentlessly
and with a bit too much vicious fervor. I
drew Jeanette's attention to the roughhous-
ing. Tactfully, however, I did not single her
son out as the perpetrator.

"Don't worry," Jeanette said. "Jake's
used to wild kids. His cousin, Colby, is a
handful, too."

"Hunter," I said, "c'mere a minute." I
crouched over the pool, which was lined
with a lovely dove gray slate. "Are you all
right?" I asked, when he was hanging on to
the slippery side. He nodded, but I know my
kids. "Do you want to get out for a while?"
He shook his head. "Why don't you two do
some races? I'll start you. And Mrs. Peabody
can judge the finish."

"Mrs. Peabody! That makes me feel so

old!" Jeanette hopped off her chair athletically and swooped Ivy up to carry her to the finish line. "I don't think anyone even calls my mother-in-law Mrs. Peabody. Possibly Mrs. P. Anyway, your kids have to call me Jeanette. You don't want my kids to call you Mrs. MacMillan, do you?"

I did, actually. Or Aunt Letty would be all right, if it seemed I would become a permanent part of their lives. "You are old," I wanted to say. I trace the loss of civility in modern society to adults' efforts to hold on to their youth by instructing three-year-olds to call them by their first names. However, "Letty's fine," I said.

"So," she said later, when the kids were eating a wide variety of sandwiches— Jeanette gave them choices, which I hardly ever do. "Allowing children to express their preferences, within reasonable boundaries, of course, develops their sense of autonomy," Jeanette said. This is probably true, but it also creates a great deal of work for the sandwich-maker, in this case, the nanny, Carmelina. Jake, by the way, requested peanut butter and jelly on rosemary ciabatta—Anyway, "So," she said, "I always *thought you'd be a producer, or actually, station manager somewhere, by now."*

"You did?"

"Sure," she said. "I was just sort of filling time at the station after college. You know, trying to figure out what I wanted to do. But you seemed really to get it. To understand what made good radio. You were always coming up with those story ideas, remember?"

I'd had probably six ideas in the two years I worked at the station, only one of which—a weekend-long demonstration in which participants constructed a colony of sand-castles and then filmed the tide washing them away to show solidarity with the homeless—a reporter pursued. (Radio was perhaps not the best medium for a story centering on water disintegrating sand structures, although we recorded some great-sounding waves as background.) Still, when she said that, some small, ridiculous part of me thought—"Yes, yes! She's absolutely right! I was a budding radio genius, who gave up fame and fortune, or at least dignified cocktail party chat, to focus on potty training! What had I been thinking?"

"Aren't you ever bored?" she asked, pushing a heavy silver fork made to resemble the sort one would find laid out on fresh white paper over a white linen tablecloth in a French bistro through the multicolored layers of a vegetable terrine.

"No," I lied. *"Are you?"*

"Bored!" She laughed and shook her head before sipping her freshened iced tea. *"I'm under way too much pressure to be bored. Every event brings a whole new set of demands—staff problems and food preferences and venues I have to get special permission to use. And people always want themes. I did something for the Philharmonic—everything . . ."* She drew an arc with one hand in the air here, *"modern classical music."*

"How did you do that?"

"Japanese," she said. *"Exotic vegetables julienned. An asymmetrical cake with pure black frosting. Every taste very distinct, inharmonious. But delicious. It was a challenge. But that's what I love about this job. It taps both my practical and my creative sides. It combines business and art. And I meet a lot of celebrities. Which is fun, because you can talk about them later.*

Discreetly, of course." She giggled. "It's hard," she went on, sighing, luxuriating in self-pity. "But I love it. It's my life, really. After Charlie and the kids, of course."

Love,

L

CHAPTER 12

Margaret

"Margaret Snyder! Of course, I remember you. How's the war going?"

"It's all right. Almost finished, actually." Why was I lying to Irving Wolcott? "How's your book?" I asked this, although I believed it morally wrong to encourage someone like Irving, whose novel resembled a Hardy Boys mystery without the plot.

"Oh, you know. I'm giving it a break for a while. Recharging my batteries."

So he was stuck, too. It disturbed more than reassured me that he and I were in the same boat. Not only that, but I was about to ask to share his paddle. "Irving, I'm calling about your business, the card you gave me? You know, your freelance group?"

He laughed. "I know my business, Margaret."

"Well, of course, but . . ." I couldn't think how to ask what I needed to know. Perhaps my communication skills were not quite what I'd assumed.

"You want to do some freelancing?"

"Well, I thought I'd look into it."

"That's great, Margaret! We're always looking for smart people like yourself."

I was flattered.

"You know, I loved the comments you gave on my work. First chance I get, I'm going to try reorganizing the way you said, putting the action up front and so on."

"Oh, good," I said. "I'm glad they were helpful." And helpful to me, too, maybe, if they'd given him the impression I was smart.

"We're having a networking meeting next Thursday at the Hilton. You should come, see what's out there, and we'll match you up with some employers."

∽∽∽∽∽

Ted was skeptical. As usual.

"But you've never done anything re-motely businesslike," he said. He was sit-ting on a stool in the bathroom over several sheets of newspaper, while I cut his hair with electric clippers. Unfortunately, this would not save us any money, since we'd been doing it for years.

"That isn't true, Ted. That summer I worked at Just Desserts I completely re-designed their menus. That would be mar-keting."

"That would be a summer job."

"And I was the faculty liaison with the parents' association. Public relations."

Ted sighed.

"Look," I said, raising my voice over the sound of the razor, "I've been reading and writing for years; I'm pretty sure I can han-dle any work that makes use of the English language. Also, I could translate for ancient Assyrians."

Ted laughed. "I just worry that you'll lose your momentum on the book. This other thing—whatever it is—is never going to be a career, you know."

"I know," I said with irritation. "Hold still."

"If you want to give up on the book, you

should give some serious thought to what you want to do with the rest of your life, not run around after part-time work you don't even understand."

"Damn it! I said to hold still. Now look what I've done."

I had let the clippers sink too close to his scalp and an inch-long white gash appeared in the dark hair on the side of his head. He held up the hand mirror to study it. "That's all right," he said. "It'll grow back."

"I'll color it in."

This sort of thing had happened before and we'd learned that I could disguise it fairly well with black Magic Marker as long as I worked in little hairlike strokes.

"Look, Ted," I said, marker in hand, "I'm not giving up on the book. I just don't want it to cost us everything, so I'm going to spend a few hours a week earning a little money. Aren't you the one who said we needed more money?"

"I thought we figured that out together."

"Anyway," I said, razoring around his ears now, "I won't let it take time from the book."

〰〰〰

The next morning, as I blew the curl out of my hair, I wondered if I would soon be writing investors' newsletters for a Wall Street bank or composing the text to accompany the installation of new works by an up-and-coming artist/welder in Tribeca. I told myself, however, that the book was merely stalled, and that I should on no account take on too many projects. No more than fifteen, absolutely no more than twenty, hours a week. The novel was still my priority.

When I exited the elevator on the windowless floor that housed the hotel's conference rooms, I was somewhat dismayed by the banquet tables tiled in name tags and the overeager crowd clutching Styrofoam cups of coffee lightened with nondairy creamer. Was I to be the sort of laborer whose sweat, induced by pressure from the bosses and overheated cubicles, remained a clammy secret under an ill-fitting jacket? I reminded myself that when I published my novel, whatever paper pushing I'd do as a member of this group would make a charming story for radio interviews and smiled at the woman who sat behind the "Freelance Network" table. It wasn't her fault that this was the best she could do.

"Can I help you?" She smiled back and placed her fingers on the faux wood veneer in readiness.

"Well, I'm hoping to find some sort of freelance work. I'm quite skilled in anything that has to do with manipulating language. I majored in English at Penn and completed all the requirements for a major in Near Eastern archaeology, except for statistics. I know archaeology might not sound helpful, but, in fact, it teaches one how to think logically better than most disciplines. And, of course, there is a lot of language work, mostly with dead languages, I admit, but that teaches one grammar, you know, from the inside out . . ."

"I meant," she said, interrupting me, "can I help you find your name tag?"

My armpits prickled and I shifted my shoulders in my ill-fitting jacket.

"Oh, sorry. Margaret Snyder."

I peeled the tag off its wax backing and stuck it to my lapel. All around me, people were shaking hands and chatting in little clumps. I guessed that this was what was meant by networking but felt, after my blunder at the signing-in table, unequal to introducing myself around. Luckily, I had forms, titled "Experience and Expertise," to fill out. These subjects were divided into several categories, such as computers, finance, sales and marketing, and information science. We were supposed to check all that applied.

Unfortunately, nothing applied. My ability to write a decent sentence under any circumstances counted for nothing here. I couldn't even understand the terms used to describe the know-how these people apparently used every day. While I'd been trying to get teenagers to discuss why Bartleby "preferred not to," others had been acquiring the skills that made the world go around. I had shunned the gold-carpeted, the name-tagged, and the banquet-tabled for years and now they would not have me.

I raised my wrist in front of my face, dropped my jaw and struck my forehead with the heel of my hand to convey to whoever might observe my premature departure that I'd just remembered a pressing engagement across town and slunk toward the elevators.

Since it wasn't rush hour, I easily found a seat on the subway home. Clearly, I, unlike most people, had nowhere to go at any par-

ticular time. In August, when I'd been a con-
temporary beatnik in charge of my own life,
I'd reveled in this sensation. Now that I was
essentially unemployed, I loathed it.

I spread the twisted forms I'd been holding like a baton on my lap and wrote
"Employment Possibilities" on the back of
one page. By the time the train reached
Carroll Gardens in Brooklyn, about half an
hour beyond my stop, I'd compiled a fairly
reassuring list. Most promising was tutoring, the new refuge of starving artists and
intellectuals, among whom I figured I could
now count myself. Traditionally, of course,
tutoring had generated only a starving-
artist's wage, but I had heard that things
were different now, what with the meritoc-
racy inflating the value of college educations and parents convinced that every
dollar pitched in the general direction of
securing their child a spot in one of the few
socially anointed institutions was a dollar
well spent. Morally, of course, I deeply dis-
approved of using my intellectual skills and
experience for something as mercenary as
giving superprivileged children an even
greater edge than they already possessed
in exchange for their superwealthy parents'

money. I was not, however, in a position to indulge such qualms. Promising myself that I'd tutor for free a needy child for every one whose parents paid me seventy-five dollars an hour, I called Neil, my former department head, as soon as I reached home.

"Margaret!" he said, when he returned my call several hours later. "It's so good to hear from you. How's the writing going?"

How deeply I regretted telling anyone of my plans. How earnestly I wished I'd quit my job to do something simple, like raise a child. "Great!" I said. "Really moving into the home stretch now. I mean, there's still a lot of polishing to do, of course . . ." I trailed off, having dumbfounded myself with the facile substitution of "a lot of polishing" for "basically still have to write the whole damn thing."

"Oh, sure, of course. The polishing will be fun, though, I'd think." His wistfulness made me wonder if he might also once have had a novel that never reached the longed-for polishing stage. "You know, Margaret, I'd love to read it. When you feel comfortable with that, I mean."

"That would be really nice of you, Neil," I said, and so struck was I with gratitude that someone I respected would want to read what I'd written that for a fleeting, warm moment, I forgot that there was, in fact, nothing to read. "As soon as it's polished," I said. "But, listen," I went on, "since I'm so far along with this now—you know, really done with the hard part—I've been thinking that I could afford to spend a little time away from it."

Neil understood my need for a refreshing change of scene and a few extra dollars. He reminded me that the wife of Sherman Sterling, the head of the Upper School, ran her own college counseling and tutoring business. "I'm sure you met at the Christmas party," he said. "Statuesque, dark chignon, looks stunning in red. She's always trying to find new people."

I didn't clearly remember Kate Sterling until I heard her rich, bronze voice over the phone. It was the sort of voice that should be worn with a pashmina shawl.

"Hi," I said, in my own, somewhat tinny timbre. Reading from a script I'd prepared, I explained my connection with her and the purpose of my call. "So," I said, "since I'm so far along now, really done with the part that demands the most sustained concentration, I thought that it might be nice to get out and do some work that involves others . . ."

"I'm glad you got in touch with me, Margaret," she interjected smoothly when I paused, hoping my gasp for breath was inaudible. "And I'll have to remember to thank Neil for sending you my way."

This sounded encouraging. I pressed on. "I don't know what you need exactly, but I certainly could do English for the SAT. Probably math, too, if I boned up on it a little. I did fairly well on the math section myself. I really didn't fall down in that area until statistics. And I could help students with their coursework in any of those areas. I'd prefer that, actually. The idea of coaching these superprivileged kids to help them get into superelite universities . . ." I broke off. This was obviously not the best opportunity for debating the ethical merits of my potential employer's business.

"Speaking of colleges," Kate said, "where did you go to school, Margaret?"

I had a good answer for this.

"Penn . . . hmm . . . well, lots of my kids end up there. It's a very good school."

I was surprised that this did not go without saying.

"But parents would be happier with a tutor who went to a place *they* couldn't get into. Like Stanford. Or Brown. You sure you don't have an advanced degree from Brown? Lots of our tutors do."

I was sure. I helpfully explained the strength of Penn's Near Eastern archaeology program and the reasonableness of my choice. As I spoke, I heard the telltale click of e-mail being answered.

"But anyway," I finished quickly, "at this point, how much does it matter? That was years ago."

"Well, we can get around that if you did something interesting after college. Did you work in publishing? Have you ever been a consultant?" she asked hopefully.

"No, I taught," I reminded her. "In D.C. and at Gordonhurst."

She sighed. "Yes, but those schools . . ." She paused and began again. "If you'd been at St. Albans or Brearley or Trinity, then we'd have something."

What that something would be was still unclear to me. Would I be better equipped to advise teenagers to write vocabulary words on index cards if I'd presented my lessons on *Hamlet* in a building on First Avenue instead of Third?

"But Sherman is at Gordonhurst."

"Yes," she said, dryly. "Of course, he does have other qualities. I'd be happy to put your name on our list," she said, "and if anything appropriate comes up, we'll call you."

I could not pretend, even to myself, that this was not a discouraging setback, but it would be May before I exhausted my re-sources and learned my lesson.

In February, I met with an editor Simon knew at one of the biggest houses, a man who went through several assistants every year and so was always looking for new ones.

"Maggie," he said, nodding from behind his desk at the chair I was to take, "Simon says very good things about you."

"That's very nice of him," I said, and then added, inanely, "I say very good things about him, too."

"What I'm not clear about is why you want this job."

I launched into a speech I'd composed the week before describing my fascination with the publishing world beginning with the buying and selling of ideas, touching on the discovery and nurturing of talent, and ending with the democratization of art in America, to which he quite properly did not pay complete attention. Instead, he flipped through a pile of mail with one fingertip as I spoke.

He interrupted as I was talking about the formative books of my youth. "You understand you'll mostly be answering the phone?"

"Of course," I said. I had not understood this.

The phone rang then and I wondered if this was a test of my initiative, but he picked it up before I could do more than raise my hand toward it. "Jack!" he said, "hang on a moment." He cupped his hand over the receiver.

"You know," he said to me, "I've thought about it and I just think it's not going to work. This is a job people tolerate because they want a start in the publishing business.

It's not worth it if you don't have years to spend climbing your way up. It's not for you." He swiveled his chair sideways to indicate we were through. "Jack!" he said again into the phone.

My knees shook as I waited for an elevator full of young, smug creatures with stylishly dirty hair and cardboard cups of coffee. Down we went, stopping at nearly every floor, letting them out and in, in and out, their easy inclusion announced in every slouching curve, while I stood straight at the very back, arms crossed over my chest.

I kept my arms in this position when I reached the sidewalk, so as to contain the fury that hissed and sizzled and popped within me. I started walking fast, my head tucked down and forward, a battering ram aimed squarely at this city and its inhabitants, a large proportion of whom were now forcing me against the pipes of a block-long stretch of scaffolding we were all squeezing through like ground meat in a sausage casing. Though somewhat hobbled by the crush of the crowd, I marched the six blocks to Simon's office, intending to rail at him about the sort of people he knew in publishing.

In the quiet of his building's blessedly empty elevator, however, my anger began to dissipate, so that by the time Simon appeared in the narrow chute between *In Your Dreams'* two rows of cubicles, I was ready to rally once again.

The offices of *In Your Dreams* were not nearly so plush and coordinated as the publisher's had been. The gray carpeting was thin and industrial-looking with a large, rust-colored spot that might have been blood Rorschached near the middle. The copy machine had a sign that read "Please Fix Me" taped across its top. The lighting was fluorescent. As editor in chief, Simon had a private room with a door but no window.

Simon's floor was a mosaic of books and journals, bristling with yellow Post-its; mail, opened and unopened; and pages escaped from manuscripts. His orange plastic molded guest chair stood unevenly, one foot on a padded mail pouch that appeared to be full. I slid a stack of books from its seat to my lap as I sat down.

"I understand you have an internship program," I said as casually as I could.

He frowned. "I thought you were going to work for Red Lewis."

"No," I said. With my fingernails, I scored small lines in my palms.

"The thing is, we're looking for students, Margaret. You know, people who actually believe that putting a few months' worth of work here on their résumés is compensation enough."

"But you pay something."

"Believe me, Margaret, you'd be stuffing envelopes and typing. You'd hate it. Anyway, I know I've said this before, but don't you want to concentrate on finishing your novel?"

I tossed my hand in the air, as if batting his words away from my ears. "You see, I don't need mental stimulation," I said. "I've got the novel for that. And I will finish," I added. "I just need to make a little money in the meantime, Simon. Doing anything. I won't hate it. I promise."

Simon sighed. "The problem is we've already got people lined up."

Several of the books began to slide off the top of the stack in my lap. I joggled them back into position. "I'm sorry," I said, getting up. It was difficult now to resettle the stack on the chair. "I shouldn't have put you in this spot."

"That's all right," he said. "I really wish I could help you with this, Margaret, but I'm just the editor." He laughed at his own joke.

"OK, well, thanks," I said helplessly, standing. Balancing the stack of books on the chair took a steadier hand than I possessed. "Thanks," I repeated. "Thanks, anyway." The books slid against each other in their slick jackets.

"Listen, Margaret," he said, finally taking the books from me, "why don't you try tutoring? I hear you can make loads of money that way and it wouldn't swallow all your time."

I saw myself out, down the hall, over the blood, into the elevator, where I rested my forehead against the green metal doors. On the sidewalk, I stood still for some minutes, letting people bump me impatiently as they hurried past. Moving forward seemed beyond my powers and it appeared unlikely that I could get myself home. Even picturing the series of tasks I would need to perform—making my way to the subway entrance, digging in my coin purse for a token, dropping it into the slot, winding my way through the tunnels, standing on the platform—it was too much! And, after all that, I would not yet even be on the train.

Slowly, I began to stagger mechanically in the direction of our apartment. Without meaning to sometimes I stopped, my brain so knotted with inchoate ribbons of thought that there was no room left even for the nearly involuntary action of putting one foot before the other. In this manner I eventually did reach our living room, where I lay face-down on the couch, wondering, between frenzied bouts of self-recrimination, whether it was possible to suffocate myself with a sofa cushion, and waiting for Ted to come home.

Ted opened the door at seven-thirty-five. By seven-forty, I'd confessed, albeit inarticulately, to delusions of grandeur, months of wasted time, and the fact that my life as a productive member of society seemed to have ended. I cut deep and I cut wide, including the chronic lateness with which I had turned back student papers, my C in Swift and Pope, and the time I'd left a six-year-old Warren alone in a movie theater. "I think maybe," I concluded, "that the best thing would be for me to go back to school."

As I spoke, Ted had slowly lowered his briefcase to the floor and then, pressing his back against the wall, followed it with his body. He slumped forward now and rested his head on his knees. His hands lay slack, palms upward, beside his feet. Finally, he spoke, he voice muffled in twill. "To school for what?"

"I don't know. Some field in which the rules are clear. Medical school, maybe."

Ted raised his head and stared at me. "You want to go to medical school?"

"I don't *want* to go to medical school, I just recognize now that there are clear tracks that a person is expected to follow to get somewhere. I've been slugging it out in the brush and I want to get onto the path."

"But you haven't done premed. You never even took chemistry!"

"Well, not medical school necessarily," I admitted. "How about law school? I have verbal skills. I think logically."

"I thought we were planning to have children."

Ted wanted children. I did, too, I suppose. I had thought, though, to put them off until I made my name. Letty often described herself as "just" a mother, to which I always replied that being a mother was the most important job, along with various other platitudes. I did, actually, believe this in a way. I believed it was an essential job and a difficult one, and all that, but at the same time, I couldn't help but think that pretty much anyone could do it in some fashion.

"We are," I answered. "Lawyers have children."

Ted had pushed himself back to his feet now. He lay one hand on the kitchen counter for emphasis. "But, Margaret, think this through. You're logical." He said this a little meanly, which was not like Ted. "The earliest you could expect to start law school would be a year and a half from now. You're in classes for three years earning no money—in fact, paying out huge amounts of money we don't have. When you finish, you'll be thirty-nine; we'll be in debt; then you'll have to work eighty hours a week for seven years as an associate to prove yourself to a firm. Margaret," he said urgently— and although we stood several feet apart, it felt as though he'd got a handful of my shirtfront and was twisting it in his fist. "It's too late."

While stroking my head in a soothing

fashion (I had somehow ended up in my dramatic full-flung posture back on the couch), Ted gently suggested I try to get my job back at Gordonhurst. "That way you don't have to give up on the novel," he said. "You'll still have spring and summer to write, and maybe by September, you'll have made enough progress that you'll even be able to continue writing during the school year. You could get up at five," he added, encouragingly. "Sally Sternforth says she does her best work before dawn."

We both knew that my recalcitrant book would not progress once I could legitimately apply my time and effort to other work. The idea that I would continue with the novel was only a face-saving fiction. Still, Ted had a great deal of advice on how I could better approach teaching, so as to get more done in fewer hours—systematize my grading, for instance, and offer only one paper topic. Keep strict office hours, instead of agreeing to meet with kids willy-nilly (his term) throughout the day. "I'd be happy to write these up for you, if it would be helpful," he said. "Oh, and Margaret, every year I see you rereading the same books for those classes. Couldn't you just wing it with what you remember? It's only high school, after all."

Which was, of course, exactly the sort of comment that had made me want to quit in the first place. Nevertheless, the prospect of doing anything other than writing had become irresistible. I called George Temperly, headmaster of Gordonhurst Academy, the following day.

"George? This is Margaret Snyder. I used to teach English for you," I added helpfully.

"Of course, of course!" he exclaimed. "Good to hear from you, Marge! What've you been doing with yourself?"

This would have been an excellent time to make something up along the lines of the Peace Corps, but I perversely dragged my frustrated project once again through its public paces. "Well, I left Gordonhurst, you might remember, to write a novel. And I'm nearly finished." This was not necessarily a lie. I did not say that the book itself was almost complete. Metaphorically speaking, I *was* "nearly finished." "But you know how well first novels sell. Or rather how poorly they sell," I said, and then added, "heh, heh," a chuckle at my own self-deprecating drollery. "And so I'm looking for a teaching position in the fall and wondered if the English department might have an opening."

"Well, that's marvelous! Marvelous!" He had a habit of wringing his hands, and I could imagine him doing this now, the phone clenched against his jaw. "You know it looks like we might. Yes, this might be excellent timing for both of us. We'll have to set up a little interview for you with Neil McCloskey—just as a formality, you know. Can't have it be said we didn't follow procedure, now, can we?"

I assured him that I was happy to follow procedure and hung up the phone feeling as if I'd been thrown a life buoy that would save me from the sea of my own hubris.

My "interview" with Neil began equally well. "You know we'd love to have you back, Margaret," he said, gently pounding three packets of saltines with his fist and then pouring the crumbs over his chili. We were lunching in the familiar Gordonhurst cafeteria, the wood paneling worn slick along the wall where students had slumped for decades, waiting for the line to move. "And it would make the school look good," he added kindly, "having a published writer on the staff."

"Mmm," I said, leaning over my souped-up baked potato.

"Margaret!" Evelyn Cook, the Latin teacher, who'd long held the position of celebrated writer among the faculty on the strength of a self-published account of her trip to Rome in 1963, was beelining across the room as fast as the obstacles created by thirty or so long tables allowed. "When does the great American novel come out?"

"Nice to see you, Evelyn," I said. A bacon bit sprang away from the pressure of my fork like a tiddlywink and landed in Neil's bowl. "No definite date yet," I mumbled.

And then we were off: me, limping gamely through the grass, leaving a trail of sweet blood with every step, Evelyn in hungry pursuit.

"I can't wait," she exclaimed, "to go into a bookstore and see your name on the cover of a novel! Who's your publisher?"

"Well, you know, since the book isn't quite done, I haven't got a publisher yet."

She pressed on, nearly drooling. "Was it hard to find an agent?"

"Margaret's thinking of coming back to

us," Neil interrupted, digging up a spoonful of chili. He seemed not to have noticed the bacon bit.

"Really?" Evelyn cocked her head and raised her eyebrows dramatically. "I'd assumed you'd set your sights well beyond our little pond," she said. "Of course, I've found teaching to be conducive to writing myself. You may remember the sketch that was printed in *The Charioteer* a couple years ago. 'Tuscany in the April Breeze'? But maybe that was before your time." *The Charioteer* was Gordonhurst's literary magazine. "You know, Jimmy Smithers, over in the math department, writes poetry. Maybe we could all get together. Form a little writing group. We could serve wine and hors d'oeuvres. Tea for the nondrinkers."

"That would be nice," I lied. How pleased Evelyn would be, I thought, when she realized she would never have to read the name Margaret Snyder in print, not even in *The Charioteer.*

Obviously, I reflected later, as I walked one of the intimate, shadowy cross streets toward a Lexington Avenue subway station, returning to Gordonhurst had its drawbacks. Still, such a position was infinitely preferable to being an intern at a barely sol-vent magazine, as I told Simon when he called several weeks later.

"Do you still want that internship?" he asked. "One of them isn't showing. Her par-ents surprised her with some graduation trip to China."

"No, thank you," I said. "I'm going back to teaching."

"Well, that's good, Margaret. At least it's a dignified job, not making copies at less than minimum wage, which is what we'd have you doing here. But what about your book?"

I explained the efficacy of the five- to six-a.m. slot, but we both knew the novel was over.

I spent March and April rereading the fa-miliar texts, marking passages for discus-sion, reviewing sticky points of grammar, and devising assignments for which *CliffsNotes* would be useless. I decided that when George Temperly called to discuss my salary and benefits, I would demand a raise. As a known quantity, I should certainly be worth a great deal more to the school than I had been as a cipher from Virginia. I also outlined a spiel I intended to deliver to every colleague, well-meaning and malicious alike, who asked me about the status of my novel. It included phrases like "getting some distance" and "taking time to truly understand my characters." In early May I called Neil, and though I was actually quite eager to begin and so leave the ruin of the previous year behind, I affected a weary sigh.

"Just organizing my calendar, here," I said. "I've bought the latest in picks and shovels at Bloomingdale's. When do we head for the salt mines?"

"Margaret!" Neil's terrier, Montmorency, barked in the background and I heard a soft thud, like a book falling from a table to the floor.

"Neil? Have I missed a meeting?" Although August was usually the month boobytrapped with faculty meetings about inexplicable insurance alterations and whether this would be the year to crack down on those who'd neglected their summer reading, occasionally such housekeeping occurred at the end of the school year. As someone who knew the ropes, I would probably be expected to attend.

"Margaret . . . no . . . you haven't missed anything."

"Good," I said. "Listen, I think I'm all set for September, but are we doing *Jane Eyre* or *Great Expectations* this year?"

Neil cleared his throat several times, as if a bit of popcorn had lodged there. "Margaret, have you been out of town?"

Why did he keep repeating my name? "No," I answered.

"And no one has called you?"

"Called me? No. Why? Has something happened?" I imagined a fire set in the corner of a science lab by a pressure-crazed junior or a flood among the precious records in the basement. Maybe George Temperly, or perhaps Evelyn Cook, had suffered a heart attack.

"No, no, nothing's *happened*," Neil said. "I mean, it's just that . . ." He cleared his throat again. "Well, the thing is, Margaret, we hired someone." Montmorency began to bark again.

I did not immediately grasp the significance of this. "You mean someone else?"

"Well," he said. "Yes."

"Instead of me?"

"Montmorency! Be quiet!" The dog continued to bark. "Well, you know, she's just gotten her Ph.D. From Brown, actually. She's very nice. Kind of bubbly, but smart as a whip. Very interested in Faulkner. I think you'd really like her."

I experienced a strange squeezing sensation in my chest, as if I'd held my breath underwater for too long. I closed my eyes, trying to shut out the sound of his voice.

"I'm sorry, Margaret," he was saying. "We really should have called you."

"OK, then," I managed. "Well, thanks for telling me anyway." My voice was high and unnatural. "I think the water is running. Or the stove. I better go."

He said something about lunch or brunch. I could do no more than nod. "OK, well, better go," I said again.

But he was relentless. ". . . writing group," he was saying. "Thinking of taking a semester off to write it up. It's sort of a mystery, but literary, of course, set in a private school. The head of the English department," here he laughed modestly, "solves the murder."

So many ways I could have gone, so many choices I could have made. If I'd studied French instead of cuneiform. If I'd taken a computer class instead of Intro to Chaucer. If I'd gone to those recruitment meetings, if I'd gotten a Ph.D., if I'd become an electrical engineer. Behind me, doors opened onto gorgeous vistas and intriguing corridors. But somehow I had missed these and had instead wormed my way into a glorified closet with a window on an airshaft, from which there seemed no way out.

And, so, I became an intern, a second-choice replacement for someone still eligible for graduation gifts.

CHAPTER 13

Margaret

A year ago, despite my public protestations to the contrary, I'd been pretty sure that an elevated place in the world had been reserved specifically for me. I'd assumed that I only needed to reveal my long-hidden talent, to throw off the bushel basket, so to speak, and those who had disdained me would gather round in awe to admire my light. But what if, after all, I had no light? What if the basket had been a useful cover allowing me to pass among those who otherwise would discern my undesirability? I now had to consider the possibility that I'd thrown off my bushel basket and lay naked on the grass and still people stepped over me as if I were a clod of earth.

On a Sunday in late May, when Ted had gone into his office—he did this regularly now on the weekends to avoid the sullen, snarling creature I'd become—I crawled into the back of the bedroom closet and ex-humed Robert Martin from his cat-fur-clouded box. I'd intended to use the backs of my manuscript pages, having just alpha-betized a list of potential advertisers for *In Your Dreams* and run out of paper to feed the printer. But there, with one knee pressed uncomfortably on the straps of a run-down sandal, I determined that I was not finished yet. All the public and private humiliation I had suffered would only fuel my renewed efforts. So what that the list of those to whom I now had to prove my worth had grown? I would show them all.

If only I'd given up. If only I'd cleaned out the closet, applied to teach at another school, and devoted my creative energies to amateur theatricals.

I recognize now that I'd have gotten off cheaply then. A year, a stalled novel, and a few callous rejections were not so high a price to pay for clear-eyed disillusionment. But no true gambler stops just because she's run through her wad, not when borrowing, begging, and stealing remain. I didn't see it that way then, of course. My illusions bruised but essentially intact, I mistook my folly for strength. I clenched my teeth and shook the printed pages in my hands. I would use my desperation, marshaling it to speed my fingers forward. I would write a novel, I told myself, or die in the attempt.

As if it were only a matter of will.

I sat down at the table with the manuscript. I opened my legal pad to a fresh page and turned on the computer. I watched the screen alight and waited while it worked through its various procedures. I opened the file called "Novel."

And the familiar malaise settled around me like a fog.

For forty-five seconds or so I stared at the last few sentences I'd typed in February. They were trite and flat. I deleted them. I drew a cube on the legal pad, and then another on top of it. I constructed a tower of cubes. I shaded alternate surfaces. Then I checked my e-mail.

There was a single message, from mac-family; subject: westwoodho.

While fortunes, such as they were, had steadily declined over the past year for the Hansen-Snyders, they'd continued to grow for the MacMillans. In January, Letty had dropped all pretense of "just seeing what was out there" and had begun to house hunt in earnest. So far, the process had been as disillusioning as my search for employment. On New Year's Day, she'd written, "There are certain things we want, otherwise it's just not worth moving." These included location on a quiet, tree-lined street on the Westside, a good school system through high school, which instantly ruled out all of the Westside other than laughably overpriced Santa Monica and Pacific Palisades, a house built before 1950 *unless* it had been designed by a well-known architect, a formal dining room, a decent-sized yard, a bedroom for each child plus a study, at least three bathrooms, hardwood floors, and no aluminum-frame windows. They were willing to forgo a fireplace, if all other criteria were met. A guesthouse would be a plus.

After the first weekend, the five essential bedrooms had been whittled down to four, and there was no more talk of guesthouses or fireplaces. By February, they would settle for three bedrooms and an attic or garage that could be converted into a study, if everything else was "perfect." In March, they agreed to make do with two bathrooms, as long as one, at least, had a tub, and decided that Michael's office at the museum gave him plenty of space to work.

Letty's descriptions of the houses they examined had at first been long and detailed, full of careful weighings of pros and cons. More recently, however, they'd deteriorated into snippets of faults that rendered the places "unlivable," although mostly these were difficult to remove errors in taste: bathrooms large enough to host spa weekends, walls covered in mirrors and marble, "Ionic columns in the living room again!" and wet bars, wet bars, wet bars. By May, she was ready to consider a three-bedroom, one and a half bath seventies ranch backed against a ninety-degree weed-covered canyon wall—basically the same house they now owned without the yard but, since it was located in a tony neighborhood, a house that "cost more than a mansion in Kansas City!" A house that would, in fact, be only slightly better than my "starter" job with *In Your Dreams.*

They carried a lot of debt, which was probably inevitable given the fact that they lived in a major metropolitan area on one academic salary and were raising four children and which was certainly exacerbated by their good taste and haphazard accounting habits. Letty and Michael were the types who, rather than recording checks diligently in their register, made frequent, frantic calls to their twenty-four-hour automated banking system to find out their balance. Also, Michael tended to be rather acquisitive. On what they considered their first date, a campus movie and coffee, Michael drew his credit card from a vintage billfold of supple calfskin but was unable to cover the cost of Letty's cappuccino. "I hoped you'd order a latte," he said, digging into his pocket to display a handful of change. "I had enough for that." However, three weeks ago, when they were preapproved for a home loan, Letty was pleasantly shocked.

M—
The bank says we can afford way more for a house than Michael and I thought we could.

Isn't that great? Not only that, but we can get a loan through the bank the Otis works with that'll let us put only five percent down. Of course, the interest rate isn't the most competitive, but this way, once we sell the house we're in now, we really will have enough to look at some decent properties.

L

"Properties." This was how one began to talk when one had been house hunting for nearly half a year. Letty did not seem to realize that the bank didn't care if her kids went to college or if she ever ate out in another restaurant. So long as she had enough to meet the mortgage, she could "afford" it. Not surprisingly, being given permission to spend more than they possessed greatly accelerated the house-hunting process, and within days Letty sent the following:

M—
We've found it, the house I've been looking for my entire life, at least since January. That's not to say it's perfect. I admit that the house I pictured while resting my head

against the steering wheel, waiting for Marlo's Girl Scout troop to finish decorating their egg carton jewelry boxes and trying to shut out the "wheels of the bus go round and round," had a porch with roses twining around the railings and the beach within walking distance and bedrooms with huge windows hung with gauzy curtains that billowed in the breeze—in other words, a house in a commercial for feminine products. But if a house like that even exists in this city, it costs at least two million dollars and the windows in its single bedroom look directly into the bedroom of the house next door.

This real house is a 1920s Spanish style in Westwood, north of Wilshire. Did you get that last key phrase—north of Wilshire? Yes, south of Sunset—but who wants to live in a dark canyon, anyway? But north of Wilshire. (Must learn how to work that into all casual conversations—"Oh, you know, north of Wilshire, where we are, the traffic isn't so bad.") I know, I know, so much for a decent public high school. But elementary is superb and we have to compromise somewhere! Anyway, we'd already decided on private for Marlo and her top choice—

single-sex, with lots of scholarship girls so there's almost the same economic diversity you'd find at a public school and with cars in the student parking lot that aren't signifi-cantly different from those in the faculty spaces—is right down Sunset. You've seen the campus in movies.

What I love about this place is the neigh-borhoody feel. The quietness. It's on this pretty, hilly block where I'll wave from the window to the kids as they run over to their friends' houses, just like we did, although I don't actually remember my mother ever waving. The gorgeous, exotic shrubbery is expertly maintained by exploited illegal im-migrants—but we won't have to continue that. We'll water our own lawn, thank you.

Beverlywood, where Letty lived now, was also a neighborhood of well-constructed sidewalks and reasonably safe streets, al-lowing children easy access from house to house. Of course, Beverlywood houses contained ordinary Game Boy–playing, skateboard-riding, TV-watching kids. I sus-pected that Letty envisioned some different breed of neighborhood child in Westwood.

The house has great bones (that's real estate speak) and an impressive carved wooden door that's recessed into the wall, so it sort of feels like you're entering a cave, except in a good way. And it's big, Margaret, substantial—almost three thousand square feet. It's not a mansion, but it's a "real" house, a come-to-our-place-Brad-and-Zoe kind of house. It needs a few adjustments to make it work for our family, but nothing too daunting. Our turn to ruin a place with tasteless renovations!

The living room (where we would serve Brad and Zoe drinks) is dramatic, really the size of two rooms, and it feels even larger because it has a vaulted, beamed ceiling. It also has hardwood flooring, a good-sized fireplace, an original Spanish-style chandelier (my favorite feature) and sconces—Peri says it's easy to get replacement bulbs. The living room is the house's best space, which is good, since we'll really have to live in it, there being no family room for the TV, the paperbacks, the puzzles, and possibly the miles of Hot Wheels highway (although for now I've told the kids there will be no plastic beyond the bounds of their bedrooms, I know I'll eventually cave on that). We'll want to add French doors that'll lead out to a patio—once we build a patio. What's the point of living in southern California without indoor/outdoor space? Also, the wet bar has to go. Nice formal dining room, not at all cramped, also "en-sconced." The kitchen, I admit, is dark and poky—BUT there's a dark and poky laundry room next to it, so once we take down the connecting wall and maybe add a window, the two rooms together will be light and airy. We'd want to replace the cupboards, the counters, the appliances, and the flooring anyway, so it's really not such a big deal that we'll be re-configuring everything in a new and improved space.

Four bedrooms upstairs—well, three right now, one big one for the boys, a small one each for the girls (incredibly hideous emerald green carpeting throughout—what were these people thinking?—but hardwood underneath), and a bathroom for the kids to share with the original 1920s tilework and tub—super long with a rounded corner. I could see buying this house just for that tub. We'll have to add a shower when the kids get older, but a tub's best for them right now, anyway. Also, something very funky

*going on with the lighting in that bath-
room—I'm not even sure it's safe to have
these fixtures in a room with running water.
We'll have to redo that, obviously.*

*The upstairs is actually a little tighter than
you'd think when you look at the outside of
the house, because, of course, there's no
upstairs over the vaulted living room, but it
should be fairly simple to put a master with
a bathroom (complete with shower) "en
suite" over the garage. That kind of renovation is going to be pricey, but Peri says if we
do it "to code," we'll more than get our
money back if we ever decide to sell. Which
we definitely won't. I'm envisioning a balcony off the bedroom just big enough for
two chairs and a little table, a private retreat
for the two of us, where we can have early
coffee or a drink in the evening. You know,
the kind of thing that's supposed to put romance back into a marriage.*

*The yard, Peri says, could be "emotional,"
with the right landscaping. She's right that
we'll have to landscape, eventually, and we'll
have to put up a fence right away for the
dogs, but there's a decent amount of space
and a fig tree—I've always wanted a house
with a tree—and we can use the fruit, make*

figgy pudding, or whatever it is one does with figs. Maybe the kids can set up a fig stand. And there's room for a pool.

One other minor problem: a dip in the driveway that's already taken a bite from the Tercel. Some molded plastic thingy dislodged when I was pulling out. Pretty sure it's superfluous, but it scrapes along disturbingly at all speeds. I think I can reattach it with twine.

It was hard to figure out what to offer, since money this big doesn't seem real. Adding or subtracting thousands feels like tossing dimes around. And it really is dimes if you listen to Peri, who pointed out that ten thousand dollars is really only ninety-one cents a day when you spread it over the life of a thirty-year loan. The kids could contribute that with their fig stand. Shall I tell you how much we decided on?

She named a price that made me laugh, but as there was no more to the e-mail, I had to assume this was, in fact, the amount of money they were prepared to spend on this house.

Although I knew that "working on a house" smacked of self-absorption and materialism, it was fun to think about. More fun than thinking about post-Vietnam nihilism. Maybe Robert could do some house hunting and fix up a place for himself. It would, at least, provide some action. I would do an architectural rendering, to make sure I could visualize everything—maybe when the book was finished, my drawing could be reproduced on the end papers. But, first, Robert would have to have a real estate agent. I'd never had a real estate agent, only New York apartment agents who were generally less polished than Peri had been.

I scrolled back through my in-box. Letty had sent me a description of Peri after they'd met in November. I would use it as an exercise, a jumping-off point from which I would then create my own character.

I began simply by copying the relevant portion of Letty's e-mail into a document I'd entitled, randomly, "Chapter Six." *"My real estate agent is a tiny woman in a monstrously large car. Of course, this describes much of the population of the west side of L.A."* I changed "my" to "Robert's." Would Robert be looking for a house on the west side of Los Angeles? I changed "Robert" to "Lexie," a new character, an intriguing character, a character who, just as the how-to-write books had promised, suddenly seemed to be knocking on the inside of my head demanding to be let out.

All afternoon, Lexie searched for houses, while Robert languished as he always had at his kitchen table, a table, I now realized, I'd never quite envisioned. I could see Lexie clearly at hers. Lexie, in fact, did not have a kitchen table, because her kitchen was too small to eat in. She had a dining el, in which she'd put an old enamel-topped table, before they became trendy and overpriced.

Why did Lexie want a new house? This was complicated, and I was not yet sure I understood all the factors involved, but I explored the issue obliquely and implicitly as she looked, rejecting one place after another that had columns and marble and aluminum window frames and had been hideously renovated by someone less tasteful than she.

By late afternoon, I'd written five pages. Well, to be honest, I'd written about three and Letty had written two. Later, I'd change the sentences I'd borrowed from her, and she would be pleased, I thought, to know she'd been my muse. I read her latest e-mail again, snipping for myself details here and there describing the house that had finally attracted Lexie. It was during this reading that my brain, by now so well trained by Ted, came to understand what should have struck me immediately.

"Letty, Letty, Letty," I said to myself, "you shouldn't buy this house."

I knew exactly what Michael was earning, including possible bonuses and the criteria for such bonuses, because Letty and I didn't keep this sort of information from each other. I knew what private schools cost, a consideration Letty and Michael were obviously not taking fully into account. I knew what they'd spent redoing their old kitchen and I knew what they'd probably get for their old house. I considered property taxes and estimated likely repairs. I assumed at least two of the children would need orthodontia and all of them would go to college. I computed the probable increase in the value of the property against what they were likely to earn if they invested their money conservatively in the stock market. All of this did not add up to financial disaster, but it did entail a close-cutting that allowed for no mistakes, no accidents, no family vacations, and very little retirement savings. It also required that all colleges be strictly state funded. In short, they would for all practical purposes be overextending themselves just when Michael's new income might allow them to relax a little about their tight finances.

I spent the next hour and a half composing a reply to Letty's e-mail, detailing my findings and concluding that she would be better off with a less expensive house, or at least one that needed less work or was in a neighborhood with public high schools she'd feel comfortable sending her children to.

Ted came home just as I was finishing.

"Writing away?" He was unable to conceal a note of sarcasm. Perhaps he did not attempt it.

"Actually, this is an e-mail to Letty telling them not to buy a house they want." I explained my thinking and figures to him briefly and he nodded.

"Sounds right to me," he said.

"But, Ted," I went on, "I did write almost five pages today."

He pretended to be absorbed in looking through his briefcase.

"I know I've told you lots of times before that the writing was going well, but today— I don't know—it was different. I wasn't straining to put something on the page. The character and the story felt almost real."

I was not insane. Of course, I knew that at this point Lexie and her house felt real because they were real—or at least had real-life counterparts, Letty and her house. But this was only the foundation from which I would build my own story. Tomorrow, I would decide who Lexie was, why she did what she did, what she would do next. Whereas Letty would decide these things for herself.

"I'm not sure what there is to eat," I admitted. "I was writing so late I forgot to think about dinner."

"That," Ted smiled, "is the best thing you've said in months."

Before we left the apartment, I printed out my five pages and laid them facedown by the computer. "I'm going to do this every day," I said, tapping the little stack with my forefinger, "so you'll see I'm making progress." Then I shut off the laptop. I'd not sent Letty my reply.

The next day being Monday, I had to spend business hours in the offices of *In*

Your Dreams. By the time I sat down at my own computer and collected my e-mail that evening, Letty and Michael's offer had been accepted, so my warning, even had I sent it, may have arrived too late anyway. And how the MacMillans chose to arrange their budget was really none of my business, was it? This is what I told myself as I sent my calculations to the trash.

M—
They accepted our first offer. This means we should have offered less. Michael keeps reminding me that if there's something horribly wrong with the place, the inspector will tell us and we can back out, but I fear there may be something lurking, hidden in the walls. What is radon again? All I know is that the house we have now doesn't have it. Can we get lucky twice?

I look at that vaulted ceiling and that chandelier (which, unfortunately, the previous owners are taking) and the thick kelly green lawns that roll out in all directions on those hills and I feel like a real person would live in this house. Not the sort of person who would repair a car with string.

My mother disapproves, of course. She

and my father came over to see "what you kids are getting yourselves into"—my father's words, obviously—and she was frowning when she got out of the car. "What do you need with all this space?" she said, blinking in the sun.

I'll admit only to you, Margaret, that I wanted to hurry her in, out of sight of the neighbors who would surely note that her jeans have elastic at the back of the waist and her shoes, chosen strictly for comfort, have laces dyed to match the leather. My father's hair is too carefully combed for this neighborhood. And when did he start wearing Sansabelts?

"Mother," I said, "I have four children. We're going to have to send a couple of them to a farm, if we don't move into a bigger place."

She clucked around the kitchen, pulling drawers out. "It's awfully dark in here, Letty. You're not going to like that, especially in the winter months. Have you thought about the winter months?"

I explained about eliminating the wall between the kitchen and the laundry, the additional window and the new, light cupboards, counters, and flooring we plan to install.

"*Michael must be doing pretty well now,*" my father said, rapping his knuckles against the wall I'd said we'd be taking out.

I showed them the space where we're adding the master bedroom with the bathroom en suite. "*We were always just fine with the one bath,*" my mother said. "*You don't want to use too much water in Los Angeles, you know. It's wasteful.*"

I wanted to protest that six people would use the same amount of water whether it came out of one showerhead or two, but my mother doesn't respond to logic.

"*This must be quite a job Michael has,*" my father said.

In the backyard, as I was describing our plans for the landscaping, my mother said, "*But you can always use our pool, honey.*"

It's nice of her, I know, to want us over there, but I wish she could appreciate what it means to be buying a house here. I wish she'd just be happy for me.

"*Michael must be doing all right, then?*" It's killing my father, the worry that we're irresponsible teenagers, blowing our nest egg.

I finally put him out of his misery. "*Dad,*" I said, "*Michael has a very important position at the Otis. He's doing very well. We're doing very well."*

Parents, how do you—

Hold on. Phone.

Jeanette. Asking if Hunter and Noah can go with her kids to see the butterflies next week at the Natural History Museum ("living, levitating, landing on your nose"—according to the banners along Wilshire). Have I mentioned that Jake and India are not the least bit bratty? At least not discernibly more so than my own stay-at-home-mothered children. It's very distressing. And they speak fluent Spanish. Unfortunately, the boys will love going. I had to say "yes." And "thank you." And also, in a moment of competitive lunacy—"and maybe Jake and India would like to join us when we go down to the Long Beach Aquarium next week." No, we had no aquarium plans!

Must close now and sew lips together with dental floss.

Have you heard from Gordonhurst?

Love, L

So they could still back out of the deal. I was glad I hadn't deleted my trash. Before retrieving my letter, though, I opened my

"Novel" file. Letty was really onto something with those kelly green lawns, and although I was sure she'd not meant to allude to the green breast of the new world in *The Great Gatsby,* it was an idea I could make use of for Lexie.

Lexie, I wrote, drives through the coveted, unattainable neighborhood, her short blond bob (nothing like Letty's hair!) whipping across her eyes (this to suggest a sort of blindness—*not* the sort of blindness that actually indicates a greater-than-mortal understanding of the world—the kind I'd given to Terry, wise, old buddy of Robert's—but a blindness to her own situation, the failure, in other words, to take into account the high probability of her children's need for braces). Or perhaps Lexie's child would need glasses, or an expensive eye operation, thus implying the blindness would extend into the next generation!

But I was losing track of my story in the symbolism, a fatal error I'd made before. Learn from your mistakes, I told myself sternly, and, making a quick note of the portentous surgery, I returned to Lexie in her air-condition-less Mazda 323, with its dragging muffler that generated tiny sparks as it scraped against the pavement. In the window of the house in which she is to meet her real estate agent, Merrie, she sees a green light, in fact, a string of green lights, in the shapes of palm trees—no, too tacky—maybe only a greenish flame, leaping up when Merrie lights a cigarette—no, no real estate agent would be caught smoking in Los Angeles. It was the window itself that glowed green—yes!—the stained glass windows flanking the front door of a charming Craftsman bungalow!

I paused, fingertips hovering over the keyboard. Comparing Lexie to Gatsby was somewhat misleading. No matter what Gatsby did, he couldn't change the fact that underneath he was still James Gatz, a nobody from the Midwest, and therefore unacceptable to the posh Ivy Leaguers and their crowd. He got to blame fate and society for his unhappiness. But now, in a world in which any girl from Glendale could go to Yale if her SATs were impressive enough, who did Lexie, or Letty and I, have to blame when we discovered we were not who we wanted to be? Only ourselves.

I stared at the screen for a moment, flummoxed, but then I plunged forward.

Somehow, Lexie's children had cleaner faces when she imagined them putting their educational toys neatly away in the solid wooden cupboards she would purchase for this house from a catalog specializing in furniture for kids. In this house, their beds would always be made. Their manners, decent now—they said "please" and "thank you" and held out a hand when introduced—would become polished. They would learn to play chess and tennis with the kids next door, games they could enjoy for life. She and the other neighborhood mothers would organize trips to the art museum and to the kids' music series at the Hollywood Bowl. All of this she sees in the future as she stands on the porch, peering through the green windows, waiting for Merrie to let her in.

That night I printed seven pages and added them facedown to the stack.

Margaret,
It's Friday night and Michael is working again. Or else he is having an affair. What is it wives are supposed to look for? Lipstick on collars? Victoria's Secret on the Visa bill? (I have actually spotted the latter, but the

lingerie is mine. I'm wearing it.) It's not that he didn't work a lot of hours as an academic, but most of those were at home (the advantage of having a hateful office). Of course, then we didn't splurge on the lacy undergarments.

You say you remember me complaining about Michael's working so often at home? The difficulty of keeping the children and the dogs quiet, the irritating requests for snacks at inconvenient moments.

This job, though, just swallows time, what with breakfast meetings and drinks with donors. And that's not counting the hours devoted to upkeep. Have I mentioned the biweekly stylish haircut? He used to be satisfied with Vivian Lu at Terrific Cuts, in the mini-mall just down the street—$8 a trim. Every time he went, he'd take one of the children and Vivian would give them tiny, crunchy fish to snack on, sort of the multiculti 1990s L.A. version of the Norman Rockwell barbershop experience. Recently, however, Michael has decided he's embarrassed to walk around his office with a "terrific cut," so he has to drive every two weeks to West Hollywood and park in an unvalidated lot, so that Lance at The Razor's Edge can give him a $45 cut with "edge." OK, I grant you, this cut has more style, but not $37 more!

Speaking of haircuts, I just spent over a hundred dollars on trims for the two boys and lunch. Jeanette called the other day and begged us to go with her to the Calliope, this salon especially for kids in Santa Monica (is it called a "salon," if it's for kids?). I would have thought the only excuse to go there was to prepare to have a Christmas card picture taken at Sears, unless you're of Jeanette's ilk, in which case you go there any time your child needs his bangs trimmed (and you hire a professional photographer to come over to the house in September). She was having a hard time with Jake, who said he wouldn't go without Hunter, which made India say she wouldn't go without Noah, so Jeanette wondered if we'd go, and then, she said, we could all have lunch afterwards. Fool that I am, I said, "Sure." I've been cutting the boys' hair myself since Michael stopped taking them to Vivian and they're getting a little raggedy. I could use a professional line to follow. Lunch, I assumed, would be chicken nuggets. After all, we'd have the kids.

   These haircuts ended up costing more than I've ever spent on my own hair. And while Jake and India sat on their little carousel horses sweetly sucking their lollipops, Noah decided he was deathly afraid of carousel horses, except possibly the red one, on which another child was sitting, and Hunter tried some sort of rodeo move, in an effort to impress either Jake or the stylist—probably both—and fell off his steed.

   Still, their hair looks so much better than it ever has. Hunter and Noah look, really, like different children, like children who might, in fact, need head shots, if I ever became that kind of mother—which, of course, I wouldn't! I can see now that they even may have looked a little dorky before, the way I was doing their hair. I would say that doesn't matter, especially since they're boys. Especially since they're seven and four. But probably that kind of thinking isn't fair to them. Probably they should look their best. Jeanette says it's good for their self-esteem to have great haircuts. She says we owe it to our kids to make the best of their looks, because although we may hate it—and, obviously, any thinking person has to hate it, but the problem is that there are a lot of un-

thinking people in this world—looks do matter. They even affect the way teachers treat a child in school. They've done studies to prove this. I mean, I don't want to put my children at a disadvantage, as long as we can afford not to.

"I can't believe you cut your children's hair!" Jeanette said. "I'd never have the time!"

This is presumably because she has more important things to do, like drive the children to the salon, wait while someone else cuts their hair, and then go out to lunch.

Jeanette, by the way, has a spectacular cut, sort of understated, obviously stylish without looking like she copied it from a sitcom actress. I asked her where she gets it done.

"I'm so glad you asked!" she said. "Edward is amazing with color."

(I leave you to draw your own conclusions about why exactly she was glad I asked, but I'll admit that I wished I were wearing a hat at that moment to hide my rendezvous with Miss Clairol.) Anyway, I now have Edward's number. He's in Beverly Hills.

Jeanette wanted to have lunch at the sort of café that turns out a lovely bruschetta. "I promised the kids," she told me, when, having emptied our checking account preparing my children for their acting careers, I countered with Hot Dog on a Stick. Apparently, Jake and India are small Jeanettes, preferring sit-down restaurants and cloth napkins.

And then there's that whole nightmare where you know you're going to split the bill, so you have to order at least as much as the other person or be stuck subsidizing her lobster. "Dessert?" she asked, so we all had to have one. The kids, of course, ate two bites of theirs and you can't take "freshly churned ice cream topped with a seasonal assortment of wild berries" home.

After lunch, we straggled along Montana for a few blocks, admiring the French infant sleepers and the Nepalese yak-milking stools in the windows. It was Noah, actually, who pointed out the African ceremonial mask, carved of dark wood, fitted with straw and feathers, a long, almost Modigliani-like face with almond-shaped holes for the eyes. Michael, I knew, would love it. He would love it, and he would never buy it for himself. Jeanette was already two stores farther on when I called her back.

"I just want to take a look at this," I said.

Jeanette agreed, when the saleswoman had unhooked the mask from the window and brought it to the counter for us to examine, that it was special. She held it up to her face. "You can never have too much art," she said.

"Let me see it," India said, so Jeanette bent and held her masked face close to her daughter's.

"No! Let me see it," India said, by which she meant touch it.

For a family whose livelihood depends on art, we own pitifully little: those two small drawings we bought on our honeymoon in La Jolla and a painting I couldn't resist at the flea market. Other than that, just framed posters.

"I'm going to buy it," I said. "For Michael." He'd finally bought me an engagement ring after he got the Otis job, but I'd never gotten anything really nice just for him.

"Congratulations," the saleswoman said. "This is one of my favorite pieces." She wrapped it carefully in yellow tissue paper and then laid it in a box.

"Let me see it!" India insisted, pushing up on her toes next to the counter.

The first time the saleswoman swiped the card, she smiled and shrugged her shoulders. "Sometimes we have trouble with this machine," she said.

The second time, she frowned. "I'm sorry." She handed the card back. "Is there another you'd like to use?"

Jeanette politely began unnesting a set of nesting bowls somewhere on my left.

"You mean it was declined?" I said. "I don't see how that can be."

"Sometimes they don't like it if you use it twice in one hour," Jeanette said. "That's happened to me."

"Maybe I should call," I said, "I can't have reached the limit on that card."

By now India was lying on the floor of the shop, her heels and fists pounding the kilim-covered floor. "I want to see it!" she wailed.

The saleswoman handed me the phone.

"India, honey," Jeanette said. She turned to the saleswoman. "Would it be all right if we took it out again?"

"You saw it," Jake told his sister impatiently.

"I want to see it!" India screamed.

I was on hold. Ivy, luckily, was asleep in her stroller, but Noah picked up a small carving and tried to give it to India to appease her.

"Noah!" I said too sharply. "Put that back! It's not a toy!" Which made him start to cry.

The woman unwrapped the mask and Jeanette held it up to India's face. "Here, honey, here," she said. "You can see it."

It turned out I had reached my limit on that card, even though it was the one I saved for big purchases, the one I'd never come close to maxing out before. I'll have to check the next statement scrupulously and make sure there's no mistake, because I don't understand what could be on there. Luckily, there were other cards in my wallet.

Michael loves the mask as much as I knew he would. He's already hung it in the living room. The straw bits are supposed to be uneven, so the ones India broke off aren't obvious.

We've cut a corner on the house expenses because my cousin, Paula, and her husband from Pittsburgh are visiting my Uncle Frank next week and he has no idea what to do with them. My mother suggested that he inspect our house—he does do something in construction, but I always thought it had mostly to do with cement pouring—in exchange for a personal, Michael-led tour of the museum. I'm officially annoyed with my mother for meddling but also a bit relieved, given that the tickets to the aquarium, not to mention the cafeteria lunches, are going to pretty much gut the inspection fund. And who's more likely to have our interests at heart, the Peri-recommended inspector or Uncle Franky?

What if he finds something horribly wrong? I will collapse in a crumpled heap. I couldn't stand to start this process over.

L

Start over? No. Lexie does not want to start over. Lexie cannot afford to spend the next fifty pages rejecting houses, getting nowhere like Robert. Where would the dramatic tension be in that? Whatever Letty and Michael did, Lexie and her husband, Miles, were committed to buying, so they could start their new and improved life as soon as escrow closed. In fiction, it's easy to find money to pay an inspector. Lexie borrows from her children's savings accounts and pushes her fingers into the crevices of the couch, groping for change. Lexie also delights at the way the stylists transform her children at the Merry-Go-Round and vows no other scissors will touch their precious locks, as long as she draws breath. Also, because the most basic element of a wardrobe is a good haircut, she gets her own hair trimmed and foiled at a salon two blocks from Rodeo Drive. Her hair is short, so she'll have to return every four weeks to maintain the shape. I printed five more pages for my stack.

"Dear L," I replied, *"treat yourself. Go to Edward. You should have hair at least as stunning as your four-year-old's."*

∽∽∽∽∽

Letty's color had, in fact, looked a teeny bit brassy at Christmas, and though I agreed that it shouldn't matter, I suspected that this would put her at a disadvantage at those museum parties. People formed their impressions. There was no stopping them.

∽∽∽∽∽

As it turned out, neither Uncle Frank nor Lexie's inspector found anything to excite major alarm, although they both amassed a respectable list of minor essential repairs to be made by the current owner, so as to justify the hour or two they'd spent in the house. Purchase proceeded as planned (one and a half pages).

Inspection went less well for both of them when it came to the house they were selling. Letty and Michael had to pay for a new roof, while in Lexie's case the roots of a ficus tree were destroying the foundation. The foundation had to be shored up and the tree chopped down, prompting Miles, a philosophy professor at Clear Mountain University, to hold forth for five pages on the antipathy between man and nature, thus bringing my total for two weeks' work to twenty-five and a half pages.

For several weeks, Letty wrote infrequently, being busy with the packing, although she did describe the trip to the aquarium with seven children—everyone except Ivy got to invite a friend—for which she had to rent a van and hire a babysitter to accompany her. Jake vomited his fifteen-dollar lunch on the return trip, which meant the van had to be kept for an extra day to allow for professional detailing. I appropriated the aquarium trip for Lexie, resetting it at Griffith Park Observatory.

So, at first, this was all I was doing, borrowing bits and pieces, using Letty's experiences as "inspiration." Or at least that was how I thought of it. Gradually, though, as *The Rise of Lexie Langtree Smith* began to take shape, I did more. I reread all of Letty's letters from camp, for instance, the ones I'd retrieved from my parents' attic, and used them, often verbatim, to create a past for Lexie, childhood experiences in which she'd learned the subtle but decisive cues communicated by elements of appearance and behavior—a particular brand of shoes, a certain style of shorts, a disdain for Jell-O salads with pieces of canned fruit floating in them. Letty, in fact, had been partial to that salad when it was served in the middle school cafeteria, but at camp she learned to know better.

Letty would want to help me. That's what I told myself. I did not, however, tell her. Instead, I asked her questions. My e-mails probed for details. What brand of paint had she chosen? Did she want a convection oven? What ideas did she have for landscaping?

M—

India is learning Japanese. Jake has devised an experimental protocol for determining the frequency of specific hybrids. Have I mentioned that they are four and seven? Is this freakish, or should I worry about my children's elementary school? We've pretty much resigned ourselves to private high school and probably middle school, but if Jake and Hunter are competing for a spot, who's going to get it, Peewee Mendel or the kid who's all excited because the marigolds that got the water and the sun grew?

L

What good, I wanted to respond, did it do a seven-year-old to understand genetics? What would be left to learn in third grade, let alone in the fancy private high school? But Lexie was also concerned with these issues.

I'd toyed with giving Lexie five children, but settled for two—Alberta and Saskatchewan—since I doubted my ability to keep track of more. If Allie and Sas went to local, public elementary schools, how good a chance would they have of getting into the best private middle and high schools? And, in a way, weren't the elementary years, during which children learned the most basic study skills and developed a lifelong attitude toward education, the most crucial?

Margaret,
I never thought about it that way. You're right—maybe Hunter isn't excited about school because his school isn't exciting. Even though this is a good public school, maybe it's just not good enough, especially since elementary school is, as you say, the time for him to acquire the tools for learning that he'll use the rest of his life. Jeanette says she can get Hunter into Jake's class at Curman. The Director of Admissions is her cousin Rosemary, and Rosemary has told her that some movie director is withdrawing his child from second grade—he's taking the whole family to Hungary to shoot a movie (a move which, according to Rosemary, is really a misguided effort to round out the college admissions packet of an older sibling)—and Curman is refusing to hold the second-grader's place for fear of establishing a dangerous precedent. Anyway, Hunter is in, if we please. I'm not

sure we do, but if we have the money, isn't it wrong not to invest it in our children's schooling? I mean, our children and their futures are our top priority, and Curman could definitely give Hunter more one-on-one attention than he's getting. What it comes down to is that you're right when you say we can't afford to make any mistakes with his education. Unlike Marlo, he's not going to teach himself. Anyway, he'd look adorable in the navy shorts and white polo shirt. I always wanted to wear a uniform.

L

Letty had not always wanted to wear a uniform. In fact, I distinctly remember sitting on her front steps, idly separating the strands of fringe on our cutoffs, and discussing how lucky we were that we didn't have to go to the East Mountain School for Girls precisely because we would have to wear that uncomfortable-looking plaid skirt and white blouse every day. We didn't know how those girls could stand it. It seemed silly to me, then, the school's concern over what its students wore, although I thoroughly approved of it now that today's children's clothing struck me as infinitely sillier. I wondered, though, about Letty. Did she just imagine she'd wanted a uniform to make the idea of her son having to wear one attractive? Or had I never known how she truly felt? Had I only paid attention to myself? This was a troubling thought, but the notion of some-one long desiring something for herself and securing it for her child seemed useful for my novel.

Lexie, I wrote, had always wanted to wear a uniform to school, so she is pleased when her son, Sas, so impresses the ad-missions director with his experiment prov-ing the existence of gravity that he secures a highly coveted place for himself at a pri-vate elementary school that requires its stu-dents to wear blue shorts and white shirts in the manner of Christopher Robin. Pages describing fictional experiment, fictional eucalyptus-laden grounds of fictional pri-vate school, and fictional uniform (despised by young Sas): two and three-quarters.

On Saturday, I was worrying a passage in which Lexie holds a yard sale and watches with mingled sadness and relief as various shabby but sentimentally valuable items are loaded onto the beds of pickup trucks or trundled off by old women with wagons in exchange for a handful of rumpled dollar bills, when the telephone rang.

"Margaret, we had an accident!" Letty wailed.

"Are you all right?" I was practically shouting at her, and Ted hovered at my elbow. "Is anyone hurt?" This was, I am relieved to say, all that occupied my mind at first.

"Yes, yes, we're all fine. It was just me and Marlo and Ivy in the car—poor little Ivy, strapped in the back. The Tercel is completely wrecked, though."

"Just car damage," I said to Ted, who nodded and opened the refrigerator.

"Not 'just' car damage," Letty said. "Total car damage."

"Yes, yes," I said. "I understand. What happened?"

"Do we have any bread?" Ted asked. His head was under the counter, where the bread was never kept. I carried the cordless phone into the kitchen, opened the bread box, and put the loaf on the counter.

Letty described the terrifying minutes and then the tedious hours they'd endured the previous afternoon. She'd been sandwiched between a Suburban that she couldn't see around—"I couldn't anticipate anything; I couldn't even read the road signs. I'd already gone three blocks out of my way without knowing it!"—and a Lincoln Navigator, driven by a woman on a cell phone who'd been too engrossed in her call to put her foot on the brake when first the Surburban and then Letty stopped. "I saw it coming, Margaret. This huge grille in the rearview mirror, right behind Ivy, and I'm honking my horn, and I have nowhere to go, because the back doors of the Surburban are right in my face. I hate SUVs. They're a menace. People who drive them have no sense of civic responsibility. I mean, how can you deliberately choose a car you know is very likely to kill other people in an accident? They're selfish beyond belief."

Having heard this rant several times before from Letty, who had been feeling increasingly besieged in her tiny, tinny car over the past few years as four-wheel-drive vehicles, used almost exclusively for trips to the grocery store and to chauffeur small children to soccer matches, inflated around her, I was able to give a good portion of my attention during this tirade to the preparation of Ted's sardine sandwich.

"And I'd just seen that show where they tell you about the insurance scams where people deliberately make you have an accident," she went on, "which of course isn't really an accident then, so I was afraid I was being conned or maybe about to be carjacked, so somehow I pulled Ivy out of her car seat with one hand, while holding Marlo by the wrist with the other, and kind of propelled myself out with both of them to leave the car for the carjacker—except part of me is outraged because I thought the one good thing about driving a Tercel was that I'd never be carjacked: who would want to carjack me?"

"So you were carjacked?"

"No, no. I was just hit by a careless woman with overstyled hair in a Navigator, but the trunk of my car crumpled like a rag. Like a potato chip bag."

Was that an effective image? A potato chip bag? I jotted it down on a paper towel. Would it be better using a specific brand? How about a bag of Fritos?

"So Miss Cell Phone finally hangs up and slides down from her SUV. 'What are you doing?' she yells at me. Now she's slapping the air with the phone. I just stare at her. I don't understand what she's getting at. 'You just backed into me,' she says. I'm still just standing there like an idiot. And, of course, everyone's honking at us by now. I look around. No witnesses are coming forward. 'What are you doing, backing up in the middle of the street?' she demands. 'See, that's what I mean,' I say, although I haven't said a word up until now and so can't possibly have meant anything, 'what you're saying doesn't make any sense. Why *would* I back up in the middle of the street?' 'I don't know why you did it,' she says. 'Can I read your mind?' "

"So she's not going to pay for the damage?" I asked.

"Nope. Also, get this—she lives just a block away from our new house."

"How did that come up?"

"It didn't. I saw her in her driveway this afternoon. She lives in the house where they were filming that commercial for long distance last week."

Given that no one had been hurt, I felt no moral qualms in seeing this accident as a fortuitous beginning for Lexie, a symbol of the old life destroyed so that the new could take its place.

"Maybe you should get an SUV," I suggested.

"Ugh. No!"

But there were plenty of arguments in its favor.

It took Letty and Lexie only five days to make a purchase.

M—

It's a Ford Explorer. I know, I know, I know— no sense of civic responsibility, selfish beyond belief, etc., etc. But if you'd seen that behemoth looming behind little Ivy, you'd understand. I mean, like you said, it's irresponsible of me to put my children at risk, just to uphold some moral principles. If we can't keep other people from buying these things, we have to buy one ourselves or be squashed like bugs. I'm convinced now that this is why all these mothers I see climbing down from them at Ralphs buy them.

We did, after all, need a bigger car. That's obvious. And even though the Explorer costs more than we've ever spent on a car, it'll pay for itself eventually, as you pointed out. No more van rentals, for instance.

In answer to the important question that

no doubt plagues you: forest green, like the trim on the new house.

L

Lexie buys a Range Rover after she has an accident that seriously damages her Mazda 323. She isn't very upset about having to replace her embarrassing car (one of its doors was held shut with a coat hanger). The Range Rover will look more appropriate than the 323 in front of her new house. It's gray to match the shingles.

And so, with charming houses in very desirable neighborhoods, children in private schools, and vehicles suitable for young, successful West Los Angeles matrons, both Letty and Lexie were well-equipped to embark upon their new and improved lives.

Letty

We canceled all but two of our credit cards before we tried for the home loan. I read somewhere that they count anything you can borrow against you, even if you don't owe it yet. Afterward, though, when the offers arrived, stiff envelopes with low interest rates printed on the outside, and return addresses to places like Delaware and North Carolina, I checked the "yes" boxes. Why not? I thought. I didn't have to use them. I would just have them, a little brightly colored bundle in a drawer like Hunter's baseball cards, money we could use, if we needed it.

With a new house, a new life, it seemed there might be things we would need.

CHAPTER 14

Margaret

M—

Packing proceeds! Transformation of life fully under way! Today I disposed of our "linen closet," five milk crates, originally stolen in 1982 as receptacles for record albums. Noah has decided I've crassly given up a family heirloom. "But, Mom, I love those," he said, looking mournfully out the window. I stacked them in a neat tower near the sidewalk, but some kid on a skateboard pushed them over, or else they spontaneously collapsed in passive protest at being discarded. I told Noah we shouldn't be selfish; it was time we gave someone else a turn. So far, however, no one has leapt to claim such a treasure.

Last weekend I finally traded the plastic Tom and Jerry cereal bowls (surprisingly valuable) for green milk glass ones at the flea market, and the children shook the dregs of their last box of Lucky Charms into them this morning. In the new house, we will eat only healthy breakfasts: fruit (purchased fresh from the farmers' market), organic yogurt flecked with wheat germ. When I prepare this meal, I will already have showered and if I haven't dressed, I'll be wearing an attractive housecoat. I'm envisioning lavender waffle-weave with some sort of satin sash. The morning sun will bathe my Mexican-tiled countertops. The granite I put in the old house I now believe was a mistake—too sleek and modern looking—too "of its time." This little store on Melrose sells tiles in antique-looking colors, muted blues, greens, and salmons, but treated with some kind of twenty-first-century, unchippable coating, so that you can set dishes microwaved to unnaturally high temperatures on them.

I also bought an orange-picker at the flea

market, so we'll be ready when the oranges come. This will be some time after we plant the trees against the side fence. Which will be after we install the side fence. Which should be sometime next week. One cannot buy fruit north of Wilshire from the shopping carts of illegal immigrants, at least I've not seen any yet, so I've decided we'll grow our own. The children can pick the oranges for juice, after their morning tai chi workout with Michael. I'm going to enroll him in a class that meets in Glenview Park at dawn next month and once he gets the basics down, he can teach the kids. This, in any case, is my plan, although it means that Michael will have to become an early riser, which may be too much of a transformation of life. Maybe there's a sunset class and the orange picking could take place in the evening. I could get some kind of graceful pottery bowl, maybe a sort of Craftsman olive green, for the oranges to rest in overnight. A lemon tree would be good, too. And a lime. Possibly there's room for a small orchard. I'm not sure. I assume there has to be a certain amount of space between trees for root growth. And branches.

L

Lexie pulls out of the narrow driveway of her old house for the very last time, one tire of her Range Rover rolling of necessity over the grass. Allie twists as far as she can under her seat belt, gazing sadly out the back window at what was once her dresser—a pile of pink gingham-papered cardboard boxes, now a ruin, sagging on the sidewalk. She is the kind of child who doesn't like change. "Goodbye, Ozymandias," she whispers. Silently, she promises the old house that when she grows up, she will return to buy it back.

I hoped the reference to Shelley would appeal to the PEN/Faulkner judges, although Allie seemed a bit young to be conversant with the Romantics. Perhaps I would change it to "Oz," a name she would surely know and a term that would still carry the echo of the monument in the sand, man's futile attempt at immortality, and so would constitute a subtle, sly wink to my more astute readers.

M—

I waited a week to cut into a promising honeydew, left it to roll around on the mantel next to the dog leashes and the jar of pennies, the half-burned-down persimmon-colored candles (impossible color to replace!), the silver polish, three egg cups, one of Ivy's shoes, a whisk broom, and a remote control that may belong to our former neighbors. Just a few of the items I've not yet found a place for. Anyway, I waited a week and this melon still has the texture and taste of a packing box. Of course, everything in this house either resembles or in fact is a packing box just now.

I'm having some trouble keeping track of paperwork—work orders and bills and bank statements—things like that. Some mail hasn't been forwarded yet; some bills were on a counter that no longer exists; some documents seem to be duplicates. I need to organize a system, but it's so hard when there's no table, no chairs, no pencils in evidence. I made these incredibly detailed lists of what was in each box as I packed, but I now I can't find the lists. I may have packed them. So irritating! It doesn't help that we're all camping in the living room at the mo-

ment—the wood under the emerald carpeting upstairs turned out to need serious repairs, and Michael and I won't have a bedroom until the addition—as yet not even started—is finished.

The kitchen is completely gutted. To prepare breakfast, I squat over the toaster on the living room floor. It's probably best that I've not yet purchased aforementioned lavender housecoat, since it would draggle in the plaster dust. Also, having difficulties choosing appliances, despite, or more probably because of, immense social pressure to buy one particular pricey brand of refrigerator (with double-sized freezer) and another particular, equally pricey, brand of oven. How much of a difference do the perfect cooling and heating elements make to the final quality of a meal? Although, when you're redoing your whole kitchen and for a few thousand dollars more it can be exactly what you want, practically and aesthetically, it's difficult to resist. Remember, even ten thousand dollars over thirty years is only ninety-one cents a day. Anyway, no refrigerator means no yogurt, organic or otherwise. Also, no kitchen sink is kind of gross, what

*with the chunks of food stuck in the tub
drain.*

Love,

L

Shepherding her children from movie theater to ice-cream store, Lexie pauses in
front of a window display of attractive office
supplies, the kind one's company does not
purchase for one. Not that Lexie has a company, being a stay-at-home mother.

"Mo-om," Sas whines, pulling on Lexie's
hand with both of his. "C'mo-on."

Lexie, however, is transfixed by a canary
yellow accordion folder, tied shut with a yellow satin ribbon.

Lexie rarely buys things for herself.
Always she thinks, Sas needs a calculator;
Allie needs Cray-Pas. Not to mention shoes,
movie tickets, and ice-cream cones. Miles
likes to split half a bottle of wine at dinner.
The money could be better spent on someone else. But she wants this.

"Just let me look at one thing," she says.

Inside, there are felt-tip markers to test
on a little pad of white paper. The children
test, while Lexie asks a clerk, "The yellow
folder? In the window?"

It's fourteen dollars. A ridiculous amount to spend on brightly colored cardboard. But it's so pretty. And useful. And, after all, fourteen dollars is not so much in the scheme of things. She won't buy a cone for herself. Then the folder will only cost twelve dollars and fifty cents.

In the ice-cream store, she laughs at herself. She has forgotten they are rich now. She buys herself a black raspberry cone.

At home, Lexie has a pile of magazine clippings, articles with titles like "Colluding with Color" and "How to Introduce Frogs to Your Garden Pond," pictures of sunny rooms full of fresh flowers and large bowls of ripe, unbruised fruit, bunches of grapes unmarred by spiky stars of degraped stems. These are what she puts in the yellow file, instructions for making life better.

Margaret,
Michael and I drove the Explorer (some sort of light lit up on the dashboard—is it possible to be in four-wheel drive without knowing it?) to the furniture stores on Beverly Boulevard. Just to explore. I now understand Michael's affection for his office, for I have fallen in love with a table. My darling is

elderly and caramel-colored bird's-eye maple in the shape of an octagon. It's not by a known designer or anything—it's what they call a "generic"—but I still think it's what the articles call a "special piece." You're supposed to buy one or two special pieces and decorate the rest of your house around them.

"Imagine," Michael said, "the prongs of a fork clutched in a tiny fist." He made small stabbing motions at the chocolate-whorled surface, which turns out to be an excellent method for attracting sales help.

Here's something. I've been in these stores before, but I have never attracted salespeople, except once when Ivy was screaming and Noah tracked dog poo onto the carpet—which was really not his fault. Anyway, somehow they can sense, these salespeople, when you are in a position to buy, as opposed to the times when you are using their showroom as a sort of free museum. In two stores, Michael and I were offered cappuccino. In another I saw a version of our former selves, the woman tentative, touching only the tip of one finger to the leather, frowning thoughtfully but unconvincingly at the wood and the chrome, the *man, reaching for the price tags, flipping them over, actually emitting that classic whistle, albeit quietly.*

We are in a position to buy, but we won't. I mean, special as this piece is, it is, in the end, only a surface on which to eat, and as such is ridiculously overpriced. We could furnish the whole house for the price of this table.

L

P.S. and while we're tabling—thanks for the House and Garden articles! Definitely going to do the antique-table-to-vanity conversion for the master bath you highlighted. Also must find one of those worktables for the kitchen. I'd make my own bread if I had one of those.

M—
Club chairs. Where are all these clubs? Who belongs to them? Why do they all have the same chair? We went back to Beverly today to look again at the table and discovered the chair du jour. Right now, you cannot be wrong, you cannot be gauche, you cannot even be particularly snobby, if you buy one of these. People like Zoe and Brad (you re-

member them, marinated goat cheese, Baby Hannah in Baby Guess, smugly commenting on their peek at my plastic-laminated drawers in the privacy of their own car) are guaranteed to nod and approve. They will slouch in the leather seat and smile, welcoming us to the world of safe good taste. These chairs are not cheap, of course. But nor are they too expensive, and that is part of what makes them the ticket to decoratal correctness. You can buy designer versions, but you can also buy them used, rescued from an actual club in France, the arm leather smoothed by decades of French elbows. And you can buy high-end knockoffs in high-end chain stores. You can even order them from catalogs. Someday, you will see them in traditional furniture stores, stores that do not also sell iron candleholders and kilim-covered throw pillows. They will be covered in Naugahyde and squat next to the La-Z-Boys. Probably they will be La-Z-Boys, with footrests that shoot out when the sitter reclines. Then it will be too late. But not now. Now they are right, right, right. If you own one, it will effortlessly testify to your membership in the vast club of those who know better; the tasteful, not

the show-offs, the progressive, not the rad-
ical (don't forget the leather).

Why are floor lamps so expensive? Does
it have something to do with wiring? If we
buy the table, we'll have to get dining room
chairs. Of course, we'll have to get dining
room chairs no matter what table we buy.

God, I know—what were our parents
thinking, renting instruments for us filled
with other children's spit? Yes, certainly, I'd
love to get a piano for the new house.
Although, I worry that it may already be too
late for Marlo and for Hunter. I gather from
Jeanette that children begin lessons at four
now, and maybe earlier, perhaps as soon as
they can sit up straight on the bench. I suppose this encourages their fingers to grow in
the optimal curves, their hands to spread to
cover an octave.

Love,
Letty

Margaret,
I told Michael what you said about the table
being a work of art and an heirloom we can
hand down to the kids, and he completely
agreed. Its value will only increase. We were
lunching late at a place on Robertson

Michael's assistant recommended, and we decided between the grilled oysters and the squid ink spaghettini with sun-dried tomatoes to go ahead and buy it. One nice piece, as a base.

The setting may have clinched the deal. It was not the sort of restaurant I'm used to, which would be the kind where you slide a tray along the counter and pile sweet mayonnaisey pasta salads onto your plate until curls of macaroni topple off the rim, the kind that includes soup and a frozen yogurt sundae bar, all for $6.49 per adult, $3.49 per child, if you've carefully clipped your coupon and remembered not to leave it in the junk drawer at home. I felt like I was having an affair with my own husband, in large part because Michael valet parked.

There was a giddy, honeymoon quality to our meal. We shared our appetizers. Michael consulted me before he ordered the wine. We took a walk—a walk!—before collecting our car. (Although I suspect this might have been to take full advantage of our valet parking. Is after-meal walking allowed when you valet park? I kept my head down until we were a block from the restaurant.) I think we both looked at one another and thought with

relief and pride: "Here is a person who understands the advantage of a club chair."
And perhaps: "Here is an even more special person who appreciates a one-of-a-kind, bird's-eye maple, octagon table."

I guess we're going for the high-end knockoffs with the club chairs. That's right, plural. Michael agrees with you that we really need two. Anyway, knockoffs or no, they're lovely—comfortable without being oversized, traditional without being stuffy, leather without the cheese.

A party for the museum people is a brilliant idea. Something outdoors, obviously, since the kitchen is still just a shell and Michael and I will be sleeping in the living room (where, as I've mentioned, I also make toast) at least until Christmas. We just have to put in a terrace and some plants, which we were going to do anyway. Scheduling a party will give us a firm deadline, so we'll avoid the trap that lots of people seem to fall into, letting projects like this go on and on.

Right now I'm thinking an aged brick— you can get bricks that they've buried underground or in ash or acid or something—or possibly large terra-cotta tiles, arranged maybe in a fan shape radiating from the

French doors we're installing in the living room. I've always wanted a barn-wood deck, but I think I relinquished that dream when we bought a Spanish-style house. I've also seen a sort of green slate that would be lovely, but I'm not sure how much weight it can take.

Digging currently under way for the pool. It'll take up a good portion of the yard, but it'll be great for the kids. Marlo and Hunter are both on swim teams and could really improve their times with some extra practice. Hunter's already talking about water polo. Plus, I like the idea that they'll eventually want to invite their friends over to our house for pool parties, where I can supervise.

L

"The rich are no longer different from you and me," Lexie says to Miles, as they sit in a candlelit restaurant sipping champagne.

No, that was going too far. Letty, or rather Lexie, was not exactly rich. Certainly not as Fitzgerald had meant it. Her wealth had only caught up to her social class. She and Miles were now, they felt, where they ought to be, spending what they ought to be able to spend, given their talents and educations.

No champagne for them, except on the most special of occasions, but instead a nice California merlot, only three times more expensive ordered in the restaurant than purchased off the discount liquor store shelf. But also three times more delicious in the former setting.

Lexie and Miles, perhaps not seated at the best table in the restaurant everyone was breathless about, but certainly not seated at the table near the restrooms, where a couple of tourists obviously from somewhere like Iowa or Wisconsin had been shunted, gaze at each other with re-newed love over their caramelized calamari and seckle pear appetizers. "Here," each thought, with a sense of relief and pride, "is a person of taste and sophistication. A per-son who understands that as long as one must have things in life, they might as well be things of beauty and history, things that will enrich the senses even as they provide a comfortable seat and a surface on which to set a glass of chardonnay."

M—
The kitchen is finished! Well, not finished, exactly, but done enough so that I could

spend the day arranging the dishes in the new—made to look old—birch beadboard cupboards, and stocking the refrigerator— half of one wall is taken up by shiny, stainless-steel doors, in anticipation of the kids becoming teenagers. The distorting mirror effect they create will also promote weight loss—I can't stand to open those doors once I've seen myself in them.

I'm sure you're right about this renovation saving us money in the end. The freezer has cubic feet enough to preserve a whole cow, if the various cuts are properly configured (this was actually demonstrated to us when we bought the appliance), so I can prepare meals late at night and store them—no more running out for expensive takeout. And then, as you say, we can entertain easily now, so we won't be wasting such ghastly amounts in restaurants. In fact, one could argue that we have a restaurant right here, what with the size of this oven, in which I am, even as I write, preparing a toastless meal.

Do you really think I should have them do the flooring over in pine? Jeanette's does look wonderful—it's so gorgeously scrubbed and worn—very Maine-coasty.

And they do have all their equipment here right now. It seems a shame after so much time and money not to get it right. And I could donate the tiles to a school or a shelter and write off the mistake.

Michael just came in grumbling about having to put the top up on the car and affix "The Club" to the steering wheel—the garage hasn't had room for cars since the armoires were delivered. "Armoires?" you ask. Indeed. Who can live without an armoire these days? Seriously, we plan to really "live" in our living room, as I think I may have said, but not having a TV room means we need some other way to hide our association with that vulgar appliance. Hence, the first armoire.

To counter the fact that this decorating technique will not be peculiar to our home and may make our living room resemble an upscale hotel, we thought we'd buy from a boutique and maybe come up with something a little bit special. Ha! All of the Westside has the same notion of how to ensure their furnishings will be unique. (Buying a "unique" armoire turns out to be akin to naming one's child Hunter.) Do not shop at that country French place on Montana on a

Saturday; it's like trying to fight your way through a Van Gogh in Arles show. We did find one that charmed us, though, made of 100% reclaimed antique French wood, although the piece itself was hammered together by a company in North Carolina last year. They offered to do us a deal on a second piece—French Canadian (both wood and construction) 20% off—which Michael figured was too good to pass up, since we'll need something to house the TV in the bedroom. Once we have a bedroom.

I know we're getting ripped off, buying from a store on the trendiest, classiest shopping street in Santa Monica instead of finding these things in the loft of someone's barn in Quebec, but at least this way we avoid shipping. Anyway, what with these, plus the bed, the bookcases, the dressers, and the Indonesian temple door we're converting into a desk, the garage is pretty full.

This morning a strange man parked his pickup in the driveway and mowed the front yard. It turns out that he comes with the house. At least, if I want to stick to my "no gardener—I'll do all the work myself" plan, I will have to fire Ramon, who says he's been working here for seven years—not, in one *sense, the most persuasive argument, since I don't like what he's done with the place.*

L

While Letty and Michael, and Lexie and Miles, lolled in their success, I met only with further humiliation. Throughout my month of drudgery at *In Your Dreams,* I'd been look- ing forward to June 30, when the second in- tern was due to begin work.

"I think you'll really like her," Simon had told me. "She's young—I mean, she just graduated from college in May—but she has a very mature sensibility. And she's a terrific writer. I think you two will really get along."

In generous anticipation the evening be- fore, I stopped at a store on Sixth Avenue and splurged on a celadon-colored coffee mug free of kitschy sentiments to present to my fellow intern as a welcome gift. I was, in fact, actually seated in her cubicle, trying to compose a clever accompanying note, when I heard Simon's voice behind me.

"You get your own workstation," he was saying, "or, as some of us refer to it, a desk."

I turned and rose, mug outstretched, to greet my new colleague.

"Ms. Snyder?"

The mug bounced slightly when it hit the soiled carpeting.

"Ashleigh?"

"You two know each other?" This was from Simon, the only one whose face did not reflect some measure of horror.

"OhmyGod! Ms. Snyder! It's so great to see you!"

Her initial dismay at coming face-to-face with a former teacher in the place where, I assumed, she'd been planning to make her first mark as an adult was almost instantly replaced by delight. I had, as I may have mentioned, been well liked in the class-room. And I had liked Ashleigh Cohen, whose hair, once slicked back into a girlish ponytail, was now mussed in a fashionable way, and who was wearing the de rigueur metropolitan black pants that made my out-dated sundress look particularly jejune. I re-membered as we embraced that she'd been sweetly eager, impressively bright, but also charmingly deferential. Yes, I had liked her very much as a student. Still, it was highly disturbing, not to mention loathsome, that she seemed to have become my equal.

Or worse, my better.

"Ashleigh's only going to be with us full-time for a couple of months," Simon said, as I knelt to retrieve the mug that had ended up under the desk. "She's going to start her MFA at Columbia in the fall." He turned to her. "And what happened with your story?"

"They took it!" she squealed.

On my feet again, I looked at them both, head slightly cocked, feigning what I hoped was a perky, quizzical expression. "Who took your story?"

"*The Paris Review*?" she said, as if I were obviously so far removed from the world of literary publications that I'd probably not heard of it.

"It was really brilliant, Margaret," Simon said. "Ashleigh sent it to me as part of her application and I knew they'd want it. I submitted it for her. With Ashleigh's permission, of course." He smiled at his protégée.

Honestly, how was I expected to live after this sort of news? But, unfortunately, although the word "mortification" suggests death, it does not actually cause it. Rather than spontaneously burst into flames or melt in a greasy puddle at Ashleigh's feet, I had to show her the Xerox machine and explain the idiosyncrasies of the fax and the filing system. We spent the rest of the morning Xeroxing the magazine's standard rejection letter, several copies of which fit easily onto a page, and then cutting the pages into pitifully narrow rejection ribbons: "sorry . . . not right for our pages . . . please try us again." I cringed with empathy every time I dropped one of these into a "self-addressed stamped envelope" to return a manuscript, envisioning the recipient poring over those final four words, weighing their encouraging invitation against the discouraging fact that we were obviously unwilling to spend even a full sheet of paper on our reply.

Ashleigh, already among the chosen, Ashleigh, who'd not even had to supply the self-defeating SASE to land her work in some of the most sought-after publications in the country, prattled on about various members of her high school class with whom she'd kept up and her boyfriend who was taking her out to lunch at one o'clock. I ate a peanut butter and banana sandwich at my desk and, driven purely by my envy of a twenty-two-year-old girl, added several paragraphs to Lexie's story.

Until Ashleigh appeared at *In My Dreams,* I'd had lingering qualms about Lexieing Letty. Whenever my pages had surged ahead, infused with Letty's reactions, even sometimes with her own words, I'd reminded myself that this was only an exercise, a means of teaching myself how to create a character, a skill I would then apply to a far different character in far other circumstances. My reunion with my former student, however, wiped away all such niceties. A novel must be produced. Quickly. And this one was clearly well under way.

In fact, it occurred to me that it might even be a very good novel. The story that was emerging from Letty's e-mails was a parable of American consumerism. Like Madame Bovary, Lexie was attempting to conjure for herself the elusive life she thought she glimpsed through other people's French doors by copying their furnishings down to the doors themselves. It was a simple notion, really, but had it not led, at least once before, to a masterpiece? That it had led also to the agonizing demise of its

protagonist was a detail I somehow managed to overlook.

Margaret,
It turns out we can't have a pool after all.
We've been informed that no matter where
they put it in the yard, the heating mecha-
nism will somehow interfere with our plumb-
ing system, and it's way too expensive to
redo the plumbing. This was only discov-
ered after the pool pit had been dug—no
surprises there. Everything is for the best,
however, since our landscape designer says
we must build a hill "to take charge of the
runoff," and the pit and its displaced dirt will
apparently come in handy in this process.
  The kids and I now spend most of our
days in what was once a lush green back-
yard and is now only an ill-defined space
erupting in mounds of soil. The boys and Ivy
insist it should remain this way, a giant, filthy
sandbox, indefinitely.
  Originally, I thought Ramon and I would
do the landscaping work ourselves. (Of
course, I couldn't fire Ramon. He's very ex-
cited about the plans, by the way, and has
excellent ideas about where to place plants.
He does know the yard intimately—its pat-

terns of light and shade, dryness and comparative damp—and claims the former owners stifled his creativity.) But what with the hill and the hole, it just seemed like too much. Building a hill involves equipment. And it should be done right. And, as you say, we want to be able to enjoy the space in our lifetime.

At the moment, there is much lifting and shifting of dirt with backhoes or front-end loaders, or whatever those large, loud, usually yellow pieces of equipment are called. This activity seems to my eye as aimless and make-worky as the stuff you see a road crew doing, but is, according to Hazel (the landscape architect), actual hill-building work. She says when it's done, we'll put in drought-resistant plantings to heighten the "oasis effect." She also wants us to build a garden wall to suggest secret spaces in Marrakech or Babylon, along which we'll plant the ten fruit trees we've already purchased. We thought of doing four, one per child, but that seemed to be asking for trouble. What if one didn't take? And then, when we got to the nursery, those little saplings looked, well, so little. I mean, they won't bear fruit for years! So what's the point?

Again, this is when we're living here; this is when the kids are young and should be able to enjoy picking the fruit—I don't want Ivy coming back from college to harvest her first lemon—so we decided to go with bigger ones, practically full-grown trees. This way we can also take advantage of the fact that we have three guys with hole-digging equipment hanging around our yard all day eating our taco chips.

We've also ordered twenty-four-inch terra-cotta squares for the patio from a family of potters in Guadalajara, who promise to make them all slightly irregular to emphasize that they are hand-formed. They should arrive by mid-August, in plenty of time to be installed by Labor Day, if we put in floodlights and pay overtime for night labor. The neighbors, of course, will have to be plied with expensive champagne, given free parking passes for the Otis, and invited to the party.

Long discussion yesterday on how said party will be funded. Even though Michael could get museum money for it—it's for museum people, after all, and for people museum people want to entertain and impress—we're leaning toward being more classy by just putting the whole thing on our-selves. As you say, it would be sort of an in-vestment in good feeling. I wouldn't do anything too complicated—finger foods, a nice wine, that kind of thing. It's going to be outdoors, after all.

Speaking of parties, can you believe $600 to attend a benefit dinner for Marlo's school? Well, we could get in for $300 a couple, but that wouldn't put us on the "pa-trons list," which will be printed in the pro-gram. We have to be on the list, don't we? I mean, we don't want people to think our daughter's education isn't important to us. Especially, since, as Michael pointed out, a lot of the other parents will know we're put-ting all this money into the house right now. Anyway, it is important to us. Otherwise, why would we be spending so much money to send her to school?

L

I gave all of Letty's landscaping and terrac-ing to Lexie, whose landscape designer is named Hazel Nutley. I thought this a clever, Dickensian touch. I also gave her a little Moroccan-tile fountain to cover the traffic noise, nearly ubiquitous in Los Angeles.

M—

No, you're absolutely right. No point in get-
ting second-rate or even aesthetically un-
pleasing appliances when we're spending
99% of our waking hours in the kitchen. Not
to mention the energy efficiency of the bet-
ter models. I think we'll go with the German
dishwasher. Also, a fountain! What a great
idea! Thank you!

L

Letty

Margaret asked a lot of questions about the house. She wanted to know every detail of my plans. I thought she was just being nice, a real friend, expressing an interest in my concerns, although her interest seemed at times to encourage what I considered my baser, or at least my more frivolous, instincts. Did we really need, for instance, to outfit our bathroom with antique-like porcelain fixtures?

Margaret had always been different from everyone else, but no longer. Now her voice seemed to join a chorus that resonated exhilaratingly through me. At the same time, however, I found myself more than once un-easily recalling a passage from *Confessions* I'd translated years before. It seemed that to Westwood I had come, where there sang all around me a cauldron of unholy loves.

And yet, even fixtures that looked like they belonged in a cheap motel cost far more than we wanted to spend, so it was not so hard to justify investing more in something we really liked. After all, as Margaret reminded me, this house would be the place our grown children would remem-ber when they looked back on our lives as a family.

CHAPTER 15

Margaret

"Margaret!"

"Letty?" For an instant, I had the disconcerting feeling that I was talking to my character, rather than my friend. It was six-thirty in the morning, extremely early for a call from the West Coast. Early even for a call from the East Coast. I'd had to scramble out of bed for it. There was a breathy sound on the other end of the line.

"Letty, what's wrong? Are you kidnapped?" I'd been woken from a sound sleep.

"No! I'm trying . . ." The phone dropped

to the floor. "Oh, crumb!" It was certainly Letty. It would not occur to anyone else I knew to say "crumb."

"Letty, what's going on?"

"It's all right now," she said in a more normal, although still quiet voice. "I'm in the addition. It's just really dark over here."

I could not imagine any scenario other than an ax murderer in the main part of the house that would force her into the addition at three-thirty in the morning. I was now standing at the kitchen sink, inexplicably turning the tap on and off in my nervousness. "Should I call the police?"

"The police? No. Why?"

"Why are you in the addition?!"

"I really don't want Michael to hear this."

Disgustingly, a tiny part of me thrilled to the idea that as soon as I could get the computer turned on Lexie would be having an affair.

"What is it?" I whispered.

"It's terrible. Really, really, terrible. I don't know what to do."

I waited quietly.

"Are you there?"

"Yes! Tell me what's going on!"

"I found the folder with the lists yesterday."

"Lists?"

"You know, what's in which box."

"Oh," I said, "great." I glanced through
the bedroom door at Ted sleeping undis-
turbed beside the mass of comforter and
smashed pillow that marked where I had
been. I was overwhelmed suddenly with a
sense of loneliness so powerful it brought
tears to my eyes.

"Margaret." The urgency in Letty's voice
made me forget myself and return to her.
"Along with the lists, there were bills." She
said this as if it were a wondrous event. "I
guess I put them in there when we were
moving and forgot about them." She
stopped, breathed deeply, and went on.
"There are others, too. I keep finding these
piles of paper and envelopes—some of
them aren't even opened! There was a
bunch in a box of videotapes, and there are
some at the bottom of my purse. And last
night, when I went to call my cousin Jane
for her birthday, I found three major credit
card statements in my address book.
Honestly, I don't remember ever seeing half
of these before. I mean, I knew about the

ones in my purse—at least I know I kept dropping them in there, thinking I'd look at them later—but these others . . . it's like they're self-generating. I'm afraid to keep opening boxes. There might be more."

"Where were they in the address book?" I asked.

"What do you mean?"

"Which letter were they under?"

"They weren't under any letter. They were inside the front cover. What difference does it make?"

"I was just," I faltered, "wondering if you'd put them under 'B' for bills." Why had I asked this? Was I fishing for details, trying to find out how to write the scene in which Lexie discovered her misplaced and forgotten bills so that it would read as if it were truly happening? I shook my head, trying to push Lexie out of it, to concentrate on my real friend.

"Letty," I said, "I really can't believe this is so bad. So you're a little late with a couple payments."

"I'm not worried about being late with payments. I've been late with payments a lot; believe me, I know it's not the end of the world. In fact, after you pay the penalty, they usually just give you more credit. But this . . ." She groaned.

"Breathe slowly," I said. Letty had had a habit of hyperventilating when we were young. I'd carried a folded paper lunch bag in my back pocket just in case.

"I can't even make myself add these up. I started and then, honestly, I thought there was something wrong with the calculator, the numbers got so high, so fast. I thought I was going to pass out. I just pushed them all under the futon."

"But I don't understand how this could have happened."

"That's what I'm trying to tell you. I don't understand it either. I mean, Michael is making so much now that we should be able to live like . . . well, at least like Zoe and Brad! I'm wondering if I forgot to deposit some checks or something. This just doesn't make any sense to me." Before I could respond, she went on.

"If only Duncan would hurry up and raise Michael's salary like he promised. I keep telling Michael he should ask about that, but he doesn't want to seem pushy or ungrateful for what he's already gotten from the museum. I can understand that." She sighed.

"You know, when I couldn't sleep I wrote down everything we've bought this year; everything I could remember, anyway. It's kind of disgusting—the sheer quantity of material goods. But, really, it's just the standard stuff everybody else has. We didn't even have cable until this year. It's not like we put in a home theater."

"At least you didn't buy a DVD player."

"We did, though." She laughed, a small, pitiful sound. "I just haven't unpacked it yet. In fact, I'm not sure where it is right now."

Again, looking back, I would not be honest if I didn't admit that I saw, with at least one of my eyes, and certainly with my heart, exactly what should be done at this juncture. Scissor blades should bite firmly into plastic, the octagonal table should skedaddle back to the showroom, the best should be made of the really quite decent Westwood public school system, perhaps with the help of a supplemental reading list I could supply. With my other eye, however, I gazed at the growing pile of pages beside my laptop. The increased tension of Letty's (soon to be Lexie's) situation seemed almost to make them quiver. What harm could it do to go a little further? In a few weeks, Michael's salary would rise and would cover the most pressing bills. Why could Letty not endure a little discomfort, perhaps dodge a few creditors' calls, and so continue to feed my novel until then?

Still, even once Michael's salary was refreshed, it was clear to me, the spouse of one who recorded even the purchase of chewing gum, that the MacMillans would continue to be in debt. As a trusted and consistently bossy friend, I should, I knew, eschew self-interest and urge frugality and a sweeping reevaluation of priorities. The previous year, before my grasp had fallen short of my reach so often that I had become fearful of holding out my hand, back when I was a person of infinite resources and possibility, I would certainly have done so.

But now the novel whose title I'd just amended to *The Rise and Fall of Lexie Langtree Smith* was the only chance I had to save myself. Did I have to give that up, just because Letty and Michael didn't know how to manage their money? It was too much to ask.

I began anew. "Look, Letty," I said reassuringly, "this is not the end of the world. So you have to pay interest for a while. These are special circumstances. You've just bought a new house; you're going to have to accept some debt."

"I can't even pay all the minimum balances. We have twelve credit cards."

"Twelve!" This shocked even Lexie.

"Or fourteen. There might be some in my other purse, although I'm not sure how much I've used them. And that's not counting credit lines at individual stores." Fourteen credit cards. I wrote the number on my legal pad.

"I suppose I could return some things," she said.

"Like what?"

"Maybe some patio furniture. Michael just found two chaises very reasonably priced in this sort of retro/modern place on La Brea. You have to see them. They're Italian with a brushed metal finish on the frame and these gorgeous colored bands—pinks and oranges and lime green. And they're super light. Ivy could fold them up and carry them off. And there's teak stuff, too. Armchairs and little cocktail tables."

I hesitated; the sense that I was betraying

Letty squeezed my throat closed. I swallowed. "But what about your party?"

"Party?"

"The museum party. Labor Day. What are people going to sit on?"

"Maybe," she suggested, "they could just stand around. It's supposed to be informal, remember?" she added, a touch defensively.

"Won't it be kind of empty and cheap looking?" I prodded. "Just a blank terrace? Unless you have dancing. But even then, people need to sit down. In fact, it's probably even more crucial to have seating if you have dancing than if you don't. Are you going to hire a dance band?"

"Um . . . I don't know. I hadn't thought of it."

"Well, it just seems a shame to return the stuff before this party, since it sounds so perfect with the cocktail tables and all." My words slithered, unstoppable, from between my lips. "I mean, aren't these the kind of people who'll notice if your party looks half-baked? It might affect how they perceive Michael."

She was quiet for a moment. "You're right," she said, finally. "I can always return the stuff after the party."

And even though convincing her had been my intention, I was surprised to hear her agree, since, obviously, I was wrong.

"You're lucky, Margaret," she went on, "that you don't care what other people think."

Shame rose in a dark wave in my chest. Futilely, I closed my eyes against it. I wished that what she'd said were true. And then, I had a flash of brilliance, a plan to help us both.

When I'd hung up the phone, I started for the bedroom, but stopped just before the door. The story pressed at me from within, pushing me back irresistibly toward the closet/study. I turned on my computer and waited impatiently through its hemming and hawing. At last the screen was blank and my fingers pounced upon the keys.

At nine, Lexie is sipping a late cup of gourmet mocha java, ground only moments before her German-made coffeemaker dribbled steaming hot water through its fragrant dust. She's created an oasis for herself on her new, cordovan-colored, leather-covered loveseat, apart from the chaos of renovation, the whine of the saws, the pounding of the hammers, the swearing of the sweating construction workers. With anticipation, she pours forth from the canary yellow accordion folder a sheaf of clippings to garner ideas for the next stage of her grand project. Onto the red-brown leather slide a photo of a slate shower, directions for building a backyard gazebo, guidelines for ordering special rocks from a special canyon in Montana with which to frame the fireplace in the master bedroom, and also a cache of envelopes, some stamped in scarlet "Second" or even "Third Notice."

That morning in Los Angeles Letty (and Lexie) fished three credit card offers that had arrived the day before out of the trash, so as to take advantage of their cash advances, and at nine-thirty in New York (six-thirty in San Francisco), I called Warren, knowing he'd be in his office when the market opened.

"About that Genslen," I said. "How good is it?"

"Why?" he said. "Have you been putting in a little overtime with the ol' knife and fork?" I always cringed when I talked to the persona Ted and I referred to as "Office Warren." While at home my brother was dry and reserved, at work he was a jovial, slap‑on‑the‑back, throw‑around‑lines‑from-movies kind of guy and I couldn't reconcile the two.

I explained Letty's need to make money quickly.

"Dumb idea," he said, in his most investment-bankerish, least brotherish tone. "Stocks are too volatile. You don't want to monkey with them unless you can hang around for the long term."

"I know all that," I said. "And, of course, I agree, theoretically, but Letty's really in a bind. She needs cash in the next few weeks."

"And if the next trial bombs and the stock tanks, then what will she do?"

"Now, Warren," I said, employing the slightly exasperated, big-sister tone I'd developed in our childhood and honed as a teacher, "do you really think that's going to happen? You have Dad invested in this stock."

Warren sighed. I could hear in that exhalation the struggle between the portfolio manager and the younger brother.

I pressed my advantage. "How many trials have there been so far?"

"Two." He answered guardedly, as if he worried I might trick him into revealing information he'd rather keep secret or drawing conclusions he'd prefer not to face. Such things had been known to happen in our collective past.

"And the drug performed well in both of those?"

"Yes," he allowed.

"I know there's always some chance that things will go wrong, but as I understand it—and I do read a great deal, Warren; I'm up on my current events—the FDA is always overtesting these drugs. People are dying and the government won't let them take a pill in case it turns their fingernails blue." Given that we were talking about a diet drug, the last point was excessive, but still, I reasoned, rhetorically effective.

"Well, this wouldn't be the FDA," he said. "It's not that far along."

I regrouped and charged again. "Still," I said, "it's been tested twice. Aren't the chances good that the third test will get the same result?"

"They're good," he agreed. "But they're not guaranteed."

"Nothing's guaranteed. All I'm asking is that you give Letty the same chance for a good return on her investment that you're giving our parents. You've known her as long as you've known them, you know."

The downside of younger-brother pliability was younger-brother defensiveness. "Margaret, Genslen's only a small percentage of their portfolio. I'm managing their money in a responsible, well-diversified way."

"No one said you weren't," I broke in, but Warren was having his say now.

"Letty can buy the stock, if she wants it. No one's stopping her. I just don't want to be responsible if she loses her money."

"Oh, for heaven's sake, Warren. Don't be so dramatic. *I'll* be responsible. And when she turns a huge profit and solves all of her financial problems in one simple transaction, you can't take the credit for that either. Anyway," I assured him and myself, "Michael's expecting a big salary jump within the month. If, by some wild chance, they lose this money, he'll be able to make it up."

Warren therefore agreed to open an account for Letty and to buy the stock for her, if she wired him the cash.

∾∾∾∾∾

Over the next few weeks, Genslen continued to rise at a breathtaking clip, and this, together with the money Michael was bound to get any day now, made Letty more comfortable with their immediate financial state. Lexie, after a morning of panic, during which she used her cell phone to place an hour and a half call to her sister, Mary, in Iceland, bought a stock called Genlock, well on its way toward regrowing hair, and also relaxed. Once she'd purchased the stock, however, it wasn't very interesting to watch her simply keep track of her growing fortune on the monthly statements. There's only so much a writer can do with the opening of an envelope, the satisfied nod, the sips of black decaf while pondering: should I sell now or hold? I stretched various poker metaphors this way and that; I put a letter opener shaped like a tiny saber in her hand; I let one statement get lost in the mail for a few tense days, but the chapter grew dull, Robert-like. I sent an e-mail. *"Letty,"* it read, *"what's going on over there?"*

Dear Margaret,
Unbelievable. People seem to think that as guests they can actually order the party of their choice. Even more unbelievable—it seems they're right, because I am indeed listening to their demands. "It looks like we have to have a full bar," Michael said the other night. I was tucked in bed, or actually in futon, which, you may recall, was our bed when we were first married, and which func-tioned most recently in the old house as a safe infant play zone. It was supposed to become a dog bed in this house, but we got rid of marriage bed #2, the one my Aunt Pearl gave us when she bought herself the adjustable kind advertised on interminable late-night TV commercials. Anyway, we or-dered a new bed, an original Case Study bed, zinc and maple, very understated (we

toyed with the California king idea, but it sounded excessive, and then we would have had to buy new pillows) but, as I think I've mentioned, it's in the garage because it would look ridiculous in the living room, and, as I've probably noted several times, we have, as yet, no bedroom. So the old futon is, for the time being, our bed once again, shoved into the one corner of the living room that isn't occupied by the toaster and the jar of Tang (did you realize that you can still buy Tang?) and the coffeemaker and the half-emptied boxes. (We're working on the kitchen again.)

Anyway—in said futon, I was diligently paging through year four of five years' worth of Bon Appétits, *marking with Post-its the pages of recipes for unusual finger foods. "But I thought we decided on sangria. Remember? Summery, festive, fruity?" I shuffled through my pile of magazines, looking for July 1991, in which I'd seen pitchers of ruby liquid, shot through with yellow, green, and orange, arranged on stone tables under olive trees, from which peered adorable, tree-climbing goats. I reminded Michael that we were leaning toward a "Mediterranean" theme. "Full bar sounds* more like Monte Carlo to me," I said. "Besides, I already bought the pitchers." "I guess a lot of people don't like sangria," he replied, tossing his trousers on top of the other clothes that we've mounded on the club chairs. (This is just until the closet is finished upstairs.) "You took a poll?" "No, but apparently Harvey Price did. We had lunch together today." (Harvey Price is in charge of twentieth-century sculpture acquisitions—very glamorous.) Our conversation veered then into a list of what they'd consumed for lunch, still a subject of perpetual fascination for us (scallop enchiladas, saffron rice, ginger flan—Michael; grilled vegetable salad with shrimp, chocolate bread pudding—Harvey; and, by the way, cottage cheese on leftover toast—me. Ivy is currently obsessed with cottage cheese, so it's handy; also, have not quite mastered quirky settings on new Italian-design, chrome, six-slice toaster, so have much leftover toast, some raw, some extra-crispy). "So how does Harvey know people don't like sangria?" I asked, returning to the important subject. "He's assuming," Michael said, carefully tucking the blankets on his side tightly under the futon. (You know how he

likes to sleep in an envelope of bedclothes.)
"Actually," he went on, "I think he's the one
who doesn't like sangria specifically. But,
still, he made clear that people expect a full
bar at these things. He very deliberately let
me know his favorite single malt."

Yes, a full bar will be horribly expensive,
but remember that this whole party is an in-
vestment, so it won't really be like we're
throwing that money away. I mean, there are
intangibles to consider: goodwill, and gen-
erosity of spirit (and spirits, ha!). The worst
would be to spend a lot of money on the
sangria and nevertheless have people as-
sume we're chintzy. Michael, of course, not
being up on his Scotch, doesn't remember
Harvey Price's favorite single malt. I'll have
to do some investigating. Do I also have to
find out every other bigwig's favorite brand?
Is there a corporate list? Or is it safe just to
buy the second from the top in every cate-
gory—Johnnie Walker Black, for instance,
but not Super Black (I assume there is a
Super Black)?

It occurs to me that we can't have Marlo
and her little friends circulating through the
crowd with trays of mixed drinks. This is
going to have to be a catered party, with the

sort of caterers who won't need to heat or refrigerate anything, since the appliances are no longer attached to energy sources. They can, however, assemble trays in the kitchen, since we do, at last, have counter-tops. I've never had a catered affair. I could ask Jeanette for advice, but then, I fear, it would become her party, a museum "event," rather than a casual, albeit catered, low-key, albeit wonderfully tasteful, romp.

Also, Gerald, the hill man, now says he can't go on with the construction until mid-September—something about his back, or his eyes, or his elbow—the malady changes with every conversation, perhaps it's exten-sive nerve damage, so I now must figure out how to disguise the not-yet-transformed-into-a-hill pool-hole. Hunter suggested cov-ering it with branches to make a trap. I think it may be better to erect a sort of leafy bar-rier with huge pots of bamboo.

Hazel says Ramon won't do, by the way. My new drought-resistant plants are too del-icate, it seems, to be nurtured by an illegal alien with a lawn mower and a pickup truck. Mr. Nakasoni starts next week.

L

In my novel, which I was now working on nearly full-time in my cubicle at *In Your Dreams,* Miles convinces Lexie to hire a catering company for a book party they're throwing for someone who's not quite a friend and for whom they nevertheless feel they must perform a significant favor, because they offered to do so in a fit of generosity brought on by a single dinner at which a bright rosé capped off by a smoky single malt conjured the illusion of intimacy. "You're a terrific cook," Miles tells Lexie. "But, honey, you're not a professional. Besides, you won't be able to enjoy the party, if you're cooking all day and running in and out of the kitchen all night. Besides, we don't have a functioning kitchen." Lexie and Miles are, of course, redoing the kitchen in the house they bought. All cupboards and countertops are being covered in narrow strips of Thai bamboo, shellacked with a special substance to maintain their pale greenish hue.

"Margaret?" Simon was standing in the doorway of my cubicle. Quickly, I snapped the cover of my laptop down, eliciting a furious beeping from the machine. I reopened it and clicked the file closed. "Subscriber list," I muttered nonsensically, and then added, equally meaninglessly, "next Tuesday."

Simon, however, was preoccupied with the papers in his hand and oblivious to my subterfuge. "Margaret, I love this piece, but it seems familiar somehow," he said. "Would you do some nosing around? Make sure it hasn't been published anywhere else?"

"Sure." I set the manuscript on the shale of paperwork layered across my desk and then turned back toward the doorway, ready for small talk. Simon, however, had already gone. Well, I was quite busy, after all. Briskly, I opened my computer and continued with Lexie's party plans.

Dear Margaret,
"So what do you do?"

This is Duncan's wife. She's sipping a vodka on the rocks—thank God we went for the full bar!—and trying surreptitiously to scrape what is probably a wad of Hunter's gum off the bottom of her exquisite sandal onto the Guadalajaran tile.

We've had this conversation before, at the Christmas party, but she's forgotten that we've met. I, unfortunately, am not quite sure of her name. I think it may be "Holly"—but this may only be an association with said holiday shindig. (Michael and I usually review key names before these social things, but because of the last-minute flurry of preparty hosting chores—he had to run down to Westwood Village to pick up another bag of lemons; I had to assure my mother that Noah's giraffe is an imaginary creature and she could call my father off his search of the yards between their house and the Big Juicy.)

"Oh, I'm a stay-at-home mom," I answer. And then I add, "for now." I've been tacking on that qualifier with certain types of people for—what?—nine years. It's despicable, isn't it? I've always wanted to be one of those mothers who announce their stay-at-homeness with pride—"I'm raising my kids!" I would say, defiantly—or probably I would not even need to act defiant, so confident would I be in my choices. If only I could squeeze in some volunteer employment. "Of course, my duties as school board president take up a lot of time," would be pleasant to announce. (Although perhaps less pleasant to perform.)

"I so admire that," she says. *"I'd be bored out of my skull if I spent the whole day with Kiley."*

"I'm sorry Kiley is such a dull child," is what I'd like to say to this sort of comment.

It's true, certainly, that *"working"* with one's children can be boring. But what work isn't boring, at least some of the time? And when did being bored become a fate worse than death?

"So what do you do? When you're not with Kiley?"

"I'm the director," she says, *"of the Center for Democratic Change."*

"Mmm," I say, sipping my own drink. *"And what is that?"* Obviously, I should know, but I'm already pretending to remember her name and there's only so much fuzziness one conversation can take. (I always find such situations difficult. Should I look somewhat stupid and ill-informed right up front, so as to save myself possible greater embarrassment down the line, or act like I know what we're talking about now, and risk having to feign sudden deafness later?)

"Essentially, we form a bridge between

progressive political causes and the enter-tainment community."

So I have revealed my ignorance but am still no wiser—the worst of both worlds. I abandon clarity in favor of enthusiasm. *"That must be interesting!"* I gush. I hope by the excessive politeness of my response to show her the rudeness of hers. As always in these circumstances my ploy fails.

"It is," she agrees. Then she holds up her empty glass. *"I'm going to get myself an-other of these,"* she says, and walks away. My only consolation is that the gum is throwing her gait off.

I should consider myself lucky she wasn't one of those who believe I am a marine bi-ologist. Michael confessed minutes before the first guests arrived that he'd given that impression to several people lately. *"Not full-time,"* he assured me, *"just occasional projects. I got tired of telling them you don't do anything but take care of the kids,"* he admitted. *"They weren't getting the right idea about you."*

"And now they have the right idea?"

"In a way, yes. Now they think you're an interesting person, which is true."

"I may," I said, *"be an interesting person.*

But I'm not a person who knows very much about fish."

"You specialize in plankton," he said. "No one knows anything about plankton. Just say it's, you know, worrying, the way it's disappearing, what with pollution and global warming."

I pointed out that global warming would probably increase plankton.

"That's good. Say that," he said. "It really doesn't matter what you say."

"Just so it has nothing to do with diaper changing."

"Letty," he said, "you don't talk about diaper changing anyway."

Obviously, he'd not caught my sarcasm.

Earlier, before the caterers arrived with their trays of rolled meats and whipped cheeses, their splayed herbs and skewered vegetables, I stood looking out our French doors (so new they're still raw around the edges) at the setting we'd created. White lights cavorted playfully among the bamboo branches, waiting for dark when they would become a backdrop of reachable stars. The lightly distressed terrace flooring evoked a nineteenth-century Mexican courtyard, and the two missing tiles where the fountain will *eventually be installed were cleverly hidden by a strategically placed teak table. Ramon (of course, I didn't fire Ramon—what kind of a person do you think I am? He comes on Thursdays; Mr. Nakasoni comes on Tuesdays) turns out to have a talent for arranging furniture. He created cunning conversation clusters with the rest of the teak pieces and the Italian chaises, leaving plenty of open flow for mingling, the passing of hors d'oeuvres, perhaps even dancing. (Brilliant touch, by the way, thanks, M!)*

Meanwhile, real life went raucously on in the house behind me. They've begun a stage of the master bedroom/bathroom project upstairs that apparently requires the continuous whine of a circular saw. Yesterday, I thought I needed new glasses, but it's only the sawdust fuzzing the windowpanes. The saw whining was accompanied by the scream of nails being yanked out of the walls in the kitchen. This was the second time I've had to listen to this, the first being when they pulled off the old paneling. This time they were pulling off new but incorrectly installed cupboards. It seems they needed a practice round.

I cleverly positioned the club chairs and

their burdens of clothing with their backs to the windows. From certain angles, guests could catch a glimpse of heaped fabric, but I hoped they would assume it was pillows. The futon I rolled into a cylinder and draped with the new Turkish carpet—well, new to us, I mean—it's from one of those places in West Hollywood that we used to be afraid to go into because we thought someone would make us buy something against our will—or maybe even without our knowledge. The museum's textile expert helped us choose it and spoke Turkish to the dealer, so I honestly think we got a great deal, and its value will appreciate, as long as not too many Tootsie Rolls are smashed into the weave. I have to say that I had hopes of coming out of that store with more than one carpet, but even the one cost more than we'd intended to spend on three. But, as Michael pointed out, this is really a work of art for us to enjoy for the rest of our lives. We can get a cheap one for the dining room—that's where the food is really going to fall—and we'll do cotton in the kids' rooms.

I hid the accoutrements of the "breakfast nook" under the duvet. The trail of ants the jam jar attracted followed along nicely.

Despite my efforts to tidy at least enough so that people could get by to use the bathroom, the inside of the house, I have to admit, is squalid. In the dining room, the bird's-eye maple is invisible under the muffin pans, the plastic action figures, the boxes of files, the field trip permission slips, etc. The rest of the room is crammed with book boxes. The children's rooms are no better. Ivy's crib is the only space free of flotsam. The others sleep on tiny cleared patches, among toys and clothes, CDs and measuring spoons, linen napkins and beach towels; items that have been pulled from boxes and have no place yet to go.

I thought I'd weeded so much junk when we moved, but still we seem to have belts with no buckles and "important" T-shirts with ripping seams and a Monopoly game with no money and endless hair baubles and single tennis socks and flea combs with missing teeth and plastic containers without tops and pens that won't write and a black-and-white TV that's stuck on channel four, and boxes of broken pottery with which I've long intended to make a mosaic-topped table whenever we finally put in a patio. Now we have the patio and it's far too nice for any table I could construct.

You're scrolling forward impatiently. The party, the party, you're muttering. Let's hear more about the party. But the fact is nothing much happened at the party.

It was a fine party. Actually, a very good party, I think. People seemed happy with the copious mixed drinks and they consumed nearly all the pretty food. Seating the jazz combo among the fruit trees was a nice pastoral touch, and although the sod we laid last week is trampled beyond repair, it was worth it for one lush evening. A couple of er-rant guests—Harvey Price and an intern—managed to tumble into the pool pit—but everyone, including Justine Price, was merely amused. Yes, overall, it was definitely a success. Duncan, gesticulating with a skewer of chicken satay, told me that he wants to bring Michael in on the "big-picture planning" for the museum.

But. I thought the evening would be dif-ferent somehow. I thought, first of all, that I would be different. More witty, more gra-cious. But I was just the same, hiding be-hind"Swordfish-and-mango-salsa-in-a-blue

-corn-tortilla-cup?" when I could think of no conversation and feeling left out when, as it almost always is, the talk was art-world gossip. My exhaustive knowledge of important human affairs, gleaned through hours of dedicated flipping through People magazine during checkout-line waits, is useless at these affairs.

Unfortunately, the party rendered most of the patio furniture unreturnable. When Harvey and his intern fell into the pool pit, they took one of the superlight Italian chaises with them and the frame is pretty bent. We can still use it, but I doubt I could get my money back. A teak cocktail table was burned when a lantern tipped over and there's a large greasy stain on an armchair where someone dropped his or her shrimp scampi. (Actually, I happen to know it was "her"—Duncan the director's wife—and a director in her own right, of course. Her name, by the way, turns out to be "Hollis," as I discovered when I rashly gave "Holly" a go as they were leaving. You don't think my blunder will keep Michael out of the "big-picture planning," do you?)

L

Letty

I'd wanted to go to the senior prom ever since seventh grade when I'd seen the pictures in Lottie's high school yearbook. The king and queen, the hokey theme, the corsage pin that ruined the bodice of the dress, the photos of me with my embarrassed date in his Easter-egg-colored tuxedo standing in front of the fireplace; I wanted it all. When the time came, I also particularly wanted to wear a dress I'd been working on as an advanced home ec project, a short, shiny, even somewhat ruffly, disco-influenced shift in midnight blue silk that I was sure would make me feel like those girls who pressed their shoulders and the sole of one foot against a locker, while chatting casually with certain boys.

Margaret scoffed at the prom. By the end of sophomore year, she was merely cheerfully condescending to finish high school. She was, however, willing to coach me. When Craig Whitehead asked me to go with him, she advised me to turn him down. Not without provocation, I admit. I am ashamed to say that I cried when I told her about his offer. Craig and I had tracked along in the same math classes since freshman year, swapping pencils and test prep questions. He kept his pressed blue oxford-cloth shirts buttoned at the wrist and his hair parted and combed, never charmingly disheveled. I was not so shallow as to care overmuch about looks, but Craig wasn't particularly handsome. He laughed at my witticisms but did not have many of his own and his undisguised diligent application to schoolwork barely earned him B's. All in all, he had nothing to recommend him but relentless decency, a quality I didn't value in a prom date. I was flattered but also appalled to discover that he'd secretly admired me since my braces had come off.

"It's a waste of a prom," Margaret agreed. "And it's going to cost him a bundle for the tickets and the tux, not to mention the dinner before and the breakfast after. It's really not fair to let him go through with all of that if you're not happy to go with him."

"And the wrist corsage," I said. This was how I'd determined to avoid the damaging pinholes.

"Whom do you want to go with?" Margaret asked.

This was a difficult question, since by my senior year, all the boys I'd admired from afar had graduated. After much consultation and listings of pros and cons, we chose a boy in Margaret's history class whom neither of us knew very well. He was universally liked without being wildly, and unattainably, popular, had performed in an amusing skit in the fall variety show and ran track. Some athletic skill, we agreed, was a plus, as long as he wasn't a "jock." Margaret could vouch for his intelligence, at least in the realm of AP U.S. history, and he wore hightop Converse All Stars, which were definitely not "in" at the time, a pleasing stylistic quirk.

"You should choose the person you want to go with," Margaret said. "Why do boys get to do all the asking?"

He turned me down. He had a girlfriend at another school. They were going to her prom. That's what he told me anyway, which was a lot nicer than what I'd told Craig, which was that I just couldn't bring myself to like him "that way."

Craig and I ended up going to a party Margaret had on prom night, along with a weird mix of people too cool for the prom and people who couldn't get dates.

"This is better anyway, isn't it?" she said to me more than once that night.

But to me, in fact, it wasn't. And I never did get to wear that shift.

CHAPTER 16

Margaret

"You win some; you lose some," my father said. "That's the game of life." In Genslen's third trial, overweight mice who'd been dosed with the drug began to experience patchy baldness. The stock had plummeted.

"It may come back," my father said. "After all, you lose some; you win some."

"That depends," my mother said into the extension, "on what you lose. Get it, Margaret?"

I suspected they'd already rehearsed this

jolly repartee several times with their friends.

"Anyway," my mother went on, returning to her usual, practical vein, "that money was all on paper."

"It was a nice chunk of paper, though," my father said.

My father could afford to be wistful. As Warren had told me, only a small percentage of his portfolio had been invested in the stock.

The same could not be said for Letty. I waited a few days, but when she didn't call me, I phoned her from my cubicle. Her answering machine advised me to try her cell phone. I'd not been aware that Letty owned a cell phone.

"J. Peabody and Associates, Letitia speaking."

"Letty?"

"Margaret?" Her voice sounded distant, but I attributed that to the technology.

"Where are you? Who are you? Who is J. Peabody?"

"That's Jeanette." Her voice slipped away from the receiver. "The light is green! Drive, lady, drive!" Letty, I realized with a mild ping of alarm, had become her own enemy, the woman on the cell phone in the SUV. "Didn't I tell you?" she said to me again. "I'm working for her now. I'm an events consultant."

She had not told me. This omission hurt, although I deserved it for the part I'd played in the Genslen debacle, a subject we both seemed to be avoiding. "So now you're a professional party thrower?" I meant it as a joke but not an altogether kind one. Letty, however, was always generously slow to take offense.

"Associate events consultant, with a con-centration in the philanthropic sector. I'm not exactly sure what that is yet, but it sounds like something an interesting person might be, doesn't it? Essentially, I now have a career, because Jeanette liked my party. She said that I, and I quote, 'provided an environment of heightened awareness and pleasure.' "

"Sounds risqué."

"It's apparently a prerequisite for the suc-cessful associate events consultant. Also, she just got a contract with the Otis to do this big medieval-themed Valentine's Day benefit for the illuminated manuscript collec-tion, and she said it would be helpful to have

someone connected with the museum—
even by marriage—on her team. Mostly I'm
running errands so far, which, I have to say,
is one of my most practiced skills. This
morning I had to be at the flower market at
five and now I'm making the rounds of a
bunch of fabric stores to collect swatches,
so Jeanette can choose one for the indoor
tent she's planning for the Center for
Democratic Change's Christmas Kickoff.
Oh, and here's an irony you'll enjoy—I'm
keeping the books. Apparently, Jeanette re-
members that I was a whiz at budgeting
when we shared an apartment." Her laugh
had a bitter edge I tried to ignore.

"Were you?"

"Sure. So much for a shower curtain. So
much for the communal half-and-half. It
was easy back when we thought we were
clever and chic for using a flowered sheet
as a tablecloth. This kind of budget, though,
is entirely different. You'd be shocked at
how much these people spend on things
like nasturtiums for salads. It's kind of sick-
ening. Meanwhile, we're going to miss a
house payment next week," she said with
false brightness. "That's how well I'm doing
with my own budget."

Genslen could be avoided no longer.

"Letty," I said, "I'm so sorry about the stock. It was a really dumb idea."

I'd intended to say much more. My words could not replace her money, but I'd hoped we could at least talk the incident through, chew it down, until we felt comfortable with each other again. Her call waiting, however, muscled between my sentences and my call waiting leapt in between "dumb" and "idea."

"Margaret, I have to go. That's probably Jeanette. She hates it when she gets voice mail." She severed our connection without waiting for my response.

My call was from Simon. This time he wasn't even bothering to visit my cubicle.

"So is the Donaldson OK?"

The Donaldson? I stirred the papers on my desk with my free hand. I'd not looked at the piece since the day he'd given it to me nor searched other magazines to see if it had been published before, as he'd asked, but Simon would certainly be annoyed if I said I needed more time. I'd already been late in faxing edited manuscripts to authors and mailing checks, and I knew my tardiness was becoming exasperating.

"I haven't seen anything like it," I said, truthfully, vowing to make a thorough check that evening.

"Great! Then we'll run it." And he, too, hung up without saying goodbye.

Late that night, Letty began communicating with me again, for which I was grateful.

Margaret,
This job, I assume, will eventually pay fairly well, although we haven't, as yet, discussed firm figures. But for the first few months, it turns out I'll have to spend money to do it. People tell me this is normal. Meeting with clients, for instance, requires a whole new wardrobe. Jeanette hasn't quite said this in so many words, but she's offered to spend a day shopping with me. Also, I'll have to get a full-time sitter for Ivy, someone with a driver's license who can pick Noah up from preschool at noon and Hunter at 2:30 and Marlo at 4:00, unless she plays soccer, in which case, 5:30. Maybe I should get a chauffeur and a sitter. Tomorrow, I'm interviewing Jeanette's nanny's sister, Ofelia. Jeanette supplies Carmelina with a car. As she says, "Then I know she's not driving

around in some clunker without seat belts that's ready to break down at every inter- section." Actually, she said "some old Tercel"—I'm pretty sure this was just coinci- dence though.

Last night Noah's school held a benefit auction, a little treat to amuse us after the dessert and coffee portion of a three-hun- dred-dollar benefit dinner. (We figure that's fifty bucks for the espresso—but, as I re- minded Michael, that coffee only comes to four cents a day over the course of thirty years.) Michael and I managed to sit coolly smiling through the restaurant meals and the light plane rides and the special screen- ings and the bottles of wine, pretending we were waiting for the next lovely item, or, toward the end, that we'd bought early. But there was no resisting Noah's own hand- print, or "fingerpaint fingers on copier paper," as Michael put it. Every child had made one. ("Made" is stretching it. I'm the first to laud my children's art, but it took them all of five seconds to slap their palms in the paint and then onto the paper for this project.) Every set of parents, needless to say, met the outrageously high opening bid *when their offspring's handiwork hit the auction block (and thank God, although not surprisingly, no one bid against us). Yes, we all have fifty more just like them or better at home, not to mention the original hands themselves, but who could bear to give the impression that they did not want their own child's little print? Whoever came up with this idea is a genius and should use her power for good! I feel sorry for the parents of twins.*

I'm trying to talk myself into believing that taking this job with Jeanette is a really good idea. I did enjoy planning that party, and it was a success. Maybe this is my calling— providing opportunities for the rich and famous to mingle "in an environment of heightened awareness and pleasure." After all, someone has to do it. Mostly, though, I'm afraid I'm just weary of the sort of social chagrin I described in my last e-mail. Could that possibly be a good reason?

Certainly, I would have to consider that a good reason, seeing as how I'd sacrificed the last year of my life attempting to vault beyond the reach of social chagrin. But while our goal seemed uncomfortably superficial when presented that starkly, we were really striving for the world's respect, and this, I knew, was far more than a party trick.

Of course, I don't blame you for the Genslen. I know it was your idea, but it was my decision, my money. That's the nature of the stock market. You win some; you lose some, right? If you happen to talk to Michael, though, don't say anything about it yet, OK?

L

She did blame me, of course. And I blamed myself. Not precisely for Genslen's fall—I couldn't have predicted that—but for my despicable sense of excitement now that it had happened. I tried to bury this reaction in my anxiety for Letty, which I also felt quite acutely, but it remained, tingling like the pins and needles of blood rushing to circulate in a limb folded too long. As a novelist—yes, that is how I saw myself now—I even yearned to open the vein of tension she'd exposed in her admonition not to tell Michael. What would happen if the ante were upped, just a bit? If there were, for instance, a bit of a scene between husband and wife, revealing old wounds, deep-seated disappointments, betrayal, and shock?

Lexie, whose very life had the advantage, like my parents' stock gains, of being "all on paper," had also been hard hit when the drug in which she'd bought shares exhibited a disturbing tendency to make the bald gain weight. So far, she, too, had not confessed to her husband the full extent of their financial slide.

Lexie accepted a position with a company called Have a Ball. Ten pages and three days of neglected work at *In Your Dreams* later, she'd purchased the wardrobe—heavy on silk blouses—and handed the keys to her Range Rover to a whiz-bang Salvadoran nanny, Miss Carmel, who was willing to drill Spanish verb conjugations with Allie and Sas during the ride to and from school. She had also begun to shop for a sportier, but still substantial, car for her own daily use. Perhaps a Passat. At that point, my manuscript, like an old Tercel, stalled once again. Without Letty's dispatches about Jeanette, for instance, I couldn't get a handle on Lexie's employer, Janet.

Luckily, for me and Lexie, things continued to happen to Letty.

M—

We are rotten at the core. The rug, in fact, the very floor, has been chewed out from under us.

"Mom, what's this?" Marlo asked. This was three days ago. We were about to paint her new bedroom (we were forced to choose a designer color for this since none of the less expensive brands produce quite the right shade) and she had volunteered— volunteered!—to wash the trim.

"What's what?" I was pulling packing boxes away from the wall.

"All these little holes. Is it a special kind of wood?"

"I didn't do it!" Hunter said.

Marlo was right. The windowsills, all of them in her room, and, as it turned out, most of them in the house, were pitted with tiny holes. The effect was lovely—lacy like Indonesian carving—and horrifying. Uncle Frank, it seems, does not know a termite infestation when he sees one.

And it's not just the window frames, which would be bad enough. It's everything, beams and underpinnings, floorboards and rafters. Studs. Half the wood in the house needs to be replaced or it will all collapse in a rain of sawdust when we least expect it. Or when we most expect it. Our expectations, in fact, have nothing to do with it. Such repairs, needless to say, are expensive.

I have begun to hide the children's books, in hopes of discouraging their college matriculation. It's too late for Marlo. She's already mastered long division and the basic elements of five Native American cultures. But maybe Ivy, at least, will be content to be apprenticed to a paper hanger.

I have, in truth, borrowed a bit from the children's college funds, but we'll put it back by spring. Still, this probably means we shouldn't have bought that table or at least ought to have forgone the club chairs. It's hard, though, to return things once you've moved them in. Impossible, actually, in the case of the table—they won't take it back. Also, Miss Wiggins has used one of the club chairs as a makeshift litterbox. Apparently, she's not completely sanguine about the move. Anyway, if I returned the chairs, we'd have nothing to sit on. I've gotten rid of all the old wicker and foam.

L

CHAPTER 17

Margaret

M—

It's two in the morning and Michael isn't home. I haven't heard from him all day, not since eight-fifteen a.m. when he asked why my coffee was always so bitter. It isn't. I mean, it was this morning for some reason, probably the pot wasn't clean or the water was "off" or something—you know how sometimes it just is bitter, but it's not like it's always bitter. Usually I make very good coffee. I get the beans from that place in Venice. (Venice, California. I'm not that extravagant.) And, really, what I wanted to say to Michael was "make your own coffee!" Especially now that I have a job, too. In fact, I'd already been to the flower market and back by the time he got up, so I'd already had my coffee. Which maybe was why it was bitter, since, now that I think of it, I didn't really make him coffee. I just microwaved a cup of the stuff I'd brewed in the dark, hours before.

Wait . . . is that the car? No. It's the Infiniti next door.

All day I ran on anger, but now my fury is down to fumes, and he's still not home.

Michael wasn't really upset about the coffee, of course. He was angry about what happened last night, which, as far as I'm concerned, started way before last night, but yesterday I was particularly tense, what with the Genslen fiasco and then Marlo getting another C on a math test. I know this is not important. She's only in fourth grade, for God's sake. But Marlo and I spent two hours studying for that quiz and it seemed to me that we understood the concept of common denominators perfectly well! Was she not paying attention? Doesn't she realize that she'll never get into Stanford without a clear *understanding of fourth-grade math? Or, failing that, an A. Also, Barkis chewed the heel of one of the shoes I bought for this new job so thoroughly that it's now a mule, and clearly I erred in correcting him, since when I try to get him to chew the other one to match, he just whines and runs into the other room. And it turns out they misrouted the pipes to the en suite bathroom when I made the switch from plastic to copper, but nobody noticed the problem until yesterday when they installed the shower in the wrong place. Even now they're pretending it's not a problem. "If you change your mind, Mrs. Letty," Hector says, "we move it." I have not changed my mind! I never wanted to have to stand behind the toilet to use the sink, which this configuration forces one to do. (It's difficult to explain, but it's obviously wrong.) But somehow, because I did change my mind about the piping material, we're going to have to pay for the rerouting and rearranging and replumbing.*

So last night all of this was weighing on me, while I lay there on the futon that smells like dog, which is not entirely unpleasant, but is still not the way one would like one's bed to smell, waiting for Michael to sand-

wich himself between the covers so that we could get this day over with so as to be ready to start another one in a few hours, and I could actually hear the crinkle of all those damned unfillable envelopes under my shoulder. Michael was standing in his underwear and his socks, neatly creasing his pants preparatory to neatly hanging them over the back of a club chair for the night, and suddenly I just felt so angry with him. I wanted to snatch those trousers from his hands, crush them into a ball, and hurl them at his head.

"Michael!" I said.

My feelings must have been clear in my tone, because he jumped. "What?" He looked right and left wildly, as if I were alerting him to the proximity of a black widow.

"What about that money?"

"I know," he said miserably. He covered his eyes with one hand and kneaded his forehead with his fingers. You know how long his fingers are? They're freakish! A child could snap them in half.

"Honey." I punched the pillows so I could sit up. I punched them hard. "That money was one of the reasons we decided you should take this job. Maybe the main rea-

son. I'm not sure it's worth all the time and effort, all the disruption of our lives, without that." I carefully skirted the main issue, which was that if he didn't hurry up and get this salary increase our lives would really be disrupted, what with the bankruptcy court and all.

He looked around nervously, trapped between a nagging wife and several heaps of items that belonged in a bedroom that seemed likely never to exist.

"Honey," I tried again, "I know you don't want to make unreasonable demands, but it's not unreasonable to demand what you've been promised."

"Well, last week, Duncan was saying—" he began.

Duncan! I loathe Duncan! And his wife with her tented, celebrity-fawning, far-from-democratic change!

"Michael," I interrupted, icy-smooth as vodka, provided at a full bar, paid for by me, "have you ever heard the expression 'talk is cheap'?"

And, after that, it only gets worse. I shamed him, Margaret. I told him he was an irresponsible father and a coward. I told him *he was weak. "Duncan," I concluded, "may like you, but he can't possibly respect you."*

It worked. Oh, yes, I got what I wanted. Thoroughly browbeaten, Michael swore he would confront Duncan today, or what was today until two hours ago when it became yesterday.

I've been trying for the last eight hours to pretend that I didn't say all those things flat out, or, at least, that my saying them was for his own good. The truth, untwisted by frustration and panic, is that Duncan overlooks his promises to Michael because Michael makes it easy for him to do so. Michael is not the sort of person who cares only about the bottom line and what's in it for him. He is a generous, modest man, who doesn't know his own worth. But that, I'm afraid, is not what I said. I'm afraid this money, when he gets it, will be tainted with my insults and demands and will no longer be something to celebrate.

But, tainted or no, it will be money. First, I will pay the bills. Then, I will fix our marriage.

Car. Yes, a familiar Saab.

Letty

I wanted to take them each by a hand and explain one to the other. Michael, I was sure, would forgive Letty her desperate accusations were he to know what lay under her shoulders every night. After all, they had spent the money together; they should work together to pay their debts, as well. But while I felt a steady pulse of empathetic unhappiness for them both, I could not help but recognize that what Letty had done— provoked a fight and yet held back the truth to maintain the tension—would be a remarkably effective plot device. Once again, I was dependent on Letty and her remarkable talent for living her life—at least the last six months of it—in a novelistically interesting way. It was far too early to call Los Angeles, so I assured Letty via e-mail that she was not a monster, but only driven beyond the limits of human endurance by fear. Perfectly understandable. Not to mention (as, of course, I did not) ideal for exploring the uncharacteristically manipulative behavior an otherwise sympathetic character might exhibit in a state of panic. I was all for giving credit where credit was due: I took a break from the novel and set to work on a draft of my acknowledgments, expressing my thanks to Letty.

Although I was selfishly pleased about their fight, I was also reassured to discover myself relieved that, thanks to Letty's exasperated prodding, they'd finally be getting the money they'd been promised and their serious financial worries would be over. Necessary as Letty's suffering was to my novel, I didn't think she could stand much more nor could I bear to watch. I was fairly well satisfied with my book anyway at this point. My characters had careened to the brink of bankruptcy; they had looked deep into their souls and discovered heretofore unacknowledged weaknesses; but I had no desire to write a tragedy and suspected readers would have no heart for it either. The strength of Lexie and Miles's relationship would prevail, I decided, and for this they deserved a happy ending. They would recognize where they'd gone wrong, promise never to be tempted by Mammon again, and squeak by in the eleventh hour to live more simply ever after.

Such a conclusion, however, did not take into account the inevitable perfidy of others.

M—

Duncan, the great and powerful Duncan, has gotten an offer from the Metropolitan Museum. He'll be gone by Christmas. He's sorry, but he's sure that Michael understands why he can't make any promises right now. His replacement may want to hire his own people. Duncan will put in a good word, of course.

Forgive me, if I sound bitter as six-hour-old coffee.

I think of Duncan now at that party, the party Michael threw for him—to thank him, to impress him, to demonstrate a commitment to him and the museum. I think of him cramming those cubes of dripping chicken into his mouth. Had I another chance, I would push the skewer down his throat.

It frightens me that Michael isn't angry, or rather that he isn't acting angry, because I know he's seething. He wouldn't look at me as he told me what Duncan had said, but I could see his fingers shaking, as if at any moment his fury would fork from them like lightning.

Obviously, I should have told him about the debts long before this. How can I tell him now? I'm glad, at least, I've told you,

Margaret. It's too frightening to know this alone. All day I've been thinking about that wad under the futon. It's like living in a horror movie, the camera always sliding to that corner of the room. "Under there, it's under there," the camera says.

L

I called, first Letty's home number, then the cell phone, and left messages on both machines. I e-mailed. I called the airlines to see how much an emergency ticket would cost. Unfortunately, although I explained the situation to a very pleasant agent named Cecilia, and also to her somewhat impatient supervisor, Tammy, and offered as incentive in each case to name a significant character in my book after her, they both claimed there were no special discounts for flying to the aid of friends in financial trouble.

Ted did not see the point of rushing to Los Angeles. He sat on the couch as I paced between the bedroom and the living room, arguing with Tammy, removing from our suitcase the sweaters we stored there, digging underwear out of the hamper. "Did she ask you to come?" he wanted to know.

I had to admit she had not, that, in fact,

she'd not even called back. By three a.m., however, when I got up to check my e-mail, she'd responded.

M—
Michael will not come out of the addition. I found him there in the space that is to be our bedroom, sitting cross-legged in front of the framed hole that is to open onto our private balcony, but which is now just a rectangle of sky overlooking the pool pit. He would not speak to me. I told the children he was working and took them to McDonald's for dinner, although even the Happy Meals now strike me as extravagant. I ordered a small Coke and ate the ice.

Later, when they were in bed, I crept into the addition with a flashlight and the bills, the mess from under the futon and two more that arrived today, still in their unopened envelopes. I've never added them up, not thoroughly, not with a calculator. We'd do it together, I thought. We'd lay it all out on the plywood; we'd face it side by side; we'd form a plan.

But Michael had hauled the cushions from the club chairs up there while we'd been away and was sprawled over them, sleeping. I went down again with my pile of paper. Alone.

And now I'm watching out the window as the Explorer is repossessed. As I type, a tow truck is jamming its hook under my bumper. I'm relieved, glad even, to see it go, along with its "reasonable" monthly payments. Although—wait!

Thank God, I remembered Percy Penguin sitting innocently in the backseat! I also removed the car seats, an umbrella, my Thomas Guide, a partially consumed package of Altoids, a comb, three plastic fork/spoon combinations, and a handful of Handi Wipes—no sense giving them more than I owe. I left loose french fries, orange peels, gum wrappers, grocery receipts, and an empty Diet Coke can. The repo man accepted an Altoid and a wipe. It's greasy work, hauling people's cars away.

An Acura Legend pulled into the driveway across the street while I was shuffling toward the house with my pitiful pile of worldly goods. Its driver looked over his shoulder, his chin grazing the leather bomber jacket he had hooked over one finger. "Car trouble?" he called across the road. We've not spoken before, but cars, like pets and children, bring people together. I nodded. And then I went into the house and shut the door.

Still, I could hear the whine of the electric winch, pulling the cable taut.

As it turns out, we're not Explorer people. We can't sit in spacious, climate-controlled leather interiors, and roll over the rough and rocky terrain of life as if it were merely grass.

I sat down then with the bills and a glass of excellent bourbon. We have so much liquor left over from the party—such quality! such variety! The pages are creased like failed origami sculptures now from the weight of us on top of the weight of the futon. They look like garbage, like paper meant to be thrown away. But I spread them out.

I've often told the kids—Marlo and Hunter, anyway, who are old enough to have homework—that when problems are clearly organized, they don't seem so bad. On this theory, I sorted and piled, keeping only the most recent statements. The stack did look more manageable when I'd crumpled first notices whenever there were seconds, seconds when there were thirds. It was only math, after all, and far easier math than I'd tackled with Marlo. And then I added the to-tals.

It seems I've lied to my children. Some-times when things are organized, they seem worse. That is because they are worse, worse than anyone could have imagined. As of October 10, we owe $145,685.64.

I don't understand. Michael makes so much money now—not as much as we ex-pected, but still, so much. And I've been paying all along, paying and paying, tuition, mortgage, the dentist for Michael's root canal. How could this have happened?

I have to go. I'm not sure where. To bed, possibly. I can't go much farther than that, given that I no longer have a car.

L

I knew how this had happened. Paging back through Lexie's expenditures, I could clearly follow her ruinous trail. Of course I could. Had I not known that was where my story was going from the moment I began it, the moment Letty and Michael bought the house? Had I not, in fact, gently pushed my friend along that path, egging her on when she balked, choosing colors and applauding designs, encouraging her to pursue a life that would make her feel the equal of her friends and the better of her enemies, who, in the case of Jeanette, at least, often seemed to be the same person?

Margaret,
I told Jeanette my car was "in the shop" today with some unspecified malady and she lent me one of hers, a Navigator, much nicer, actually, than the Explorer. Of course, our financial status is none of her business, but I was still surprised by how easy it was to lie. Tomorrow I will say the problem is still undiagnosed, the next day that the garage has ordered parts. The parts will take a long time to come. Then they will be the wrong parts. This, in fact, has truly happened to me, so I know it's believable.

It's three o'clock and I gather from the messages on the answering machine that Michael slept all morning. His assistant called at nine-twenty to remind him that he had a meeting at nine, and again at ten-fifty to ask if he should cancel another one at eleven. Michael left a note for me at noon: "I've gone to eat my free lunch." In case you're as worried as I was that this meant

*something too awful to consider, I've spo-
ken to him at his office. He meant it literally.*

*I am alone. The children are being shut-
tled by Ofelia to ancient Greek club/soc-
cer/play date, respectively. Ivy is just being
shuttled without destination. Peri has come
and gone. Did I tell you I called her? I think
we'll have to sell the house. Although, according to Periwinkle Scott, it won't do
much good.*

*She walked through, her mouth making a
little moue of disapproval that I'd never noticed before, even when she took us
through places with hideous gold-textured
wallpaper and lime green shag carpeting.
She wouldn't even go into the master bedroom–en suite bathroom addition, just
poked her head between the two-by-fours
that make up the framework and clicked her
tongue against the roof of her mouth.*

*"Look," she said, finally, when we were
standing in the living room at the foot of
the futon, "I'm happy to sell it for you, but
wouldn't be honest if I didn't warn you
that you're not going to get what you paid
for it."*

"What are you talking about?" I said.

"What about the improvements we've made? What about the addition?"

"I told you to do it to code."

I protested that "to code" ended up costing so much that we'd given up.

"Well, you won't get a penny of it back this way," she said. "Look," she went on, "I can see it's going to be fabulous when you're done. If you finished all these things—the kitchen, the master, the floors, the landscaping . . ." She flapped her hand back and forth, indicating the various undesirable areas. "The bathroom," I added. "Then," she went on, "the place would be gorgeous. That would be a different story. But people don't want to take on other people's projects. You can understand that. It's . . . messy. I'm only thinking of what's best for you guys." She launched a modified version of her old, perky smile toward me. "Why don't you finish it up first? Think of it as an investment."

I convinced her, finally, to put it on the market, "just to see." "But, really," she said, turning in the doorway, her sunglasses poised just below her chin, "you guys are going to lose a lot of money."

L

M—

Michael is sleeping enough for both of us, which is a good thing, since I'm barely sleeping at all, what with my cache under the futon stabbing me in the gut all night. There is, however, very little gut left to stab, weight loss being an unanticipated benefit of intense and constant worry.

I'm finding it difficult to concentrate on creating an "environment of heightened awareness and pleasure" for the Otis benefit when I despise that museum and all who wish it well. Mostly, all I think about now is numbers. If Marlo and Hunter quit their Saturday soccer leagues, how much will we save? If I stop buying presliced cheese for Ivy and Noah, how much will we save? Do they sell American cheese in blocks? It seems to be born individually wrapped. Although delis have it in blocks—maybe I could buy it wholesale. This is what takes up all the space in my mind. I get lost now. I try to go to Encino and end up in Reseda.

This morning, while Michael slept with his head between two pillows, I vacuumed the Turkish carpet and removed an amoeba-shaped blob of some brown substance from its center. Marlo helped me to roll the carpet into a heavy tube and together we heaved it into Jeanette's Navigator. "Is it because Noah spilled pudding?" she asked, as she climbed over the backseat, so as to tug while I shoved. "He won't do it again. I promise."

Mr. Wallace, proprietor of Eastern Carpets, similarly mistook my motive when I appeared in the doorway of his shop, bowing under the heavy roll. "Mrs. MacMillan," he said, "so good to see you again!" He hurried to the front of the store, while motioning with one hand for his underlings.

I'd found a parking spot only half a block away and had felt embarrassed to ask for help in lugging the carpet to the store, knowing the purpose of my errand, but my position now, I realized, with my face closing in on my toes and sweat beginning to make the back of my neck slippery, was far worse. My knees were trembling slightly from fatigue and hunger, my breakfast having been a scant handful of damp Cheerios stolen from Ivy's high chair tray.

"Here, here, let my men take that," Mr. Wallace scolded, and his henchmen whisked it from my back, as if handling a duvet, and lowered it to the floor. Mr.

Wallace himself bent to unroll a few feet of the carpet he'd sold me only two months ago. "Ah," he said. "Yes. One of my favorites. Very wise of you to bring it in for special cleaning. I warned you," he raised one finger playfully, "with the children, a special piece like this will need special cleaning!"

"I wish I were bringing it in for cleaning," I said. "I mean, I'm sure you do an excellent job. But it's not dirty."

"No?" He scratched with one manicured nail at a dime-sized sticky circle I'd missed. "Have you brought it in as a guide for choosing another? In a complementary pattern? Perhaps for an adjoining room? Or sometimes people use two in one room. That's a very sumptuous look, I think."

"Yes," I said, "that would indeed be sumptuous."

"Good!" he said, clapping his hands. Last month this signal had prompted two assistants to leap about the room, selecting various carpets at Wallace's behest, and unrolling them one on top of the other, but at angles, so that the corners still showed for the sake of comparison. Michael and I "oohed" and "aahed," as each gorgeous

rectangle was revealed, as if we were watching fireworks at our feet. We nibbled ginger cookies and sipped tea, while our friend Omar advised us about which carpets to prefer and dickered over the price.

"No, no," I said quickly, before the leaping could begin. "I can't buy another carpet. I'm afraid we're having some problems."

Mr. Wallace frowned at me. I doubted that cookies would appear this time. "Well! I know you're not having problems with the carpet! This is one of our very best carpets!" He smoothed his palm over the fibers, as if the rug may have been offended by my words and required soothing. Then he looked up at me, raising his eyebrows and tilting his head to indicate a question. "Unless, perhaps you would like to exchange? This one is perhaps too small for your space?"

"No, it's perfect for my space," I admitted. This was turning out to be more difficult than I'd imagined. I thought resentfully of Michael, a long lump beneath the covers.

Mr. Wallace waited. He did not smile. He did not offer tea.

"Mr. Wallace," I said, "the problem actually is that we should not have bought this *carpet. We thought we could afford it, but as it turns out, we can't."*

"But, Mrs. MacMillan, that is why you used a credit card." He laughed, somewhat patronizingly. "So that you would pay only a little at a time."

"Well, it turned out to be a lot at a time," I said. "Too much."

"I'm sorry." He shook his head and rerolled the length of carpet he'd undone. "But I can't accept returns. I would like to help you personally, but, you understand, if I accepted returns, then everyone would buy, return, buy, return. Today, I need a blue carpet for my Picasso party," he said, assuming a false, high-pitched voice. "Tomorrow, the party is over; I return the carpet. Next week, my mother is visiting. She prefers a red carpet. Ah, now my mother has gone home; I will return the carpet. You see?" He smiled, a hateful smile. "I would have a library, not a business." He held both his hands in the air.

"No, I understand. I understand. You couldn't make it a policy. But I hoped you might make an exception. For a special case."

"No," he said, firmly. "I can't make an ex-

ception. Everyone, you know, would want to be an exception." He mocked me, his voice rising again. "I am special. You must help me."

His words on top of my meager portion of Cheerios made me feel physically ill. He was right; I had thought I was special. I wanted to grab up my carpet and run from the store, but I could not have lifted it again, and, in any case, his foot was resting on the roll now, holding it symbolically in place.

"I would like to help you," he said, resuming his old tone, now that he saw he could frighten me. "You are a friend of Omar's, and Omar is my friend. Perhaps you would like me to buy the carpet back?"

"Yes." I nodded eagerly. We'd paid almost ten thousand dollars for that carpet. I thought he was suggesting a return under another name. "Maybe you could buy it back."

"First, I have to be sure you have not damaged it." With two easy motions, he directed his men to carry our carpet to the middle of the floor, where they unrolled it briskly. Mr. Wallace paced up and down its length, bending now and then to touch the fibers.

I have to admit, Margaret, that, beautiful as that carpet is, it looked slightly scruffy, exposed there, under Mr. Wallace's scrutinizing eye.

"I will give you," he said finally, "three thousand dollars for it."

Three thousand! Three thousand! My mind kept repeating the dismayingly inadequate number, leaving no brain material available to form an answer.

"You think I'm not being fair," he said, "but I don't need this carpet." He waved his hand over it dismissively now. "I'm happy with the ten thousand dollars you paid me. When I pay you, I'll have only seven thousand, and I'll have to store this large carpet again. Who knows if I'll sell it?"

"But if you do, you'll have made seventeen thousand dollars!"

He shrugged. "Perhaps," he said. "That's my business."

Three thousand dollars. Three thousand out of 145,685. It was nothing. It would barely allow me to go on buying individually wrapped sliced cheese. But I accepted his offer. I didn't think I had any choice.

Here is a fascinating, albeit disgusting, fact. The museum is spending a week's worth of the money it owed Michael on mushrooms alone. According to Jeanette, the mushroom, "with its earthy, exotic flavor," is very "medieval." When I suggested that the price might be somewhat excessive, she reminded me that these are not regular brown mushrooms, but wild chanterelles. She said this as if I, perhaps thanks to a fondness for hot dogs on sticks, might never have heard of this special fungus. In any case, she explained that a major institution like the museum would find it unseemly and even counterproductive to worry about cutting costs when planning a major benefit. "Donors want to feel like they're contributing to an organization of substance," she said. "Not some fly-by-night nickel-and-dime operation. You'll see. They won't object. In fact, I'll bet you lunch that they worry we're not spending enough on the wine."

L

The following day, I'd been typing furiously for three hours, describing a stout banker named, with delicious irony, Mr. Mercy. His lip curled in disdain as he strolled through Lexie's house, rapping his knuckles against the wood paneling and calculating what the bank could expect to realize from the house's sale after foreclosure.

"You have remarkable powers of concentration," Simon said, startling me. My fingers bounced off the keys. "I've been standing here for five minutes." He held his wrist up as if to show me the face of his watch.

"Oh!" Quickly, I slid my mouse to the menu and clicked on save. "Did you want me to do something?" I turned sideways in my seat and smiled up at him. Although other members of the staff had swivel chairs, as an intern, I was obliged to make do with a metal folding chair.

Simon did not smile back. He held out a copy of the most recent edition of *In Your Dreams* opened to the page on which Frederick Donaldson's article began. "Yes," he said. "I wanted you to see if he'd published any part of this piece anywhere else."

I pressed my palms to my cheeks to cool their sudden warmth. I had forgotten about the Donaldson story.

From under *In Your Dreams,* Simon slid a copy of the January issue of *Harper's* and held it open toward me. "And this," he said, "is reprinted from *Zoetrope.* He even used the same title, Margaret! Did you even check LexisNexis?"

"The same title?" I exclaimed, despite myself. "How did he think he could get away with that!"

Simon stared at me. "The point is, he did." He sighed. "And several writers have complained that they haven't yet gotten their author's agreements, incoming faxes haven't been sorted since last week, and Nadine says you never gave her the clippings she wanted. What have you been doing?"

The list of mindless tasks he expected me to perform conscientiously, coupled with my shame at failing to complete even this busywork, drove home the unbearable indignity of my situation. I tried to remind Simon that he'd once considered me more of an artist than a gofer. "You might recall," I said, sitting tall in my folding chair, "that I have been writing a novel."

"The Vietnam thing? Margaret . . ." He broke off, shaking his head.

"No," I said, standing, pulling my pride around me like a bath towel, "another 'thing' entirely."

Simon sighed again. He closed the *Harper's* and then the offending issue of *In Your Dreams.* "Well," he said, finally, "maybe you should devote yourself to this book full-time. I mean, as your friend, I have mixed feelings. I don't want to let you go, but I honestly think you need to focus on your real work." He paused and looked at me steadily. "As an editor, of course, I have to think of the magazine."

It was unpleasant to be fired, and particularly unpleasant to sense that Simon had not been quite as enthusiastic as I'd supposed about my novel, but that, I reminded myself, as I marched indignantly down Lexington Avenue, had been a different book. Also, feelings of shame aside, it didn't matter now that I was out of a job, the novel—the very venture I'd been supporting with that humiliating internship—was nearly finished. And it was, I reflected, tapping the disk on which I'd saved that day's work, wonderful. It was rich in detail, full of tension, a scathing commentary on modern life. All it lacked was a dramatic ending.

〜〜〜〜〜

When I got home, I watered the plants. I washed my face and then mixed a glass of Ovaltine to sip as I worked. None of this demanded privacy; nevertheless, it was disconcerting to open the door to our closet/study and discover that I'd not been alone.

Ted was seated at the desk. My manuscript lay before him in two stacks, the larger one print side down. My heart jumped, jostling my arm and sending Ovaltine in a wave over the lip of the glass. Somehow, although I'd been piling pages on that corner of the desk each night to prove my progress to Ted, it had never occurred to me that he might read them without my invitation.

Ted's, I realized with some confusion, as I hurried back to the kitchen for a sponge to wipe up the spilled milk, was the opinion that mattered. Ted's and, it occurred to me, Letty's. Their judgments mattered more than those of agents, more than those of editors, more than those of *New York Times* reviewers, more even than those of the Pulitzer Prize committee. I was puzzled that this should be so, since it contradicted much of what I'd striven for throughout the year.

"Ted?" I whispered.

He turned. In the currents of air his movement stirred up, two pages wafted to the floor. He was shaking his head.

"What?" I said. "What do you think?"

"Oh, Margaret!"

"Tell me," I insisted. My hands were shaking now. I was glad I'd left the Ovaltine in the kitchen. "What do you think?"

"Well, I haven't finished it," he began infuriatingly.

I clenched the doorframe with both hands. "But so far. So far," I prompted.

He turned back to the manuscript, riffling the edges of the turned-over pages with his thumb. "It's very well written," he began.

"Yes?" I interrupted, encouraging him to continue. "Well written. Yes."

"Although the allusions might be a bit heavy going once in a while. Once in a while," he repeated, holding up a hand when I groaned. "But what's remarkable about it is these people!"

"You mean the characters? Lexie and Miles?"

"I mean, it's unbelievable! In a good way.

In a good way," he added hurriedly, holding up both hands now. "It's a great story—the expensive house, the new schools, the SUV, the Teutonic dishwasher. But the best part," he said, "is that they have no idea how they got themselves into this disaster. That's so realistic. That's why the ledger is so important, Margaret. By the way, you must have used a couple of inkjets printing this out. Did you record those? And all this paper?"

I was standing at the desk now, peeling back the pages of my "remarkable" work. I brought choice bits to Ted's attention. How did he like this scene? Wasn't this a clever metaphor? Had he noticed the sly way I'd structured a particular sentence so that it segued into the next chapter?

He nodded. He appreciated. "It's really very good, Margaret. As I said, it's very realistic. On every other page I just wanted to jump in and warn those poor people."

Blood rushed to my head at these words. My ears rang, as if Ted had struck me. Stunned, I stared down at my feet, waiting for the sensation to pass. I was wearing a pair of narrow green flats with pointed toes, shoes I'd had since college. They'd seemed so right for me that I'd never been able to give them up, but instead got them resoled and polished, year after year. I noticed now, for the first time, how scuffed and misshapen they'd become.

I'd talked myself out of vague misgivings. I'd overridden moments of shame. Finally, however, I realized the key fact. It was not Jeanette who was Letty's enemy. It was I.

CHAPTER 18

Margaret

While Ted slept that night, I sat in the closet/study. I'd told him I wanted to work, but the manuscript, slumped in a slovenly heap on the desk after Ted and I had pawed through it, repulsed me. I snatched it up, and, holding it at arm's length, I carried it to the kitchen and pulled the bin lined with the clear recycling bag from under the sink.

But recycling was far too good for the hateful thing. I wanted it gone. I grabbed it back out of the bin in handfuls and marched again to the closet/study with it, the pages turned in every direction and doubled over on themselves.

Getting the window open was more difficult than I'd expected. I had to pound the corners with the stapler and stand on the desk for leverage, but, finally, the old paint cracked, the iron weights sighed in their casements, and it slid open. The air shaft was sharply cold and smelled of mortar and something metallic. Crouching on the desk, I leaned out as far as I could without losing my balance, held my novel in both hands over the darkness, and let go.

Having disposed of the incriminating pages, I felt cleaner, more calm, almost as if I had jettisoned the deceit that had gone into their making. I slammed the window shut and went to wash my hands. Then I showered.

"So I won't be a writer," I told myself, vigorously working my fingernails into my scalp. Lots of people weren't writers. They found other, worthwhile things to do, work that endowed their lives with dignity, work that did not necessitate their feeding parasitically off their best friends.

I brushed my teeth, thinking of all that I

had swallowed in college, in the prep schools where I'd taught, in the very atmosphere of this city. I'd let these environments and the definitions of success they espoused poison my better nature. In the morning, I would convince Ted to leave New York for someplace more wholesome and together we would do something that did not stink of ambition. We could open a bed and breakfast in Oregon or a diner in Ohio. We could bake pies. Letty and Michael could join us. We could live on a commune and raise goats. Such modest endeavors, however, would earn nowhere near $145,685.

In the morning, when Ted had gone to work and all that was left in the coffeemaker was an amber glaze, I checked my e-mail.

M—

It turns out that Lottie's still paying for medical school. "Hematology isn't a high-paying speciality, you know that," she said. She's very proud of choosing her field without concern for its earning power.

I'd only asked for enough to help us through the immediate month, but my request set off her usual rant.

"You know, if I'd wanted to make money, I'd have gone into ophthalmology or derm. Everyone assumes doctors are rich, but it isn't true. Not anymore with all the managed healthcare."

I interrupted. "Yes, yes, Lottie, you've explained all that. HMOs, malpractice insurance, et cetera. I just hoped you might have some to spare just now. Something sitting around in a money market, not really doing very much."

"Are you talking about my wedding account? Because if you are, you should know I used that. I went on that trekking trip to Nepal. That's where that went. Except the deposit I couldn't get back on the dress."

"Rod should have paid that. I can't believe he didn't even have to pay for that."

"Letty, I'd give it to you if I had it," she said. "I wish I had it to give." Then she brightened, assuming her big-sister tone. "You know what I do, Letty? You might want to try this. I save my change. Every time I break a dollar, I take the change home and put it in this really nice antique apothecary's jar I got at the flea market. Then every month I have all this extra money."

I wanted to explain that it was not more

than she would have had had she spent the change and not broken another dollar, but who was I to claim any insight about finances?

"But I thought you said Michael was doing well." This, of course, was my father's first line.

"He is, Dad." It's all so predictable—his lines, my lines. This being an unprecedented situation, I had hoped it might go differently.

"Then why do you need money? And why is he sending you here to ask, instead of asking me himself?"

Wait—let's not forget my mother: "I knew it! I knew you just had too much stuff. You always had to have the best, didn't you?"

"When, Mother? What are you talking about?"

"In home ec? You had to have the silk? When I told you the rayon. And the rayon had the better pattern—you even said that at the time—'I wish I could get this pattern in the silk,' you said."

"I'd earned the money, Mother. I'd saved it myself."

"There were better things to spend it on."

"Better than a prom dress?"

"When you don't go to the prom, I'd say yes."

"Letty," my father said, *"you just bring your account balances, your credit card statements, all that type of thing over here. I'll get you kids sorted out."*

"Louie, she doesn't want to show you her bills, for heaven's sake. She's a grown woman. What do you need, Letty? Five thousand? Fifty-five hundred? Just write her a check, Louie. We should be happy we have it to share with our kids. Although, Lottie would never ask for money."

"Lottie asked to go to medical school," I pointed out.

"That was different. That was education. Teach a man to fish," my father said.

"Never mind, Dad," I said. *"It's not such a big deal. We don't really need it. Michael's doing really well, you know."*

"Are you sure?" my mother asked.

I could see they were relieved. It's not the money. I'm sure they could easily spare five thousand dollars. But they don't know if giving it to me is right. Are they helping or spoiling me? Hard as they try—and often I suspect they aren't trying at all—I will always be a child to them.

Obviously, Michael's mother can't help us. We've been sending her checks since 1989. She already subsists on tuna and toast. When we're bankrupt, it'll just be the toast.

L

I opened the window again. I knelt on the desk and squinted down at the pages glowing white and sharp-edged in the grayish indistinguishable matter that lined the bottom of the air shaft. I might be able to dispose of the evidence of my guilt, but this did nothing for Letty. And then, as I hovered over that filthy abyss in despair, inspiration slalomed, sure and swift as a cab down Tenth Avenue, into my consciousness. Why not use Lexie's story to redress both my obscurity and Letty's poverty? Struck by the perfect, circular perfection of this plan, I nearly lost my balance. If I finished the novel, if the novel was as good as I suspected it might be, as good as Ted, an extremely discriminating reader, said it was, I could give my advance to Letty! Ted would understand. My interest, after all, had never been financial gain.

Luckily, pitching a manuscript into an air

shaft, while a satisfyingly dramatic gesture, didn't mean what it would have in an age before computers. I opened my laptop and set to work to fix all of Letty's problems by eloquently compounding Lexie's in the final chapters of *The Rise and Fall of Lexie Langtree Smith.*

Throughout the course of that day, I scarcely left my desk, and each time I did, a compelling idea or the perfect word tugged me back within minutes. When I grew hungry, which in earlier days would have sent me scurrying to the gourmet market or the A&P, likely both, for a diversionary half hour, I spread sour cream on saltines to simulate herring and carried a plateful back to my desk. By seven-thirty, when Ted got home, I was in the middle of a scene in which Lexie's house, the quintessential symbol of the new life she and Miles had spent so hard to create, burned to the ground after the cord of the six-slice, chrome-plated Italian toaster, having been stepped on so often during its sojourn on the living room floor during the kitchen renovations, frayed and sparked.

During the succeeding days I regained the intense focus I remembered from my childhood. Now that I was writing with a purpose beyond my own aggrandizement, I was able to devote a large portion of my brain, which had previously been occupied only by anticipation of critical and social reaction, to telling a good story, and my novel proceeded so quickly it seemed to sheet off the screen like a heavy rain off a roof. I only needed to catch the pages as they fell from the printer and add them to the pile. Even without Letty's sketches, I found I could envision scenes and tap my way through the course of the action. I was at long last a writer, although I could not spare the time or the attention to enjoy the role.

In two weeks, I was revising. By the end of the third week, I'd written something magnificent. A few scenes needed polishing; a couple of secondary characters needed sharpening; some of the language could have been more precise; but overall, it was a fantastic novel.

I'd wanted to wait until the book was sold, until the check was in my hand, before I offered Letty the money, but it seemed suddenly crucial to let her know there was hope—that it was, in fact, nearly certain that if she could hold on a little longer, she would be able to pay her debts. Some of them, anyway. Most of them? All of them? And then some? Sally Sternforth had bought a co-op on Carnegie Hill with her advance. I'd heard of people getting half a million dollars for their first novels. Why not me?

"Can you hear me?" I asked, after I'd delivered the gist of my news. Letty was on her cell phone again, edging her way through Mulholland Pass on the 405. Twice so far I'd found myself talking to dead air and had to wait for her to call me back.

"I'm not sure. Did you say your book was done? You finished it? Let me in, damn it! Sorry. Lane change."

"Yes, and, as I said, it's much better than I expected it to be," I repeated modestly, in case the mountains had cut this off earlier. With the hand that was not holding the receiver, I turned over random pages of my manuscript, admiring sentences here and there.

"Margaret, I'm so happy for you."

"But, Letty," I said, "you're not understanding me. This is good for both of us." And again I pressed home the prospect I'd offered her. After she finally understood that I was presenting her with my advance, we were cut off and then, when she called back, we had to slog through all the "Margaret, I can't let you do that"s and the "This is incredibly generous of you, but no"s. It was tedious, but it had to be done. And, finally, she had to agree. She had no other options.

"It might take us a long time, you know, to pay you back," she said.

"Letty, you don't need to pay me back. What's mine is yours. And, really, I owe you. You've helped me more than you realize with this book." I was about to confess the nefarious means by which the novel had taken shape, when the connection severed again. If she tried to call me back, she didn't get through, and I made no such attempt. She would read everything soon enough.

Letty

I didn't understand, at first, when Margaret told me she would loan us her advance. I know we're close friends, best friends, but still it sounded crazily excessive, a far larger favor than I would ask even of my parents. I told her it was impossible, of course. I laughed in that uncomfortable way one does when one doesn't know how to respond. Obviously, Michael and I couldn't accept such a gift. Still, she insisted and insisted. It was almost as if she were as desperate to give it to me as I was to have it.

I emphatically did not want Margaret's money, but obviously, I did want money from somewhere and I had come to see over the past few months that there was no other source. As I edged past the exits, Ventura Boulevard, the 101, Victory and Sherman, creeping farther and farther into the Valley in search of a gross of grape-flavored licorice whips for a post-premiere party, I started to think this was not such a crazy notion, after all. If Margaret and Ted could spare the funds for a while, wasn't I just letting pride bully my family out of relief, if I refused to accept their loan?

At the same time, I didn't take Margaret completely seriously. It wasn't like she was standing in front of me, cash in hand. We would see what would happen, when she actually got the check. It would do no harm to accept it now; I could always thank her and refuse later, if some other way presented itself. "Thank you," I said. My hands trembled with giddy relief on the wheel. "I'll pay you back." She started to answer, but the phone cut out. I let it drop from my shoulder to the floor and, as the tension of the past months began to dissolve, cried as well as I could while maintaining my stutter-step among the fast lanes.

Margaret

I didn't have time to hunt and peck through the agent world, nor was I confident that Simon would be helpful, given my recent failings at *In Your Dreams* and the disparaging tone I'd detected in his mention of my aborted novel. I found Sally Sternforth's number in Ted's address book. The agency she worked with was small, Ted had once explained to me, but prestigious.

"You might remember," I said, when I'd got Sally on the phone, "that I mentioned I was working on a novel?"

"Oh, that's right," she said. "Something about breakfast in Vietnam, wasn't it?"

I batted aside the familiar onslaught of humiliation and exasperation. I had no time

for self-indulgent feelings now. "I'm calling,"
I went on, "because I finished my manuscript." I hoped this piece of information
alone would elicit an offer to introduce me
to her agent. It did not.

"Oh. Well, good for you," she said.

I thought of Letty and her desperate
need. I could not allow tepidness to deter
me. I gathered myself, as if I were about to
leap over a gorge. I closed my eyes.

"Yes, well . . ." I began, the running start.
"I was wondering . . . that is, would you be
able to . . . I mean, would you mind . . ."—I
sprang off the cliff—"recommending me to
your agent?"

The wind swirling up from the bottomless
crevasse screamed in my ears as I hung in
midair. I couldn't hear. Was she answering?
What was she saying?

"Well, you know, Margaret . . ." she
began.

Oh, God. Could I go back? My arms
flailed. My legs churned the empty air. It
was too late.

"She's awfully busy," Sally was saying. "I
don't even know if she's taking any new authors. In fact, I'm pretty sure she's not."

It was difficult to breathe, what with the

rapid falling, the frequent changes in air pressure, the whipping about of the rag-doll-like limbs. "Oh, of course, that makes perfect sense. Well, never mind then," I chirped.

Sally softened. Effortlessly, she extended a net to break my fall. "Listen, why don't I give you the name of someone else over there? She's just starting out, but she's up-and-coming. You can say I told you to try her."

"Thank you," I gasped. I wrote down the name. I had no other options.

CHAPTER 19

Margaret

On the morning of December 5, I nestled *Lexie* in a fresh box and dressed myself in a writerly black skirt and turtleneck. I debated whether the sterling silver earrings shaped like two tiny Everyman editions my parents had sent for my birthday blared presumption or suggested whimsy, and put them back in the drawer. Real authors probably wouldn't wear tiny books on their ears. I let my hair curl to create the impression of unkempt artistic seriousness, but added a necklace of pink beads to announce that I was not a memoirist, about to put my head in the oven. I limited myself to a single cup of coffee, in case Heather Mendelson Blake offered me more.

The Hope Perdue Agency offices, on the third floor of a townhouse on Charles, were encouragingly literary. The stairway was dark, possibly even sooty, and the treads, under a worn Oriental runner, each creaked a distinctive, individual note. Upstairs, books and manuscripts were stacked in front of shelves crammed with the same, so that the hallway was reduced to a narrow, zigzagging path, along a floor that tilted charmingly, if disconcertingly, toward the back of the building.

A girl was on the phone in the front office. The ends of her long brown hair swept the top of her desk as she nodded. "OK," she was saying, "OK. Well, don't worry, Alice, we'll take care of it."

Alice? Alice Walker or Alice Munro? Or maybe McDermott or Hoffman. It was exhilarating just to be standing in that atmosphere. I wrapped my arms around my manuscript and pulled it to my chest. It was the key to this world, the secret handshake that would secure me a place beside the Alices.

"Can I help you?" the girl asked.

"My name's Margaret Snyder," I began.

The girl said nothing.

"Sally Sternforth suggested I come," I continued. "She said I should ask for Heather Mendelson Blake. That she would be interested in my novel."

"Oh," she said. "How nice of Sally." She tossed her hair over her shoulders and held out both hands for my manuscript. "OK, well, I'll make sure Heather gets it."

I transferred *Lexie* to her ink-smudged fingers, and that was it. It was over. I had no more business there. I lingered at the office door for a moment looking back at the block of pages that now would have to speak for themselves. And then I was back down the atmospheric stairs and out onto the gray sidewalk with nothing to do but clean the apartment and devise this year's Christmas gifts while I waited.

I assumed I would have to give Heather Mendelson Blake at least until Wednesday to finish reading it, and then maybe another day or two to decide which publishers to send it to, to make copies of it, and perhaps to get it copyrighted or whatever agents did. Realistically, it would be well into

December by the time an editor saw my novel. I worried that editors didn't buy much over the holidays, what with book parties, Christmas parties, and ski weekends. "I don't think we can count on a check until January," I told Letty cautiously that afternoon. "Can you hold out until then?"

"Margaret," she said, "I don't know what to say. I can't believe you're doing this for us."

"You'd do the same for me," I assured her. I was certain that she would, but I was happy to know that things would never work that way when it came to Letty and me.

Letty

Margaret likes to think that what happened was her fault. She wants to be the one with the story, the one who says how it goes, as if the rest of us couldn't rub two sticks together without her. This part, however, she can't tell, because this part, unfortunately, is mine.

On the night of December 4, I had to pay

for the rushes. Once Michael had fallen asleep watching *A Charlie Brown Christmas* and the children were in bed, I sat on a step stool at the newly constructed, mosaic-tiled breakfast bar and sorted paperwork for Jeanette. It was an especially busy time for J. Peabody and Associates, and there were various invoices to reconcile with canceled checks and several final payments on venues and to caterers due. The Otis event was not until February, but nevertheless deposits had to be made. One of these was for rushes.

Jeanette had discovered that authentic rushes of the very kind once used to provide warmth and softness underfoot and to hide all manner of refuse, such as chicken bones and saliva, on the floors of the great rooms of medieval castles could be purchased from a small, family-owned business in France and shipped to Los Angeles via a Chinese import/export firm based in the City of Industry. To secure the quantity we required, I had to send a check for thirty-five hundred dollars to Wang Ho Company.

I didn't mean to pick up the pen filled with erasable purple ink. However, given that it was the only writing implement the children were not allowed to use and hence were discouraged from depositing in an undiscoverable location, among the roots of the fig tree, for instance, it is not surprising nor even entirely random that it was the first pen that came to hand after I'd emptied two drawers, checked the pocket of Michael's jacket, run my fingers under the club chair cushions, and dumped my purse. An erasable pen writes like any other inexpensive, medium-nib ballpoint, and I filled out the check without thinking of anything beyond the exorbitant price of an outdated floor covering.

The next day, Jeanette signed the check, and I would certainly have deposited it on my way to collect Noah from a playdate that evening had Ofelia not been summoned to her own daughter's school to discuss a biting incident with the principal at two forty-five, which meant I had to cancel my afternoon appointments and return home after a lunch meeting with the Otis planning committee. It was during my twenty minutes at home, while I was forcing Ivy into an outfit appropriate for her three o'clock session at Toning for Tots, that I happened to pick up a call from Steve Carlson, who'd installed our plantation shutters. "Listen, Letty," he said, "I like you and all, but I'm going to have to take you to court if you don't pay me." "How much do I owe you?" I asked, distracted by the difficulty of working Ivy's resisting arm into a fresh T-shirt, but also being disingenuous. In fact, I knew the precise figure, having been informed of the amount four times by letter, three times by phone message, and twice by means of "casual" drop-by visits when Steve was working on other neighborhood window treatments. This time, however, Steve refused to play along: "For Christ's sake, how many times do I have to tell you?" "OK. OK. I know," I confessed. "Three thousand, four hundred and fifty dollars." "And Letty, if I don't get it by next week, I seriously am going to take legal action. I hate to do it to you, but my wife—" I interrupted. I couldn't stand to hear him make excuses for demanding his own money. "I'll pay you! Please, Steve, don't tell me these things!" He didn't need excuses. He was right; I owed him. I had, in effect, stolen from him.

The envelope was already in my purse, sealed and stamped, ready to mail. My fingers pushed it back and forth as I rummaged for the car keys. It was strange that the amount was so nearly the same as that on the check I'd written for the rushes. It was not such a large amount either. Enough, it seemed, to provoke legal action, but still not more than I could easily send to Wang Ho on my own the next week, after Michael and I got our paychecks. While Ivy wormed her way back out of her T-shirt, I took the envelope out of my purse and pried the flap open.

The pen, with its own eraser conveniently attached, lay on the counter next to the coffeemaker where I'd left it the night before. At the time what I did seemed reasonable. The money needed to go to two people; but the one who'd been in my house, who'd drunk my iced tea and used my bathroom, was demanding it right away, while the other, the anonymous Wang Ho, could easily wait a week. It seemed sensible to pay the one that needed paying now, even if the money I was using was not quite mine yet.

The actual "embezzling"—it still seems wrong to think of it that way, although I see now that that is precisely what I was doing— took less than ten seconds. I erased "Wang Ho and Company" after "Pay to the Order of" and wrote in "Steve Carlson," and I put my name in the memo, so he would know whose shutters it was for. I addressed and stamped a new envelope. I sent Steve thirty-five hundred dollars, fifty more than he'd asked for as a sort of good-faith apology, from the account of J. Peabody and Associates.

Margaret

Although I'd told Letty not to expect any word until the middle of January, I spent the next two weeks picking up the phone to check for the telltale beeps of a waiting voice mail message and leaving the apartment to give the phone a chance to ring.

"Do you think I should call?" I asked Ted.

"What for? When she's read it, she'll call you."

"But can it hurt to call? Just remind her that it's there? See how it's coming along? Maybe she has questions."

"Did you put your number on the title page?"

"Of course."

"Well, then, she'll call you."

"What if she misplaced the title page? I think I should call. Do you think I should call?"

"All right. Go ahead and call."

"But they say not to call. That and the SASE. They're like the rules of agents."

"You think if she loves it, she's going to throw it out because you called?"

"If she hasn't started it, maybe she'll send it back. Maybe she'll think I'm too much trouble."

"Don't call then."

On December 23, I sat down at my desk with a cup of coffee and a square of crumb cake. I would be brief and nonchalant. I would not be a bother. I would merely inquire in a businesslike fashion as to the status of my manuscript.

"This is Margaret Snyder," I said, presumably to the girl with the long brown hair. "I left my manuscript for Heather Mendelson Blake earlier this month?"

"Mm-hmm," she said. It was impossible to tell by this whether she remembered me or whether she was just politely marking time until I committed myself to some specific piece of business.

"I don't want to bother her, but I was just wondering if someone, maybe you, or . . . someone, could tell me if she's had a chance to read it."

"Hang on a minute."

I hung on for more than a minute, allowing me ample time to drop several chunks of sugar and butter from my crumb cake into my lap. As I began to ease my napkin out from under my coffee cup without setting the receiver down, a voice I didn't recognize came on the line. "Hello?"

"Hello?"

"This is Heather."

"Oh, hello!" I sat up straighter, and in doing so, dislodged the napkin too abruptly. The cup overturned. "This is Margaret Snyder," I said, snapping to my feet and clamping the tail of my shirt against the edge of the desk to stanch the rushing spill.

"Yes?"

"I'm calling . . . well, I know I'm not supposed to call, but I thought maybe you wouldn't mind. I mean, I just wanted to make sure you got my manuscript." The coffee was headed now in two general directions, west toward my laptop and south toward the household ledger. I released the dam I'd constructed of my shirt and dragged my computer to safety. "I could easily get you another copy," I said. "It would just take me a couple of hours to print and then I could run it right over. I live very near. Of course, I don't know how long you're planning to be in your office with the holidays and all."

"What did you say your name was?"

I repeated this information and slid my legal pad under the stream of coffee that was now running onto the carpet. "Sally Sternforth told me you might be interested," I added helpfully.

"Oh, yes, I have to thank Sally for the referral," she said. "I'll tell you, I've only gotten through the first few pages. You know, with the holidays and all."

"Yes, I know you must be busy," I managed.

"But it looks first-rate. That opening scene," I heard paper rustling, "with the grass. Just lovely."

"Thank you," I said. "First-rate. Just lovely," I scribbled on a blank page of the ledger. I wanted to be able to report her precise words to Ted. "I'm hoping," I continued aloud, "that the allusion to Gatsby works sort of as an undercurrent, almost at a subconscious level, because I don't think Lexie is really . . ."

"Right, right," she interrupted. "Exactly. Anyway, I have to go to London just after New Year's, so I won't be able to get to it until after that."

"After New Year's is fine," I assured her. "After New Year's is wonderful. Just wonderful."

My hand was shaking as I replaced the receiver and I'd forgotten to wish Heather Mendelson Blake a happy holiday and a good trip. It was happening. My novel was on its way to being published. I'd dreamed and despaired of it; I'd worked around and toward it; I'd strained my marriage, tarnished my relationship with Simon, given up a good job and lost a bad one for it. Worst of all, I'd nearly—it still made my breath shallow to think of it—done irrevocable damage to my dearest friend for its sake. But all of that was over now. This post–New Year's business was a nuisance: I would have to tell Letty to push back a bit the date on which we could expect to see money. But only by a couple of weeks. We were saved.

Immediately, I called Ted and was forced

to leave a breathless message on his machine. "She says its first-rate!" I announced.
"Ted, isn't this unbelievable? It's really happening! Heather Mendelson Blake likes my
book! She likes the grass!"

While I sponged the coffee off the carpet,
I called Letty and left a similar message on
her cell phone. I called Simon, my parents,
Warren, Sally, Neil, and several teacher
friends, leaving versions of this message all
over Los Angeles, D.C., and New York. I
e-mailed Brooke in London. The faint brown
stain that remained after my efforts to clean
up the spilled coffee would function as a
souvenir. When we had people over, I could
point to it and say, "That happened the day
the process of publishing my novel began."

When I could think of no one else to tell,
I burst from the apartment and ran down the
stairs. I had no purpose other than to feel
the cold, fresh air on my face, and to walk
the city streets, full of other people—a
woman pulling a wire handcart; a man in a
camouflage-patterned parka; a cab driver,
peeing into a bottle; a man in a cashmere
coat, the skirt flipping back in the wind; a
girl applying lipstick; a mother with a little
boy on each hand, one hanging back to ex-

amine the cab driver and his bottle—who belonged there, as I finally felt I did. I nodded to people as I passed them. I was worth their notice now.

Giddy, I wandered down Sixth Avenue, feeling as if a cocoon that had grayed and muffled my days had fallen away, leaving my vision clear and my skin tender and new. I plunged through the gourmet groceries, Balducci's and Jefferson Market, and bought a pomegranate, three limes, and a wedge of Parmesan for their colors alone. I stood on the corner of Eighth Street and breathed in the incense. In the drugstore, I spread a ginger-scented lotion on my hands. I wanted to exult in all of it, to dunk myself in these few blocks, to claim them. *My* fancy foodstores, *my* overpriced pharmacy, *my* quaint hardware store, *my* city. I may even have hummed a few bars of "New York, New York." After gulping an achingly sweet hot chocolate at a window table in a corner restaurant, I skipped across the street to the library, just to sit again at the table where I'd worked the summer before. I stroked the woodgrained Formica gently with my fingertips. I was a different person now.

Letty

Michael and I were both paid the week after I diverted the funds for the rushes to Steve Carlson and, as I'd promised myself, I sent Wang Ho a check from our own account. It was difficult to part with that money, however. The next semester's tuition installment was due January 1 along with another house payment. Housing and education were obviously more important than medieval floor covering. Also, Ofelia clearly deserved a Christmas bonus. I told Jeanette that I was troubled by the idea of the museum crowd stuffing its collective faces with special fungi, while my nanny had had to borrow from loan sharks when her daughter fell off a slide and broke her arm.

"But, Letty," Jeanette said, "you're not seeing the bigger picture. This is a benefit, a charity event. With the money it'll raise, the museum will be able to display pieces that people otherwise would never see and enjoy. This event is going to enrich the city in a way that's almost incalculable. I mean, how do you measure the effect of a work of art on a child? Yes, access to medical care is important, but if your nanny's daughter spends an afternoon with a Delacroix or a Frank Stella, who knows how it'll inspire her, how it will change her very way of looking at the world around her?" She took a sip of her macchiato and shook her head. "That's what I love about this job. We're helping to make the world a better place."

That afternoon, with the erasable pen, I changed a payment for cocktail napkins printed with scenes from the unicorn tapestry to cash and presented the bills to Ofelia in an envelope I helped the kids decorate by cutting designs in raw potatoes and inking them on stamp pads purchased for event consultant purposes by J. Peabody and Associates.

Then, for a period of several days around Christmas, I was granted a respite from what had become relentless calls and letters from contractors who hinted at Mafia connections, credit card companies who helpfully suggested that I borrow from other credit card companies, and Hazel Green, the landscape architect, who wept.

We bought the children Christmas gifts. It seemed too cruel and strange, too much an admission that nothing was as we had expected, to ask them to do without. Whatever ground I'd gained with my economies—withdrawing Ivy from Toning for Tots, filling Jeanette's tank with regular gas, using baking soda to brush our teeth—was sucked away in the vacuum of the holidays.

The Christmas reprieve ended on January 2, when the world seemed resolved to collect what was owed. The bank's foreclosure notice arrived that day, as did a request for "outstanding payment" from Marlo's school. "Perhaps," they diplomatically suggested, we'd "misplaced" the most recent balance statement in the "holiday chaos." They were "happy" to enclose a duplicate. They were also willing, they said, to "work with us to meet this obligation." I asked to meet with the headmistress.

"Mrs. MacMillan," Mrs. Drake said, coming around her desk with her hand outstretched. I was ashamed of the vanity of clear nail polish—even though it was only a brand available in drugstores and I'd applied it myself—when I took that large competent hand. Its masculine nails were clipped, not even filed.

"I wanted to talk to you," I said, when I

was seated in the visitor's chair, "about this." I took the letter from my purse and held it out to her.

She didn't bother to read it. She knew our case. "We're so pleased," she said, "to have Marlo as a student. She's just the sort of girl, I believe," she looked at me significantly here, knowing that what she thought mattered to me, "will truly benefit from the creative vision we offer here at Wheatley."

They did not like to lose students once the year was under way. They counted on our tuition.

"I believe so, too," I said fervently. "We've been very happy so far."

"We were not made aware of any financial difficulty when you applied to us."

"No, you wouldn't have been. I mean, there wasn't any then. It's just . . ." I paused. As had been the case so many times in the past few months, I had no explanation for why we could not pay a bill that we seemed obviously able to afford. Was it because we'd purchased the more mature fruit trees? Or was it because we'd installed a retro showerhead and a pedestal sink? Or was it because we'd given too many bottles of wine with attractive labels and recogniz-

able names to those who'd vouched for
Michael's expertise to the museum's hiring
committee? Yes, all of these expenditures
were extravagant, but none seemed particularly over-the-top. We had not, for instance, given Dom Pérignon, wired an
outdoor sound system, or lined the shower
with slate. Michael drove a Saab, not a
Mercedes. We'd not even bought jewelry,
aside from my engagement ring, which,
honestly, was embarrassingly overdue and
sported only a very modest sapphire.
Unless the light was right, you could barely
see it.

"Your husband is still at the Otis?" Mrs.
Drake asked.

"Oh, yes," I said. "That's why I'm here. I
hoped we could address this," I gestured
subtly toward the folded letter that now lay
on the desk between us, "creatively."

"Certainly." Mrs. Drake nodded and
opened her palms upward, expansively, as
if inviting me to lay my idea in them. "You
know, we always encourage our students to
think outside the box."

"Let's hope it rubs off on the parents." My
response wasn't particularly amusing but I
may have giggled. The headmistress merely

waited, a technique she must have found useful in working with preadolescents. I continued, soberly, "I have, actually, recently become an events consultant. I work with J. Peabody and Associates. I'm one of the associates."

Margaret had laughed at this, but Mrs. Drake did not. Perhaps I'd mistimed my delivery. "Anyway, I thought we could do some kind of event for Wheatley at cost. I'm sure the Otis would donate their plaza. I've told the new director quite a bit about you—although, of course, he knows Wheatley by reputation. He has a daughter in sixth grade. In D.C. So they'd be looking for an appropriate school." I had done no such thing. I didn't even know if the director had children of any age.

The headmistress nodded. "Well, thank you. We'd be quite interested in a project like that. We do expect our parents to help out around here to the best of their abilities. Tuition doesn't cover nearly as much of the cost of running a school as people think."

"Oh, I know. I know," I said sympathetically. "And I know we'd have to work out the details, but, in principle, you would consider something like that in lieu of, say, a semester's tuition?"

"In lieu of tuition? No." Mrs. Drake sat back in her chair and laced her fingers together so that her hands formed a meaty ball on the desk. "No, I'm afraid we couldn't do that." She rose, signaling the end of our meeting. "We can only accept a donation such as the type you're suggesting if it comes strictly from the heart," she said, placing a hand on her chest, "with no strings attached. Otherwise, you know, it wouldn't be fair to the others who can't afford to be so generous."

I stood on cue. I'd been out of the box long enough for one day.

"We would certainly be interested in an event like the one you proposed, however," she said brightly, opening the door. She handed me the dunning letter I'd left on her desk. "You need to keep a copy of this," she said. "Perhaps a payment plan would be helpful. Shall I ask Christie to set up a meeting for you with our business office?"

I drove by the bank on my way home, but bankers, I knew, would not accept a party in place of a house payment.

The school and the house were not the

only things that did not truly belong to us. On January 12, the contractor threatened to pull our kitchen cupboards out. "I'd sooner use 'em in my own place," he said, "than let you keep 'em. Even though that glass is for idiots. Ever heard of earthquakes, lady?" "It's Letty," I said. Although I understood his frustration, I did not appreciate that tone from a man for whom I'd squeezed blood oranges for midmorning refreshment. "And take the damn cupboards," I said. He did not want the cupboards. He wanted cash.

The demands came incessantly now, from all directions. "Don't answer it!" Michael shouted and clamped a pillow over his head whenever the phone rang. I'd started to grind my teeth in my sleep and woke every morning with a headache. We ate only puffed rice now for breakfast, purchased from a wholesale company in plastic bags so large they had to be stored in the garage. When Noah complained that he missed his Tom and Jerry bowl, I made him eat his cereal dry.

The calls grew more angry, the weeping, both Hazel's and mine, more hysterical. With Margaret's advance in mind, I assured everyone that by the end of the month I could pay them all, but they all said, "Too late," even Ramon, who stood outside our kitchen window one morning cursing us in Spanish. That was the day Jeanette called to announce triumphantly that she'd secured the Commedia della Luna to entertain at the museum party. "A private party is not something they normally do, which is the best part," she said. "They're only doing it for us because my college roommate's husband is their business manager. And the other best part is that it's not going to be formal or on a stage or anything. I mean, they'll have their tent with the trapeze and all that, but they'll also mingle with the guests, while they're eating fire and doing those great contortionist tricks and standing on each other's heads. It'll be fantastic! Very Brueghel."

"Is that medieval?" I asked.

"Oh, those dates are fluid—late Middle Ages, Renaissance, early Modern, who's to say when one period ends and another begins? Listen, though. We've got to pay them everything up front, and this is going to be a little more than the museum wanted to spend on entertainment. I want you to talk them into it."

"Jeanette, I can't—" She cut me off.

"Listen, Letty, they really like you over there and they trust your judgment. If you approach them, they'll understand that we're suggesting this to help them, to give them an event everyone'll be gushing over for years. Right now, their image is a little stodgy. You can remind them of that, but they know it. People feel they have money, but they don't know how to spend it. You know what I mean? Tell them that something like this could really change that impression."

I quailed at the responsibility. I was an errand runner, a check writer, an occasional mushroom-taster. I had no experience in sales. "But why don't you tell them? Listen to yourself—you're very convincing."

"If I go to them about this, they'll just think I'm after publicity for my company, and, whoa, guilty as charged over here. I mean, think how this is going to sound in *L.A. Magazine.* Think of the pictures! The masks! The saturated colors! Maybe we could get *Vanity Fair* to cover it. Anyway, they're much more likely to believe you're looking out for them, because of your connection to Michael. It's not going to be difficult, Letty.

People are dying to be told that it's in their interest to spend money."

As Jeanette had predicted, it wasn't difficult to convince the Otis's event planning committee that this was the best use of even more money than they'd originally intended to pay. Especially when I mentioned the Brueghelness of it all. They wired forty thousand dollars to J. Peabody and Associates' entertainment account the following day.

It was indeed a large sum. Enough to make one question one's choice of career, no matter what one was doing, as long as it wasn't swallowing swords. Not enough, of course, to pay everything we owed, but more than enough to pay all those who were clamoring for signs of good faith.

I called the Commedia contact to arrange to transfer the funds to them. Jeanette, it turned out, had been misinformed. For an entity as trustworthy as the Otis, the group would accept a small deposit and collect the remainder on the night of the party.

I was dialing Jeanette to clear up the confusion and ask whether we should return the Otis's money until it was needed, when the call-waiting blips sounded on the line.

"I have some people who want to look at your house," Peri said. "Can I show it tomorrow? They're not expecting any of the work to be finished," she added, "but you might want to pick up a little."

"Tomorrow?" Children's books were strewn like colorful paving stones across the living room floor. I collected them as I listened to Peri.

"It's a young couple from Chicago," she was saying. "She's very up-and-coming with Huebner—you know, 'Get Drunk on Life.' " She hummed a few notes of the jingle. Huebner had created a stylish, edgy ad campaign for bottled water, famous for featuring real homeless people from Santa Monica. "They want her out here yesterday, so they're prepared to move fast. You're not going to get your price, though. Don't expect it."

I felt dizzy, as if I were hyperventilating, though my breathing was slow. I walked around the room with a fistful of *Madeline*s and *Curious George*s. There were no bookcases on which to shelve them. "Tomorrow?" I said again. The humiliation of admitting that we didn't belong in this house made my tongue thick. Others were up-and-coming. We were down-and-going. Why hadn't Michael or I turned out to be the sort of people Huebner wanted here yesterday?

Although, obviously, selling the house, slipping out of the onerous monthly payments and the improvements suspended at stages that made daily life miserable, would be a relief, it was, I recognized now that it seemed possible, the last thing I wanted to do. This house, its neighborhood, even the renovations we'd begun, the paint colors we'd chosen, and the bathroom fixtures we'd installed, made us the people I wanted us to be. With these accoutrements, we had clearly succeeded in life. Without them, we had failed. It was as simple as that. When we sold this house, everyone—Brad and Zoe, Duncan and Hollis, my parents, Jeanette, Lottie, even Ofelia—would know that we were not the sort of people we were supposed to be.

"I'm sorry, Peri," I said. "I should have called you. I've changed my mind."

"You mean you don't want to sell?" She sounded slightly exasperated.

"No. I mean, yes, we don't want to. Not just now."

Peri blew her breath out loudly to make clear to me that her work was hard and I was not making it any easier. "Well, I wish you'd called," she said. "But I have to say, I think you're doing the right thing. I'd hate to see you lose money."

I have never been a gambler. Michael and I once spent a weekend in Las Vegas; we won three hundred dollars and I hated it, hated the actual winning. It felt wrong, like cheating. The very sensation that delighted everyone else—getting away with something—appalled me. Honestly, before we desperately needed the money, were I to have won the Publishers Clearing House Sweepstakes, I would have wanted to give it back. Why should I have what others did not? Why should I get lucky?

But I didn't believe our being in this house was a matter of luck at all. We were smart; we were sophisticated; we were tolerant of other cultures; and, especially now that the Explorer had been repossessed, we trod lightly on the earth. Michael, it was true, had smoked, but only for a couple of years in college. I wasn't flashy. I didn't demand or even desire luxury. But I did want what was appropriate for our station in life. We didn't belong in a two-bedroom apartment in Palms, with lipstick ground into the carpeting and hollow closet doors that fell off their tracks and freeway noise through the aluminum frame windows. We didn't belong in a split-level way off in the Valley with do-it-yourself kitchen cupboards from a building supply warehouse chain store. And we didn't belong in a ranch in Glendale with a cement patio. I didn't look down on people who lived in those places. I was sure they were perfectly nice, decent human beings. I had been one of them for years. But I wanted more. I believed, sincerely believed, we deserved more.

And that is the only way I can explain why I did not call Jeanette nor the museum to inform them that a large amount of money would in fact not be required until February 14. Instead, I took that money, as easily as I'd taken the previous sums. I wrote a check to the Commedia della Luna in erasable ink, and once Jeanette had signed it, I paid it to the order of me. Of course, I knew it was dishonest. The interest on that money belonged to the museum, or perhaps to

Jeanette, if she could convince the museum to see it that way. That interest, however, was all I ever intended to deprive them of. I believed I had arranged for the museum to grant me only a short-term loan. Long before February 14, Margaret would have sent me her advance and I would replace the money as secretly as I'd taken it.

CHAPTER 20

Letty

We were saved. As soon as I had deposited the check Jeanette had signed into my account, I began writing checks of my own. I'd brought the bills with me to the bank in a tidy sheaf, together with several books of stamps commemorating our nation's wildflowers, and I stood at one of the little ledges with a pen attached and paid them. Our most frightful creditors—the bank, the schools, the utility companies—and those with faces—Hazel and Ramon and Mr. Nakasoni, the contractor, the dentist, the vet—I paid in full. I also paid the library (we'd lost books in the move). To the credit card companies, I threw sops to buy us another month. It was a relief just to touch the cool vinyl of the checkbook cover and know that I could open it, that I had recorded a figure in the register from which I could subtract. I pulled each check slowly from the book, taking pleasure in the meaty sound of the tear. I savored the sweet adhesive as I licked each envelope's flap.

Over the past months, I'd forgotten I am a tall woman. I straightened my shoulders now as I left the bank and lifted my chin. My jaw felt so loose I wanted to yawn. I tucked three singles into the cup the man beside the ATM machine held out to me.

Being saved is a lightening, a stretching, a lifting. Now that we were saved, I was euphoric at the sight of the palm fronds that arched over the Wells Fargo sign, so lovely were they, etched against the blue sky, playfully trying to scratch the drivers off their stagecoach. Though I was in Westwood, five miles from the ocean, I could feel its cool breath. And what matter if I only imagined the smell, the whisper of brine under the blare of car exhaust and the bleat of onions from Tommy's chili burgers? The scent was in my nose, whether it came from the Pacific or from my own head.

I was distinctly aware that I owed the museum and Jeanette for our salvation, and would continue to owe them for the next couple of weeks, until Margaret received her advance and sent it on to me. While I waited for Margaret, I vowed I would redouble my efforts for the event, so that the Otis would get its money's worth and more.

Margaret

When Heather Mendelson Blake didn't call by January 10, I wasn't worried. I reasoned that she'd barely had a chance to unpack; there'd be piled-up paperwork to attend to; possibly ornaments and wreaths to return to their storage boxes, depending on whether her family was more Mendelson or Blake. In fact, even the Mendelsons were likely to have a tree to dispose of. I had to allow her time. By January 15, however, I was becoming nervous, and on January 17, I took my shoes to be reheeled, had an extra key cut for the apartment, purchased a single croissant and then returned for a second pastry, in four separate trips that brought me, legitimately, within half a block of the offices of the Hope Perdue Agency. On January 20, I discovered twelve pages from chapter sixteen under the dictionary. Were they part of the earlier draft I'd dropped down the air shaft? I stuck my head out the window. By now, the once-white pages had grayed and begun to distintegrate, settling into their bed of cigarette packets and pigeon feathers and a slick of snow. Were the pages missing from the manuscript I'd delivered to Heather Mendelson Blake?

"This particular scene," I said to Ted, "is crucial for the plot. Do you think I should call and make sure she has these pages?"

Ted obligingly shuffled through the papers I held out to him. "I can't believe," he said, "that she'd turn down a book because it was missing twelve pages."

"But this is where Lexie tries to return the carpet," I said, pointing to a passage. "It's the beginning of her desperate period. I'm not sure that what comes afterward makes sense without it."

"Let me guess," Ted said. "She gets more desperate."

"So you don't think I should call?"

"I think that if Heather Mendelson Blake thinks that she can't make a decision without those pages, she'll call you." He turned back to his work, practical and confident.

I took the phone into the bedroom and closed the door.

"Hello?"

I wished I knew the name of the brown-haired girl. "This is Margaret Snyder," I said. "May I please speak to Heather Mendelson Blake?"

"She's in a meeting right now. Would you like to leave a message?"

"I'm afraid the manuscript I gave her might be missing some pages. Twelve pages, actually. It may not be. They may belong to the manuscript in the air shaft, but I can't check since we're on the sixth floor. I'm not sure, actually, if I could even check if we were on the first floor. I suppose I could ask the people in that apartment if I could crawl out their window, although I would hope it's still pretty far off the ground, because the stuff down there really shouldn't be close to human habitation. For sanitary reasons. Well, you can imagine the kind of stuff people throw out their bathroom windows. Anyway," I finished, "if she needs those pages, I could bring them right over."

"Twelve pages. Meg Snyder. I'll leave her the message," she said.

On January 25, Letty called. We talked for some minutes about how visible downtown Los Angeles was from the freeway that day and the fact that the clementines had been sour all season. About nothing, in other words, that mattered.

"No," I said, finally.

"Oh," she said. "I thought mid-January."

"I know. I'm sure she'll call any day now. Probably she'll call tomorrow."

"But this is just the agent you're waiting for, right? I was hoping that by now it would be out to editors. Isn't that how it works?"

I experienced an unpleasant prickle of defensive irritation. She was right. I had assumed my novel would be in publishing houses by now, if not already sold, then nearly so. I did not like Letty, the one whom I had wronged, pointing out that I'd not yet righted matters. That she did not intend to point this out (since she did not, in fact, realize I'd wronged her) somehow made me feel worse. "That's how it works," I said, "but she had to go to London."

"Over Christmas."

We were both well aware that Christmas, even if you stretched it to the New Year, had been over for three weeks.

"It probably takes a while to get revved up again," Letty said. "After the holidays."

"I know you need the money soon."

She was suddenly sobbing.

"Letty, shh," I said. "Shh." But I was crying now, too.

"God, Margaret, I can't stand this. Taking money from you. I just . . . I don't know what else to do."

"This," I said. "This is what you should do. Listen, I'll talk to her today. I'll tell her we have to get going on this. Time is of the essence! When do you absolutely need a check?"

"The fourteenth. The fourteenth of February. Well, really before that would be better, but that's the latest. That's the very outside."

"Why? Is it the bank, the house?"

"Really it's everything. Everything comes due then, and it's important I pay on time," she said in a decisive tone she rarely used and one that did not encourage me to question her further.

Letty

It didn't seem fair for me to worry Margaret with how desperately I needed money by February 14. That was my doing, after all. My problem. When I hung up I went into the laundry room, where the spin cycle covered the sound of my emotion, a weak, exhausted wailing that had recently begun to escape from me in periodic spurts.

The relief I'd felt writing those checks had evaporated as the event approached and the space of time, like an artery, squeezed more tightly shut with each day's relentless passing. Don't think about it, I told myself, helplessly, illogically, closing my eyes for seconds at a time, even on the freeway. Since thinking about the situation did me no good, I convinced myself that not thinking about it would work some magic. Margaret would call with encouraging news, I told myself, only when I was engrossed in other plans, not while I was slapping the cell phone against the car seat, trying to pound a ring out of it. To this end, I focused on the benefit with an intensity that made me ball my hands into fists and dig the shredded remains of my nails into my palms. I attended animal training meetings to find out how to keep the greyhounds from mixing it up with the peacocks and the falcons and how to keep all three species from snatching minia-ture sausage tarts off the guests' plates. I arranged access to secret rooms on the museum's upper floors, so that the lighting designers could make the massive, widely spaced, sand-colored buildings suggest the crowded streets of medieval Florence. I au-ditioned children to play ring-around-the-rosy to create a haunting reminder of the Black Death, and mediated a feud between the a cappella singers and the recorder group. Surprisingly, for whole hours at a time, I entirely forgot that the end of the world was at hand.

Margaret

On February 5, beginning at nine a.m., I strolled casually up and down the street in front of the Hope Perdue Agency. Most agents, I figured, would not start until ten-thirty or so, but I couldn't risk missing

Heather Mendelson Blake. In fact, I couldn't risk missing anyone who went into the building, since I had no idea what H.M.B. looked like.

At nine forty-five, I stopped the first woman who'd approached the door. She had regal gray hair and carried over her shoulder a satchel made of Tibetan fabric. "Ms. Mendelson Blake?" I said, hopefully, blocking her access to the building. She looked like someone who could represent all of the Alices and the Anns besides.

She stepped back, startled. "No," she said quickly, shaking her head. "No, no."

At ten, I tried a short woman in a camel-and-black houndstooth pea coat. "Heather won't be in until at least eleven," she said impatiently. She made a tiny jump to reset-tle the enormous black leather knapsack on her back before she started up the stairs.

At ten-thirty, my bottom lip had begun to bleed where I'd been fretfully chewing at it. My fingers had numbed and I could no longer feel my toes. I went across the street for a hot chocolate to go, but kept my eyes on the door. The brown-haired receptionist and two men went in while I waited in the shelter of the café for my drink.

At eleven-fifteen I'd been back at my post for forty minutes, when a girl in black stretch, low-slung trousers and a short, black, belted trenchcoat came toward me. Her hair streamed around her face in long waves and she was carrying an oversized cardboard cup. No, I did not dismiss her as far too young. I had come to expect such things.

"Ms. Mendelson Blake?"

She cocked her head, puzzled. "Yes?"

"I'm Margaret Snyder," I said, thrusting my hand toward her. She shifted her cup to her left hand, and shook my right, politely. "Yes?" she said again. "Have we met?"

"You have my manuscript," I said. *"The Rise and Fall of Lexie Langtree Smith*? I'm not wedded to that title."

She frowned. "God, things have been so busy. The holidays, you know."

"And you had to go to London," I added.

She looked surprised. "That's right. How did you know that?"

"You told me. We've spoken on the phone. You loved my opening. The grass?" I prompted. "Possibly you're missing twelve pages."

She continued to frown, her eyes watering in the wind. With one finger she hooked a lock of hair from between her lips where a sudden gust had blown it.

"The thing is," I said, going boldly on. "I really need to get this show on the road." Why was I talking in clichés? Why did I sound like Warren? "You see, a good friend of mine, my best friend, actually—we've known each other since infancy—is really counting on whatever I can get as an advance. She needs it ASAP," Warren finished for me.

She smiled, her teeth perfect and white between her glossed lips. "Sure," she said. "I'll call you," she said. She turned away from me to go into the building.

I had taken enough. The time had come, for Letty's sake and for my own, to assert myself. I did not step squarely in front of her—I am not a threatening person—but I did move forward. I did hold one palm, if not exactly on the door, then at least in a gesture that indicated I did not want her to open it just yet. I spoke quietly but firmly. "I don't think you understand," I said. "My friend needs this money and she needs it now. If you would jimmy a few hours into your overcommitted schedule to read my manuscript you would see that it speaks eloquently to our age and so has a great deal of commercial potential, something I would think, if you are any kind of agent at all, would interest you as much as it interests me and my friend."

Her eyes widened as I spoke and she reeled back a step. Then she pushed past me through the door. "You'll hear from me," she said.

I did not.

~~~~~

I heard from Letty, however, in phone calls that became increasingly frequent and incoherent. We tried to talk about other subjects, but our anecdotes and petty concerns could not hold our attention. "But you'll be sure to call, right?" she said, at the end of each conversation. "As soon as you know when you'll be getting the money?"

Letty

It's funny the way you can convince yourself of an eventuality you long for: the house you're searching for will be the next one you view, the bus you're waiting for will come in the next two minutes, the next man you date will become your husband. So vividly can you picture the event in your mind, that even if it would not have happened spontaneously, the power of your envisioning it seems sure to make it so. This is the way I was with Margaret's call. I was sure one day that she'd leave a message on our answering machine between two and four, so I went to the market deliberately then to give her a chance to do so. Other times, I was certain I'd heard the cell phone ring and pushed talk, only to hear a dial tone. You would think these failures of my premonition would make me doubt myself, but, in fact, the opposite was true; my convictions grew more vivid. Since she had not yet called, I thought, it was all the more likely that she'd call today or perhaps tomorrow. There was, after all, very little time left.

I stopped sleeping on February 7. I had not been sleeping well before then, but that night I stopped altogether. Which was all right for the first few hours. While Michael slept beside me, I ate a Rice Krispies treat that I'd found in Hunter's lunchbox and watched Tom Snyder chat amusingly with Bonnie Hunt about the bratwurst he ate in Racine, Wisconsin, in 1952. Then I watched the ABC late-night news show. While the anchors, knowing no one important could be watching at that hour, traded their comfortingly informal comments, I wondered what Hunter had traded for the treat. I hadn't been packing anything that I would have considered tradable for months.

As long as Thalia Assuras was up, sporting her nifty glasses, it seemed all right to be awake. But after that, since our cable had been cut off a month ago, I was faced with jowly men and frighteningly tanned women talking with false and forceful cheer about exercise equipment and kitchen devices, and the fellow who insists you can make a fortune by placing classified ads. I turned off the television and shut my eyes. Why hadn't Hunter eaten the treat, if he'd traded for it? What if he'd found it? Had some child killer laced it with poison and left it on the playground?

I turned the television on again. An elderly nun with a black patch over one eye was hawking an enamel crucifix from the right side of her mouth, while the nerveless left side drooped disapprovingly. Down the street a car door slammed and an engine started. Birds began their restless morning hubbub. At nine I would call Peri. Maybe the Huebner wunderkind was still looking. Maybe someone else was. Another car started on its commute. But to sell a house took longer than a week.

At six I got up and went out to the garage. Margaret would call at eight, I thought, scooping puffed wheat out of its industrial-sized sack with a coffee can. There was a time not so long ago when I did not buy coffee in cans, but in bags from its own special store. Probably, we should have given up coffee altogether.

I stopped eating on February 10. Not altogether. I still began meals with a few swallows, as if I meant to go on, but then I somehow couldn't. Worry had tightened my stomach into a golf ball.

Margaret

Since, obviously, I would have made a nuisance of myself had I called the Hope

Perdue Agency every time Letty called me, I allowed myself only one call a day and varied the time, in the hope of getting someone other than Brown Hair, which occasionally worked. I kept my messages pleasant and brief. I suspected I may have gone a bit far that day on the sidewalk, and I didn't want to make things worse.

"Just checking," I would say. "Just wondering if she's gotten to it yet." Once, however, I lost my temper. "I gave it to her before Christmas," I said. "How long does it usually take?"

"Well, you know she's very busy," the woman on the other end said. "After the holidays and all."

Letty

I was supposed to report to the museum at dawn on February 14 to prepare for the event, but by the time the pirate nun was rasping on about the merits of an amber rosary, I felt legitimately ill and one of my eyes had begun to twitch.

"I can't," I whispered into the phone to

Jeanette, so as not to wake Michael. "I'm very sorry, but I just can't. I'm too sick."

"But this is the fun part!" Jeanette exclaimed. "You must at least come tonight. Have Michael carry you here on a stretcher. You cannot miss this. This is going to be the event of a lifetime."

All day the phone lay quiet—no, that's not true—there were calls, a friend of Marlo's, my mother, the *L.A. Times* trying to renew our subscription, but not the call from Margaret. It was too late for money. The Commedia would not be paid that night. But if Margaret called I could at least promise that payment would be swift. I could blame a short delay on the bank, a computer glitch, a transferring error. I could have misplaced the company checkbook. It wouldn't make perfect sense, but it would be far better than the truth.

I called her, nine, ten times before I lost count and began to hit redial compulsively. I stopped leaving messages after the sixth call. I could think of nothing more to say.

I couldn't sit still nor could I concentrate on a single task but careened like a pinball from one activity to the next. I laundered; I scoured sinks; I creamed butter and sugar for cookies; I disassembled the stove. I flattened the end of the toothpaste tube and rolled it neatly. With the toothbrush, I begin to work on the grout between the tiles on the bathroom floor. I Windexed; I vacuumed; I recapped markers and Play-Doh; I stripped the beds. I sprinkled yeast on water for pizza crust. I sorted Legos by size into plastic containers.

Michael got out of bed in time to prepare for the party. I perched on the rounded corner of our extralong tub, still one of the best features of our house, and watched him shave. "You're sure you can't go?" he said, wincing against the pain of the razor. He used plain soap now, instead of special, soothing emollients. "I'd rather not go without you."

I worried they would corner Michael. His back would be pressed against the railing that keeps visitors from diving into the canyon. "Didn't she say anything to you?" the acrobats would ask. They'd swipe a torch through the air near his throat. "Didn't she give you a check?" But he would be innocent and ignorant. He would explain about my illness. Perhaps by that hour a vessel would have burst in my head.

Perhaps the museum would have crumbled in an earthquake.

"Come home early," I said.

Ofelia arrived. I'd forgotten to cancel her. It didn't seem fair to send her home without paying her and, under the circumstances, it didn't feel right to pay her without asking her to work. "Stay," I said. "I'll go."

I had no idea where to go, but it was a relief to be on the move, to be pushing the accelerator with my foot and feeling the cool winter darkness on my face. I drove Jeanette's car west on Sunset, winding through the eucalyptus groves of Bel Air, past the private school campuses of Brentwood, under the clean sky of Pacific Palisades. Without traffic, Sunset is fast; the lanes are narrow; the curves can be tight. In the right lane, branches from untrimmed hedges scratched at my windows; in the left, lights from oncoming cars made me blink. It's a good road, if you want to keep your mind on the driving and away from other, more dangerous subjects.

When Sunset emptied into the Pacific Coast Highway, I turned right and drove up the coast, my phone mute on the seat beside me, like a sullen passenger. I bought gas in Malibu, so that I would be prepared if I decided never to turn back. Soon after Point Dume, the stoplights ended and for long stretches, mine was the only car on the road, and my world was reduced to a few yards of gray pavement and painted lines studded with reflectors. On my right, the hills were dark. On my left, the ocean was black. It was difficult to keep my foot from pressing harder and harder on the accelerator as I hurled myself into this vacuum, into space itself. But space is limited here. In half an hour or so, civilization would begin again. I'd be in Oxnard, then Ventura, then Santa Barbara, each successive community more like the one I'd escaped.

I toyed with disaster. I imagined driving up one of the canyons and over the edge, but even as I envisioned the winding climb, the wrench of the wheel, the free fall, I knew this would never be more than a comforting thought. I couldn't leave my children. And after I'd stolen from Jeanette, it hardly seemed fair to total her car, too.

It was the thought of my children that made me U-turn, cautiously, at Point Mugu. They, at least Marlo and possibly Hunter, would find out soon enough that their mother was a thief, but at least she would be a thief who took responsibility.

I wasn't dressed for a party. My hair, unwashed for days, pressed close to my head and I had only my teeth to give my lips color. When I got out of the car, I slipped the cell phone into my sweater pocket and covered it with my palm to warm it, to coax it to spring to life. It was late in New York, but not too late for Margaret to call.

Jeanette, I saw, had a genius for party planning. Although I'd chased down most of the evening's elements and had even come up with the idea for several of them, I'd not have guessed that the whole would be so magical. The museum's plaza was transformed. Thanks to the lighting designer and several strategically draped lengths of painted fabric, the monolithic, desert-hued surfaces of the museum's buildings somehow did suggest a clutch of two- and three-story wooden dwellings huddled against one another at the center of a medieval town. Torches, the only light source actually visible, crackled with real fire at intervals along the "streets," wide paths Jeanette and I had marked out with wattle in the pattern of a maze to encourage and inhibit traffic flow at critical junctures. (One of Jeanette's specialities was keeping people from getting jammed up near the food.) The torches created the effect of a low-tech strobe: guests appeared brightly lit on one side, shadowed on the other, for seconds at a time, and then disappeared in the surrounding darkness. If the museum burned would the performers still have to be paid?

On the walls and on special kiosks, enlarged reproductions of details from the museum's medieval collection hung: three hunters stalked a deer under an archway, a lady-in-waiting sidled along one wall, a burgher slapped another on the back just beyond the door to the gift shop. The recorder group was playing as I arrived, their notes at once plaintive and sprightly. The air smelled of wood smoke.

A greyhound daintily mouthed a meat tart from my hand. "No feeding the animals," scolded a man in a smock and leggings. The dog was discreetly leashed and lay down when it had finished its snack in a soft, gray ring on the rush-strewn stone floor. Near the fountain, a peacock spread its tail. Waiters in white smocks and waitresses in muslin aprons carried food about on trays the weight of which was relieved by coarse leather straps around their necks. Across the plaza, I saw Michael laughing— laughing—with a squat man I'd not seen before. He caught my eye and motioned me over, but I turned away, as if I didn't understand his gesture. I had to concentrate on willing the phone to ring and then on my confession. I could spare no resources for chat about plankton.

I helped myself to a handful of blushing yellow Queen Anne cherries, conscious of their grotesque expense and wanting to be sure I got my share. I lifted a heavy tumbler from a waiter's tray. The expensive wine we'd purchased was mulled with spices according to the abbot of Kent's fourteenth-century recipe I'd found in the UCLA library. We weren't able to duplicate every flavor, but the final taste was sweet and sharp at once, strange enough at least to seem authentic. We'd also brewed a hard cider. I looked around for a tray of that.

I was surprised I'd not noticed the Commedia della Luna performers before because suddenly they were everywhere, tumbling through the air and walking on their hands, wearing long-beaked and snouted masks, ebony feathers and white ruffs, capes and short jackets and tights striped scarlet and violet, indigo and goldenrod. Some rippled their legs and torsos like looped ribbon; one juggled bones. In several cases two had clamped on to one another in an unnatural configuration more Bosch than Brueghel in which feet grew from ears and hands stretched between legs.

I found a tray of cider. As I reached for a pewter tankardful, a contortionist crab-walked face upward on all fours with roach-like speed between me and the waiter. How much had the tankards cost the museum? I couldn't even remember that check.

With my right hand, I raised the cider to my lips, while I slid my left into my pocket to be sure the cell, quiet as a stone, had not slipped out.

In front of me, a raven in crimson tights gulped globes of yellow fire. When he saw me staring, he held out the torch. "Try some, miss?" His voice was rough, his accent unplaceable. He wore shoes with claws. I shook my head and backed toward the garden, where the children I'd hired were trampling the plantings and plucking the petals. Every few minutes they gathered in a circle and recited, as they'd been instructed, tumbling to the ground with the final line. Jeanette's makeup artist had rendered the kids I'd seen in the studio on Santa Monica Boulevard unrecognizable. Those had been manifestly healthy, twentieth-century Americans—with gleaming teeth, shiny hair, and straight limbs. These children were different. They seemed stunted somehow and their hair was dull and ragged. They smelled of garlic and grease, even yards away. One of them limped on a clubfoot. How had Jeanette managed that?

I wandered into the crowd, and the recorders gave way to a chant ensemble in monks' robes, their faces deep in their cowls.

"Alms, miss?" I felt it thrusting against my shoulder before I turned, the stump of an arm in a bandage caked with blood and dirt. The man leaned on a stick wrapped in rags. "Alms?" he said again, exposing his empty gums. Who was the makeup artist and why hadn't we discussed these actors? Jeanette obviously had not shared all the secrets of her business with me. I dropped a precious cherry in the beggar's cup. "Eight dollars a pound," I said.

He scowled and spit on the floor deliberately on a spot where there were no rushes to hide it.

"Ring around the rosy." The children's piping voices overlaid the chant.

A small animal scuttled through a patch of torchlight. It was certainly not a dog or a peacock. Had Jeanette added cats? Where was its trainer and its leash?

Where was Michael? We should not have been here. We had to go home. We had to pack; we had to sell. I hurried along the paths, pushing my way past a woman who'd turned herself into a hoop. A trick of architecture made the children's voices louder, although I was moving away from them. "A pocket full of posies." The maze dead-ended against a guardrail, and the dark canyon gaped before me. In the distance, well beyond my grasp, the city lights mocked me with their spangle. At my feet, a bold rat feasted on a chicken wing. "Ashes. Ashes."

It was over. I knew suddenly and with certainty that Margaret was not going to call and it was over. We would not be saved. And then my cell phone rang. Or rather it emitted the theme from *The Lone Ranger* in a high, mechanical tone.

"Letty?" Jeanette said. "Are you here? Can you come help me? This woman insists we still owe the Commedia."

I could hardly hear her over the voices of the strange, stunted children: "We all fall down."

I was balling socks, remnants of my laundry binge the day before, when the police arrived the next afternoon. They did not let me finish.

Margaret

The envelope I received from the Hope Perdue Agency in March was so light and flimsy that it might not even have contained a sheet of paper. Heather Mendelson Blake was sorry, but she just didn't have the passion necessary to give my work fair representation. If I would send money for postage, she'd be happy to return my manuscript.

AFTERWORD

Dear Judge Brandt,
It's kind of you to take an interest, especially considering that you already favored Letty and me with so much of your time at the hearing. I got the impression that you were slightly exasperated with my testimony. I seem to recall your saying that one's day in court should not extend to a week, and, then, when you concluded that my involvement had no legal bearing on the case, I thought—well, perhaps the chafing of some other judicial matters was responsible for your irritation. I do see now that, as you said, bringing every quiver of my conscience to the attention of the court may have been more tedious than enlightening. This is the sort of lesson I have learned in

the painful aftermath of the State of California v. Letitia MacMillan.

The Otis, as I understand it, was generous with Letty. To avoid public embarrassment, it paid the Commedia and allowed the MacMillans to return the money in small installments at a low rate of interest. Michael was fired, but that could hardly be otherwise.

No, you will not soon be able to purchase a copy of The Rise and Fall of Lexie Langtree Smith. *Lexie is gone. I dropped the disks in the public trash can on the corner of Greenwich and Sixth, deleted all chapters from my hard drive, and left my laptop on the curb. I wish luck to whoever picks it up. After Heather Mendelson Blake demurred, I sent my manuscript to several other agents, still hoping to make the money to help Letty pay her debts. Apparently, however, the publishing community is running low on passion these days. I put it this way to show you I have not lost my sense of humor. What I mean is that I am a failure. Despite the early evidence to the contrary, it turns out that I am merely a dull penny in the cash drawer of life. And it turns out this is not the worst thing a person can realize about herself.*

Recognizing New York's invidious effect on me, Ted accepted a job in Columbus, at some cost to his own career. He now leads a research group funded by Ohio State that specializes in the problems of Appalachia. I found work here monitoring subjects in a sleep study lab. Mainly, I attach electrodes to people's heads and collate the pages that spew from the machines all night. I also bring people juice, if they want it. Ted says I should audit some psych classes and learn to read the data. He thinks I could run the lab, if I wanted, in a couple of years. But I'm through with ambition.

Relieved as I was for Letty when you sentenced her to community service rather than to prison, your comment about her friendship with me being punishment enough hurt me deeply. I did not set out, after all, to do her harm. These past months watching people sleep, however, have afforded me a great deal of time for reflection. I understand now that I have never been the friend to Letty that Letty was to me. It was not that I did not love her. I did love her. I do. But I never gave her my full attention. I never thought of her without being distracted by me. Encouraging her debt was my most egregious betrayal of her, certainly, but it was not the first time I'd plundered her story to advance my own. I would be happy now to be dull, and I wouldn't mind having failed, if I could be a true friend to Letty. But it's far too late for that.

I send her checks, a portion of my pay every month. So far, none of them has been cashed. It is, in any case, a comfort to me to write her name on the line and then again on the envelope, to know that this paper at least will enter her house.

For details about the MacMillans, I'm afraid you will have to apply to them directly in Winnemucca, Nevada, where, according to my mother, Michael is teaching at a junior college. This past Christmas, I sent Letty a card, nothing sentimental, just a snow scene. When we were young in winterless Glendale, we used to wonder what such coldness would feel like. She has not yet written me back.

Yours sincerely,
Peggy Snyder

Dear Judge Brandt,
I appreciate your attempt to intercede for the sake of "a lifelong friendship," as you

call it, but I'm afraid Margaret's testimony spoiled all that. Fancying herself a Svengali! That's Margaret all over. You were absolutely right to point out that she had no power over me, that my desires and decisions were ultimately my own.

You ask me to consider whether it was the prospect of living in Margaret's reflected glimmer, and thereby taking on my own glow, that attracted me from the start. If I am honest, I must admit there is some truth in that. Still, it is certainly not her failure, as you suggest, that makes me turn from her now.

That in her mind she will always be Robinson Crusoe and I will always be Friday, I can forgive. Who is not, after all, the heroine of her own life? But that she cared for the world's regard more than she cared for me, how can I forgive that?

We live now in a rented, prefabricated house on a country road outside of town. Margaret sends me checks here, small ones, drawn from an account in Ohio. On the memo line, after the printed word "For," she writes "redemption." I keep the checks, along with her Christmas card, in a small ca-

nary yellow accordion file. They are a tie to her, however tenuous, and so I cannot bear to cash them.

Yours sincerely,
Letitia MacMillan